Praise for *The Electrical Field*

"Sakamoto is a master of repressed tension. . . . Miss Saito is a powerful creation, a twisted mixture of repression and yearning. . . . Using her to narrate the events surrounding a murder is a balancing act, a feat that marks Sakamoto as a writer to watch and makes this dark, layered novel difficult to forget."   —*Chicago Tribune*

"A slow-burning Miss Smilla. . . . For those who like their books to have that subtle, Peter Hoeg feel, here is a burning, enigmatic addition to the genre."   —*The Independent*

"[An] ingenious debut novel."
—*Time Out NY*, which also named Sakamoto
one of "99 people to watch in 1999"

"Hypnotic, haunting, and utterly original. From within the mind of a woman scarred by war and injustice, Kerri Sakamoto illuminates that shadowy terrain where history meets illicitly with sexuality and human longing."
—David Henry Hwang, author of *M. Butterfly*

"Beautifully written. . . . With great mastery, Sakamoto has structured a novel around the twin mysteries of Asako's crippling guilt and the fate of the Yanos."   —*San Jose Mercury News*

"Rarely does a debut novelist exhibit the skillful use of narrative that pervades this work. . . . Highly recommended."   —*Library Journal*

"Kerri Sakamoto has given us a haunting, harrowing tale that illustrates, more powerfully than mere polemics, the ravages of history on hearts and lives."   —Joy Kogawa, author of *Obason*

"Sakamoto has designed a mystery, but more, she has created a mystery out of her painfully isolated characters and, in doing so, asks, how do we manage to communicate when so much of our actions and desire mean something other than what is spoken? This poetically rendered novel translates a world of Japanese North Americans, after the humiliation of internment. What a brilliant and radically new way of seeing the effects of this history."
—Kimiko Hahn, author of *The Unbearable Heart*

THE ELECTRICAL FIELD

Kerri Sakamoto

W. W. Norton & Company

New York • London

Copyright © 1998 by Kerri Sakamoto

First American edition 1999

First published as a Norton paperback 2000

Library of Congress Cataloging-in-Publication Data
Sakamoto, Kerri.
   The electrical field / Kerri Sakamoto. —1st American ed.
      p.   cm.
   ISBN 0-393-04692-3
   I. Japanese—Ontario—Toronto—Fiction. [I. Japanese—Canada—Evacuation and
relocation, 1942–1945—Fiction.] I. Title.
PR9199.3.S163E44   1999
813'.54—dc2I

                                                    98-30649
                                                    CIP

ISBN 0-393-32048-0 pbk.

W. W. Norton & Company, Inc., 500 Fifth Avenue, New York, N.Y. 10110
www.wwnorton.com

W. W. Norton & Company Ltd., 10 Coptic Street, London WC1A IPU

1 2 3 4 5 6 7 8 9 0

FOR MY PARENTS

AND IN MEMORY OF
JUJI MATSUI
1923-1942

THE ELECTRICAL FIELD

I HAPPENED TO BE dusting the front window-ledge when I saw her running across the grassy strip of the electrical field. I stepped out onto the porch and called to her. I could tell she heard me because she slowed down a bit, hesitated before turning. I waved.

"Sachi!" I shouted. "What is it?"

She barely paused to check for cars before crossing the concession road in front of my yard; not that many passed since the new highway to the airport had been built. Shyly she edged up my porch steps to where I stood. She was out of breath, her eyes filled with an adult's burden. "I don't know," she said, panting. "Maybe it's nothing."

The sweat glistened on her, sweet, odourless water, and it struck me as odd, her sweating so much—a girl and a nihonjin at that; we nihonjin, we Japanese, hardly perspire at all, and the late spring air was cool that day. I sat down to signal calm and patted the lawn chair beside me. She sat but kept jiggling one knee. Finally she stood up again. "Yano came and took—," she began.

"Mr. Yano," I broke in, though everyone called him Yano, even myself.

"He took Tam out of class this morning. Kimi too."

"Tamio," I corrected her, as if I could tell her what to call the boy, her special friend. As if I could tell her anything. "A doctor's appointment, maybe?"

She shook her head as a child does, flinging her hair all about. Though at thirteen going on fourteen, she no longer was a child, I reminded myself.

"Yano looked crazy," she went on. "Like I've never seen him. His hands were like this." She clenched her fists and gritted her brace-clad teeth: a fierce little animal. "He hadn't taken a bath, not for a long time," she said, pinching her flat nose and grimacing. "Worse than usual. Everybody noticed."

She almost pushed me away when I patted her brow with a paper towel, then smiled meekly as I smoothed out her thick black hair. I felt the tangled nest of it at the back of her neck but stopped myself from getting a comb. I gave her a glass of juice and a cookie and made her sit still until she cooled off. I gazed across the field at the Yanos' green-roofed bungalow, identical to the others in its row except for the overgrown lawn and the curtainless front window.

Suddenly Sachi was at the bottom of my steps again, peering up at me. Like a child with no mother to clean her up: crumbs scabbing her chin, and her skin dirty in the light. She made me think of a scraggly urchin we'd passed on the road leaving the internment camp after the war, Papa and me, long ago. I was unhappy that day as I recall, because we were not going to the sea, I would not see Japan; we were staying in Canada. Leaving the mountains, going deeper in to a place that Papa could barely pronounce. "On-ta-ri-o." Standing in the back of that crowded, rattling truck, I gazed down at the urchin, her lost eyes. Left behind. I was glad at least not to be left behind.

"I have to see if Tam's back," Sachi was saying, her knee jiggling again. I dabbed around my chin until she did the same, backing onto my lawn. "How's your mother? Tell her to come by," I said, and immediately felt foolish.

I warned her to watch the road, but already she'd scampered across it, back to the field. "Let me know what happens," I shouted, remembering why I'd called her over in the first place. She waved her thin arm at me without turning, afraid I'd make her come back. I felt a tinge of loneliness as she crossed to the other side, to those bungalows in a row that kept one another company. Not like our house, built by a veterinarian decades before, sitting at the edge of the field, up from the creek, all on its own.

Nothing that unusual, I told myself, a father taking his children out of school for the afternoon. Not at all. He might have needed them to lick some stamps, give out flyers for one of his redress meetings that no one came to. Maybe a last-minute treat, an outing. Yano was capable of that much.

I watched Sachi wait at the Yanos' door for a moment or two, all she could stand, then run home to the grey-roofed bungalow a few houses down. I could not help thinking of the games she liked to play, with me and with herself, and how convincing she could be. But I told myself her worry was not to be taken lightly. Sachi was a perceptive child, gifted, really. She reminded me of myself in a way: a finely tuned receptacle for others' impulses and confidences. I often caught myself telling her thoughts better kept to myself, at least until she was older. It was the knowing way she had about her, the way she carried an understanding in that wispy girl's body. She wasn't muscular like most nihonjin, with hard, dense flesh. Even I with my restful life, old enough to be her mother, had flesh more taut than she.

When I went back inside, the smell seemed worse than usual. After all these years, I'd never grown used to it. It was Papa, his body whittled away upstairs, the smell of the sheets, the pillow, no matter I'd just changed them. There was his moan calling for one thing or another, coming steadily down the stairs like a creeping vine; quickly I passed by, plumping up a cushion on the chesterfield before sailing through the kitchen and out the back door.

In the garden, my flowers were coming up nicely, in spite of the frost we'd just had, not unusual for mid-May, I suppose. My tulips and daffodils in the far corner, my peonies and irises coming up on both sides. I caught the scent of my narcissus, potent, I thought, for such a delicate-looking bloom, its pale colour. It went straight to my head when I put my nose to it, like a drug. Stum had mown the grass short and even, as I'd asked, and swept the walk of clippings. I spied a hardy spiked weed sprouting in one corner of the garden, and was about to get up when I felt a sensation rise inside me that would not go away.

It was Yano, the thought of him, wild, crazy man in the middle of my placid afternoon, riling me. He was forever

ranting about something, raking back his hair with his dirty
fingernails; his hair that was too long, like a teenager's, his
clothes too tight at the armpits and crotch, so they showed
his bulge. Standing at the foot of my steps, where Sachi had
stood, his dog peeing in my flowers. Over and over he'd ask
me about the camps. He'd say the government owed us money
and an apology. Badger me with where this, when that, and
how long. "How long were you there, Saito-san?" For the
tenth time.

"I told you," I would scold back, not keeping the impatience from my voice.

"Each time you say different," he would say. "Four years,
five, which is it? When was it you left? Forty-six, forty-seven?"

When I didn't answer, he'd come up with more to taunt
me with. "Why didn't you leave sooner? Right when the war
ended? Why did you wait, Saito-san?" I could have asked him
why too, why didn't he stay in Japan? Why did he come back?
But I did not. Really, it mattered little now. Thirty years gone
by, and still it was fresh in his mind.

Whenever he came to me with his petitions, his flyers
for meetings, he'd stand so close and I'd have to breathe
through my mouth because he smelled. Even out here, in
the open air. It wasn't like Papa, a slow, seeping odour coming down the stairs, settling on you; it was alive and pungent, insistent, a man's odour probing you all over. How I
wanted to shake it off, shake both him and Papa off me, but
I couldn't.

Instead, I reached under my skirt and unhooked my
stockings. I was careful with them because they were expen-
sive. These days it was nothing but pantyhose in the stores.

I left the stockings in beige pools on the stoop and stepped onto the cool, cool grass. I even forgot to yank out the weed.

It was the first time in a long while that I'd given myself over to such an impulse, gallivanting in my garden, barefoot. Beyond the fence of the yard, the bushes and grass seemed thick as a jungle leading down to the creek.

Later that evening, after dinner, I noticed one of my stockings hanging out of Stum's pocket. "What are you doing with that?" I demanded, and took it from him. He smirked a little. "Where's the other?" He pulled the second from his pocket as well. "They were there," he said in his drawling way, pointing to the stoop where I'd left them. His fingers were gentle and slow giving it back.

I knew it wasn't the first time he'd touched a woman's things. Years ago, I caught him with his nose inside my underwear drawer. Since then, as far as I knew, he'd held only day-old chicks, just so in his palms, squeezed and scrutinized so he could tell their sex. One after another, eight hundred in an hour, so he said, separated out to do their business, the males from the females. He'd never brought a girl home.

"You snagged them," I said, examining the stockings. This kind, thick yet fine at the toes and heels, was not to be found in the stores any more. I'd bought two dozen of them when we lived in the city, before we'd moved here, and taken out a new pair every two years over the past twenty.

"Go check on Papa," I ordered. "See if he wants dessert." Stum could be an obedient little brother at times. He and his lopsided cheeks and his tiny eyes, and his legs that met from their tops to the knees, so you'd hear the *vim vim* of his trousers as he walked. He'd be turning thirty-three this year but he was still my baby brother, my ototo-chan.

At my window I noticed that the Yanos' car was still not there. At the Nakamura house, farther down, the drapes were now drawn and their car was parked in the driveway. I thought of Sachi inside, waiting under its grey roof. I took one last look before finally closing the drapes for the night.

I stepped out onto the porch in the morning and picked up the newspaper. I treasured this hour in the fresh early air, Stum gone and the routine not yet started up with Papa— feeding him, cleaning him. When, without a glance at the world's dreary front-page news, I could, at my leisure, turn to my word jumble and my crossword at the back of the want ads, near the funnies. I was not far into it when I looked up to find Sachi racing through the field towards me. She was screaming something but I couldn't make out the words. I folded up my newspaper and set it aside, trying to resist the chaos she was bringing. I could not help seeing then that the Yanos' car was not back, and the light from last night still burned in the living-room. Sachi flew up my steps, two at a time. She grabbed my arms, screaming in my face: "Tam! Where's Tam!" Her hair swarmed round her unwashed face; her breath was rotten.

I pushed her away. "Shush, shush, now," I said, but she only screeched louder.

"Where is he? We have to find him!" She was hysterical. "He could be down there!" She pointed to the back of the house, her hand shaking, her whole body shaking; down at the creek, she meant. I drew back. I could hardly stand her clawing me like this; where was Keiko, her own mother? She should have known better, she should have sensed what was rising in me, but she was coming closer, about to grab at me again, and I slapped her, not hard, but enough. As if I'd been waiting for an excuse for some time. In all her confusion, she sensed that too. The air carried the sound, the smack of it. The sleeve of her top slipped down her shoulder, exposing the brown nut of a newly sprouted breast, her hair hiding her eyes. She wasn't the untouched child I'd sat with here yesterday; I had no wish to soothe her, to comfort her. Tam would be back in no time, with the others. No time at all. She just couldn't stand the fact of them gone somewhere together, a family, without her. I almost said so, but didn't; I bit my lip.

"You don't care about him," she said coolly. "Maybe he's dead and won't you be glad," she seethed. She ran along the side of the house and down towards the creek, then turned back. "But he's not! He's not! You'll see!" she cried.

"Sachi," I called out. "Come back here, now!" I shouted, but the words seemed to drop to my lap, little fish leaping from a tank. She'd got me riled up in spite of myself. Hurriedly, I slipped into my shoes, calling up to Papa, though he couldn't have heard. I headed down to the creek after her.

I ran, my feet tangling in the uncut grass, until I reached the trees that thickened by the creek and fanned the water, and the bushes hung in bunches over the edge. I thought I caught a snatch of black hair through leaves, a shadow sliding over the dirt path that followed the creek. I stopped; aside from my own heaving breath, there was only the held-in whisper of the woods I knew so well. My feet were hot and swelling inside my shoes, my stockings snagged. I touched a hand to my face to find it curiously damp; I was grateful no one could see. Mosquitoes circled close even as I swatted them, drawn in by the sweetness of my body, my blood. I took a last look through the bushes at the creek, the murky water quite still except for circles of current tracing the surface from its underside and pinpricks of insects that touched down here and there. I called out. At last I spied her lying by a weeping willow that leaned off the bank, her thin stomach wriggling to catch some breath. She looked pale and sickly: a strange little island there. Her eyes were black holes, shot out by the sun. But her face strained up, her back arched up too, up to the burning bright sky. Then she cupped one hand over that nut of a breast.

"He's not here" came out of her small, cold lips. "Go back. You can't stay," she hissed. "Not this time," and her eyes stayed with me, as if to ward me off, as if telling me she'd found me out. Then she curled up, wrapping her raggedy arms across her chest, pulling up her thin legs so they stuck out at her sides. She made me think of those straddling insects you often saw here this time of year, with their jutting wings, getting ready to mate in mid-air. Abruptly, she jumped up onto the bank and danced across the creek on stones; faced me from the other side with the sun blazing behind. Now her face wasn't pale any more; it was tanned, too tanned in this light, her eyes gone gun-metal. She was that urchin again, belonging to no one.

"He's not gone," she called across, all the hiss let out. "But you don't care. You don't give a shit about any of them."

For a moment I didn't reply. She was hysterical, she made no sense at all. I could have said something, something to calm, something to hurt back. She was a girl, after all, and I was a grown woman. "I'll say a namu amida butsu for Tamio that he's all right" was all the answer I gave, ignoring the strange and angry look she cast me. I dabbed my forehead with a crusty tissue I'd finally found tucked up my sleeve. "You'll be late for class," I said stupidly, as if she cared about school, and headed back to the house.

When I climbed my front steps, I saw I'd left the door wide open. Anyone could have walked right in, taken whatever there was to take. I made a mental note to go and dust off Buddha's figure dark in the altar in the dining-room; to say a prayer, needless as it seemed. It would be the first time in a long, long while. I would do it for Sachi's sake, in spite of how she'd spoken to me. Papa was calling for me; I could hear him even through the screen, that low intermittent groan that must have started long before my return. I left my mud-chunked shoes on the porch. Chotto matte—in a minute, in a minute, I thought, sliding my feet into cool slippers. The groaning went on. Everything had the dull sheen of the indoors you see after coming in from bright sunlight. I made my way to the kitchen and drank a cool glass of tap water before heading upstairs.

I hesitated the slightest bit at his door before stepping in; it happened every once in a while. His eyes shifted to me as I stood just inside the doorway.

"Nani?" I finally said, coming up to the bed. What, what? Knowing what he wanted, making him wait a moment more. He closed his eyes and I moved in, all shameful efficiency: I yanked back the sheet from his shrunken body; I hitched down his pyjama bottoms without flinching at the sight or the smell, unpinned, wiped, and changed him. He gave a thread-fine shudder at my final movement: tucking the cooled sheet back over him. His mystery, power, gone.

Downstairs, at my window, a lawn of silvery fine dust had already appeared on the ledge I'd wiped just yesterday. There was still no sign of Yano's Pontiac. I reminded myself to drain the soybeans I'd been soaking overnight for dinner, and to slice and salt the cucumber for sunomono.

The beans had bloated up to the surface, along with the moulting husks, tiny corpses. I poured them into a sieve, all clustered against one another like a hive. I shivered at the sight. It was turning into the kind of day, I felt, when nothing looked quite the same. I dropped the beans into the sink, and went back to the front window.

There she was, my Sachi, crossing the field as I'd seen her on a hundred other days when she'd been skipping school to run off with Tam. Already wise to life, wiser about its possibilities than I'd ever been. I could never fool her, never keep her with my silly folding cranes or my heaven-earth-and-man flower arrangements, my pretend readings of tea leaves. I could never be angry with her for long. No wonder her mother didn't know what to do with her.

She was halfway across the field when she turned as if she knew I was looking out, though with the sun casting a glare over the window she couldn't possibly see me. Her hair was a dark blot, nothing blacker on that field. I came out onto my porch. She raised her hand to her mouth and I saw there was a cigarette clipped between her fingers. She looked foolish and mean, her one shoulder bare where her top slipped down—a summer top, too thin, too skimpy when it was only the middle of May. I fought the feeling welling in me as I saw her tiny hip jut through the cotton of her skirt; I detested that stance with everything in me. She puffed furiously in quick spurts, a little engine revving. All of a sudden she froze, spotting something where the glinting electrical towers marched like giants past the houses and into the distance. Then she ran. She stopped short at the base of a tower, the north one, closest to Mackenzie Hill. So small against the giant, yet I could read everything there in her posture, her turned hip, the way she held her head. Again she glanced back, daring me, knowing I wouldn't step down from my porch to stop her. She swung herself up the first rung. She was climbing, a slow struggle because the rungs were diagonal and widely spaced even for her gangly legs. Her skirt hitched up to expose the gleaming white of her underpants, white as the clouds.

I put my hand to my mouth. I was about to utter something. An awkward sound? Her name? "Get down here this instant," like the concerned mother I could never be? I held my hand there as she struggled higher and higher, higher than I'd seen her climb with Tam, up into the cut of the sun. Then she stopped and leaned her skinny neck and shoulders towards the creek where it curved down behind Mackenzie Hill, holding on with one arm wrapped around a steel beam. I knew she was looking for Tam, and hoping he'd be looking for her. I felt wet at one corner of my lip—my mouth was still open—and I knew the word just as my lips pushed against one another: "Baka!" I cried. Papa's word. Stupid! Get down! I'd taken another step when shouts from the far side of the field drowned me out. It was him, Tom, Nakamura-san, her father, on his day off, striding across the field, stopping himself from running. "Hey, hey!" he yelled, the way he always did, without using her name, as if she were anyone to him.

He arrived at the base of the tower, and once she saw him there she gave in instantly. As if all she'd wanted, all along, was for him to come for her. I knew it, for hadn't I felt that impulse, used that child's ruse, myself? She tugged at her skirt and began climbing down, almost daintily now. But just when she was about to reach him, she balked. She screamed and pointed past my house towards the creek. I heard Tam's name cried out, and her legs bounced, poised to climb again. Then he grabbed her. I'd come down my lawn by then, crossed the road, and as I hurried onto the field I saw that man's brute fist grabbing Sachi's skirt, pulling her as she screamed and screamed, her eyes darting and blinking all at once, like the light inside a siren. Once he got her, he slung her over his shoulder as if she were one of his two-by-fours to be nailed down in his unfinished basement, only she wasn't a piece of board, she flopped and kicked. He nodded at me as I ran up, some sort of polite gesture. His face was heated, red, his eyes only half rising from the ground as he kept his balance. "Sorry, Miss Saito," he called, and as he swung towards their house, Sachi glared at me through the web of her hair. She raised a finger in a rude gesture I'd seen other schoolchildren use with one another. "He's back there!" she screamed. "Go look! Go! For me!" And she strained over her father's shoulder, tethered there, almost diving into the field, except for the strong carpenter's hand that clamped her back.

In a few moments they'd disappeared into their house, and I was left standing alone as usual, the ridiculous one. The girl's cries rang in my ears and I half turned to head for the creek, but I stopped and marched myself back to the house. I bristled at Tom calling me Miss Saito, like some old thing, some old schoolmarm, when he could hardly be much younger. Even Yano called me Saito-san. I shook my head thinking of what Tom would have to contend with once he got her home. Hands grabbing at door handles left and right, holding on with all her might; legs kicking and banging, fighting him in his arms with each step he took down the hall to her room.

It was half-past eleven. Already the sun was overhead. They were somewhere: Yano and Chisako, driving with Tam and Kimi in back, a family. Down a pretty country road, green, with tips of spring colour sprouting in the ditches, somewhere together, for once. A little holiday on a whim, a day or two taken off work, the light in the living-room forgotten, who knows what else. I might have even urged Yano to do just that, had I thought of it.

More chores, and at last I sat down to read my paper, folded as I'd left it. I opened the paper and there it was. I remained calm, numb to it, I suppose. I ran my hand over the picture of Chisako, smudging it with my fingertips, which were suddenly damp. Awful picture. It was her, but before. Beside her, a hakujin, a white man, behind big horn-rimmed glasses so you couldn't really see him. Couldn't see his deep-set eyes, or his wavy hair that was dark but not quite black, or how tall he was. Her Mr. Spears. *Woman, man shot in lovers' lane*, it said.

In the chest, both of them, him once, her twice. *Husband, twin son and daughter missing.* It blurred as I tried to read on. *Found by boy and his dog Wednesday evening.* Inked in thick and black, their names for strangers to see: *Mrs. Chisako Yano, Mr. Donaldson Spears. Tamio and Kimiko, Mr. Masashi Yano.* Masashi. Who called him Masashi?

The field was silent. Children should have been out by now, on their way home for lunch, calling to one another, baby birds weeping to be fed. Something was wrong. Come out, come out, I wanted to call. Across the way, the rows of houses were straighter than ever, drapes drawn except for one. Closed eyes. Cold shoulders. Where were the children? No jeers, not even a *hey, chink lady.* Deserted. Nothing.

I ran into the field. Seized, I wanted to be seized. Like that girl, like my Sachi was, instantly and firmly. I ran until my heart was pounding, but still I felt shallow and light. *Shot twice. In the chest.* I touched myself there; the beat was slowing. I held out my hand but it was steady.

I found myself at the feet of the giant, where Sachi had stood, among the weeds. Cool and dry. I leaned and the cold metal shocked me at my hip. I held the rail and squeezed. Yards away, smoke spiralled up. I could not mistake the acrid smell from the grass, how something that is moist with life held in it smells when it burns. Suddenly children swarmed the south end of the field. In the distance, the middle-school bell rang. I ran to the spot of smoke and ground my heel over Sachi's stub of cigarette and the smouldering blades. The children were calling out to one another, rushing in as I backed away; quickly I returned to my porch.

I stepped inside the screen door in time to hear Papa's

faint wail. *Sa, sa, sa.* A lulling sound that brought me back to my life. I was not Chisako. No matter how many times I had wished it. Nor was I that girl pining for her special friend. I took a last look at the sky through the screen, and the flood of schoolchildren, like gulls come in from the lake when it starts to rain. The sky was blue as ever, with white puffy dashes. As I tried to keep Papa's call at bay, I kept seeing those dashes in blue, a ghost's hoary eyebrows raised at me. Whose, I could not say.

I went into the kitchen to prepare lunch. I noticed that the clock on the stove already said 12:16. No wonder Papa was wailing for his lunch. The school bell must have gone off late.

"Chotto matte," I called up to Papa. Just a minute. I heard my own voice, cheery almost, forgetful. Steady. There with my tray at the doorway. Then Chisako came to me again, the thought of her, and I had to set it down. Chisako. Dead. I'd have to say it to myself aloud, to make myself understand.

Some time later, I sat down to rest on the chesterfield for a moment or two; I did not go to my window. I noticed the newsprint that stained my fingertips, the pitch that had not come off through all the chores of washing and wiping and dusting I'd got on with. I marvelled at that, the consolation of my quiet life, the getting on: my calm. My grief, oddly removed from myself.

For I had long ago understood that you had to live in the midst of things to be affected, in the swirl of the storm, you might say. And once you did, only then could you be for ever changed. You couldn't simply sit and watch, imagining from time to time how such-and-such would feel, would be, what happened to others and not to you.

I hadn't spoken to Chisako in a long while, or so it seemed. It felt as though months had passed, and yet it could only have been days, perhaps not even a week. I had not said what I would have wanted to be my last words to her.

TWO

STUM CAME HOME A little later than usual that evening. I'd read that newspaper over and over, searching for clues, but nothing had come of it. Even the air was staler in the house, the way I could imagine the inside of an airplane, though I'd never been in one. Stum must have been sitting in the living-room for several minutes before I realized he was there. He was still sitting, staring at nothing, when I came in to tell him dinner was ready. At dinner, he began to mash the beans between his teeth.

"You cooked them too much," he said, frowning. "And the rice." He let the grains drop from his chopsticks.

"You were late coming home," I said, calmly taking the dishes away. He groaned and pushed his plate back. The clatter of our two dinner plates against one another sounded more hollow than usual.

"You heard?" His voice popped out then, seemed almost

to disappear. I nodded and continued clearing. As I bent over him, I noticed the tiniest feather on his shirt collar, and it took my breath away; I felt it furry and sodden in my throat, blocking my passages. I reached down and flicked it off.

Stum brought down Papa's dishes after feeding him. I was watching the window of Yano's house, the blue Pontiac still missing. As it grew dark, the light burning in their empty living-room seemed harsh, almost obscene. All across that one block of houses, drapes were modestly shut, cars in driveways, shelved for the evening, including the Nakamuras'.

"They won't be back." Stum's voice came in a hush, and for a few seconds I was inside Yano's empty living-room, alone with nobody home. Standing like this, we were both trespassers, peeping Toms. I stepped away nervously. Where were the police? Why hadn't they come around yet?

"Nobody's coming home to close them," Stum said, meaning the drapes on the window.

"There aren't any," I replied. In four years Chisako had never hung drapes. Not that Stum noticed such things. Briskly I closed our curtains, leaving us in darkness. "They'll be back."

"If you say so."

"He took them some place safe. Safe from whoever did this."

"If you say so." Stum flopped down onto the chesterfield.

"Stop it." I punched the cushions beside him, smoothing out the creases.

"Whatever you say." He slid to the end of the chesterfield, sifted into shadow. After a moment, he got up, shuffled towards the kitchen, his lazy feet snagging the carpet. "What do I know?" he muttered over his shoulder.

I turned on the lamp. Eiji's portrait on the end table was lit beneath it. My nii-san, my older brother; I was so much older than him now. He didn't look himself tonight, his young smile seemed callous. A thought struck me.

"How would you know? Did you talk to him?" I moved to the doorway of the kitchen. "Did you?"

Stum shook his head, his back to me.

"Did you speak to Yano?" I stepped in front of him as he tried to pass, munching peanuts.

He held his hands up to his face like a fence, his shoulders slinking down in that imbecilic way he had. "You know I didn't. I don't talk to that weirdo." As I took my place at the window, he added: "He's a kamikaze Jap." He smiled, a vulgar smile, sucking in his lopsided pincushion face. "You know that." He wheeled out to the backyard, screen door twanging like a sinew in my heart. My brother, a fool, the foolishness of my life. The cold slapped against me.

It was sometime later in the evening when I sensed Chisako there with me, floating through my house in her vibrant colours. I was relieved to feel her presence, as if it were a sign—of what, I didn't know. I could see her now as she had been when she visited me in my home two, perhaps three weeks earlier.

It must have been those colours she wore, like flower bursts, that convinced the neighbours she was the real thing, from Japan. While I had my quiet browns and navies. On one or two occasions I saw hakujin men slow down on the street just to watch her, to try to catch her eye. A true Japanese lady from a samurai family. That was what she told me, her lowly lady-in-waiting. That was what I was, but I didn't mind. The Saitos were samurai too, but I kept that to myself, letting her have her moment. I knew what it meant to her, for all her nonchalance. That day, she wore a cherry-red scarf at her neck, less fine than her usual style—tie-dyed by her daughter, by Kimiko, she told me. There were rings inside rings on it, all bleeding into the centre, staining the white parts. It seemed to trick my eyes, the rings heaving with tremors, and I couldn't decide whether the red was staining a white piece of cloth, or the white was bleaching out the red. Then, stupidly, I realized she was sobbing, and her shoulders were convulsing.

"Chisako, what is it?" I flapped around her, not daring to touch. "You're tired," I said. "I've kept you too long." I glanced at the front door of my modest home, which I now so wanted empty, to myself. Her sobs were too messy and loud in my ears. She waved her hands in front, as if groping for a wall in the dark, the edge of things, and her crying subsided. It was then that I heard Papa's low whine resume upstairs, the buzz of some rickety appliance. For once welcome.

"No, no." She shook her head, and a strand fallen out of her bun caught between her teeth—that thick nihonjin hair, strong as dental floss. In a second it snapped. "Asako," she said, grasping my name tightly in her mouth, not wanting to let it go. As if it were the first time, the last time she would say it. "No, no," she repeated. All I could do was stare out my window at the towers glinting in the afternoon sun, as Chisako began sobbing again. I urged her to sit down.

"It's him," she said. "Yano." Even she, his wife, called him that. Not Masashi. Not Masa. "Hidoi hito," she whispered, squeezing more tears from her eyes. "He's a monster." She groaned, clutching her left side, and bowed her head in pain.

"What is it, Chisako?" To my surprise, I felt tears in my own eyes; I shed them as if they belonged to a stranger, not knowing whom they were for, or why. When she saw my wet eyes, Chisako's lips curled into a smile. "You are so kind," and again she said my name, this time with tenderness. She moved closer to me on the chesterfield, as if wanting to whisper in my ear, though we were alone. I was about to assure her of that when her dainty fingers began to loosen the blouse tucked inside her skirt. I watched, unable to look away.

"Last night, when he came home, he was crazy. Hidoi hito," she repeated. "Look." She lifted her blouse and her fingers, yellowy-white at the tips, the nails barely tinged with blue, spidered over her ribs. The skin was white, pale as snow; it took my breath away. There were only faint marks where the band of her bra had bitten her skin. The orb of one mesh-covered breast hung over it, full for a nihonjin woman, I couldn't help thinking. She heaved a sigh. "Well?" she said, suddenly impatient. I looked again over that paleness, and saw nothing, no blemish, no scar, no bruise or discoloration. I blinked, waiting, hoping for some sign. I murmured some noise, something, and she dropped her blouse like a curtain, those dainty fingers tucking it back in. She glanced at me, then turned away.

"Don't worry. It's not as painful as it looks," she said, now quite matter-of-fact.

"I see." I was about to offer her green tea when she sank back into the chesterfield. Limp. Not like her.

"Don't worry yourself over me, Saito-san," she said sharply. Then, soft and low, she added: "I know what I have to do." That was so like her, to be harsh one minute, then kind the next: cold and hot. She looked down at the high-heeled shoes she hadn't wanted to leave at my door, stared at them, digging their soiled pointy toes into my carpet. "I'll leave him. I don't care what anyone says." Something must have shown on my face, for she smiled. "It's all right, Saito-san. I know people say waru-guchi about Yano, even the children say bad things. The Nakamuras. Maybe your brother too. The people who never come to his redress meetings. All he does is talk about the war and the camps when they just want to forget. They think he's crazy, I know." A thought seemed to dawn on her. "But you couldn't stand it either, could you? That's why you chose to be on your own, isn't it, Saito-san?" She didn't wait for my response. "You're brave, Saito-san. Kashi-koi, smart, ne?"

I wanted to tell her it wasn't true, I wasn't brave at all. I hadn't chosen. What had I made of myself?

Chisako had made herself a beauty. Had grown into one, miraculously. She hadn't been one in the beginning. When she first came, she was plain, almost as plain as me. To see her, I didn't feel so badly about myself. Slowly it happened. It wasn't difficult to put your finger on, like some changes. It was little more than a year ago, when she took a part-time job in the mail-order department of some manufacturing company. She withheld bits of information from me, like the company name, where she took the bus to three

afternoons a week, what precisely she did there; from the
first day, it was to be her secret life. I dared ask if it was
nihonjin she worked for, but "Oh, no, Saito-san," she
replied, with a touch of disdain I could not mistake. Pinning
her hair in an upsweep, her black, black hair that had no grey.
Dabbing white powder to her face, red lipstick and black eye-
liner. At first it seemed too dramatic, to see her standing at
the bus stop at noon in our little suburban neighbourhood.
But I grew used to it, and the makeup that seemed to float
over her features soon melded into them: her skin grew paler,
her eyes more slanted and round, her hair a lacquered black.
Little by little there were more changes. The hand cupping
her mouth when she laughed, the downcast eyes, the dainty
steps. I found it irritating, even laughable, in my living-room.
But one day I saw her out on the street. She'd stopped to
look at something, and the way she held her head just so, her
bony white neck showing with her coat open, even in winter.
Seeing her that time, I thought to myself that she didn't
belong here at all.

When I looked at my own face in the mirror, I found I
could no longer bear it. My faults glared back at me: my eyes
hidden and small, my mouth pinched and drooped. My
plain self had grown ugly even as Chisako had blossomed. In
my daily routine, I could not help watching my body as if it
were apart from me, growing ugly and growing old: my
stubby hands passing Papa's yellowed sheets through the
wringer, the crêpy pull of skin on my forearms when I
reached into the high kitchen cupboard. I took baths in the
dark to avoid seeing the changes happening to me. My thickening toenails, the short hairs that fell from my head to the

bathroom floor, more and more, some a wiry white. I was past the age for long hair, and it was now too thin. I no longer wondered, even in my most capricious moments, what man might touch my skin that was becoming dark and rough. Like nori, I laughed bitterly to myself; I was shrivelling to dried seaweed. And yet, seeing those men watch Chisako, I imagined how I might disgrace myself.

That day, Chisako paused in her sobbing and looked up; her makeup melted away to show skin almost as flawed as mine, and her eyes swam through, pink at the rims, and black and small as minnows in her face.

"What is it, Chisako?" I asked gently, though I'd wanted to push her out of my sight, to the bathroom, to fix herself up. Instead, she went to my living-room window, to my chair there. I stood at her shoulder as the light poured in, seeing through her eyes what I saw each day. My clear view of the houses on the other side of the field, including her own with its gaping front. I felt exposed, felt a small panic at being discovered. Afraid that Chisako might, in spite of being preoccupied with her own worries, grasp the little life spent here at my window, day after day, with only the comings and goings of others, of herself, to entertain me. Yet I was relieved that someone else might know, might perceive the worst of me. I did not mind if it was her. Papa may have made a noise then, crying out to be changed, but I ignored it, as Chisako graciously did.

"I should put up drapes, shouldn't I?" was all she said. "Keep our secrets to ourselves, ne?" She clucked her tongue. "Those towers are such ugly things. Does it depress you, Saito-san, to wake up to those each morning? They're cages, ne?"

Before I could respond, I spotted two figures struggling out to the middle of the field, black heads bobbing amid the waves of grass. "Look. I'll bring them in for cookies," I offered, eagerly reaching for my sweater on a nearby chair.

"No, no," Chisako said quickly, pinching my forearm as if I were a child who'd unknowingly done something to be punished. She grimaced as she released my arm, then her smile returned. "Let them go on. They have their secrets. You remember what it was like at that age." We watched them as they crossed, Tam's strides carrying him a little farther with each step, Kimi half running to keep up.

"Look at them," Chisako said, folding her arms under her breasts. "So chiisai, ne? So insignificant. They must be the shortest in their class." She did not try to hide the disgust in her voice. She disappeared into my bathroom for several minutes, emerging as her old elegant self, her face evenly powdered. She thanked me many times, and apologized for her outburst. "I'm urusai, I know. Don't mind me."

"No, no," I said, "not urusai, no bother at all. Never."

At the door she bowed dowdily, avoiding my eyes.

As I recall, the afternoon light fell on Eiji's portrait in a particular way after Chisako left that day. His smile there, his arm flopped over the armchair in our Port Dover living-room, long ago, before we left Vancouver Island and the sea that he loved. Before everything. He might have just turned sixteen. As I looked into his face, he called to me with his smile. Asa-chan. The sound of my name—no one else ever said it that way, not Mama, not Papa, not Stum. It brought feeling into my heart for Chisako.

I greeted her eagerly on the street the next time I saw her,

anxious to show my sympathy. She was just stepping off the
bus. I searched her face for signs of distress. "Chisako, genki?"

"Yes, yes, I'm fine, thank you, Saito-san," she replied
brusquely, amid the squawk of the departing bus. Her eyes
flitted over my coat, my drab coat that could hardly have
been to her taste. "Specials on ika and sashimi downtown,"
she said with a cold smile at the ground, adjusting her many
shopping bags. "Very fresh today." She murmured something else too: a hasty goodbye, I thought, but she did not
leave. I looked away too, out to the field, to the giants,
Chisako's cages—the electrical towers. How people could
have it in their heads to build such hideous things was beyond
me; on that afternoon they reminded me of giant ika, standing in the field with their long squid legs. I edged away,
nearly bumping into a woman—a big-boned hakujin woman
in a kerchief passing at that moment. I recognized her as
Keiko Nakamura's next-door neighbour. "Hello ladies," she
said, her hand with its large knuckles tugging delicately
at the kerchief, and we answered in unison, sounding sweet
and obedient. She and Chisako exchanged a smile. Chiisai,
we're chiisai, I thought, so small, so insignificant, like Tam
and Kimi. I saw my house in the distance, the porch light
I'd left on by mistake tunnelling into my eyes in bright
daylight. Flashing a message of my loneliness. But Chisako
was beautiful, I saw that again, like a newly discovered fact.
She was beautiful in anyone's eyes. A wife, a mother. With
bags of groceries for her family. "Saito-san," she started
to say, but by then I'd moved away, to cross the field for
home, and even as I saw she was hurt it was too late. I called
out something about getting back to Papa. Getting back

because I could not endure myself in her presence for one second longer.

"Ne-san!" It was Stum, staring at me, concerned. In his little-boy moments that was what I was, his ne-san, his older sister. But I saw myself in his eyes, slumped back on the chesterfield, looking lost.

"Nani?"

"It's Papa. Something's wrong." I listened but it was unusually quiet, no whine or hum from upstairs. When I stood up, my knee buckled, still asleep.

"What happened?" I followed Stum up the stairs.

"He made a funny noise, and then..." His untucked shirt-tail flapped at the back, his belt slapped his thigh as we hurriedly climbed and his muffled voice fell back in my ears. I crossed the hall into Papa's room, pushed myself past the doorway. I closed and opened my eyes once to feel something that fit together. The room was silent, the air sucked right out. He lay still, too still, his head back farther than usual. His lips and eyes were clenched shut, but saliva shone all around his mouth, puddling on his pillow, more than usual. I heard the toilet flush and Stum came up behind me, leaning over my shoulder.

"I was on the benjo when I heard it," he whispered shakily. "He's leaking." He pointed at Papa's lips as if that were the sign, instead of the fact that he wasn't breathing.

I stood there, watching, waiting for the slightest rise in his chest. "Do something," Stum hissed in my ear.

Slowly, I leaned down and listened. Holding my own breath. I did not touch him. Seconds passed. Do something,

I told myself. I felt Stum pinch my elbow, hard; I'd have a bruise by morning. I reached down to Papa's neck, what I'd seen the nurses do. His lips were more purple than ever, and gummy. I would not, could not press my lips to those, even to save him.

"Ne-san, do something!" Stum repeated, only louder. He put his hand on my back to push me down closer. As he did, Papa's eyes flickered open and a whistle of air streamed from between those lips onto my cheek, and saliva bubbled up. It smelled sour, as sour as Eiji's had been sweet, up until the very last moment.

A whole day passed without word or trace of them. Late that night I finally fell into a deep sleep, but in the morning, watching Stum pull out of the driveway, I was suddenly tired. I'd managed to keep everyone from my thoughts except Sachi. It was all I could do. I tried to let each moment sit, then move on, tick tick tick. But each hour brought me closer to the possibility of what Stum had said being true: they were gone, every one of them. Then the tick tick grew fierce.

Today was Saturday. The field was quiet. The Nakamuras' front drapes remained closed. She was in there, shut inside her room. I worried about her alone, trapped there, her nerves squeezed tight. I wondered if she might hurt herself. I had no faith in Keiko or Tom to prevent it, much less help her. I knew the way they were with her, she didn't have to tell me. They'd come home to her tired, with no patience, no understanding to coax her still, no words.

The window of the Yano house gaped wide as ever, as if its occupants had been evicted. A police car was parked in front but there were no signs of anyone around or inside the house.

I went out back to the garden to look at my peonies. They were all blooming at once now, so many of them, on both sides of the yard. My climbing pink roses were budding, and my irises were rising stark and rich. But the sight made me a little sick at heart, all the lush pink and purple and pure white coming up around me, because in no time they'd be brown and curling, ruined. As I cut a few stems, I imagined Sachi beside me, wincing with each snip of my scissors and letting of sap, like the first time she'd visited. I brought the flowers inside and the smell in the house seemed to sweeten at once, in spite of Papa.

It was around this time of year when Sachi and I had our first visit together. She was much smaller then, only nine or ten. Truly a child. A hot spell had tricked my hybrid tea-roses into early bloom; the nights were still cold. I'd brought out my tall glass bottles and covered the blossoms close to the ground, gently bending their heads as a protection against the night frost that would surely come. I was considering plastic wrap for the taller buds when I noticed one or two broken off, the stems oozing their fluid thicker than dew. I touched the stickiness and brought it to my mouth, as if to stop the flow of blood from a finger cut. It tasted bitter instead of sweet.

By the fence at the far end of the yard, I spied the gaudy yellow and red stripes of a candy-bar wrapper in the grass. I was reaching to thread my arm under the slats and grasp the wrapper between my fingers when I heard a rustle, and breath sipped up, little by little. Instinctively I glanced up at

Papa's window, where, on good days in the past, he sometimes struggled to sit, but he wasn't there. It was then I found
her with me in my garden, twisting the flower off one of my
hybrid teas with her stubby little hands. There were two
more by her feet, the pink heads already wilting. "Stop that!"
I snapped. I was furious but instantly felt sheepish; she was
just a child, I told myself, she didn't know any better. She
let my rose droop on its half-broken stalk and stood up.
She held her hands behind her, as if offering herself pris-
oner. On the pale yellow blouse she wore, I noticed two
round shadows where her breasts were starting, like spreading stains. I was more than a smidgen taller than her, but I
could tell from her long neck, thin as my rose stems, that she
would grow.

We knew each other. We'd been seeing one another for
years now on opposite sides of the field. I'd seen her with her
mother, a short woman with thick, muscular calves and dark
skin. I'd see Keiko tug Sachi along on the street, gripping
tight as she struggled to break free. The child fixed on me as
I took my morning walk through the field, among the electrical towers that Keiko warned her away from. Wondering
what I was to her.

I took Keiko Nakamura for Okinawan because of her
swarthy complexion, which stayed through winter. She was
like me, nisei, that was obvious. Perhaps it was that look of
toughness, being the second generation in Canada but the
first born here, I don't know. The wind first carried her name
to me when the husband, Tom, called from his car in the driveway, half getting out: *Keiko, nan-to you wa*, complaining about
something she hadn't done his way as she stood holding the

screen door half open in the morning. *Kay, come on in for a coffee sometime, won't you?* from that big-knuckled woman next door. Neither Tom nor Keiko knew what to do with the child, unruly, wilful child, I saw that; even I knew better.

"So?" I said to Sachi as she stood in my garden that day. I didn't know how I meant the word, in English or in Japanese, or if she understood it could mean something in both. She stared, then thrust out her arms and her hands holding my broken blossoms.

"Sorry," she blurted, not sounding sorry at all. Like a rebellious child being told to give her teacher flowers, though they were from my own garden. "Miss Saito," she added, knowing I'd be surprised, even flattered she knew my name. As I took the flower-tops from her I noticed small cuts on the backs of her hands. They were too long to be pricks from thorns; some were fresh. I winced. It had started back then, the small tortures in the kitchen at night while her parents slept.

"Itai? Does it hurt?" I asked, eyeing her hands.

She shook her head. She was still clutching one flower that had stayed furled tight, an eye shut against the light. "They were gonna die anyway," she declared. "When the cold comes back at night." Without blinking, watching me with each word: "Then they shrivel into old babies."

Inside she sat on the chesterfield as I dabbed iodine on her cuts. She didn't flinch. After a moment she sat up. "What's that?" It took me a moment to realize she meant Papa. It was the low buzz I carried in my head all day, even when I left the house. Even in my sleep. I barely thought twice.

"Nothing," I said. After a moment I added: "Just the fan upstairs." She paused, listening closely, glanced at me, then kicked her legs against the couch.

"There. No need for bandages," I said. "Let the air heal them. That's the best thing." I tightened the cap on the iodine bottle and pushed it aside. She slipped her hands out of mine and sat forward, knowing I was going to ask her about the cuts, how she got them. The flower heads lay in a pile on the coffee table in front of us.

"Does it hurt them?"

"What? Oh, no," I assured her. She was staring at the short stems, ragged at their ends. She eased herself away from me as if I were something she'd broken off too.

"Well, maybe a little," I said, watching her mouth wilt at the corners. Her lips naturally drooped into a frown. "But no more than when they're cut in full bloom," I added, conscious of my own meagre smile.

Sachi pointed to where the stems had leaked their bitter fluid onto the coffee table. "Look," she said, and her voice quivered. "They're bleeding."

I laughed.

"My mom says they bleed to death when I pick them," she said. A cruel thing to tell a child, I thought, just to keep a garden. She lowered her head and stared into her lap, where her hands fidgeted. Without thinking, I reached out and held one in mine. Her small fingers were stiff; they wouldn't collapse inside my clammy palm. I wanted to say, they're only plants; not flesh and blood, like you. I wanted to pinch her and hold her. I yearned for it. This was different from when Stum was a child. Holding him, my own body young yet, I

didn't wonder then how it felt to be a mother, to have someone grow inside you.

I'd held on too long. Sachi pulled away gently. I drew
back, my hand hanging cold.

"That's why I picked your flowers instead of my mom's,"
she blurted with a mean smile. She could change in an
instant; be almost pretty, then brutally plain. She bounded to
the foot of the stairs, put one foot on the first step, glanced
back at me with my pounding heart. "The fan sounds tired,"
she whispered, blowing on her finger.

I tried to draw her back to me, bringing out my ikebana
things from the dining-room cabinet, clattering the porcelain
vase onto the coffee table to drown out the whine from
upstairs, but she stayed put. She watched me trim and stab
the short rose stems into the kenzan. Hesitantly she made
her way over. "Earth, moon, stars," I said, and I hastily held
a cluster of leaves this way and that under the flowers. "My
mom says it's heaven, earth, and man," she said, and I felt the
heat in my cheeks telling me I'd got it wrong. Then she
leaned in close to the three roses and moved her lips slightly,
whispering again. "They're dead now," she said. Then, after
another moment, asked, "Can I go now, Miss Saito?"

I watched her from my window as she waded into the
field. For an instant I thought about calling Keiko to say her
daughter had been with me, in case she was worried, as I'd
be, wondering why Sachi was late. But Keiko wouldn't like it,
not one bit, me knowing more about her daughter than she,
even for an hour one afternoon.

Sachi dawdled through the field that day, stopping to
gaze up at an electrical tower gleaming in the light. She slid

her hand along the rail, along its edge. If Keiko could see, she'd be yanking the girl away from the tower, back home, disgusted with her brooding and dawdling.

The memory of her in the field, looking a little lost, looking everywhere but back at me to find her way, stabbed at me. I kept telling myself that it was Tam and Kimi who were in danger, not her, but I couldn't help fearing that something was happening to her, at this very moment, when I couldn't be with her. I couldn't help telling myself that if I had kept Sachi close, these terrible things would never have happened—a ridiculous thought that made no sense. My living-room, where I always waited for her visits, felt empty without her; even the sound of Papa upstairs became a comfort I'd had and lost: a bridge that once held my weight, now collapsed. I felt useless.

Slowly I made my way up to his room. He was sleeping deeply, his breathing clear and even with the drops Dr. Honda had prescribed over the telephone last night. "You fuss too much, Saito-san," the doctor had said. "He's old." I sat down on his bed, careful not to wake him. I always stood, bustling around him with something to do; I never sat. The mattress had grown too soft, like sponge-cake. He shifted and groaned and I sprang up. I would not want him to find me like this. But he slept on.

My chest began to ache and I realized I was holding my breath. This room made everything stop.

In the bathroom, I sat down on the cold seat under the open window. My shikko came out slow and warm, a deep yellow almost like green tea, and took for ever—a relief I'd withheld from myself all morning, until I'd finished my chores. Downstairs there was a banging on the screen door, then Sachi calling me. I looked in quickly on Papa; I shut his door partway, then hurried down. At the sight of her lurking outside the screen door, some feeling welled up in me—gratitude, relief, I wasn't sure what, but I was happy to see her. I was careful, though; she'd detest me if I let it show. She seemed fine, rested even, and she was wearing a little pink T-shirt with jeans. I let her in. Without the mesh between us, I saw that her eyes were actually puffy as though from too little sleep. But this time her face wasn't stained with dirt or food. She smelled of soap; Keiko must have made her take a bath. She looked neat, but she was ticking away.

"Miss Saito." Her eyes were black and searching.

"Sachi, you're right," I started to say, "Tam is fine, he's—"

She stopped me cold. "I need you to take me in your car, Miss Saito. Right away."

"My brother takes the car in the morning. You know that." I chided her as if she should know my life, the smallest details of it, by rote. She stood there, aloof, tolerating me, without a word in answer. Cold to me. Cruel to me. She must have noticed something, my uncombed hair, my eyes; she seemed to soften. She was such an adult, the way she could change just like that, like Chisako in a way. Mask her feelings, her disdain for me; humour me for the moment. She tugged me close, knowing the effect that had. She drew me up to the screen door, as if to let me in on something.

"Miss Saito!" she hissed, wiggling a dirty fingernail at the driveway. There it was. I rarely saw it by day. It was hideous, really, an eyesore, with rust spots that scabbed the fender. Sachi was wringing her hands.

"Miss Saito, your brother got in at two this morning and went right back out. He left with somebody in another car." She said it like a little wind-up machine.

"How did you know?" My mind was clicking too but nothing engaged. Stum staying away all night, not calling. My sleeping straight through. Without the snap of the inside door lock to let me sleep once he got in from Sunday-night shift. The night passing with only Papa and me in the house. It was true: I hadn't seen or heard Stum leave this morning. I'd only thought I had, out of habit.

"I was watching for Tam, and I saw. Can we go now, Miss Saito?" She tugged at me, the sleeve of Mama's good mohair sweater. "Please? I'm sure your brother's okay."

"Where?"

"You know." But she didn't move.

"For how long?" I glanced up the stairs. Sachi waited several seconds before answering, so we could both listen for the quiet rhythm that came from up there.

"Half-hour, that's all." Her wilted mouth turned up at the ends but it wasn't a smile. I scurried upstairs. Behind me I heard "He'll survive."

She sat in the passenger seat, her flat shiny forehead rising a little above the dashboard, her eyes darting again. She was small, like Tamio and Kimi. Sitting there, punching her fists on her legs as she watched the streets pass. Chiisai. I saw the curve of Chisako's lips saying it.

Sachi had brought me away from my place at the window,

out of my routine. Made me do what she'd wanted. Outside here, I was lost. I saw myself wandering by the feet of those towers, back and forth for years to come, until they took them down. No Yano to trail after me, no Sachi to watch after. And now, no Chisako to come to me with her dramatic stories. What would I do with myself? The thought of Stum being gone even for a night made me queasy with panic. Where did he go? Who was his friend? Hadn't I known all along that Stum would one day leave? Even he wasn't afraid not to come home.

I hadn't driven in years. But this I could manage. Seeing the world pass on either side, my foot resting steadily on the pedal. I remembered that I liked driving, keeping between this line and that, watching for signs that warned you what was ahead. I held the steering wheel firmly at ten and two o'clock; it felt good in my hands, familiar. I pulled out to the concession road and the electrical field slid past. In my rearview mirror, the towers were shrinking into toys. Mackenzie Hill loomed ahead to the right.

"I'm sure he's all right," I said again. "His father must have taken him and his sister some place safe." I avoided saying Yano's name. "Soon the police will find—"

"Faster!" She pounded on the dashboard. "No, wait!" Sachi bolted up in her seat, twisting. "That way." She pointed right, to the gravel road that led to the hill through a flat field. I overshot it and had to back up.

"How could you miss it?" she cried as we bumped along. She gripped the dashboard with her little fingers. I'd wanted to miss it. I'd wanted to go on just like this, rolling past, behind the haze of the windshield, so that no news, good or bad, could ever reach us. At least until we were safely past the hill, that dark lump of coal on the smooth sky.

"This isn't going to help." I heard the pleading in my voice, the tinge of desperation. We were slowing down.

"Keep going! Keep going!"

My foot was now dangling off the pedal, I saw that. I saw my shoes, Mama's old shoes that I wore out of stinginess. My ankles were thickening, my fluids pooling, Dr. Honda had said. He said I couldn't stop it, I could stand on my head and it wouldn't make them slim again. The car grew sluggish, everything sliding down.

"Speed up!" She pounded the dashboard.

"Urusai!" I muttered, coming to a full stop. Nuisance. I should be doing my chores, I thought.

"Then go home. Where you belong!" She flew out the door. I called after her but she ran and ran towards the hill. She didn't turn back and I could tell from the way she plunged her body into the wind, the way it grabbed her hair ragged, she didn't care if I was watching and waiting, not this time. From this side of the hill I saw the ski lift, closed for the season, red needles stuck in the ground. I felt a shiver. Something bad. The girl running as she always was: away from Tom, from Keiko, away from me; to Tam, only to Tam, lashing her thin body with all her might. I didn't want to follow, but I couldn't let her go alone. I accelerated and, with the open door flapping, came up so close behind that I saw the workings of her shoulder blades beneath her shirt. I smelled the acrid smell that came from Mackenzie Hill from time to time; it was a hill made of garbage. It reminded me of another scent from long ago, of burning flesh.

"Sachi!" I slowed the car and stopped, but she kept running, even sped up. This time I pulled in front, stopped, and stepped out.

"Get in!" I shouted. Abruptly she marched up to the car and did as she was told.

We drove along the north-east side of the hill to where trees sprang up and thickened around an abandoned parking lot. The overgrown driveway came into sight yards ahead. She sat quietly panting beside me. I stopped and pulled her arms to me, rougher than I meant to be because I thought she'd resist, and I held out her hands. The criss-cross of scars took my breath away but there was no blood, no fresh cuts. The skin was dark in parts, brown and dull from not healing properly. Her hands looked weathered, old. She yanked them away. I thought of the game I'd seen children play with one another, palm to palm, sliding them away fast to slap the tops of one another's hands. Squealing from the excitement of it, the violence.

"Satisfied?" she blurted. She balled up her hands and tucked them in her armpits. "Now go," she ordered, as if she knew the place, had been here before.

I inched the car into the lot, branches scratching at its sides. The first time I'd driven right in. It was barely big enough for ten cars; the parking lines were long faded or ground in with dirt. We rolled over roots of trees that broke the asphalt like grasping fingers.

"Over there," she said, pointing to the farthest edge. The trees fractured the light coming in. The ground was dappled where Sachi pointed, whitish in spots over the gravelly asphalt. She opened the car door and fresh air drifted in, a slow invasion.

How I longed to be back on my porch with Sachi, feeding her milk and cookies, whispering a harmless word in her ear. "There's nothing here," I said.

"What if Tam left something?" She raked her fingers in rows across her palms.

"Don't be silly. Tam wasn't here. Why would he—"

She slammed the door before I could say more, leaving me alone with my hasty words; alone in this private place, a forbidden place where too many things had happened. Who else had known about this spot? Only the boy and dog who'd found them, Chisako and her hakujin friend. Now the rest of the world. From a distance it was just a cluster of trees at the side of the hill; in winter it was an island frozen over. The trees drooped down now, the bushes curled in thickly, knit up the sky except for a circle at the very top. A place where the sun was kept out and the wind was buffered.

Sachi was tiptoeing carefully between two trees opposite one another, looking for something; the tattered ends of the yellow police ribbon trailed from their trunks waist-high. I was queasy thinking of Chisako, remembering the stretch of unmarked skin over her ribs she'd shown me that afternoon weeks ago, what I hadn't seen. Whatever it had been, it was too late to know. She and her Mr. Spears were dead.

I didn't want to know what had happened to them here that day. I'd warned her, I could hear myself telling Chisako, exactly what I'd dared to say. At the time worried that I sounded like an old busybody schoolteacher with no life of her own.

I looked down through the steering wheel I gripped; my feet were still perched on the pedals. Inside, the air felt close.

Through the dirty windshield I saw Sachi crouched low to the ground, her head twisted back with one eye masked by her hair; she stared straight at me. She wanted me to come to her, I knew. She needed my help, she wanted it. Without a word, she was asking me to. I didn't know what she was looking for or why I had brought her here where Keiko never would, would not have let her out the door if she'd known. I looked back. *Yes, I'm coming.* I grabbed my handbag and fumbled for the door handle.

When I reached her she was crouched to examine a spot by her foot, a rust-coloured stain. She recoiled from my outstretched hand the tiniest bit, high-strung as ever. "Sachi?" My voice a whimper. All around the stain were overlapping footprints, even a dog's paws stamped into the dirt-covered asphalt. In the early morning just three days ago the police had arrived, ambulance, newspapers, the boy with his dog, pointing, leading them in. There were traces of white powder sifted in with the dirt in no particular pattern. Sachi shuffled forward on her haunches, sniffing at the ground as the dog must have. I grabbed her elbow and pulled her to her feet. She stumbled back.

"You can't do that to me!" She shook herself free, then snapped to the ground again. She dragged her finger across the stain, a delicate arrangement of dust that dispersed easily. I tried to grab her wrist but she sprang back. She held her finger in mid-air for a moment, then wiped it on her pants. I backed away. I didn't know she could be like this, this possessed, this crazed.

"What are you doing? Stop it."

"It's her blood," she said. "Tam's mom." I thought of the

black smudges on my fingertips from reading the paper the day of Chisako's death, the greasiness that wouldn't wash off.

"How do you know it wasn't...her friend?"

"He came out the driver's side." She pointed a few yards off.

"We shouldn't be here." When I reached for her again, I noticed my hand was trembling.

"I'm not going." She was peering through the trees and down at the footprints that trampled over and over themselves.

"I'll leave without you!" I stamped my foot childishly but she ignored me, waiting out my tantrum, as I would hers. She rubbed her thumb and finger together, the finger she'd traced through Chisako's dried blood. Why didn't they clean things up? She terrified me but I couldn't leave.

"I thought, of anybody, you'd understand," she said, a quiet reproach, but there was panic underneath. "Because you've seen Tam and me."

"I don't know anything!" I snapped. I would not encourage these ideas of hers, this feverishness. Perhaps I was too harsh. I saw now how she was, how desperate for some clue to find Tam. I wanted to shush her, to take her scarred hands in mine and hold her, but that was not what she wanted. So instead I set down my handbag and slowly began searching the ground for something, anything, I didn't know what, futile as it seemed. To show her I cared. She did the same, circling the spot where the bodies had lain, moving out wider and wider into the woods. We continued for some time, in silence, I afraid of what I'd see in the snarl of twigs and leaves and dirt. For I did know some of what went on in this place.

"Miss Saito," she said, still crouching. Something had changed; the panic was gone, the pleading. Her voice stole up. She stepped gingerly among low-lying bushes, circling. "You'll miss him, won't you?"

My heart stopped. Eiji? Stum? I wasn't sure whom she meant. All I could do was stare into the mess, my feet in Mama's soiled shoes. Could she mean Yano? I straightened up abruptly, brushed off my skirt. "What are you talking about?" I would not fall into her trap. I turned towards Mackenzie Hill. There it was, what I could see of it through tree trunks straight as bars. The sparse fringe of leafless trees along the top. I felt my heels sink into soft earth, anchoring me here, with her, my tormentor.

"Why did you make me come?"

"It's not like it's the first time."

I cringed at that, hoping she'd say no more. Leave it unspoken, all she knew, all I knew. Leave me be. "You could have come on your bicycle, by yourself," I said. "You seemed to know your way."

"I wanted you to see."

"Sachi, there's nothing," I said. "Nanni mo nai," I murmured. I felt safe behind those words. "Why would Tam leave something here?" With that I strode back to the car, my heels punching holes in the ground with each vigorous step.

"He knew about this place, he might've," she called out, not letting me escape.

Cold fell over my shoulders. So Tam knew. I didn't wish to ponder that, what it could mean. I stopped myself from rushing into the car, kept my pace even. I got in and started it up. Through the windshield I saw Sachi scoop up the handbag I'd left behind and scurry towards me. Already I was pulling out.

"I wanted you to come, Miss Saito," she said, breathless as she slipped into the moving car and slammed the door. She was nervous again. "I thought it would help you remember something that might help." She gritted her teeth, and the morning sun knifing between trees flashed over her braces. "Because sometimes you forget," she said.

Whatever she'd meant by that, by any of it, I pushed to the back of my mind. I would not hold her responsible for things said in the heat of the moment. We rode in silence. I let her off at the corner, and when I reached home I collapsed on the chesterfield. The fresh air had taken my energy. I reached for Eiji's picture on the end table beside me. His smooth-lidded eyes lifting, a question there, no answers. No sympathy, no solace.

I was left alone with my shuddery thoughts of Chisako, reduced to a trace of red on the asphalt. The burst of her colourful presence I'd felt floating about my house, gone now, ground to dust.

A loud moan came from upstairs and for once I was grateful. Slowly I made my way up. Papa's lips had dried to a cracked purply brown. I held his head and made him drink water.

"San kyu, san kyu," he murmured, then sank into his pillow. He was frail, just bones under a veil of skin, but he'd survive for years like this, hardy and persistent. As the powder trace of Chisako's blood was blown to the wind.

I saw them stretch out, the years of my life. Alone. Not

that Chisako ever concerned herself with my loneliness. I'd
learned to live with it, knowing that soon enough I'd be
deserted by everyone around me; everyone except Papa.

I was calm though. In the past I used to panic. The summer we brought Papa home from the hospital after his second stroke, Stum carried him up to the bedroom and a
breeze was fluttering the curtains at the window, the air was
warm, the afternoon felt so idyllic. I knew then he'd be
perched up here for ever, and he'd never come down again.

In the beginning I woke in the middle of the night and
squatted outside his doorway, my nightgown pitched over me
like a tent and, underneath, my knees hugged cool to my
breasts. I was listening, afraid he'd leave me, wretched to hear
him above my own breathing. I heard the gurgles his body
made, the fervent protests. I crept in and put my ear to his
throat, his clogged chest. The noise was muted but powerful
—like a crowd roaring. Now it was that steady fragile hum.

"Lunch, hoshii, Papa? You want?" I patted his hand and
went downstairs. I'd left a trail of dirt on the cream carpet
covering the steps and living-room, and once I'd fed Papa, I
vacuumed, then wiped it clean.

It was long past noon when I finally got to my morning
paper. I turned to the local news section knowing what I'd
find. There it was, at the bottom corner of the front page:
a photograph of the Yano family sitting in a row on their
chesterfield, Tam and Kimi flanked by Chisako and Yano. *Son,
daughter of woman shot still missing; husband sought*, strung over their
heads. Yano leaning as if he'd slid into the frame after setting the shutter timer, a lock of hair fallen in his face, shirt
bunched at his armpits as always, his flitting eyes captured

for once. I could imagine him as he rushed in front of the camera and glared into its single eye, impatient for the click. There was Tam, Sachi's Tam, curved protectively around a sullen Kimi. His narrow shoulders, that ribbon of a body; I knew how it could move, glide through the high summer grasses of the electrical field, day or night, cross the marshy ground by the creek, the rough gravel leading up to the hill. Those tufts of hair jutting above his forehead, like crab grass; his eyes downcast as usual. Eyes that, when they looked up, hardly blinked, as if seeing in a gifted way.

It was the old Chisako there, the ugly duck with her twin ducklings. Her eyes dull behind thick glasses. Her hair, too coarse and heavy, as Japanese hair could be, hiding part of Kimi's face, straggling out like hardy roots that could grow anywhere. It was disappointing, really, for the world not to see Chisako as I had, as the woman she had become. As on one late afternoon in December, when I had stepped off the bus to find her sitting on the bench, unable, it seemed, to go home, despite the cold and the snow that had begun to fall. Waiting for I didn't know whom. Her skin looked very white that afternoon; her hair, in its elaborate roll, blacker than usual. She resembled a doll, a doll dropped in the snow, forgotten by its owner. No sooner had I stepped down than she was patting the bench for me to sit beside her, as if it were spring, as if the seat were warmed by the sun. I dusted aside the snow and sat, setting down my groceries.

"I'm so glad you came, Saito-san" was what she said, as if I'd shown up by invitation, but I caught the distracted tone in her voice. She stared into the electrical field for what seemed a little eternity. I cleared my throat, about to rise, to mention getting back to Papa, for it was nearing dinner time. I'd grown fond of her, that was true, but also hurt, I suppose, that she'd confided nothing to me of her new life at work, that secret life: what had transformed her so. She sensed the irritation in me just as I was gathering up my bags, and quickly, deftly, she drew out a small thing she'd been cradling in her palm, inside her bag.

"He gave it to me," she whispered, a little out of breath. It was a glass dome filled with water; a pink rose blossom floated in it. A small bloom, really, a lovely hybrid tea, I guessed, but at certain angles it became monstrous. As I held it I saw beads of air cling to the petals, so tiny, less than a sigh held in them. Chisako snatched it from my gloved hands.

"A gift from Mr. Spears, my supervisor. For working late." She drew the dome to her open mouth and puffed on it, clouding the glass with her warm breath until the pink inside disappeared. Instantly it was visible again as the glass cleared in the cold air. "He picked it himself."

"He should pay you instead," I said.

"This means much more, Saito-san." She breathed on it again, so close her teeth touched the glass, as if she might swallow it. It disturbed me seeing her with it; already it was precious to her, this insignificant thing.

"It means nothing," I said. "It costs less than the over-time pay he owes you." I felt compelled to say this, so she would not be taken for a fool. "Give it back to him," I said. I heard how harsh and commanding I sounded. Best to be firm, I told myself. For Chisako's sake.

She held it away then, no longer trusting me, that I might not damage the silly thing. "You have no feeling, Saito-san," she said, stroking the glass, then tucking it into her bag. "No feeling at all." With that, she got up and headed down the road; no goodbye, not so much as a thank-you. I could only ponder her behaviour, her ingratitude, taken aback as I was. I sat for some time, long enough for another bus to pull up and open its doors. At my feet, my groceries were sprinkled with snow. I waved the driver on and headed across the field, thinking what a silly woman she was, how naive. For the matter had nothing at all to do with feeling, with the feeling I did or did not have. Slowly I made my way home, marking the snow with each careful step.

I pasted the newspaper article beside the previous one in my notebook, wrote the date neatly across the top of the page, matching the one written two days earlier. I glanced down at Chisako once more. I tried not to think again of that afternoon at the bus stop, of how I'd failed to nip things right then, in the bud.

I left the book open on the dining-room table for the Elmer's to dry while I went on with my afternoon chores. I could never clean this house enough, there was more dust than ever. It wasn't an old house, although it wasn't new like the bungalows across the field; yet it was disintegrating little by little, I was convinced, turning to dust, like so many things. The walls were thinning on all sides, and sound leaked in and out.

I knew Sachi would be sitting at her window watching through the night, or at least until Keiko chased her from it, but I refused to look out. I refused to let her sense me there, keeping her company.

While dinner grew crusty and cold on the table, waiting
for Stum's arrival, I changed Papa. His gibberish would cease
when I cleaned around his chimpo. There was a silence then
that frightened me. Frightened me for him.

When I was a girl, my eyes were always drawn to that
hitch of fabric in his trousers. The cork glimpsed through
the half-open bathroom door as he stood at the toilet. I
imagined a row of them pointed down into the pits at the
camp benjo. There was a time when I could not move from
the crack in the doorway, could not look away. I dreamt such
dreams. Yet the truth, when I learned it, its plainness, the
common sense of what it meant to be a man, did not shock
me. Once Papa's hips grew rickety and his bowels went, I had
to clean there with my striped washcloth every other day, and
it became a little lever on an old machine; I lifted it easily
and set it to one side, then to the other.

Finally I drew the drapes and served myself dinner in the
dim dining-room, while Stum's empty plate lay opposite me
with its watery sheen.

There were never many chances for me. I knew that from
long ago, from when we first got here. "On-ta-ri-o," Papa
kept saying with his pitiful accent. He'd wanted to come east
to the city but all he could do was huddle behind me with
Mama and Stum. With Eiji gone and Stum just a baby, I was
the first-born, born here; they pushed me out to the big city,
to the world, thrusting my homely face to it when they were
afraid. Now that it wasn't just nihonjin in the shack next
door or down the road of the camp. Ask this, say that, while
they hung back. I didn't know the right words to say, in
English or in Japanese. I cringed at how I stumbled along,

each sentence gaping like a mouth with missing teeth. It was then that I sat myself down with my books and crosswords and word jumbles. I became clear in my own mind just what I could expect of myself. Exactly what I could desire from life, even in the day to day, so I would not be disappointed.

I was refilling my cup with green tea when Stum came in. It felt late in my dining-room, hours past sundown, yet it was only early evening, and the light from outside cut into my left eye. He carried a rumpled brown paper bag under his arm, hugging it close to his side, the top rolled over.

"Dinner, hoshii?" No "where have you been, why didn't you call." It was easier this way, not to nag, only to refer to our shared routine. To remind him.

"Your favourite," I said, swishing the spoon in the stew. "Nishime." He was shuffling about in the dark hallway but going nowhere, head down, shaking it.

"No, no." He placed a hand on the rail. "I'm tired," he murmured. "It's too much trouble." He had one foot on the first step. But I wouldn't let go, not yet.

"I'll heat it up." I rose with the bowl in my hand. "No trouble." I flicked on the living-room light and glanced back. He looked startled. I expected some change to have come over him, a sign. He stepped forward. His lips were chapped, pink and swollen. His eyes tired, nearly folded double from no sleep.

"No, Asa. Not hungry at all." He said it with an adult weariness, a weariness with me, my name barely said. I had not heard quite that indifference before.

"Go then. Go on," I said, more harshly than I intended. I switched off the light and bustled into the kitchen. "And take off your shoes," I shouted. "I just cleaned the carpet." He said something back but I couldn't hear him above the running water I'd spun on for the dishes. I couldn't stand to see his face a second longer. From the corner of my eye I spied him disappearing up the stairs, then I heard the unmistakeable clunk of his bedroom door closing.

What a waste, I muttered to myself as I emptied the leftovers into the garbage. Mottai-nai. I scraped away the last of the nishime. It was Yano's phrase. His refrain. After clearing the rest of the dishes, I went to the dining-room table, where my notebook lay open. I felt the springy thickening of its rippling pages, a living thing in my hands as I closed it and replaced it in the bottom cabinet drawer.

The ceiling quaked from Stum pacing upstairs. After a while he settled down. I heard the toilet flush in the bathroom, the rush of water through the pipes across the ceiling. I sighed, glancing at Eiji's portrait again, unmoved from its spot on the end table. I sat down beside it. I know, I thought. No one but myself to blame. Indulging Stum like the baby he has always been, looking after every little thing all these years. As I would do for Sachi, if she'd let me.

I heard the rush of water close, almost inside me. I was riding Eiji as before, playing seahorse in the ocean at Port Dover, holding on. He swam in the black water, arms knifing in and out. Too tight, he cried, throwing back his head. I was holding him too tight, my hands a crab at his neck; we began to sink, both of us, my hair tangling dark under our mouths. *We won't die, we won't*, I whispered to myself. The air was prickly on my skin, there was the strange slapping noise, our flesh, the only sound. The shore was far away, where logs, Papa's logs that he stood on and rolled by the mill, floated like broken-off fingers. I dipped down into the dark then, inside a glass jar, and I saw the sun dropping into the shore, the fingers drifting away. Eiji kicked and kicked without making a sound and we came up at last, water shattering over our heads. We rode on a wave and tumbled ashore, my crab hands never letting go. *Nii-san, nii-san,* I was calling, holding onto my big brother, my strong big brother.

"Ne-san, ne-san!" My eyes flickered open. What? What? It was Stum, Stum shaking me, gripping my wrists, twisting as if I were dangerous. What was wrong with him? I saw myself caught again in his eyes, grey and fallen. I sat up. "What?" I said again, the word blurring on my lips. Stum's pyjamas were rumpled, as if he'd been roused from sleep himself.

"What is it?" I repeated, bleating in my own ears, catching up. We were still, arms locked. His hands were warm and moist on the undersides of my forearms. "It was a dream. A dream, that's all," I muttered, just realizing it myself. Stum looked startled. As if it were beyond him to fathom that I might dream, that there were things unspeakable by day. I struggled from his grasp.

"Abunai!" he cried, pointing with his eyes to my lap. There was a noise, a tinkling. "Abunai! Watch!" He released my arms and stepped back. I looked down to find Eiji's portrait in my lap, the glass broken, jagged, in pieces in the lamplight.

THREE

AFTER I CLEANED UP the stray bits of glass, I went into the bathroom and locked the door. I switched on the light and faced myself in the mirror, just like that. For the first time in a long while, more than a glance to make sure there was no mess. Tonight I saw the skin at my temples thinned and veined with my bitter thoughts. Mottling there and under my eyes, even across my hands.

As a young girl I stared in the mirror for hours and never got on with things. When I saw my short nose growing wide across my face, I pinched and pinched to stop it. I knotted strips of rags around my knees at night to make them grow straight instead of bowed like Mama's.

I watched Eiji change in a way that made me lonely. I told myself it was because they made us leave Port Dover, leave Vancouver Island; it was because they sent us to the camps in the mountains and we'd had to leave the ocean behind. But it wasn't just that. I remember the moment when I knew. It was a small thing, really, when he turned to someone else and not to me, even when I called for him. It was like summer turning to fall, a sudden creeping chill.

In the next room I heard Stum rummaging around again, knocking up against the wall, then finally settling down. I turned off the light and came down the stairs. I saw a shadow where I'd muddied the carpet during the day, but when I came close it disappeared. I ran my hand over it, and for a moment reminded myself how much I cherished my home. How grateful I was to have escaped the dark upstairs in the city that wasn't much better than our shack in the camp. After nine years of watching Mama's bowed legs climb those crooked steps and seeing her arrive breathless at the top; of smelling another family's smells drift up through the floor.

I went to my window and sat down. The darkness was turning back my reflection even as I strained to see beyond it to Sachi's house. Upstairs, Stum's bedroom door opened, then the bathroom door closed. Comforting noises I lived with day in and day out. I could not help wondering: if he leaves, when he leaves, what would become of me?

The sound of him, his voice when we first moved here after Mama died. So high it made you grit your teeth at its girlish softness; no edge, no bottom. He was not the slightest bit like Eiji; not handsome at all, not strong. He was a boy of twelve or thirteen, miserable at first, missing his mama who'd always kept him close, missing his Chinese friends in the city. His face was shapeless, shy to show itself. But it did soon enough: those grotesque sprouts of black hair not quite

whiskers, pimples erupting ripe and angry, as if contagious.
I couldn't stand to be near him. So helpless in his body;
everything showed in his big doughy face. I was twenty-eight
then, already past my bloom. It wasn't up to me to fill him
in, to tell him about his own private parts, what he should
know himself.

Of course, he had his yearnings. I poured bleach on
those yellowed stains on his boxers each week. When they
first appeared, I said to myself: it's a sign. Soon he'll be out
nights, girls will call, he'll be gone, gone. Leaving me alone
with my bitter, plain memories. The paisley of my bedspread
as I folded it back each night looked faded and limp. But for
years, a sign was all it was; nothing more. I saw Stum's eyes
drawn to my breasts, watching them, wondering; the mystery
I held for him. The way Papa and Eiji had been for me. The
lingering of his fingers on my hand when we passed dishes
across the table. He was wondering, I knew, what it would be
like to hold a woman. I pulled my cardigan together in front
and gave him a chore to do. I saw the lost gaze, the not
knowing where to look; I'd taken his anchor and set him
adrift. How relieved I was when he'd go out to rake leaves or
shovel the walk, overgrown in his winter jacket. He'd be panting, ready to burst.

I now heard Stum's slippered feet, slow and lumbering,
coming down the steps. Walking like a man, I thought, a man
all settled in life. Almost like Papa used to be. Stum had
filled out since those early days, of course, but his hands, his
fingers had stayed small and slim as a boy's. That was what
Kaz had noticed, Kaz Fujioka, who first took Stum to the
hatcheries.

I looked up to find Stum at the foot of the stairs, holding Eiji's picture. I resisted the urge to snatch it from him. Without glass it was unprotected. It was all I had left of him.

"Wish I'd known him," Stum said, coming closer, but without the wistfulness, the sadness you'd expect from almost anyone saying such a thing.

"You did. You did know him. I've told you."

"Not the way you did," he insisted. He made a low, disbelieving snort. "I was a baby. I hardly remember." As he paused, I moved to ease the picture from his hands, surprisingly strong for being slender.

"But there was something," he murmured, not quite letting go. "I remember the two of you, how you...how you'd leave me behind." He seemed bothered.

I laughed, brushing a crease from my skirt. I thought I felt a prick of glass under my hand, but nothing was there. Finally I took the photograph from him. "Like you said, you were just a baby," I reminded him. I crossed the room with Eiji's photograph and slid it inside my notebook of clippings for safe-keeping, then closed the drawer with a loud jostle. "It's late, I've kept you up."

But he went on, in a far-off voice. "I remember how well you got along," he said. "Sometimes ne-san..." I felt his eyes on my back; my hands froze on the drawer handle. "Sometimes I was jealous."

Such nonsense, I thought. Not another word, I warned, if only in my head. "You were only two," I said, hearing how frugal my words sounded, how ungiving. "Eiji used to toss you up in the air," I added after a moment.

"But what about you, ne-san?"

I began bustling around, moving a knick-knack one inch this way, then that. "You were too heavy for me back then," I said with a strained laugh. "I was just a girl, a skinny girl. Not like now." It was true I became skin and bones once Eiji was gone, nothing but worry and grief; I hardly touched Stum. His little-boy arms, grown thick before they grew long, they tugged at my neck the last day in the camp. He pointed to the big suitcase at our feet, carefully packed with Eiji's tin. Stum thought that we were leaving him and Mama behind and they'd have to live there for ever. He didn't trust that we'd send for them soon enough.

"It's late," I said again. I was waiting for him to go upstairs, or to slink out to the backyard, as he sometimes did before going to bed. But he did not.

Then it occurred to me, seeing him stand there in the middle of the room, empty-handed. A doughy boy, little islands in his face, born too early, too late, born at all. He was like me: jealous of someone he could never catch up with, not now.

My face must have lit up or reddened at this thought but Stum took it for something else. He rushed towards me from the middle of the room and suddenly he was very close, his head held against my breast, resting just so, his hands gripping my arms.

"Ne-san!" He said this with urgency, with all his yearning. Not even my name, but ne-san, always ne-san. I felt a warm circle above my breast where he breathed. In and out. "Ne-san," he said very low, wavering, as if he was scared of me; for me. I could not push the words away. "Something wonderful has happened to me. A woman." He stopped.

There was a long period of silence in which I was to say: Yes, ototo-chan, my little brother, tell me all about her. But I did not. I felt his breath catching, his head too heavy and large against me, his hands growing clammy around my arms. The scent of him rose in my nostrils. He released me.

I could not bring myself to look at him; I could only stare ahead, out the window into the night. I thought of Sachi at her window, wallowing in the darkness, waiting for Tam. Then, strangely, Chisako's smooth, unmarked skin, as she'd held up her blouse, flashed in my head, too too pale.

"For you too, ne-san," Stum said. So solemn I could have laughed, but I didn't. "It will happen someday soon," he said.

I myself knew it was too late. I'd waited too long, instead of not long enough.

I never asked Stum where he'd been that night, or who his friend with the car was. Those twin questions popped into my head as I lay in bed under my covers. Then Sachi's voice entered my thoughts, its sweetness turning sly: *Miss Saito, will you miss him when he's gone?* Even as she knelt before Chisako's powdery blood.

The night grew cold before I could fall asleep. My feet were ice; they kept me half awake, two blocks of ice that would neither sink nor melt. I curled up smaller and smaller in the middle of my bed, vast at night, the edges dropping off: a single bed whose twin was in Stum's room, but I was alone in it. I remembered how it felt to sleep two to a sagging bed, the particular warmth of another body beside mine, the glow around it, like burner rings that held their heat no matter how cold it was. I saw him sometimes, I made out his shape. I watched Eiji's shape rise on one side of me, and the cold swept in. It crossed the room and paused at the door, but did not turn its face to me.

There was more news Monday morning, ten lines. *Missing man bought gun.* A clerk at the Canadian Tire store remembered *an Oriental man, nervous. "I showed him how to use it,"* he said. Yano's name, the name of the street, the neighbourhood, they rose in blotches that spread until I could read no more. I tried to envision Yano approaching the store counter, as I had seen him a hundred times come towards me after spotting me on my morning walk around the electrical field, arriving sweaty as if he'd stepped in from the rain. But his hands would be dry as he rubbed them together; I heard them, like sandpaper. I tried to imagine a gun, long and dark, notched in intricate ways, a thing I'd never seen in real life, laid across those thick, parched palms. I could not. Much less picture it held up by those hands I knew, pointed at Mr. Spears' chest, at Chisako's heart.

"I told you it was him," Stum said when he came down later than usual, clucking his tongue. His face was puffy, thick with too deep sleep, too rich dreams. Another thing different.

"They'll find those kids any day now," he said carelessly. He pointed his finger to his head and let out a sound twice, an explosion. His mouth a gun, then a reckless smirk. Across the kitchen table I caught the spray of it like poison. I threw the paper aside and stood up.

"You!" I shouted. "Shut up!" I tasted the words, bitter, metallic. But I was crying out for Sachi, for Tam, for Yano.

For myself. Stum's face went white. He wasn't used to his ne-san like this.

"Baka!" I picked up the newspaper and swatted him like a fly. "Stupid!" I screamed. A little nothing flapping in my face. Now he was quivering with fear of his ne-san. His big cruel ne-san from years past. I'd cut him down to the little boy that he was, that he'd always be. But in an instant the newspaper I'd rolled in my hand was snatched from me. My palm burned cold-hot. He waved the paper over my head.

"You can't treat me that way!" he seethed. "Not any more." He backed away, throwing the paper to the floor beside me, trampling it. "I'm not your little boy, your baka-tare-bozu, not any more!"

He pointed to the table in the living room where Eiji's photo usually sat. "Just because I'm not him!" He kept staring there. "I'm no different." He pounded his fist on the table. "No different!"

"You'll be late," I said calmly. He was late, much later than usual. He stopped then, looked at me as if he might grab me and try to shake something out. But he didn't; his body slumped, hinges loose and broken.

"All right, ne-san. All right." He walked out, shutting the front door behind him, leaving behind his thermos of green tea and the lunch I'd packed.

It wasn't that I believed Stum about Yano and the children, even for an instant. I wasn't convinced that he did, himself. I'd only wanted to jolt him. I'd wanted to hurt him, that was it. Return him from the carelessness of his dreams, whatever, whoever was in them, to our life, to me. I wanted him across from me at meals, in bed at night in the room next to me; wanted to feel my fingers pressed by his on the edge of a plate as it passed to his side of the table, as if his life depended on it, as it used to.

I retrieved the newspaper from the floor, brushing off the dust of Stum's footprints. The look of those names in print, the names of our streets. It was disturbing and yet, I had to admit, somehow thrilling. To be exposed in this way.

I took my scissors, glue, and notebook from the cabinet drawer, clipped out the article, then carefully pasted it down. Once again I wrote in the date above the clipping. Already four days since the first news. I felt the thickening ripple of pages. It was growing. I turned back to the previous clipping and looked into Yano's face, that homely face. I saw how false the picture was. Tam and Kimi huddled in the middle, Chisako at their side. In earlier days. Pitched to one side as the timer clicked in, Yano could be a family friend, a visitor, even a distant uncle, except for the terrible resemblance between father and daughter.

I looked into his eyes as hard as I could—Yano's eyes that could be unreachable, angry. *Look within Buddha's deep waters to be healed, to forgive.* This phrase came into my head from long ago, from Reverend Hashizume when I was a girl in camp. To forgive what? Wherever he was, Yano had done nothing, that much I knew.

At a glance, they were a family, despite the stiffness, the space between their bodies. They were nihonjin, after all. But from that very first day four years ago, they were odd, even to me. It was in early December, the kind of still day when the cold seems to suck the heat from your bones with its dryness; about five in the afternoon. I remember the time because I'd just checked the clock and made a mental note to serve Papa his dinner in one hour, as usual, expecting Stum within the next half-hour.

The four of them had come out of their car, the same navy Pontiac, newer and shinier then. Yano struggled with the front door lock for a moment, then Chisako led Tam and Kimi in, eight or nine at the time. They must have been hungry and tired from their journey, wherever they'd come from. They took nothing inside except for Chisako with her handbag and small vanity case. I kept an eye out as I made dinner, walking out to the living-room for one thing or another.

When Stum arrived, he stopped on the porch to look at the orange U-Haul across the electrical field, all the while holding the door open to the brittle cold.

"Hayaku, hayaku!" I hurried him in, briskly shutting the door. I was a little more buoyant then; I had more energy. He went to the window with his coat and boots still on.

"Who are they?" he asked. I heard the boyish anticipation in his voice, the bit of hopefulness that some life might come to our lonely neighbourhood. His emotions seemed more pure then, untainted. He was less guarded and his sweetness shone through in simple ways, daily. He studied the blue Pontiac parked there with the U-Haul hitched behind it. The car sat low to the driveway, packed as it was with a jumble of items. It was impossible to discern more from this distance.

"Nihonjin," I said abruptly, walking away.

"What?" He was jittery. Excited even.

"Take off your boots," I scolded. The snow he'd trekked in was melting into my carpet.

"How do you know, ne-san? Are you sure?" He struggled to kick off his boots in the hallway. His nose was running.

"A family," I added, handing him a tissue. I could not be wrong about them being Japanese. There were telltale signs. I took Yano for a nisei right off, with the U-Haul, the toughness, everything do-it-yourself. Chisako's walk, the way she held her head slightly tilted and down; her wearing a dress instead of slacks, even for a day of moving, in winter. I knew she was from Japan. Later she would alter her walk, taking bigger and straighter steps, striding with her head held high, no doubt mimicking other women she saw. But before long she reverted to her old ways and gestures, when she came to understand how attractive they could be, tilting her head down and stepping daintily.

All that evening, Stum and I watched out the window for some sign, but nothing moved. As night fell, the house remained dark.

"Maybe the power's not on yet," Stum offered. His eyes followed the wires from the house to the electrical towers streaming over the field.

The next morning, as I dusted the windowsill, I spotted Keiko Nakamura from two blocks over, walking in her way, which was then lithe and athletic, even eager, you might say, springing off her muscular calves. Her hair was long and sleek, the fashion for young mothers then. She followed the driveway up to the house, skirting the U-Haul. In one hand she was carrying a box wrapped in a brightly coloured cloth, a furoshiki chosen, I knew, with care; with the other she dragged along Sachi, who was the same age as Tam and Kimi. Struggling to keep up.

Keiko knocked, waited, knocked again; after another moment, she set down the box in the furoshiki beside the door and left. This time she crossed in front, through the mounds of melting snow, glancing up at the wide empty window.

Five minutes later, no more, someone peeked out from the corner of the window. It was Chisako. I saw her thick black bundle of hair. I felt like a birdwatcher spying a rare, twittery bird. A moment later she appeared at the door, reached for the box, and disappeared.

Another day passed before Yano emerged, by himself, to begin unloading boxes from the U-Haul. I remember noticing then, from that distance, something disagreeable about him. A mean stubbornness. The way he took on too heavy a load but refused to put it down in order to close or open a door. The boxes tumbled from his arms two or three times, and each time he stood over them for a minute. Later I would see his broad, ugly hands in tight fists of frustration, like Papa's in years past; he was so angry at himself and the rest of the world. So many times he proved to himself with those tumbling boxes that nothing went his way, nothing turned out right, ever. Things went more wrong for him than for anybody else.

I didn't see any more of them for several days, until Chisako came out with the two children, leading them to the side yard, still clutching her handbag and wearing a dress, very ladylike. There they played on the crusty mounds of greying snow. To me, the children's coats looked flimsy and the two seemed to grow cold quickly.

I stood watch at my window whenever I could, but Papa

was growing more demanding with each passing day. Stum would shut himself away in his room. Then one morning after I'd packed Stum off to work with his lunch, when Papa lay dozing on the old green chesterfield, long since pitched out, there was a knock at the door. Not one knock or two but several, over and over, insistent.

My speechless surprise at finding him at my door might have been taken for rudeness by almost anyone other than Yano. But he was as distracted as ever, preoccupied with his own scattered concerns, yet at the same time quite focused and determined. He was someone who could only concentrate on one thing at a time. If you gave him a square inch of sidewalk to study, he'd find something in it.

"What do you want?" I asked. A little more brusque than I meant to be. I held the door half closed, as I did with strangers. Sometimes I wouldn't answer, to avoid pushy door-to-door salesmen or nosy neighbours. Yano seemed to expect me to open the door wide and invite him in.

"Saw you walking," he said in a stilted way, punching the air towards the field with his fist. It was the way so many nisei spoke, their Japanese no better, with that halting rhythm I'd worked hard to rid myself of; no grace at all. I remember that feeling, the hated awkwardness of my speech; the lumpiness of my tongue. I cringed to hear it come back at me out of another's mouth. And there were other loathsome things about Yano: his smell, of course, and how he stared so intently at you and stood so close. I closed the screen door even more, as if to shoo him away. But he stayed put, his face almost pressed to the mesh. His smell grew more pungent.

"You nihonjin?" That's how direct he was. I nodded, though I was not willing to acknowledge the slightest connection between us. "Yano desu," he said, pushing his hand inside the door, I suppose to shake mine, when Papa suddenly shouted for me. I excused myself and quickly shut the door.

"Dare desu-ka?" Papa was demanding to know who it was. I hastily shut the drapes as he strained towards the window. I did not want him to become needlessly agitated or excited. I glimpsed Yano heading down the length of the electrical field instead of across it, back to his house.

"New neighbour," I said, plumping up the cushion behind his weakening back. "Yano-san."

"Nihonjin?" he exclaimed. For what were the chances of three Japanese families settling in one small neighbourhood? I went to point out their house but realized I'd already shut the drapes. I explained that he lived with his wife and two small children in the house across the field. Papa grew excited then, and struggled up on his frail legs, but fell back. He struggled again. I could make out the outline of his legs, the jut of bones through the worn fabric of his trousers. I suppose he was hoping to make new friends. At his age. Whatever his ideas, I thought it best not to encourage them, and to keep him calm.

"Sit, Papa." I gently pushed him down. "Gone now."

"Gone?"

"Gone."

That would be the sum of one afternoon's conversation between us. Not much less than now. Back then it worried me, spending all of my time alone with only Papa and his ragged bits of English. I was reading books, books of all kinds, on all topics under the sun, one after another from the shelves of our little local library. I went through the newspaper with my dictionary every day, and began filling in the crossword puzzles to put myself to the test. I wanted to better myself. I was petrified, in spite of the progress I was making, of sliding back. In the beginning, watching me, Stum was often silent and sullen, retreating to his room.

After a time, the two of them began to tiptoe around me whenever I was reading, filling in my crossword, or sorting out my word jumble. Often they left the newspaper folded in quarters to that page for me. They saw me differently in those days, I suppose. Different from them, poring over my precious words every day.

Yano talked like the rest of them, and in many ways he seemed cruder, rougher. When he later told me that he'd worked on a road crew during the war, I wasn't a bit surprised.

One morning several weeks after his brief visit to our door, he intercepted me on my early morning walk.

"Saito-san!" His deep voice, commanding really, reached me through the faint hum of traffic from the distant highway. I glanced back without breaking my stride. I heard the trudge of his boots crack the surface of snow glazed from freezing rain early that morning. Suddenly he was at my side, out of breath, and a single bead of sweat rolled down his temple, odd in the dead of winter.

"Sure walk fast," he announced, smiling a broad, fleeting smile.

I eyed his jacket, its flimsy fabric, as he unzipped it. "Careful you don't catch cold," I said.

"I'm cold-blooded, just like the reptiles. Never get sick."

Then, as if to prove it, he took off his jacket as we walked and proceeded to roll up his shirt-sleeves.

We walked on, the towers looming ahead, marking my halfway point. Birds were swarming in the grey sky above us. I was about to say something about the possibility of more freezing rain when I heard Yano's voice lagging behind me once again, fainter this time. I turned back to find him stooped, one hand spread across his chest where his shirt opened. As I came closer, I heard his breath wheezing in and out, a rope straining through a narrow loop.

"What is it, Yano-san?" I was little help standing there in the middle of the field as he choked. He peered up at me through suddenly bloodshot, watering eyes, and pointed to his back. He'd dropped his jacket in the snow and I bent to pick it up.

"Please," he sputtered. "Chotto," and he pointed to his back, making a gesture for me to rub it. He had the strength to snatch the jacket from me with one hand, and threw it back to the ground. "Hard, like this, ne?" He showed me again as he gasped for air. I rubbed the heel of my palm over his back, behind his lungs, but my hand kept slipping. I took off my glove. His shirt was wet, and a sharp, yeasty odour rose from him.

"Harder!" he rasped and stooped lower. "Hayaku!" He meant for me to rub faster, and I tried, but though his flesh was solid and thick I was afraid of hurting him. Then, like a clearing arrived at in a forest, my movements finally found a rhythm that joined with his slowing breath. In another moment he straightened up and was able to breathe more easily. He pushed my hand away then, roughly.

"Iie, iie," he muttered gruffly, like an issei with no other words, like Papa, telling me: enough. He took the jacket I held out to him. "San kyu, san kyu," he said with a mock bow. "Are you all right now?" I asked cautiously. "Fine, fine." He took a deep breath to show me. "A little breathing problem. Nothing serious." He coughed once more. I nodded. "Well, if you're sure you're all right." I'd already stepped away from him.

He waved me off. "I know, I know. Papa's waiting, right?" He winked and fell in beside me. "Don't hold back. I can keep up," he reassured me. But I could tell he was growing tired, and I slowed down. I noticed he was staring straight ahead, up at the hill.

"You know who they named that for, don't you?"

I shook my head.

He whistled, watching me. "The prime minister. That bugger Mackenzie King."

I had no interest in that kind of discussion, of things I'd long ago left behind and made my peace with. But Yano kept on with them. I stopped at the point in the field opposite his house. There were still no drapes up, as there never would be, and the window displayed an empty space without furniture. Then, quite abruptly, Chisako with her stark black bun peeked out from the corner of the glass. She must have been there for some time. No sooner had our eyes met when she vanished. Yano seemed unaware as he put his jacket back on, and took one quavering, gulping breath that betrayed him. "See you again, Saito-san," he said cheerfully, smiling a wide-open smile that revealed a jumble of teeth in a too-small mouth.

As my little porch and my curtained front window came into sight, I heard him bellow behind me across the field. "Saito-san!" I turned and gave a short wave.

"Thank you, Saito-san! Thank you!" he shouted back.

My memories of those first meetings with Yano drifted in and out of my head, I suppose because I'd summoned them. I was haunted by the echo of that voice, that voice not heard in days, wondering when I would hear it once more. Remembering too how he unsettled me each time, repelled as I was by him. I wanted to convince myself that, repulsive man though he was, Yano was not capable of harming his own children, or his wife. Something had gone terribly wrong, it was true. But Yano was not capable of such an act. The children, I was convinced—in spite of Stum's terrible accusation —were somewhere, anywhere, safe with him.

"It's still there." Sachi was rubbing her fingers together as she had at the parking lot just days ago. Already it was Tuesday. Clutching books in one arm, she watched me closely as I held the screen door open to her.

"What is?" I couldn't tell if she was trying to torture me or herself. But I had to make her say the words.

"The blood. Tam's mom." Behind her the late-afternoon sky was growing sooty. I shook my head as I let her in.

She sniffed her finger. "I never washed it."

"Stop!" I snatched her wrist, pushed it away too roughly. I could only play the game with her so long. But she persisted.

"It gets in through your pores, see?" She held up her finger to me. I tried not to recoil, what she'd want. There was nothing to see. "Blood attracts blood," she said. "Did you know that, Miss Saito?" Peering at me, steely yet quivering, like a tuning fork. Something flared in her eyes, behind her glasses, which she rarely wore.

"I thought you only needed those for reading the blackboard," I said. So she must have gone to school, then wandered off for the last hour or so.

The books she held tumbled to the hallway floor. She was grimy, her hair mushed flat to her crown. Her braces were clogged with food bits; she must not have brushed in days. "Everything looks wavy," and she flailed her hands in front like a blind person and smiled stupidly. She was waiting for me to tell her what to do. She let the smile drop and looked into my eyes through her lenses, which widened and blurred her eyes. "If I don't go to class, Keiko won't let me out of the house," she murmured in a voice gone small. "I had to, for Tam."

I sighed and led her to the kitchen sink and held her fingers close to my nose, in a show for her benefit. "See? Nothing." Yet I imagined I did smell something, a hint of flesh gone bad. It wasn't Sachi's scent. Quickly I spun on the tap and held her hand under it. She screeched.

"It's hot!"

"All right, all right," I muttered. I turned on the cold water and loosened my grip on her hand. I turned it over in mine and saw new nicks and cuts across her knuckles, not deep: the kind that form thin scabs and easily peel off. I cursed Keiko in my head. What are you doing to her, I wanted to shout. Why couldn't they watch her? Pay her a little attention, as I did? Sachi was watching me; my lips must have been busy, she knew what I was thinking. I didn't care. I knew she liked it, my seething, my frustration.

I sat her down in the living-room. I dabbed her hand dry, again making a show of searching for traces, babying her as she seemed to want, even need. "Look," I repeated. "Nothing!" I sniffed at her fingers. "Soap." I knelt down in front of her, removed her glasses, and pushed aside her greasy hair. I smoothed her face over and over with my hands; a useless gesture, but I couldn't help myself. The softness under my palms, the velvet resilience. The newness. She watched me as I did so, unblinking, trusting my touch more and more with each stroke. Then it came, as I knew it would. Her face scrunching into a monkey's. Her mouth cracking open to an animal wail. I cupped her face in my hands. My fingers slipped over her open mouth, sticky and dark. "No, no, no," I frantically rasped above her tears, trying to stem what I myself had called forth just by touching her.

"Tam!" she finally cried, breaking free of me. "I want Tam!" Her eyes, swimming in her head, at last found me again. "Miss Saito, Miss Saito!" she screamed, wringing her hands, rubbing her fingers, her body vibrating. "What am I going to do? What am I going to do?" Her sobs rang through the maze of my house. At last she collapsed against me, holding me tight, tighter than Stum had the other night, crying for his ne-san.

She let me hold her hand as we made our way down to the creek, along the path I'd followed her on last Thursday, when the first news came. It was where the creek flowed south, away from Mackenzie Hill into a shallow ravine. It started to rain lightly after it was too late to turn back, and you could hear the drops slipping in between the reeds to small hidden places. I didn't know what we were searching for, but this was the only way I could calm her down. As our feet slid into the softening dirt, I wondered what traces were melting; whose footprints we were trampling. The rain was coming down harder, the tap tap tap on the leaves suddenly busy in my ears, and the bushes and trees along the path slowly bowing under it. I'd expected her to take the lead, but she hung back and gripped my hand more tightly as we went on, so tightly that I felt the streams of blood inside our fingertips pulse side by side; I remembered what she'd said about blood attracting blood. I felt the rain pouring down my face, saw it crowding the air in front of us, a forest of needles piercing the ground. All I could do was watch my own feet in Mama's shoes, and feel the lumpy earth through their soles, taking one step after another.

"Stop," she said. Our arms tugged as I tried to move on and she stood still. We'd barely passed the willow tree where, days ago, she'd lain in wait to taunt me. She inched us to the small clearing skirted by higher grass and thicker bushes, a spot I knew. She dragged me into the middle of it. The tap tap eased a little under the shelter of the willow, but my heart was pounding, busier than the rain. Sachi scanned the ground, searching for clues when nothing was there; kicked her foot about in the wet grass. She whispered something under her breath. We exchanged a glance, as if to say, *nothing here,* and went on, she still holding tight to my hand.

She took us back to the path, muddy as it was, and I was relieved. Relieved we'd left that too-familiar place, as hushed and quiet on certain afternoons as a closeted room with a tiny window into it. It haunted me, made me dream forbidden dreams only she could guess at. She let me go, if only for this moment, but she knew. She'd spotted me here, who knows how, when I'd always been so careful, or how long ago. Yet she'd left the secret unspoken. Released me without another glance.

I was grateful for the rain, which made me forget my body's humiliation. I couldn't tell if I was weeping or sweating or bleeding, if the dress that clung to me was my own weathered, welted skin, if the sludge under my feet had come from my body or the earth. The whole world was leaking and we were a part of it, and so were Tam and Kimi and Yano, wherever they were.

By now the creek was rising, flowing quickly with the summer rain, frothing on the surface. Sachi pulled me along one bank until we ended up where she'd crossed before, but the rocks she'd danced on then were submerged. She looked back at me, this time as if to say, *now what?* But I shook my head and we kept on along the bank, farther and farther away from Mackenzie Hill and the last electrical tower on this side of the field; away from the last block of houses, out of sight, as if the whole neighbourhood had been levelled by rain.

We kept going for an hour or more, it seemed, following the creek that swelled up its banks. I felt her hand going limp in mine with the fatigue and cold that grow as you venture farther from home with no destination in sight.

"Let's go back," I called, though I couldn't say which way was back. She shook her head. But her pace slowed.

It didn't take much to coax her. We came to an opening

and found ourselves returning into the far south end of the
electrical field, the towers guiding us in. She lagged behind,
weakened by the fear that we might never find Tam, I suppose; I had to keep tugging her, pulling on her arm as if on
the leash of a stubborn animal. "There's nothing there," I
shouted through the rain.

At home I took her into the bathroom and began peeling the clothes from her shivering body. Under the layers she
was nothing, almost see-through with cold, her skin transparent with veins like an old woman's, like mine, pinpricked
with goosebumps, her nipples shrunken purple-brown. She
stood still for me, unresistant for a moment, knowing I
wanted to look. But quickly I wrapped the towel around her;
she was so thin it went around twice.

"Miss Saito," she burst out, with energy that came from
I don't know where. "I know what happened."

"Shush," I said gently. "Go nen nen. Go to sleep." I found
myself talking as if to a child. I tightened the towel around
her. I felt the pumping of her little heart, her breath coming
in fits and starts.

"They must've seen the man," she murmured feverishly.

"What man? Who?"

"The one who took Yano's gun, the one who did it. Tam
must've seen him. Tam sees everything. The man knows it so
they had to take off."

I thought of Tam's unblinking eyes as I led Sachi to my
bedroom. "I see." I could feel her giving out, little by little.
Her body caving in.

"They're waiting for the police to catch the man so they
can come back."

I laid her down, slipping her under my faded covers, see-ing through her eyes the dowdiness of my room, smelling the musty lifelessness, the meagre stillness. I sat down on the edge of the bed. She kept her eyes open for the longest time, staring at the ceiling as she nattered on with her ideas, seem-ing not to notice any details of my decor.

"See, Miss Saito? All we have to do is wait."

This was how she was holding on. I was so used to her being taciturn, in spite of what churned below; it was like another person here with me. But it was Sachi after all, no one else.

"Miss Saito, Miss Saito." Her hand was stirring beneath the covers. She'd quietened down now, her nervous energy almost spent.

"Yes?"

"Tell me the story about Eiji."

"Which one?" I was taken aback, and touched that she should think of my brother at a time when only Tam could be in her head. It brought her comfort to hear about me with Eiji. I suppose she liked to imagine the two of us as not that different from her and Tam, though Tam was nothing like Eiji, nothing at all.

"You know, during the war," she persisted.

"It's not really a story."

"I know." She smiled.

"It's nothing."

Her wise smile, the smile I hadn't seen since we'd heard about Chisako, about Tam and Kimi gone missing, fell away as she surrendered to her exhaustion. That smile made me pour myself out. We'd spent so little time together lately.

Being with her like this, it was almost the way it had been before anything happened. Her eyes fluttered shut.

"When we got there, Mama and I...," I started to say, never knowing quite where to begin.

"Where? Got where?"

"Hastings Park, the exhibition grounds in Vancouver." Already I recalled how dizzy I'd felt from the ferry ride over, my first; sick from being inside a hulk that moved against the current while you stayed still. There was the smell in the live-stock building that made me more sick—a disinfectant used on the stalls where we slept, and the musty stink of cows and their business lurking under it. It almost hurt to smell, a sharp but burning sweet that made me press my nose to the floor the first night and sniff until my head ached.

Sachi's eyes stayed shut, but she wasn't asleep. I felt her hand rustle under the cover next to my leg, urging me on. "Papa and Eiji had been there for weeks already." Eiji was on the baggage crew, taking in everyone's shabby bags and boxes, settling us in for the months we would be there, before they sent us to the camps. I could tell he was glad to be busy, to not be thinking about what he was missing. How strange it was to say Eiji's name aloud to someone other than Stum or Papa. It made me realize how rarely I did say it, how much I kept him to myself. I was grateful Sachi's eyes were shut. I didn't care to be watched.

"We'd been there a month or two when a fair came to the grounds," I told her. "With rides and all kinds of games and candy floss." I watched her lids flicker at that but they didn't open.

"One night, after his shift, Eiji took me through the

gates." There had been no Mounties, no gatekeeper, no pass-
taker to check on us or stop us. Only an open field between
the gates and the fair, passing quickly as we ran. I had seen
the livestock building left behind in the distance, and
coloured lights turning in the sky in front. I had seen tickets, pink, in Eiji's hand. I saw it now like a dream, his hand,
his long straight fingers with the tickets held in them. It was
his face I couldn't quite see. It was like seeing through his
eyes, because there I was, a girl Sachi's age, waiting by the
ticket booth, in line for the ride. It was growing dark. We
were the only nihonjin there, as far as I could tell, yet nobody
looked twice at us.

"What was it called? The ride?"

"I don't know," I said, startled. It was the only ride
besides the Ferris wheel I'd ever been on.

"You used to know."

"Did I?" I felt the chill of confusion, but then realized
my hair was still wet, dripping down onto the shoulders of
the dress I'd changed into. I must have looked a mess.

"What's wrong, Miss Saito?" She sat up on her elbows.
Gently I pushed her back down. "Keep going," she said with
quiet authority. "Don't stop."

"It was the kind of ride," I began again, "where you sit
in little cars, two together, and hold on," I said, seeing myself
slip in beside Eiji in slow motion. I had the face of an adult,
long and thin, with too large a jaw and a high forehead, while
my body was still a child's. I watched myself slowly grip the
steel bar in my hands, one here, the other there. I loved the
ride, the whirr of it, inside and out, up and down. I heard
the cries rise and melt into the air, and I was half flung to

the sky, pinned down by my hands. Eiji was beside me and he was smiling, he loved the ride too, he loved it that I was afraid. "You were so scared," he said after, back on the ground, his eyes with the ride still whirring in them. I was never so happy, never so without care as on that night.

It exhausted me, calling up this memory, and I felt queasy all at once, as if from the motion of the dream, though I could not at that moment remember the ride itself, how the little cars moved. I found myself unable to continue; the words and pictures in my mind had vanished, and Sachi had fallen into a deep sleep, her cheek pressed into my pillow.

I don't know how long I sat there; long enough, I realized, for the rain to have slowed its pace once again. Long enough that bright light now leaked in around my blinds where before it had been dark. It was a strange thing, the day growing darker, then lighter, as if day and night were changing places. I peeked out between the blinds and gazed down at the creek. I pictured us there, two sodden figures. Anyone spotting us would have taken me for a neglectful mother, crazy even, leading my daughter out in the rain without a coat or an umbrella. Yet I had done more for her than Keiko would have, I knew that.

I could almost bear the rain's quiet pitter-patter now, sitting in this room. A room that I normally came to in complete darkness at the end of the day.

Sachi stirred but she did not waken. She turned her head from side to side and knitted her brow. I went to touch her, to soothe her, but thought better of it.

"No, no," she seemed to murmur, her breathing laboured. I listened closely, laying my head close. "That's not it! Get away!" and her arms fretted under the covers, fending off something, someone. "You're wrong, no touching." Her tongue lolled, then she fell back into slumber, her mouth clamping thinly to let nothing escape.

I'd seen her like this before, when she'd uttered such things fully awake, prickly, alive with them. I'd watched her sitting cross-legged with him, the tips of their skinny knees a smidgen apart. I'd seen the pulsing in her start, I knew when the warm lick from down there was going up through her middle to her heart and back again, and all the time their eyes stayed locked; giddy, she grew giddy waiting for the words, for his hands, until, exhausted from the waiting, the anticipation, they both dropped into light sleep in the clearing by the willow, that private room in the woods. The curl of their slight bodies there; it was Tam she was saying no to in her dream. No and yes.

"You can't touch, can't," she was murmuring now, over and over, arms folding and unfolding across her front. In my bed. "Chi-chi, chi-chi," she giggled, squeezing her little breast, taunting him with it.

But that wasn't the word he needed, he'd got that one before. He shook his head at her in his placid way, telling her it wasn't over, not yet. I saw his two fingers on his knee a half-inch from hers, and his thumb twitching and tapping, and so did she. Nipple. That was what he wanted, that was the word he needed. That was the game. Something like spin-the-bottle, with no spinning and kissing, only words and touches.

I knew the secret words and so did Chisako. I'd learned them long ago, from the schoolyard at Japanese school in

Port Dover, from behind the ofuro in camp, the boys and girls coming out of the bath wrapped in their towels, tittering. Eiji even told me some. As a girl I stored them up, whispered them to myself under the covers at night. Sometimes, as I watched Sachi and Tam, I had to quell my lips with the words on them when they got some wrong.

"I don't believe you, that's wrong," Sachi said after Tam said the word, but she was pulsing. She wanted it to be right. "I don't cheat," Tam told her. "That's the word."

"You cheat, you cheat," she cried, but she was laughing. It took me a moment to see that. She knew the word, knew he was right. Because she'd sat on my porch one day and pinched her nipple through her top, looking at me. Asking, waiting. Shamelessly I whispered the word in her ear, felt the tickle on my lip.

It wasn't that I'd planned it, to stay and watch. The first time I'd been walking as usual, a little out of the way of my normal route around the electrical towers, a little later in the day. The woods by the creek had seemed inviting that afternoon, everything soft. The sunlight veiled by clouds, my skin protected from any harshness as I crouched. I could go dizzy watching them watch each other, waiting with them, holding my breath, not giving myself away. I could lose myself.

Tam's two fingers and thumb had trembled in the air, dangling there.

"Chikubi," Sachi erupted, with such force that she woke me from my reverie, brought me back to the present. I thought she must be awake too, but she wasn't. I thought I saw her hand rustling under the covers, a small movement back and forth. But she slept on. Back in the woods, giggling with Tam, she'd taken his two fingers and thumb in hers, led them where they ached to go.

Downstairs the front door opened and closed. Heavy footsteps, Stum's slow rhythm up. I tucked the sheets under Sachi's chin, but her one arm lay flung across the pillow, the flesh of her hairless armpit exposed. When I came out to the hall, I found him looking tired, a little stooped, by the door to the room that had been his since he was a boy.

"Ara?" A little cry of Mama's, barely a word. He came closer to look in, thinking it odd, no doubt, to find me in my room at this hour, with no cooking sounds or smells coming from the kitchen. When he saw Sachi lying in my bed, the nest of her hair, her thin velvet arm sprawled out, he took an involuntary step back, but couldn't take his eyes from her.

"What's she doing here?"

I shushed him before he could say another word; shooed him back to his own room. He left his door open a crack, wide enough for his one eye and ear. I sat back down at the edge of my bed, my bed that now seemed less dreary and not my own; her hair was spread miraculously across my pillow, long and thick and black as pitch, as mine used to be. Her face was sealed tight in sleep.

Chikubi. I couldn't help thinking of my own, shrivelled and dark. The stray hairs that had sprouted there years ago. Who would touch them now, after all this time? I shuddered, remembering the press of Stum's ear against me days earlier. His longing for something so ugly. He didn't know any better.

I went downstairs to make dinner, busied myself with the rice cooker, measuring out the rice. I saw my hand disappear into the milky water as I washed the rice, then reappear. The water circling down the drain. This moment, then the next, each one bloodless. There was no death, no Chisako, no Yano, no Tam or Kimi to worry over. Papa upstairs drowsing as usual. Stum in his room. And now, Sachi in mine.

The creak of the floorboards upstairs startled me. The sound of a door opening and closing. I waited for the flush of water through the bathroom pipes but it didn't come. I rushed up to my room and found Stum there, standing stupidly at the foot of the bed where Sachi continued to sleep.

"Get out of here," I hissed. When I tried to grab his arm, he slipped away easily.

"I wanted to see, that's all," he said. He stood there dumb in my room of faded florals. I glared at him until he came out to the hall.

"I wasn't going to do anything," he whispered, suddenly sad-eyed.

I made him come down with me to the kitchen, where he padded back and forth glumly, picking at bits of raw food I was preparing. I tapped his hand. "We won't have enough."

"She staying?"

I shrugged. Stum paced around again. He picked up a chopstick, started tapping surfaces here and there, lightly at first, then louder, on pots and pans. That was the engine in him revving, all the energy kept back, coiled in his fingers hour after hour, making his movements tiny as those chicks.

He wheeled around to face me: "She's sick because she knows her boyfriend's dead."

This was his revenge, I knew, for me calling him stupid,
for me wishing he was Eiji. He was torturing me with that.
Wanting to spoil what he could for me, whatever way.

"The kamikaze did it." He banged the chopstick one last
time on my big pot, then dropped it to the floor.

"You'll wake up Papa," I said evenly, "and her." I wasn't
going to get upset the way I had the night before. What happened to the calm I'd known before all this? My nights where
I stared out at the electrical field and my giants, and the
asphalt of the concession road paved smooth and dark? This
childishness. I no longer dreaded him leaving us, leaving me.
Not one bit. Not one bit.

"What was that?" Stum was looking at me, waiting.

"Nothing."

"I saw you," and he fiddled his fingers over his lips. This
was how I'd given myself away ever since I was a girl: talking
to myself, trying to keep my secrets; it wasn't old age. "What
did you say?" His voice was rising, waiting.

I merely shook my head, got on with the vegetables, the
meat, going from here to there, not looking back.

"Did you talk to your pictures today, ne-san?" He said it
with a cruel smirk.

I ignored him; I began to hum. I concentrated on my
hands swishing in and out of the water, then draining the
rice. The way Mama had taught me years ago, without losing
a single grain. Washing it because, Mama said, of all the dirty
hands that touched these millions of grains, the hands of
men and women who dropped their sweat, their grime, even
their nose pickings into the bags. I remembered that and
saw a dozen filthy, swarthy hands reaching into my water.

Suddenly my water was dark. I looked up to find Stum close
to me. I pushed him back, picked up the chopstick from the
floor, from beside his broad feet that stretched every pair of
shoes until they ripped at the seams. I stayed silent.

"Ne-san, do they answer you back?" he jeered. "Your
pictures?" It was easy for me to ignore the fool, the baka-
tare-bozu. I almost called him that aloud, the very thing he
said he would never again be to me, but I stopped myself,
remembering the bitterness of our feud the night before; I
caged my lips with my fingers.

"Get out," I said, pointing to the back door. He slunk
out, unhurried.

He did not upset me so much. For they did answer me
back sometimes, my pictures. In their way. In fact, his jeers
made me remember that I did not have a photograph of
Chisako; only the picture from the newspaper, where the
other Chisako, the plain one, stared out of the grainy,
smudged print like a homely stranger. Not the one I had
known, who had shared some of her secrets with me.

When I finished washing the rice, the water ran clear. If
I could simply be like this, I thought, dipping my hand once
more into the cool liquid, touching the polished grains:
stripped clean; everything done step by careful step.

Just then the doorbell rang. I ran to the front hall, glancing at Stum through the back screen door. It struck a pitter
of panic in my heart, the thought of coming face to face
with her, his new friend. But he shrugged his shoulders, gave
a dumb look. He came in, went to the window, and peeked
through the drapes just as I opened the door.

It was Keiko. She stood there, a neat, solid block lit by

the porch light. It startled me seeing her up close for the first time in some years. She'd aged; her skin had darkened even more, and coarsened like sand. Her lids drooped over her eyes, giving her a sad but impervious look, as if nothing touched her. These days, her hair was cut short to the chin. I touched a hand to my unkempt hair.

"Nakamura-san." I never knew what to call her. "How nice—"

"Is she here?"

"Yes, she is," I said. "But—"

"I'll take my daughter home now, Miss Saito." She rested her hand on the doorknob, waiting. The other hand gripped a flashlight; a circle flickered from the wall to the floor, big, then small.

"She's sleeping," I announced, more bluntly than I'd intended.

"Wake her up then, please," Keiko replied coldly. "I'm sorry she's been such a bother." Not sorry at all, I thought. Furious. That she should have to come to me for her daughter; that I'd indulged the girl, shown her some care. Keiko's eyes flitted up behind me. I turned to find Sachi at the top of the stairs, her damp clothes back on.

"I'm coming," she said, in a timid little-girl voice, and bounced down the steps without so much as a glance at me. Keiko swiftly pushed her out the door and picked up the soaked sneakers left on the mat.

"Thank you, Miss Saito." Keiko held the door. "Please don't bother yourself again like this," she said—a warning, I thought. She dropped the shoes on the porch for Sachi to slide into. The lonely chirp of crickets filtered in.

"Good-night, Miss Saito." Keiko nodded, then let go of the door.

"Good-night, Miss Saito," mimicked Stum, dragging himself lazily into the kitchen.

Petty woman, I said to myself. Cold and petty. Reminding me, the old schoolmarm, of my lonely status, so different from hers. Through my parted curtains, I watched them cross the field, Keiko's flashlight pointing a long lit finger in front of them. For a moment I imagined Sachi turning to look back at me. But then she was prancing in circles around her mother among the grasses, tugging at her as she strode forward. I knew what was in Sachi's heart. I'd caught the look that had passed between them the instant they saw one another. Sachi's eyes had flared with yearning. It wasn't just about Tam. It was about Keiko. In an instant she'd forgotten all about me. Everything I'd done for her. Just as Stum would.

Once they were home, everything would settle into place, back to normal, I told myself. To the routine of it all, one thing after another, no cracks for Sachi to fall into. Keiko would not let that happen. Keiko with her strong, muscular calves flexing, going here, going there. Expecting Sachi to follow, equally efficient. Bewildered by the girl's brooding sprawl across her bed and the record she played over and over with its squealing high notes descending at the end. Thinking too much, feeling too much, as if the thoughts and feelings were special somehow. The cuts Sachi never tried to hide, from tiptoeing out to the kitchen in the dead of night. The knife slid from its block, left there on the counter. In the morning washed and wiped clean, put back in its place by Keiko without a word. Sachi would return to me as she always did, all that yearning, that faith in another, wasted.

Eiji did not console me that night. I could not bring myself to be comforted by one of my stories murmured to myself with his picture cradled in my hands, resting on my lap. I had, in fact, felt a little estranged from Eiji since I learned of Chisako's death. He seemed to have turned carelessly away from me. I took out the notebook I had begun, pressed its rippling pages to my breast, then opened it to the photo of Chisako with her family. Already it had changed: her features grown smudgy; her eyes inked in black. Already she had grown dead to me, even as I looked her in the face; my lips remained still. I tried to conjure her up, I tried to summon the peculiar light in her black eyes, that voice of tinkling crystal, but she remained a blank. All I saw was the carpet in her little room, and the spreading stain that my spilt green tea had left on its ivory surface from our very last visit. My clumsiness. For she had flustered me, after all. But beside that stain her slim legs gracefully leaning to one side like stems, her feet lifting daintily.

I sat down, trying to collect my thoughts. My thoughts that wandered, stumbled down into the night. I tried to line them up into my usual practical concerns. I thought about koden money; how much would I send? From the family or myself alone? A ridiculous thought, I realized, the old tradition of sending money, under the circumstances. Who was there to send it to? I bristled at the idea of those church ladies downtown taking charge as they sometimes did when there was no family. But Yano would return. Any day, any moment now. He would take care of things.

Stum had left the door open, and in came air through the screen, sticky and warm like exhaled breath. I stepped onto my porch. Out in the field, I could perfectly imagine her, Chisako as she was when I first met her, those years ago. She was wearing a navy uniform-like overcoat. Despite her protests, Yano was pulling her towards me through the field muddy with late-melting snows. Her hair had been severely cut, too short to twist up into a bun. It made her look younger, like a rebellious teenager or a naive schoolgirl tugging away from Yano as he pulled her along. From a distance, he could have been her father. I was walking at my usual brisk pace, counting my steps to each end of the field, when Yano called to me, waving with one hand, holding onto Chisako with the other. "Saito-san!"

I slowed down slightly, holding my count. Normally I would have kept on, but I was curious to meet her.

"Saito-san, this is Chisako, my wife," a breathless Yano announced, pushing her in front. She seemed to dangle there, as if relinquishing herself. Something told me she'd cut her hair herself, out of spite and unhappiness, for it was unevenly trimmed, in jagged clumps, hiding much of her face the way too thick, too massive Japanese hair stubbornly does unless it is kept long. We stood in silence for some moments until she finally glanced up. When she did, her spine seemed to straighten and stiffen, and she instantly appeared more robust and wilful. It was difficult to tell what she actually looked like, but I could make out her features: a fine nose, and deep black eyes that caught the light, a rare thing. She pulled her hand from Yano's with almost a child-ish grimace, and held it out to me.

"Hajime mashite. Dozo yoroshiku," I said haltingly, mustering the proper greeting learned in my girlhood classes in Port Dover. Not like my peasant bits of Japanese from Papa and Mama.

"Nice to meet you, Saito-san," she replied. Coolly, as if unimpressed by my addressing her in Japanese, insulted even.

"Wanted to show her the hill," Yano said, waving at it. We three paused to look into the distance. There it was, ris-ing past my lone rooftop, lumpy and dull. "First time she's seeing it from out here," Yano said, taking her hand again. Suddenly she erupted in rapid Japanese to him, so rapid I couldn't follow. She snatched her hand back, bowed slightly to me, and walked away, taking her dainty steps. It was then I noticed she was wearing only house slippers, now muddied and chunked with snow.

She wasn't beautiful as I'd imagined, and for that I was relieved, glancing down at my own shabby coat. I suppose I'd felt intimidated, knowing she was from Japan. It was much later that she became beautiful, like a frozen bloom that would thaw. She was simply plain at the time, pursed shut. I was about to mutter something about getting back to my walk, but Yano had more thoughts on his mind.

"Married her over there," he said. "In a temple, even." He laughed. I had to hold back my own smile; I could not imagine Yano in such a place, such a serene and sacred place. But it was unmistakeable what he was conveying: pride that he'd got himself a Japanese girl from Japan. Not like the rest of us homegrown nisei; not like him and me, neither here-nor-there stock. I looked at Yano differently then, swayed by the moment, by his pride. "She didn't have any family left."

We both watched her as she made her way up the driveway to the house, avoiding deep patches of snow in her slipper-clad feet. Yano was suddenly embarrassed. "Silly woman, coming out without the proper shoe." He seemed worried about what I might think.

"See," he said, as if he were telling me a story I wanted to hear, a story I didn't already know. "I went there after the war, after the camps shut down. That's how it was, they shipped you back to where you'd never been." He laughed bitterly.

I couldn't resist saying something. Something to remind him, as he would remind me. "They gave you a choice," I told him, "even if you couldn't go home. You could have come east like the rest of us." As I said those words, it crossed my mind that he might have been like Eiji, yearning for the ocean.

He gave a snort, disgusted with me, my comment, I suppose. Then why return to here of all places, I wanted to say, but didn't. I had no wish to start anything with Yano, any involved discussion.

"This is paradise for her," he went on, looking up at the hill, then down at me. "Paradise." He was scrutinizing me so closely, I wondered if something showed on my face. "But she's still Japanese," he assured me, reminding me of the difference between us. "On her passport it says she's still Japanese." His finger poked the air. After a moment he added: "Hiroshima-ken."

"I see," I said, wondering if from that I was to understand

what Chisako had left behind. Wondering if I'd imagined a change in his tone, a slight hush. But the moment passed.

"Anyway, thought I'd introduce you," Yano said. "Because" —he looked me deep in the eye, gauging whether he should say what was in his head—"because we have to stick together. Don't we?" He stared so intently that it unnerved me. He sighed, then pointed from me to him in a continuous loop, implying some sort of connection that was beyond words.

"She doesn't understand," he said. He pushed back his greasy, tangled hair. It resembled a black nest against the bruised sky, and his eyes were holes pecked out of his large face. "She's gone through a lot, but she doesn't know." He kicked his worn shoe into a chunk of snow, and sighed again. "She doesn't know what it feels like to be ashamed, you see." He looked to me to help fill in the words he groped for; he raised his hands as if he might grab me by the collar and shake the words out of me. As if he could claim something that was not mine to give. But of course he didn't, he didn't touch me.

"Not like you and me," he finally said, his eyes drilling into mine. "She doesn't know what it's like to get herded up. She doesn't know what it feels like to be ashamed to be nihonjin."

"But surely she knows—" My words dropped to the ground, unheeded. I had no wish to involve myself, no wish to engage his anger. I turned abruptly, awkwardly, to walk away, holding my breath as the distance between us grew. I stole a glance back as I hurried towards the south tower; he remained where I'd left him, watching the hill, that lump planted on the flattest stretch of land, frozen in his thoughts.

Once I reached the tower, I gripped the steel beams with both hands; I suppose I felt wary of Yano, though he still made no move to follow me. Through the cross of beams I watched him turn for home. I felt sheepish and sorry. We were bound together, that was true. The way Yano stood so close when he spoke with me; the way he pushed Chisako and me together as intimate family. He wanted more, much more, between us.

Now, before I knew it, I was crossing the field, my feet in house slippers as Chisako's had been that winter day long ago, sinking down to where I couldn't see. I couldn't stop myself, but I couldn't say what was driving me into the night. I plodded on, and found myself in front of the Yano house. The living-room still lit up, every detail of shabby furniture to be seen, every dusty, littered surface as I remembered it. I clucked my tongue; it echoed out to the field. Even now I was judging her, in my desperation; assuring myself that I kept my home better than she ever could have. What did it matter, now or ever? I wanted to put up some drapes, to give Chisako some dignity, some privacy, perhaps from my own petty self.

Then a light shone on me, an explosion of white in blackness in my eyes; I almost screamed from fright. A voice came from behind the glare.

"Who's there? Who's there?" The light flickered around me. "What are you doing?"

"I just wanted to see," I said, and I tried to step into the light, but it eluded me. I felt my fingers at my mouth, nervous and climbing. "I meant no harm," I called into the

blackness, and heard my voice come back at me, forlorn and
sorry, for what I couldn't say. The light shifted finally, shrank
to a small moon on the grass. A woman stepped forward. It
took me a few seconds to recognize her in the shadowy light
as the next-door neighbour. Someone I'd seen in a window,
around the yard, passing in the street.

"There's nothing to see."

"I'm a friend of the family."

"Really?" The voice sounded disbelieving. "The police
came by." The woman sighed. "He won't turn up here. She
clicked off the flashlight. "No word about the children."

I nodded my head in sympathy, forgetting she could
not see me. I cleared my throat, then murmured something;
the darkness, with its unseen rustlings and scents, swallowed
it up.

"That Yano is a strange one. You know him?"

Stupidly I nodded once again. "Only a little," I added.

"Poor Chisako. Hard to believe, isn't it?" The woman
clucked her tongue even louder than I had moments earlier.
"Wouldn't surprise me if..." She paused for a long moment,
then clicked the light back on, sliding it across my face. I
could make out only her one eye wide open, staring alone
and knowing out into the field, in the direction of my house.
Perhaps Chisako had confided in this woman. Suddenly I felt
a cold wet slither around my fingers; I gave a cry, a little too
shrill, and jumped back.

"Hey, hey." The woman flapped her arm down beside
her, patting her thigh. "Don't mind it," she said. "I've been
feeding it, poor thing. Starving in the backyard." I saw the
outline of Yano's dog, that cold white flame of a tail in the

night, but I couldn't see its eyes. I caught the tinkle of the chain at its neck.

"You live over there, don't you?" The woman swung the flashlight towards the towers. "In the old farmhouse."

I was taken aback, hearing my home referred to in that way. I looked across the field, wondering how I would find my way back.

I'd left the porch light on, after all, and that solitary light guided me home. Each step falling a little deeper or shallower than I judged. That stain on Chisako's carpet preoccupied me, inexplicably. My stain, my clumsy presence, marked there for ever. *Don't fuss, Saito-san,* she'd said, forcing me up off my knees. *It's nothing. Yano doesn't care. He doesn't come in here.* If only I'd been allowed to finish. That day she was jittery; it was so unlike her. She expected Yano home at any time, but was brimming with news as always. She wanted to tell me every detail about her Mr. Spears. She had even begun to imitate the way he talked, the way he said her name, which she found funny and charming.

"Cheeesuko, Cheesuko," she laughed, holding her side. The memory of her voice was startling as I crossed the deserted field. But that was on another visit, I realized. A time weeks before, a happier time, when she'd showed me his walk, holding her narrow shoulders high and square. I tried to laugh out loud at this memory, be carried away as I had been that afternoon. Yet all I could think of was the stain I hadn't cleaned up. The clumsy bump of my elbow. My arm twitched with the memory, how I could have prevented it.

When I got in, Papa was groaning, and I cursed Stum for not settling him for the night. "Nani?" he muttered. As I leaned over him in bed, his eyes seemed strangely lucid. A trick of moonlight, I thought, once they began darting here and there.

I heard Stum's heavy footsteps outside in the hall.

I called out, "Why didn't you—" and he was there behind me as I tucked the covers in tightly.

"What's the matter?" Stum tugged at my arm. "Ne-san, what is it?" The two of them were staring at me all of a sudden, both of them helpless, helpless children I must look after every moment. Looking dumb in the face of every detail, every chore of living, when it all meant nothing.

"Nothing," I said. My breath was quietly seizing up into a ball. I felt a familiar sensation, a release; my face was wet.

Slowly, oafishly, Stum touched his thumb to my cheek and wiped it firmly, like dirt. He did it again and again, almost digging into my flesh. I pushed his hand away and felt the drops on my cheeks, on my hands.

"Stop, stop!" he finally cried, turning his face away in shame. As if he were the one weeping.

Later I lay in bed, my broad back overflowing the imprint Sachi's slight body had left on my sheets. I was tired, my skin felt parched; it had been too much for me, I suppose, the day's events, the ponderings. I blamed my weeping spell on this state of not knowing. But I knew my exhaustion came from within, from a sense of my own responsibility in all that had happened. Yet I felt helpless. I gave in to this feeling in my weak moments; knowing that I must not surrender to it, this sense I'd carried for as long as I could remember, that I must look after everyone, as I had all my life.

The house was utterly still. The towel I'd wrapped Sachi in lay abandoned in the middle of the floor. My room had grown stifling and musty from the damp. When I opened the window, sounds from the creek rose up, faint animal sounds dotted the air. Beside me the telephone rang, shrill in the dark.

"Moshi, moshi." It was my instinct to answer in Japanese at this hour. There was a long pause, breath let out. An ear listening, a mouth pressed like mine, waiting with me in the dark. I nearly hung up.

"What about the dog, Yano's dog?" Sachi's words mist in my ear. "Miss Saito?"

I eased myself back onto my bed. My mouth was open but nothing came out, just a hole catching the blackness in my room. Through the window I could imagine a wild dog howling in the night, Yano's dog. I was a fool to let that girl drag me about, in a downpour even, unsettling me in the midst of losing Chisako. I saw myself, the trudge of my feet in Mama's shoes, cold and soaked, sinking into the mud by the creek. Desperately holding onto Sachi's hand. The hideous sight of my hair drying like an unruly wig. Sachi's capricious, steel-clad smile; Stum's jeering smirk. And Keiko's humiliating appearance at my door. Her refusal to even sit down in my home; the pride she wielded over me, the arrogance. For Sachi was her child, not mine.

Let Keiko take her, let them look after her. She belonged to no one but them.

Miss Saito, Miss Saito. Are you there? I heard the desperation in that reedy voice, the loneliness, because Keiko had disappointed her once again. It didn't take very much. I sank back into my pillow, my head the anchor to my body; *Miss Saito, Miss Saito*—her voice became bodiless, nameless, a cricket's chirp rising from somewhere in the electrical field.

Gently, I hung up the receiver.

I slept dreamlessly that night, more deeply than I had in years. Perhaps it was the exhaustion that had built up inside me, all the changes that were happening so quickly and dramatically around me. Initially I'd let myself become caught up in the drama through Sachi, and upset myself needlessly, and suddenly I felt freed. As I crept down the hall in the morning, I noticed that Stum's bed had not been slept in; he must have left after I'd gone to sleep. I tried to push away that thought, the thought of Stum spending the night with his new friend, the thought of a different Stum, his knowing body; I shoved it to the back of my mind.

The sky was smoky with clouds, and the Yano house seemed to rise out of it. The front yard squirmed with foamy weeds, fat and tangled and grown over into a jungle, exotic among the neighbouring shaved lawns. I imagined mould forming in corners everywhere inside: in the cupboards; in the refrigerator, furring old food; staining the rim of the bathtub; the thick, sour smell. Who would look after it? Chisako had no family, Yano had said. Yano had only one brother, in a Kamloops mental hospital. A man he hadn't seen in twenty years because of the strange fits he'd fall into. "He can't stand the sight of an Oriental," Yano had told me one morning when he intercepted me on my walk; when casually enough, I'd asked about his family. "Can you believe that?" he said. "It's shameful. Chinese, Japanese, man, woman, doesn't make a difference. Goes nuts." He guffawed with disgust, pointed a finger to his temple, and made a little circle like a wind-up toy. He told me it had started in the camp.

I suppose I could understand the man's illness, how easily it might begin. With the line-ups at the mess hall, the ofuro, the benjo, day after day, endless. Everybody too close. Those smells, those noises, those voices. Mountains all around. I too was sick of it, sick to death of them all, before it even began; I longed to get away, just Eiji and I, out to sea, to Japan.

Now here I was, not a mountain-wall in sight, and two housefuls of them across from me; and all I could do was watch them, day in and day out, their comings and goings. What else was there to do? Yano had kept cranking his little finger at his head, not willing to understand the craziness in his brother. "We got to stick together, see?" As if going crazy were a rational decision his brother had made. To be different. To shun the rest. Yano had looked to me with that awful eagerness, time and time again. The last time I'd seen him, I could have smacked him for that look, the same way he smacked his dog when it jumped on him.

As I headed for the north end of the electrical field, I passed the Nakamuras' house, but the drapes were still drawn, later than usual. I faltered for a moment, then carried on, marvelling at the energy in my steps.

Even Papa was livelier this morning as I fed him his boiled rice and sour plum. His eyes darted out the window.

"Up-ee, up-ee," he gurgled through the meal, pointing a

crooked finger at the window. I raised the blinds to reveal the woods leading to the ravine beneath a searing blue sky, the same view as from my window, though I rarely saw it.

"Yano-san?" His finger wavered in the air as his head strained off the pillow.

"What? Nani?" I went to the window.

"Don buro," he said after a moment, still pointing. I looked again and laughed. Down below, he meant. I looked directly down to our yard, our little rectangle of mown green skirted by my peonies, coming up lush and full, leaning this way and that. My daffodils and tulips were still in bloom, but from up here they seemed to rise out of a dark pit. My yard could be a cemetery plot; our house a slab of grey stone. The thought struck me that Stum might be right: that after three days with no word, the children might no longer be alive.

"Nothing there, Papa." I didn't think twice about what he'd said, the nonsense. I wiped his mouth and helped him slide back under the covers. He'd become almost another kind of creature, it seemed to me, his skin thin and shiny. Whenever I birdbathed him, every few days I discovered new nooks and crevices, where flesh had shrunk and bones had shifted.

He was nothing now, less than an infant. Gave me no trouble at all. Not like Stum. My resentment slipped away on a day like this. On a day like this, I might even be grateful for his company. Not to have suffered a fate such as Chisako's. To be living. Not to be alone. I would never again be that girl, helpless when Papa was suddenly no longer strong, no longer brutish, and could not rise from his bed.

Who sank to the floor outside her papa's door in the dark, curled up under her nightgown, silently weeping to be let in, afraid she'd be left alone.

I passed most of the day by the window in spite of myself, of how anxious I felt over Sachi. Wondering about the night, about the drapes at her house that remained closed. Already I felt the exhaustion return to my body, felt that it had lost its memory of deep, untroubled sleep. By dark, staring across the field, I imagined a shadowy dot behind the drapes of the Nakamuras' house to be her, waiting and watching too. It was possible that she might never forgive me for waiting there, dumb, at the end of the telephone line; in silence I had listened as she'd called for me the way she did when she was anxious for my attention, or angry with me. She'd called my name twice. Each time I remembered, it felt like the tip of a knife gouging my heart.

FOUR

I **SEARCHED THE PAPER.** It was Thursday; exactly a week had passed since the news about Chisako, and nothing. The dot I had imagined to be Sachi at her window the night before had vanished in a flood of morning light. Keiko's drapes were open wide, as was usual for this time of the morning. Wherever Sachi was, I knew she'd be twinned with me in this ritual, turning page after page, through to the obituaries. Terrified yet relieved to have found no trace.

It occurred to me that there might have been an obituary placed by Mr. Spears' family on the Friday or Saturday, perhaps notice of a service of some kind, a burial, but I'd forgotten to check. Or hadn't cared to.

I had even neglected my crossword. The word jumble provided its usual comfort: the straightening out of a mess that at first glance appears hopeless. "Given", "pitied", "whose", and "knave" were the words for the day. On certain

days, years ago, really, I would scrutinize the words, wondering if they held some clue to my life, to my future. But of
course, even unjumbled, they remained a puzzle.

I went out back to look at my yard. I stepped out of my
slippers, unhooked my stockings, and planted my feet in the
grass. The second time in a week I'd done such a thing. I was
thinking of that little girl, being inside her slight, burgeon-
ing body. All churned up like the mouth of a current, missing Tam.

The grass was warm and moist and flaccid instead of
cool and crisp: a breeding ground. I felt everything withered
and rotting. Eating itself up, though it was only late May. My
daffodils and tulips, even my peonies were drooping; my irises
no good for ikebana, I thought: each one a little ruined, a little imperfect. Even my shasta daisies were coming up with
their crowns stunted. I clipped them back a bit, hoping to
thicken their flowering. Along the garden's rim, the trimmed
stems and crowns and fallen brown petals I stooped to gather
made me think of one of my visits with Chisako.

It came to me as I dropped the bits in a trash bag by
the patio. It was those flowers, my daisies, stunted as they
were. I'd planted them years ago because their white petals
reminded me of chrysanthemums, the kind grown in Japan.
Now, as I looked at them, they seemed a flimsy shadow of
the thick, pristine blooms seen in traditional arrangements.
They took me back to those early days, the winter when
Yano first befriended me, not long after they moved into the
neighbourhood. I was coming out of the house for my
morning walk and found him standing in my front yard,
scrutinizing the amateurish ikebana I'd foolishly placed in

my window. I'd used daisies from the local supermarket, the thin, cheap, spindly kind, and they poked out of the vase along with a broken pine branch Stum had brought me. I'd struggled with it, but even from a distance one could see that it was all wrong.

I was annoyed and mildly humiliated to find him there when I'd purposely timed my walk a half-hour earlier to avoid him. He'd been meeting up with me more frequently, and I did not care to make conversation at such an hour. For it was my hour. To hear the busy sweetness of birds, the roar of the planes departing early for who knows where; even that buzz of distant highway traffic, all uninterrupted by Papa's impatient requests for this or that. In those days, confined to his wheelchair after his first stroke, he'd bang his wheels against my furniture. I savoured this brisk morning air. No one had yet breathed it, or so it seemed; after a night of snowfall, mine would be the first footprints in the blanketed field; my path, marked for me to see once I returned to my window. It was invigorating; not merely the physical exertion, but to be out of doors, not sheltered by my porch, or behind glass. I kept track of changes in the neighbourhood, however small: new drapes hung in a window; the carton from a washer or dryer discarded for pick-up.

To be greeted by Yano, first thing out my door! What was most annoying was how he would follow me a few feet behind. Some days it took a while before I noticed him there. He enjoyed that advantage, watching me, undetected. There I'd be, muttering away to myself or counting my steps. I wondered if he eavesdropped on any of it; if on some occasion I'd said anything inappropriate.

On that morning I set off at a brisk pace and, sure enough, it was not long before he was lagging behind. I turned abruptly, about to air my mind to him. I worried, too, that he might one day follow unseen and suffer another of his respiratory attacks. I couldn't be responsible, I told him, a little breathless myself at having to express my feelings so forthrightly.

"Worry? About me?" He smiled his crowded smile. "Why, Saito-san, I'm touched."

I knew instantly what was going through that unruly head of his: that I was looking out for him, after all; sticking together as he'd suggested we all do. That pleased him no end. I did not detect sarcasm in his tone.

"Gomen, Saito-san. I'll keep up," he said, apologizing, and rushed up beside me. Not granting me so much as a second to shoo him off. He waved a hand back at my house and the window, his breath puffing like baby powder into the winter air. "Chisako's good at that flower business. She can teach you," he said, falling back and catching up with me again. I simply nodded, never knowing how seriously to take anything he said.

"She was saying last night," Yano said, "wouldn't it be nice to have Saito-san over?" He laughed a little. "Don't worry." He gave my elbow a knock. "It'll just be you two girls. I'll keep out of your hair." His face was already slick from the vigorous walk and he unzipped his jacket partway. "Gotta stick together, right?" I winced at this refrain, but it no longer unnerved me. As if being nihonjin in the same neighbourhood could melt every disagreeable difference between us.

As we passed the Nakamura house, Keiko appeared in

the window. I stepped up my pace, anxious not to seem like a spy, and embarrassed, I suppose, to be seen with Yano. "What's your hurry?" Yano tugged at my coat sleeve. He stopped to watch Keiko as she stood with her muscular arms folded. She was looking out towards Mackenzie Hill. Who knew what was going through her mind? She turned away to carry on with her morning's chores, too busy to see us. Yano was taken with her, I could see, but he shrugged it off.

"Snob," he muttered.

"What do you mean?" I asked innocently. For I too had felt the brush of Keiko's cold shoulders early on.

"She saw us just now, right?" he said, pointing, though I wasn't certain she had. "What would it hurt? A little smile? A wave?" He shoved his ungloved hand through the air towards their window, pushing her away. "I went there yesterday. Talk a little, shoot the breeze. I even invited her to my redress meeting. She wouldn't let me finish, practically pushed me out the door." His voice grew wheezy telling me.

"There, there," I said absently. I couldn't help thinking of how I had shunned Yano when he first came knocking on my door. I was taken by the thought that Keiko had actually let him inside the house. I myself had never been invited in.

Yano fumed a little, and I tried to deafen myself to his muttered curses. I shuddered, wondering if I sounded anything like him with my mutterings: more than a little crazy. He stopped once he saw me watching, and gave that wheezing laugh. "Not to worry, Saito-san," he said with cheerful determination. "I don't give up so easy." He kicked his boot into the dry, frozen earth.

"I'll see you tomorrow night, won't I, Saito-san?" He slipped a flyer into my hand and winked. "Your brother too?" I glanced down at it quickly, then folded it in half. It wasn't the first such meeting he'd invited me to.

"Yano-san," I said, lowering my voice to indicate the seriousness of what I was about to say. "These things," I went on. I smiled pleasantly; I felt the steadiness of my own wisdom in the words poised on my tongue. "Our life is not so bad here. We've made our way." I kept smiling. "These things that happened are behind us now. And they are...private, ne?" Eiji entered my mind just then, as he always did when these subjects came up.

Yano was silent for some moments. His jaw twitched, and as he inhaled he wheezed slightly, but his manner was easy. His ready smile, repellent as it could be, was absent from his face. "We? What do you mean, we?" He paused. He did not intend me to answer. "So, Saito-san. You do stick together when it's good for you, right?"

I did not respond to that bitter remark either. I did not so much as alter my expression. I had no wish to share in his anger, or to make others share in mine; to blame the government, the camps, the war, the man they may or may not have named that hill after. For what life did or did not give to me. There would be no end to it.

My bitterness belonged to no one but myself. I did not share it with strangers; I did not hold them accountable. For these were private matters; family matters.

I held my smile. I turned abruptly, still smiling, and carried that smile on my face until I reached the edge of my front yard. Only then did I let it drop. Sure enough, Yano's shout rang across the field as I was about to open my front door. I felt like the guilty suspect on the television show Papa often watched, who always lets his guard down once the detective has left, only to have him return seconds later. "Saito-san!" Yano bellowed. Reluctantly I turned. He was waving frantically, his smile regained. "Your first ikebana lesson! Tonight at seven. Chisako expects you!"

Inside, I found Papa sitting in his wheelchair at the window, with the television off. He appeared more alert than usual, more restless. Even on such listless days, he refused to struggle with his cane, partly out of laziness and partly out of pride. It irritated me to see him languish like this, and it occurred to me to remind him that he had not been so proud in the old days, when Mama sent me out after him; then he had not hesitated to lean his heavy body, heavy with drink on Saturday nights, on my slight girl's frame. Perhaps in some way he was haunted by that memory, for he would not allow me to help him up the stairs, preferring Stum to do so.

Papa could watch show after show of games and soap operas interspersed with the news. *As the World Turns, Another World, What's My Line,* even *The Dating Game.* The drone of it was endless. It filled me with nausea, the gaudy flicker of colours and faces that distracted me from my reading and crossword puzzles. As a concession to me, he kept the volume low. But at that moment the television was off, a slate with our own shadows passing across it, and he was pointing out to the field and struggling with words.

"Yano-san wa..."

"Hai, Papa. Yes, that was Yano." I hurriedly closed the

drapes; the light had begun to grey unexpectedly, as it could even in the early part of the day. That shadowy cover of cloud that could easily dampen the spirit.

He was still pointing wordlessly when I said: "Tea, Papa?" Without waiting for a response, I went into the kitchen to put on the kettle. I set two cookies for each of us on a plate. When I came back, he was studying the flyer I'd carelessly left on the coffee table, using his magnifying glass. His one eye loomed insect-like through it.

"Nani desu ka?" He wanted to know what it was. I snatched it from his hands, more roughly than I meant to, and crumpled it up. These things could be unsettling, really, and for no good reason.

"A silly meeting, Papa," I told him. No sooner had I sat back in my chair than the kettle began to sing. I got up but, when I did, Papa had blocked the space between the chair and the coffee table so that I couldn't move. Back then, in spite of his legs being weak, his arms were strong enough to manoeuver the wheelchair. His face was remarkably smooth and unsunken; the skin was still thick. When he was angry, though, as at that very moment, the skin tautened over the bones of his face, and the veins protruded in an almost violent way. The kettle was screeching.

"You, baka, ne!" he shouted. That word, baka, stupid, never far from his lips. He slapped his palm on the table. I shrank back; he still intimidated me in those days. I uncrumpled Yano's flyer and showed it to him. "It's about us getting money from the government," I shouted above the screaming of the kettle.

"What for?" Whenever Papa uttered a single word or

phrase in English, he changed in my eyes. He became a different person, for better or worse. Perhaps it was because we communicated so little. He became lucid to me; less forgiveable.

"For the camps," I said.

I don't know if he understood, but he took Yano's flyer
from my hand and crumpled it up again. He started to laugh
as he wheeled himself away from me. I scurried to the
kitchen to turn off the stove.

Papa had switched on the television when I returned
with his tea. He'd turned the volume up louder than usual.
He was still chuckling to himself as he struggled from his
wheelchair to the chesterfield. He heaved himself over, his
laugh turning to a choking cough. Usually he remained in
his wheelchair until Stum came home; during the day he
wanted to remain mobile, I suppose. But by five minutes
before five-thirty each afternoon, he was waiting by the
doorway for Stum to arrive. Today he seemed anxious to settle in to watch a particular program, so I left him there. He
was so involved that later I let him and Stum eat their dinner in front of the television, while I went up to my room.

At seven I was at the Yanos' door. For the longest time
there was no answer. In the shadows outside, I chided myself
for having listened to Yano, for making such a fool of myself;
for wasting so much time deciding what to wear. I'd even sat
myself down in my darkened bedroom, breathing deeply,
calming myself before venturing out, for I rarely made visits
anywhere without Stum or Papa, except for my shopping
trips downtown. I was making my way back down the driveway, dreading the lonely return across the dark field, when
Yano called after me. It was, I admit, with some relief that I

turned back, clutching my offering of little rice cakes. He rushed to usher me inside the house.

Yano was more flustered and excitable than ever; that I sensed immediately. His hair was more unkempt than when I'd seen him that morning, and he was perspiring, as usual. I suppose he was anxious, eager at the prospect of Chisako and me becoming friends. A scent filled my nostrils; it was a mingling of Yano's pungent body odour and the not-unfamiliar smell of fried fish and daikon. This half-known thing disconcerted me; made me flush with shame at our shared habits, our odours. For my home was no less fragrant than Yano's. It was ridiculous, really, to be concerned when we had so few visitors.

I bent down to remove my shoes, but Yano insisted I keep them on, and led me into their living-room. A momentary gratitude welled inside me for his kindness in welcoming me. I felt sorry that I normally harboured such repulsion for him.

I expected to find Chisako in the living-room; I was readying myself to greet her. But the room was empty, though crowded with booklets and newspapers; a card table with a typewriter was surrounded by open books piled face down, spines cracked. The local telephone book with the odd name underlined. The dog and children were nowhere in sight.

"Wait here, Saito-san," Yano said, seeming to vibrate with impatient energy. He pointed to a lumpy chesterfield whose armrests were threadbare. "I'll get Chisako."

I scanned the room, the stacks upon stacks of papers, and saw no flowers or vases, no implements normally used for ikebana. The walls were yellowing and bumpy from old wallpaper being painted over. A calendar from the grocery store downtown hung crookedly beside Yano's table, scribbled on, dates furiously circled beneath a photo of a placid Japanese garden. On a sheet of paper in the typewriter I noticed one word had been typed, but repeated three times, each time spelled differently, then x'ed over. The last time correct: "abrogation", but x'ed over just the same. It could have been one of my word jumbles, the long and challenging kind that came at the end of the week. There was dust on the sheet, untouched for some time. I reached to flick the dust aside, as was my habit, when I heard movement behind me. I turned to find Chisako hovering at the doorway, alone, face hidden within her hair, as she'd appeared that day in her slippers out in the field.

I bowed slightly. "Hello, Yano-san," I said, offering the cakes. I was more awkward in those days, and stumbled over my greeting. "Thank you so much for—"

"No need to thank me, Saito-san," she broke in abruptly, striding into the room. Again I was struck, as I had been at our first meeting, by her shyness; it was the part of her that floundered in spite of the forthrightness of her speech. I realized that if our friendship was to develop at all, I would have to show some initiative. But in time Chisako would outgrow some of that diffidence—helped in some small way, I believe, by our meetings, which later became quite frequent. She took the package from my hands, bowing. "Lovely," she murmured, then carelessly placed them atop one of the stacks of papers.

As I stood in that room the thought came to me, like a chilled breeze, that perhaps this was all Yano's idea; that he had forced the idea on Chisako and she was made nervous by my presence and the expectations Yano had raised. Perhaps she was not happy at all to be here with me.

As if sensing my agitation, she drew back her hair from around her face and said: "Don't worry, Saito-san. I am an excellent teacher."

"I'm not…" Worried, I was going to say, I suppose. I touched a hand to my flushed face. It seemed I was incapable of finishing a sentence, uncertain of what precisely I intended to say. But she had already disappeared through another doorway, which I assumed led to the kitchen. She re-emerged a moment later bearing some implements and a bunch of flowers.

"Please call me Chisako," she said as she set the things down on the chesterfield. "I don't like 'Yano'." She frowned as she said the name, exaggerating the sound of it. "It isn't a nice name, is it?"

I was struck by how fluent her English was, but refrained from remarking on it. Instinctively I knew we shared that horror of hearing ourselves vulgar or rough in our own ears; we both strove to better ourselves. I heard too, in her l's, rolling in that telltale way, that she was trying very hard; I could imagine her sitting before her reflection in a mirror, making sure her tongue touched the edge of her teeth and roof of her mouth in just the right way, pronouncing a word over and over. *Lovely, lovely.*

She cleared off Yano's card table, without a thought, it seemed, to preserving whatever order his things were arranged in. She dropped them to the floor. "My husband is very untidy," she said, pushing the books aside with her foot. She then unwrapped the flowers and laid them on the table.

Those were the flowers that have stayed in my memory: shasta daisies, white with yellow centres, badly wilted and brown at the petals' edges. With each move she made, petals fell to the carpet. I contemplated gathering them up but left them, too self-conscious to do so. Chisako seemed oblivious, and quickly, wordlessly began clipping the flower stems to varying lengths.

She sighed now and again, as if tired, perhaps bored, and again it occurred to me that this had all been Yano's idea and that she was merely going through the motions to satisfy him. I searched for words to make a gracious exit, searched in vain, watching her slender, dexterous hands take up the stems and the clipping shears. I stood awkwardly behind her.

"Saito-san, you know all this, don't you? Heaven, earth, man?" Her hands bustled around the brown blossoms with a kind of hurried grace, indicating the three levels at which the flowers would be placed. "It's a little silly, don't you think?" She kept on busily with the task, stabbing the narrow stems into the sharp points of the kenzan as the odd petal drifted down. "There are so many schools of ikebana and everybody disagrees. In fact, I prefer the Western way of flowers in a vase, all together. It's more natural, don't you think?"

I was silent at first but then: "No," I answered, with a firmness that surprised even myself. "This is much more beautiful," I said. "Everything in its place." I don't know where these ideas came from, but as I pronounced them I was convinced of their truth, of the fact that beauty must be protected and preserved, and be given its proper place.

Chisako looked up at me with a mildly shocked expression that seemed genuine. "Why, Saito-san. That is a very Japanese thing to say. But you are nisei, like Yano. Born here, ne?" I nodded. "So, so so," she murmured thoughtfully. "How unusual."

"You studied ikebana, I suppose," I said, waving my hand clumsily at the flowers.

"Yes, every girl does. I studied the style of Ikenobo school. Very classical," she said, sighing. "It seems so far away. My school-days."

"Do you miss Japan?" I thought of those icy waves that washed over Eiji and me at Port Dover. One after another, and the elusive speck I could never see that Eiji said was Japan. Where he promised to take me.

"Samui, Saito-san?" I must have shivered, for Chisako was looking at me with concern. She hugged herself to make sure I understood. "Cold?" She reached for a man's sweater draped on the chesterfield. Yano's, no doubt.

"No, no. Iie." I tried not to flinch at the thought of Yano's sweater next to my skin. "It's all right," I added.

"No, Saito-san, I do not miss Japan," she said tiredly. "Nihonjin are so…" She searched for the word, wrinkling her nose with distaste. "So…seigen suru. Wakarimasu-ka? Do you understand, Saito-san?" I shook my head, but I could guess what she meant. "So stiff," she explained.

"Also, they are short." She held out one hand palm down by her ear to show me. I realized then that she was tall for a Japanese woman. She giggled, covering her mouth. "Yano is not so bad, of course," she said, and she moved her hand away to show her smile for the first time. "That's why I married

him. He is Canadian, not nihonjin." It was not exactly an
unflattering smile, the way her upper lip pushed up over her
slightly protruding teeth. "He's a nisei," she said, as if she had
to explain that to me.

Yano bustled into the room, and Chisako stepped up beside the arrangement with head cocked to gaze at it. "Saito-
san didn't need a lesson at all," she declared. "Look at the
wonderful ikebana she's done."

I recall when Chisako stepped back from the flowers she
alone had hastily arranged. She looked from me to her agitated husband and back to me with one knowing glance. I
felt the thrill of that conspiracy, of the intimacy between us
in the lie of that moment. We stood there, we three, before
the arrangement of sickly, wilting flowers.

"Utsukushii desu ne?" Yano exclaimed.

"Yes, it is," I said. "It is beautiful." I suppose to show that
I understood.

There was silence, then Chisako's sudden laughter, which
seemed to crack the surface of Yano's beaming face like water
poured on ice.

"What?" he demanded, the smile gone.

Chisako kept on, unable to stop. "Utsukushii," she whispered, convulsing with half-silent laughter. "Utsukushii," she
repeated, glancing at me, clutching her side. Before I could
stop myself, I felt my lips curling up, though I didn't fully
grasp what was so funny.

"Chisako!" Yano's voice was not loud but it stopped my
heart for a second, the ominous warning in it. But Chisako
ignored him, still giggling, trying to catch her breath. The
sound of his voice I could not forget; like thunder gathering

its charge. A second later he slammed his fist down on the table with such force that books fell, the floor even shifted, and the withered blossoms shook; a few petals drifted down in the aftermath. He was crazed then, his long, greasy hair fallen over his eyes. I feared for Chisako, but she remained calm as ever. The laughter had vanished, and she now appeared almost solemn.

"Gomen, Masa-chan," she whispered, as if to a favourite child. "Forgive me." She went to him, smoothing his hair back from his face with surprising tenderness. I saw what was between them. It was the only time I ever heard her call him by his given name, and in that intimate moment I longed to disappear.

Despite my protests, Yano insisted on walking me back across the field. We went in silence for several moments, with him lost in his thoughts. He erupted loudly into conversation, as he often did.

"You learn quick, Saito-san."

"You were right. Your wife is an excellent teacher."

"Thanks for coming," he said. He seemed to be looking at me, but it was difficult to tell as we fell into a shadowy stretch.

"Not at all."

"My wife is lonely," he said, still in that quiet tone. "She hasn't made friends. Her English isn't so good."

I was about to remark that her English was, in fact, excellent, but stopped myself. Instead I said: "It was kind of you to think of us, both Chisako and myself." It later struck me as an odd thing for me to say. "I had a nice time," I added.

"She's . . . difficult," Yano said, pursuing his own thoughts. I could see his broad hands flexing in front of him, that frustration I'd seen in him when words failed. "Mon ku, mon ku. Complains and complains." We'd stopped in the middle of the field.

"This is fine," I said. "I'm fine now," indicating that he could turn back. "Thank you again." There was his large, ever-gleaming face illuminated by a fragment of moonlight. I recognized the anger lurking in his furrowed brow.

"You know, Saito-san. I do what I can," he said, one fist working into the palm of the other hand. "I work hard. Try to change things for us nihonjin. It's important to try, don't you think?"

"Yes, yes," I murmured, in as soothing a voice as I could, anxious as I was to get home, away from him. Try, he'd said to try. I envisioned the one word on the page in his typewriter, gathering dust, spelled and misspelled. I felt apprehensive standing there with him, I don't know why.

"There were others who tried, but they gave up, years ago, Saito-san. I won't give up."

He turned towards Mackenzie Hill, the darker shadow of it in the sky, far off and yet so large. The moon hung flimsily over it, a white light dully glowing. "If things had been different, if it weren't for the war, I wouldn't be doing what I'm doing. Pressing collars and cuffs all day, cleaning other people's dirty clothes. Would I, Saito-san? Would I?" He wanted an answer; demanded it.

"No, no," I replied, again as calmly as I could. But I did not believe it. Not for an instant. What would you be doing, I wanted to demand back of him. What?

He started walking again, striding as he spoke. "Same with your papa, sweeping up on that chicken farm. Your brother, all those years. We'd be doing something else. Something important, ne? You too, Saito-san. All of us. We were too good. We were doing too well, so they had to set us back, didn't they?"

Thankfully, we just then reached my front porch and I scurried up the steps. He was waiting for some response, anxious that his words not be lost to the darkness between us. I heard his shoe tapping in the snow at the foot of my steps. The sound of his fist working into his palm, dry and rough as sandpaper.

I gave a forced sigh. "Well," I said, groping for words to placate him. "What's past is past." A meaningless phrase, but it seemed to frustrate Yano even more.

"No, Saito-san. Never say that. Never." He sounded ominous again. But then he stopped himself; seemed to pull himself up. He half smiled, tiredly, no longer daunting. Just another man, a shambling figure in the night. "Well, Saito-san, good-night." He gave a wave and we both turned from each other. Then, as I was about to close my door, he called back, as he always did.

"Tomorrow at seven, Saito-san! The meeting at school!"

When I shut the door and switched off the porch light, I found Stum alone in the dark, sitting by the window in Papa's wheelchair. In those days he shared my habit of staring out into the field, watching the goings-on. "What meeting, ne-san?" he asked. He must have heard Yano's shouts. I could not see Stum's face, but often it seemed he could be so transparent in his boyish wonderings. I could see the mechanisms in his head and heart clicking and chugging along, those intricate engineering drawings he sketched in his notebooks come to life. He played with the chair's wheels, turning them, wheeling back and forth.

I placed a firm hand on his shoulder, stilling him, wincing at the welts being ground into my carpet. "Oh, nothing," I muttered. "Some little meeting at the school. Nothing you'd be interested in."

"Papa said it's about money from the government for us. For being in the camp." Stum had such a curiosity then; his voice conveyed a light trusting quality. "Papa says it's stupid. Is it, ne-san?"

"I suppose it is," I said. I felt suddenly tired. I wanted nothing more than to fold myself into my fresh sheets and sleep. I yawned and indicated that I was retiring.

"Are you going, ne-san? To the meeting?" he persisted in that youthful way.

"Oh, no," I laughed. "A waste of time. Nothing will come of it."

As I lay in bed that night, in my crisp clean sheets, I was suddenly wide awake and wondering about what Yano had said, his rantings, his stacks of papers and books, his meetings. That one word on his typewriter, again and again. Abrogation. I knew what Yano took it to mean. Of rights, abrogation of rights. Blaming everything on the war, the camps. It was too easy to see things in such simple terms: cowardly, even, not to face your own personal troubles. Instead, to air them to the world and expect it to pay attention. In a way, pitiful.

The time I spent day in and day out, remembering this,

remembering that, or not remembering at all—this was how my time went by. It brought me comfort. I felt sorry for Yano as I lay in my warm bed; he had no peace of mind, none at all. In the end, I suppose, I accepted my lot as he never could. I felt sorry for Chisako too, to be with Yano in our little neighbourhood, shy and alone; no doubt missing Japan, though she'd said otherwise.

I didn't think of Yano's meeting the next day as I went through the routine of my chores. If it hadn't been for Stum's mentioning it again at dinner, it would not have crossed my mind at all.

"Will anybody go to that meeting, ne-san?" he asked, food dropping from his chopsticks. In those days, much as he kept to himself, staying in his room with his drawings and studies, Stum could ask many questions, always expecting me to know the answer. I'd summon up the best response I could, and pronounce it with all the authority of an elder sister.

"One or two at the most," I said, with a little toss of my head. Knowing Yano, he would have sent out countless flyers all over. I remembered that open phone book in his living-room—he'd picked out the nihonjin names to make his list, that was what it was. Since the end of the war, nihonjin were scattered all over. No longer any reason to settle together in certain blocks of the city, as if in a camp of our own making.

It was shortly after dinner when I felt a fullness in my stomach that only a brisk walk would dissipate. I found myself near the middle-school grounds and happened to spot a single classroom lit up. As I neared the window, I caught sight of Yano standing at the front of the class, and in the first row were two men I took to be nisei, uncomfortably seated in those child-sized desks, still wearing their coats. Yano was gesturing emphatically as if to a room full of people, as unkempt as ever, with a stack of papers on the desk before him. I was surprised, and yet not, to find Chisako absent.

"Anne! Anne!" I looked up from where I was squatting in the garden to find Stum standing by the back door rather stiffly. His calling me by my Christian name was a warning. He cleared his throat noisily and gave me a strained glance. "Anne, could you come inside, please? Someone is here." Through the grey-shadowed screen, I discerned a tall silhouette. Quickly I got up, slipped into my shoes stockingless, and entered the house behind my brother.

We sat in a circle, Stum, the police detective, and I. I was a little nervous; a lick of excitement, perhaps fear, ran the length of me as I watched the man lean his large frame into my armchair, the one whose cushions I'd plumped up just that morning. He cradled a small black notebook and held a tiny pen in his oversized hands. We so rarely had guests, let alone hakujin.

The man, Detective Rossi, raised his pen to us in a salute, sat tall in my armchair as if it were a saddle a little small for him. He was not that young, I saw, though his hair was thick and full and without grey, running like a sprouting hedge across his forehead. Perhaps ten years older than Stum, at the most. A little younger than me. I looked for signs of unnatural colour, where he might have used something like that Grecian Formula, for his face betrayed his age.

"Ma'am, tell me. How well—"

"Please," I interrupted. "It's Miss Saito." I could not endure being called *ma'am* this and *ma'am* that in my own home. Stum flashed me a look, a look that said *how dare you?*

"Please," I said, leaning forward in my seat as graciously as I could in my nervousness, "continue."

"How well did you know the deceased, Mrs. Yano?"

"She was my friend, of course."

"When was the last time you saw her?"

"Well, let me see." I tapped my fingers across my lips and ran through a flurry of dates in my head. I must have been muttering, for when I looked up the detective had stopped writing and was staring at me. Stum looked dark and small beside this man, his colourless eyes radiating kindly concern. Stum had his eye on me, waiting for me to mortify myself before our guest. Pretending a dread of it, but deep down looking forward to it. I had an urge to run to the bathroom mirror to see myself, what could be read on my face.

"Which is it, Miss Saito? Monday, the fifteenth of May, or Tuesday, the sixteenth?" He was tapping his pen on the arm of the chair.

I felt a draft on my knees and glanced down to see my pale, veined legs exposed without stockings. How hideous they looked, how mottled and old. I pulled my skirt over my knees. "It was the Tuesday then," I answered.

"That was the day before Mrs. Yano was murdered," he said, in his indifferent way.

"Murdered?" No sooner had I let that escape than I felt like an idiot.

The detective looked up, his forehead crinkling with four straight creases parallel to the hedge of his hairline. They disappeared in an instant. "Well, it doesn't look like it was an accident. It wasn't suicide."

"Of course not. It's just the word...it's upsetting, isn't it?" My face flushed hot and cold. The word stung me. Up until this point I'd heard, read in the newspapers: *dead, deceased, shot*, but never *murdered*. The violence of it. The severed yellow police ribbon dangling from trees in the parking lot, the trampled blood dust came back to me; the streak of it on Sachi's finger. Stum was watching me.

"Did Mrs. Yano express to you any fears or anxieties about anything? Anyone?"

"No, not really."

"Miss Sa-to, am I pronouncing that right?"

"Sa-i-to," I corrected.

"Miss Saito, did she confide in you about her relationship with this man who was found with her, Mr. Spears?"

It was at that exact moment that I noticed an inch-long section on my leg where the vein was actually protruding, a bluish worm halfway down my calf. It seemed to vibrate grotesquely. Incredibly, it was a part of me, my own body. How long had it been there? It seemed undeniably a sign. I closed my eyes for a few seconds to regain my composure, then opened them to find both Stum and the detective once again watching me closely. I had to pause to place myself, to register the room I was in, one that could hold these two faces side by side.

"Miss Saito?"

"Anne?" Stum kicked the side of my shoe with his.

"Yes, yes, don't rush me," I muttered. They both drew back from me.

I took a deep breath and tried for calm, but I could feel that my lips had got ahead of me, as usual. I slowed them down.

"Ma'am?"

"Yes," I said simply.

"Yes?"

"Mrs. Yano and her friend were having... an affair." As I said the word, I stroked the raised worm encased in my leg and shivered. The detective would have caught that, the telltale tremor.

Yet he seemed unaffected by my revelation. Had he heard this before? From other neighbours? From Keiko and Tom? Sachi? How many knew? He began to tap his loafer with his pen.

"And what about Mr. Yano? Did you know him?"

"Yes," I said. "I did."

"He was involved in some political activities, wasn't he?"

"I suppose so," I said. "I wouldn't know about those things."

"When did you last see Mr. Yano?"

The dates seemed to blur in my mind. For what did dates mean to me when my days were all the same, all routine, I told myself; every day is a Saturday; I couldn't be held responsible. I shook my head regretfully. "I can't say for certain," I answered. "Several days earlier, I suppose. At least."

"Tell me, Miss Saito, have you known the Yanos for very long?"

"Since they moved in. About four years ago."

"Miss Saito, have you ever seen Mr. Yano become angry or violent?"

Strangely, that evening years earlier was all that came to mind. When we three, Chisako, Yano, and I, stood admiringly before that pathetic arrangement of half-dead flowers. As long ago as it was, it was fresher in my mind than any recent encounter with Yano. I wondered what this was, this trick of memory. But there was Chisako, her hair oddly cropped as it was then, clutching her side, still giggling at whatever Yano had said. And there I was, unsmiling, tentative. Wondering what I was doing there, out of my home, away from my armchair, away from my window. Yet somehow enthralled. "Chisako!" Yano had boomed. Then the fist, that crashing fist.

"Miss Saito?"

I felt the kick of Stum's foot against mine, jolting me into the present. "Anne?" Stum was staring at me.

"Should I repeat the question, Miss Saito?"

"No," I finally said. "No."

"You remember the question?"

"Of course I do," I said. "I've never seen Mr. Yano violent." The detective scribbled something into his little notebook.

"Shouldn't you talk to their neighbours?" I pointed vaguely out the window, across the field to the house beside the Yanos'.

The detective turned his earnest eyes to me. "Is there someone in particular you think I should talk to, Miss Saito?"

"No, no," I answered quickly. "I just wondered, that's all."

"And you," he said, turning to Stum. "Were you acquainted with any members of the Yano family?"

Stum shrugged and sank farther down in the couch, playing the sullen teenager once more, ridiculous at his age. "Not much. Not like her," he said, wanting to slough things off on me.

"Is there anything you can tell me that might shed light on the deaths or the disappearance of Mr. Yano and his children?"

Stum blinked his eyes slowly, as if each time he might not open them again. "Nope," he said. Then smiled a lazy smile at the detective, who got up, brushed off his pants with one hand.

"Anything at all? You're sure?"

Stum nodded again, keeping his lazy smirk.

"Fine." The detective seemed satisfied. "Now, just a few routine questions." He gave a little smile. "Anyone else live here with the two of you?"

"No," I said, pleasantly. I felt Stum's foot bumping mine. "Ne-san!"

The detective looked from me to Stum and back again.

"I mean, yes, there is," I stammered. "Our father, up-stairs. I forgot to say...because he's very old, you see, and he barely..."

"But he still lives here, does he?"

"Yes. I only meant that—"

"And how old is he?"

"Eighty-six."

"How long have you each lived here?"

"All my life," said Stum, raising his hands and letting them drop. He turned to look out the window.

"Don't be silly," I scolded. "Only since you were thirteen."

"Twelve."

"So, how long is that?" The detective remained patient.

"Twenty-one years this September," I said softly. How long. It was painful to say aloud, a blur of time. Just numbers, telling nothing of the tick tick of it. What did it mean to this stranger, this detective who was passing through a single moment of it? And yet I knew I would be reviewing it over years to come, asking myself: What did he think of us? Did he believe what we told him?

"You've been here the longest of all your neighbours, then."

I nodded. The detective wandered to the window. I felt the heat draining from my legs, the circulation waning.

"You must have seen the neighbourhood go up, house by house." He pointed across the way. "You must have watched every one of those families move in." He seemed to be scrutinizing my face, to see my response.

"I suppose."

"School wasn't even built until '65." He was squinting to the south, where the electrical field became the football field farther up. "This is the old vet's farmhouse, isn't it?"

"It is," I said, thinking of the Yanos' neighbour; she'd called it a farmhouse too.

"I grew up not far from here," he explained, pointing north. "On the other side," he said, half to himself. He meant the Italian blocks, where large elderly women in black dresses sat on kitchen chairs on their porches or sidewalks.

"When we were kids, we'd go down to the creek." The view out the window, though it was the opposite direction from the creek, must have called up memories for him.

"We'd skip off classes, go down there…do things we weren't supposed to." He winked at Stum. Without missing a beat, Stum nodded back. Man to man, as they say. I tried to imagine this detective as a boy, his body lanky, with his bushy head of hair and an eager instead of careful face, lying on the bank of the creek, all stretched out, a cigarette in his hand like Sachi. The kind of boy who'd have taken her down there after school, then ignored her the next day in the hall.

And here was my brother, now an experienced man who gave back an assured nod to the detective's suggestive remark. Nowadays, he must understand everything.

"That's a long time in one place," the detective was saying.

"You don't notice," Stum mumbled.

As I held open the screen door for him, the detective paused, his face a foot up from mine. "Miss Sa-i-to," he pronounced carefully, with another smile that didn't stay. "I wonder. Did you see anything from your window that day? That Wednesday?" He meant the day Chisako and Mr. Spears were found, before the news broke.

"Not that I can recall," I responded. I glanced at my chair by the window, its worn seat and armrests.

The detective stared at his car parked out front, dwarfed by the towers. "It's possible we'll never find them," he said quietly. "In cases like this. People just disappear and—" The last of what he said was sheared off by a car speeding past on the concession road. I made a useless gesture for him to repeat himself, but by then he'd bid us goodbye and the door was flapping shut.

Stum and I huddled silently at the corner of the window, the way we always did after a rare guest left. The detective sat in his car, busily writing more notes, his chin squashed to his chest. When he glanced up at the house he may have spotted us as we quickly stepped back from the window, a pair of clowns. Finally he drove away, leaving a cloud of dust from the gravel shoulder in his wake.

"The way you behave!" I exclaimed, walking away from Stum and the window.

"We didn't give away anything, did we, ne-san?" He balanced on the ledge, legs folded girlishly. "We protected our own, didn't we?"

"What do you mean, give away? Protected our own? You sound like—"

Stum clucked his tongue. "Like Yano?"

"You can't believe he'd do this."

Stum ignored me, swivelling to look out the window, then swivelling back to me. "You wanted him to ask more questions, didn't you? You were disappointed not to have her stories to tell, all details, weren't you?"

"Don't be ridiculous. Don't be disrespectful, not to Chisako-san."

"Isn't it true, ne-san?"

"Just because I don't have anything to hide. Not like you!"

"Me?"

"You know something, don't you?"

"What are you saying, ne-san?"

"Why didn't you tell the detective?"

"Why didn't you?"

"If you know something, you must tell the authorities, little brother." I watched him shift uneasily. "You've been talking to Yano, haven't you? That's where you got that sticking together rubbish, isn't it?" Stum seemed unperturbed. "He's been saying that to me for years. And you take it all in, like a fool, don't you?"

Stum turned back to the window, silent and thoughtful as he stared across the field at the empty Yano house. "Yes," he said softly, after moments passed. "He was my friend."

The way he said this, so convincingly. I was shocked. Why had I not seen signs of this friendship? Barely a smile exchanged, a pause between them on the street, in the field. How could Stum have hidden this from me? Why?

"How could you be friends with such a person? The other day you called him kamikaze!" I accused him childishly.

"What do you mean, 'such a person'? You're the one who says he's done nothing."

"He's a weirdo. He smells, he's dirty! He shames us all. Even his wife."

"His wife has shamed him! She deserved it!" Stum rose angrily from the window-ledge, his fist pounded the back of my armchair. Before I knew what I was doing, I heard the smack of my hand against his cheek, clear and stark. He stood back, his face shuddering with the realization of what I'd done, in his eyes that child's look of betrayal I'd seen when Papa once struck him. More a child than Sachi, who'd been callous to it, unsurprised by the violence in me when

I'd raised my hand to her. I retreated to the chesterfield and sank down.

The echo of our shouts hung in the air. Upstairs Papa was calling out feebly, Nani-yo? Nani-yo? It was so faint, as if he were singing.

"I want the boy and girl to be safe. That's all," I said quietly. I clung to that thought amid everything.

"Is it, ne-san? Is it really?"

"Of course."

Suddenly he was calm. "I don't think so. I think you wish them all dead, even that Nakamura woman," he declared. My striking him down had made him rise up mean, almost menacing. "You want that poor girl to have only you to turn to."

"Is that what you think of me? That I'm the monster?"

"Why not?" He reeled. "You'd do anything to stop me from having a life besides you and Papa. I can't even have a friend to myself. Even Yano!"

"You sneak out like an animal at night and stay out till morning! I don't stop you!"

"Now I see. Now I see! You're jealous, ne-san. Admit it!"

"Just tell me, once and for all: What do you know?"

"What do you know?"

"I don't know a thing. Not a thing."

"Stop playing innocent!" He seemed to charge at me like a heated animal, and I reared back, warding him off with raised arms. That seemed to enrage him more, but he fell away. "Stop pretending! You're formidable, ne-san! Formidable!"

Formidable. I didn't know he knew the word. He looked stupidly victorious having used it.

"All right, all right," I said, patting the air down around us. "I only meant…you keep saying it's Yano who did it. How do you know? How could it be? Is he capable? You say the boy and girl are—"

"Dead." He seemed to blow out all his rage through that one word, then went limp.

"They can't be. Just because you say!" How irrational I sounded, like Sachi brimming with desperate puppy love. Like the girl in my romantic imaginings who dreads the boy leaving her, taking the part of her that has become his.

"They're waiting until it's safe to come out." I said this with a conviction that surprised even myself; in the same un-wavering tone as Sachi had used to convince me.

"You should know." He gave a tinny, heartless laugh.

"You sound like an old record. Over and over. Never telling me what you mean." But I didn't want to know. I edged towards the kitchen. The white light of the cloud-filled sky was blinding and cold before the window. It cast an eerie light into our living-room, as if Stum and I were at the helm of a spaceship approaching a strange planet.

"Because, ne-san." He softened as he came near, with that tentative, shy look that used to come over him when he wanted up onto my lap. His voice low. "Because you were the last one to see Chisako before she died, weren't you? Didn't she confide in you as usual, ne-san? Didn't she?"

"I don't think I was the last—"

"What did she tell you that day? She must have suspected something."

I was shaking my head. "No, no, no," I repeated, unclear about what I was refusing. "There must have been others.

There was the hakujin neighbour too. Chisako must have spoken to her that afternoon, long after I—"

"And what did you tell her, once she confided in you? How did you answer?"

I walked away from him, swung the back door, and stepped out to my garden. I had to clear my head but the air pressed closer outside than in. Stum was confusing me, spinning a web around me, making up ridiculous stories. It was merely his revenge for every single thing, for being the baby brother who was born in the camp, too early, too late. Who had nothing, no one to blame for his sufferings, for his shortcomings.

I lay down for hours, from afternoon through evening, with Eiji's photo clutched to my chest, neglecting my chores. As I tried to sort out the things that had been said, dust was settling on ledges, in corners, everywhere, so dirty. It was that woman, I suddenly realized, his something-wonderful-has-happened woman, who was influencing Stum, making him accuse me in this way. Half of me would want to demand that he bring this new woman in his life to me, so I could see for myself that she was the instigator. For it seemed his cruelty had only surfaced recently, and perhaps it was more than Chisako's death that was causing this tension between us. Bringing such thoughts into my sweet brother's head. Not that I believed him to be an innocent, but he never would have said such things to me before.

As I looked at my photo of Eiji, into his calm, knowing eyes, his smile reassured me, and I could not help seeing how ridiculous Stum was; I too had to smile. I began to laugh then, uncontrollably, from the tension, I suppose. I laughed all the harder hoping Stum might hear me in the next room. But when I stopped there was silence down the hall. Perhaps he had already prowled out once again, to see her.

When I got up, Stum's door was ajar, the room dark. His pants lay crumpled in the middle of the floor, the pants I'd ironed earlier that week. I stooped to pick them up, lining up the seams from the crotch to the ankles and stroking the creases out; I draped them over his chair. Papa's mumblings went in one ear and out the other as I fed him; even though, strangely enough, he'd begun babbling more and more about Yano in the last two days, it did not interest me. After I cleaned him up for the night, I returned to my room without going to the window downstairs. I slid into bed without washing, without brushing my teeth, and I felt the grime of the day coating my body. Yet I did nothing. It was just me alone, with Eiji clutched to my breast, as always. I closed my eyes, waiting for sleep to overtake me. Yano's voice drifted back. *My wife is lonely*, he'd said. Lonely.

Stum brought his special friend in the next evening, without warning, though I was not surprised. It was as if I'd expected it. I was in the kitchen preparing dinner, and somehow I had known to slice ample portions of meat and to steam an extra half-cup of rice. The day had passed slowly, dripping into its large empty bucket that somehow magically grew full. I'd succumbed to waiting by the window, waiting for Stum, for Sachi, but no one came by. Keiko's car passed early in the morning, on her way to work, I presumed. Even Papa was quiet. At noon children flooded the field momentarily, then vanished, their cries and laughter melting to echoes. Late afternoon, I heard the door being opened and held two instants longer than it usually took Stum to step clumsily inside. I did not look up hearing the shuffling and general commotion in the hallway, then twinned footsteps approaching into the living-room. Stum's stockinged feet appeared on the linoleum before me as I sliced chicken into bite-sized pieces.

"Ne-san." I gave a nod but he didn't seem to catch it.

"Ne-san." He stilled my hand, the one holding the knife. I looked up. Stum had that uncomfortable look, the one that asked that I speak for him, that I take the lead as always. But this time it fell away, and he held my eyes steadily.

"Ne-san. There's someone I want you to meet." I was filled with dread, sinking into humiliation, and I felt my face droop into pleading—*No, don't do this, not just now*—that he ignored. Just as I had ignored him, pushed him from my breast, refused to be his mama; refused my baby brother his heart's desire.

"Ne-san, this is Angel." A woman appeared from behind, angling around him through the passageway between living-room and kitchen. Not nihonjin, I saw that immediately. Small and dark, with a thick body; a young face, a pretty face with neat features, all in their place. She held a hand out to me. The hand gripped mine, sure and hard, my fingers strangled within it.

The evening passed as in a dream—the way I often felt when strangers entered my home. Their names, their voices made my own home strange to me. And now Stum a stranger to me as well. This too-long dream was interrupted by fits of utter clarity in which I heard Papa's faint groans upstairs, louder than ever; heard my own slow inhaling and exhaling as the only other familiar sound. What a fool I was to think I could live out my life in peace, resigned to everything.

"Miss Saito—" The girl's voice seemed to pierce the air with its unfamiliarity, its strangeness in my ears, at my table, the accent I couldn't place.

"Please, it's Anne," I said, as warmly as I could. I managed a smile, crooked on my lips; I felt it tremble.

"It's really Asako," said Stum eagerly. "I call her Asa." He smiled stupidly with the lie. Only Eiji ever called me Asa. "Or ne-san. Which means older sister."

"It's more respectful," I said. She was looking at me as if there was something to see. Involuntarily I wiped my mouth with my napkin.

"In the Philippines, where I'm from"—she paused to drape her hand across her breasts possessively—"we say *a-te*. To show respect." She smiled, and her dark face lit up from within. "You see, we're not so different, are we?" Stum was beaming too, gazing at her with a special light come over him that I'd never seen before. It changed him utterly. I melted away, nothing but air between them. Hastily I got up to refill Stum's bowl of rice.

"Asako"—she called my name out to the kitchen tentatively, trying it out—"your brother is very good at what he does." I heard giggles. When I returned to the table, she was holding her hands up, daintily cupped, level with her breasts, as if squeezing milk from them. "He's so quick. He does twice as many as the others in an hour. He can last for longer shifts, too. I have to bring the boxes quick for him." I tried to imagine the two of them, in a place I'd never seen—a barn I'd once envisioned, with endless cages and trays and troughs.

Somehow, very very clean and antiseptic. The only sound the blurry chirp of thousands of newborn chicks, a city of them, to be separated into male and female. Stum a giant among them, with a gentle giant's hands reaching down among them.

After dinner, we stood side by side at the kitchen sink. She insisted on helping, plunging her hands into the dishwater. Stum hovered listlessly at the table, looking anxious, watching me as if he didn't trust I wouldn't harm her in some small way. She wasn't so delicate, I thought, watching her from the corner of my eye as I wiped each dish she plopped on the rack. Young, but not so young. Occasionally her long hair, a brown the colour of rust, grazed the dishwater and dipped in.

"Did Tusomotu tell you how we met?" As she stumbled over the name, her smile dropped. "I'm sorry, I never seem to get it right. Tu-so-mo-tu," she repeated, still wrong. She glanced at Stum lurking in the doorway. They both giggled. "He can't say it right either," she said. "Asako, you say it," she urged. "He says you're the only one who says it in the proper Japanese way."

"Tsutomu," I said quietly.

"Yes, that's it. Tsutomu," she repeated even more quietly. She paused with her hands in the dishwater, full of thoughts. I saw my brother's name resting there on her lips.

We sat back down at the table for dessert, waiting for the water to boil for tea. Outside it was growing dark, but I could not bring myself to draw the living-room drapes against the night and the electrical field.

"He didn't tell you, did he?" Angel, young person that

she was, was growing more excited as the evening wore on. "One night the electricity went off. Everything stopped. The lamps, the heat, everything. It was all dark and quiet, except for the chicks. Their chirping got louder and louder. They didn't want to stay where they were put. They were taking over!" She laughed loudly. "For the first time in that place, I was frightened. Tsutomu, he didn't want to stay where he was put either. So we sat together in the dark, waiting for the lights to come back on, with all the chicks screeching in our ears. Can you imagine?" She laughed again, then stopped abruptly, seeing my face—my face, which must have been frozen in horror or pain or fear, I don't know which. An awkward silence fell, a silence that I knew Stum was unable to bridge. I struggled to speak but before I could she was already chattering again, like a nervous squirrel.

So the evening wore on, with the girl's animated chatter, Stum's beaming face as he listened and nodded, adding here and there to what she said. They rushed to fill one another's plates, their hands on fork handles brazen, anxious to touch one another. It was another Stum who offered me a second slice of pie, not the one who usually sat glumly at my table, expecting me to do every last thing for him. I had to look away, to look down, anything to hide my face from them until the shadows inched across the room. Her laughter rose out of those shadows, full of glee in the moment. Before I knew it, Stum was reaching to turn on the living-room chandelier.

"Stop!" I ordered, and they both turned to me, she surprised, perhaps shocked, at the harshness in my tone, the anger. He fearful that some unflattering truth would be revealed about me, about him, about us both. My hand was up in the air, to do I don't know what. My throat felt raw and my face was wet, telling me I'd shouted or cried out. I wiped my tears with my napkin and got up, smiling into the dark. "Those bulbs are out," I muttered; some such thing. "I'll get some candles." I went into the kitchen, fumbling in the drawers I kept so orderly, desperate to recall where I'd kept a stub of a candle left from a special dinner years ago.

Then Stum was at my side—I smelled him, that whiff of shoyu and ginger on his breath. "It's all right, ne-san," he said, gently as a feather floating down through the air. "We'll be going now." The girl's voice came again out of the darkness, chirping behind him but subdued. "Thank you so much, Asako. The meal was delicious."

Then they were gone. They'd called their goodbyes from the door and, when it closed, that quiet clasp of the door by its frame swept away my breath so that the house, this cage with its unbearable loneliness, was suffocating. It would soon be even lonelier, if that was possible.

I sat by the window for hours into the night. I was waiting for a visitor; longing for company. Sachi, Chisako, Eiji, I don't know who. No one came. The driveway was empty and the streets were bare. A car went by on the concession road; I watched its tail-lights wink in the distance. I found myself humming an old tune from camp days. "I'll Be Seeing You" playing on my lips, the melody off; those words, it was not my story. I clutched at Eiji's photo, staring into his face. Answer me, I demanded. Tell me. Then I laughed at myself.

Often I feared wearing out my memories of him, silly as that seemed. Looking too much might wear him thin. And even I could tire of him. Like anything—a picture, letter, card, a stub from a concert or a ride ticket. The sweat from my fingertips was acidic, eating away, little by little. I would not share him with anyone, hardly at all; only with Sachi. Her I could not resist telling sometimes, though she never seemed satisfied with what I told.

I always knew how lucky I was, how blessed. No one ever had to tell me that. To have had a brother who loved me— how many could say the same? Chisako seemed to understand, to appreciate, perhaps because she never had a brother; she was an only child. I could hear her telling me, "You are lucky, Saito-san." Lucky. Even a child did not love freely, she told me. It was obliged to love you. How else could it survive? She cupped her breast in one hand, showing me that this was all Tam or Kimi ever needed of her. Even a man, she told me, a man with his needs, when he closes his eyes you could be anyone, she said, shutting her own eyes. But a brother. Nothing, no one, made him love me.

I'd had my happy moments when I did not feel alone or left behind. There had been days when I felt hopeful. When was the moment it all changed? Of course, I knew. It was when Eiji left me.

Only Eiji had that power over me, to make me feel I was not alone in this world, that it held some promise for me. He tricked me, that was the awful truth of it.

FIVE

I AWOKE TO FIND the covers flung back, myself still dressed, my clothing twisted, and Eiji's photograph on the floor by my bed. I felt achy and spent, as if my body had been spirited away from me in the night, God knows what done with it. From the grey light it seemed very early yet, and so I stole into the bathroom to fill the tub, careful not to wake Papa.

As I shed my clothes, I noticed that the clasps that held up my stockings had left their imprint deep and red on my thighs. I let the water run hot to melt the grit of the past day from my body, though I'd done nothing to exert or sully myself. With a shock, I saw that my feet were filthy. Had I wandered off in the night after all? Made a fool of myself? Done things I could not now remember?

Then, in the midst of my panic, I remembered: I had walked barefoot through the moist grass in the backyard,

briefly, just before the detective's visit. But that had not been
yesterday, but two days ago; I hadn't bathed in that long.
What was happening to me?

Slowly I let my heart ease out of its panic. I lowered
myself into the scalding water, giving in to the heat, and as
I did, Eiji came back to me as he had in my dream.

He was showing me Japan, for the hundredth time, waving out at the ocean, way far away, and still I couldn't see it.
There was the long thin line between the sea and the sky, and
his hand uselessly flapping before it. "I'm going!" he was
shouting. "I'm going!" Now he was waving both hands,
jumping up and down. Not like my Eiji.

"I'll leave you all behind!" he cried. He looked different:
his eyes wide and big, a crazy light in them. For an instant I
couldn't be sure it was him. His hair hung in a stranger's thin,
brownish locks.

No, no! I tried to shout back, but my throat was blocked.
"What about me?" I hoarsely cried at last, only to be swallowed in the roar of wave after wave. Eiji was leaving me,
moving into the water. I started to run to him, but behind
me Papa was struggling in his wheelchair through the sand,
faintly calling: *Nani-yo, nani-yo.* That soft, senile, blameless voice.

"Eiji!" I screamed. "What about Papa?" When I looked
again, Papa had toppled over in his wheelchair and was
squirming pitifully, like a crab.

Eiji stared blindly. Not seeing me, not seeing Papa.
"Papa?" he shrieked wildly, as if I should know the answer to
my own question. "If Papa had never left Japan, we wouldn't
be here! We'd be there!" Again he waved his hand out to sea.

Then he glared angrily. I understood. It wasn't me he was angry at. I caught up to him then, and pulled him from the water onto the sand; he dropped like a clumsy, newborn animal, legs splayed. "Don't you see, Asa?" he sobbed. Sobbed as I'd never heard him, not even in his last days, as he lay suffering. "Don't you see?" The waves kept coming, roaring like lions, one drowning in the next. Then, in the way of dreams, Eiji was gone. Vanished.

There was only Papa struggling on his side, half out of the toppled wheelchair, his bony legs and arms treading air uselessly, calling me. Then he too was gone, and I awoke.

The bathwater had grown cold around me. I splashed my face to regain my senses, and called my name sharply— *Asako!*—scolding myself, pulling myself up out of the tub. I dried my body off quickly, chafing myself, if only to jolt myself to attention.

What a peculiar dream, I thought. And it struck me as I slipped into fresh clothes how deceptive dreams were: how they played tricks on you to make what was familiar turn strange, even though they were of your mind's own making. How Papa was there in the wheelchair he would not be confined to until years and years later; when in those Port Dover days he was rolling and manoeuvring logs at the mill and falling into the water every so often, after a night of drinking. That beach was the beach of my childhood, where Eiji had taught me to swim, but the waves were high and rough instead of slow and rolling. How angry Eiji was with me in the dream, angrier than he'd ever been in real life.

As a girl in Port Dover, I believed that dreams were magic; that they could tell me the secrets I longed to know.

I thought they foretold the future. How naive I was. Dreams told me nothing new; nothing I did not already know. But they sharpened my memory, making me more certain of how things happened.

"Look!" Eiji would say. He would point and point, just as he had in the dream, at some silly speck on the horizon. He was only a boy, after all. Eiji snuck me out late at night, when the saws at the mill where Papa worked were shut down. The sea spidered up to my toes, creeping higher and higher in the dark. I screamed at its icy black touch. Screamed as I did on the ride at Hastings Park. I was a child, and I did not stop myself. I remember the flash of Eiji's fierce smile in the night each time I screeched. He shushed me but he liked it; he enjoyed my fears, in his special way. He was not cruel. Eiji liked to watch my fears rise with the tide, then chase them away himself; to see the rush of relief there on my face.

Eiji knew my secrets. Even the things I hid from him, he knew, though he said nothing. Things Stum would never easily comprehend. One morning we were there early on the beach at Port Dover; the air hung heavy and grey as curtains. The moon dangled above us, more and more a shadow as the sky lightened. Eiji ran ahead, his feet tearing up wet brown clumps of sand. My little legs stretched to step into each dark hole he left. He slammed into the water—I heard the slap of his legs against the wall of it—then dived under. His head bobbed to the surface, slick and black on the colourless water, out where it was smooth. The giant saw in the mill started up then, razor sharp, searing the air; so sharp it made me grit my teeth.

I suppose that as I grew up, the happier I was with Eiji,

the more I trusted in him, and the greater my fear of losing him was. It was my dark nature that Mama and others saw in the large brooding adult face I wore as a child. But that was not what Eiji saw when he looked at me.

He was waving to me, calling. I slid into the water, paddled out calm as could be. Then a wave crested in front of me, high as a cliff, it seemed. It broke and sent me tumbling, water churning through my nose and mouth; my hair whipped my face and blackened the water. Even then, in those seconds of panic when I could not breathe, could not see, a part of me was serene and waited for him. Then his fingers gripped me, pulled me up; when I broke the surface to sky, everything was keen and still except for the lashing of my own breath, in the air where Eiji held me like a ball or a trophy. The sun was rising, barely brighter than the fading moon.

Eiji swung me on his back to play seahorse, the way we did in bed, only now the covers were waves. I was crying and I was laughing, hysterical thing that I was then; each time he dipped down, I saw my feet disappear into the water and screeched. It was like a ride: each time knowing in your heart that you would come back up, but not knowing when. But when I felt Eiji's body separate from me once more on the ride, it seemed to drift down farther than before, limp. I tried to pull him up but I was slipping, the water cuffed my neck; I arched my back to keep my head up. Suddenly I was frantic, climbing him like a tree in a flood; under my feet, his body went down the slightest bit more, and still I held him tight, trying to save us both, I told myself, but I was the dead weight. At last he surfaced violently, head thrust back. "Let go! Let go!" he sputtered, wrenching my fingers from his neck. I did what he said, and as I let go I could only stare at my hands in shock. All along, I'd been holding too tight, making him go down.

Eiji laid me on my back and let me go with the waves. "I was playing, Asa," he said, "just playing." I struggled at first, then surrendered. "Now look at the sky," he said as we both floated face-up, and that was all there was. Sky. Everything that held your body in this world, and nothing.

I lay in my bed countless mornings after, trying to regain that feeling. The way he let me on his back again and swam to shore slowly, carried by the waves. I held his shoulders gently, as he showed me. "That's what drowning people do, they can't help it, Asa," he told me, because I'd gone quiet, sheepish. Ashamed. Underwater my hands looked like sea creatures that latch on to feed themselves.

We played seahorse on the beach, Eiji running with me and dropping me on the sand, making me forget my shame, and we rolled in the sand, our whole bodies growing dark and furry. "You couldn't help it, Asa," Eiji whispered to me again on the road back. "I shouldn't have taken you out so deep." I must have lapsed into my brooding silence; that horror at myself and what I'd almost done returned. My hands seemed to have grown large and heavy, the fingers thick and swollen. They hung like anchors as we walked, and my thighs chafed one another with the sand between them.

It was that very morning, when I went to my room to change for school, that I saw it: a trickle of blood in the sand on my thigh. I was ten or eleven then; it was two years before we'd have to leave for the camps. What did I know? Mama barely came near me. She pushed me away with the repulsion you can only have for one you are obligated to love and care for. I searched for a cut, a scrape, but I knew it came from my chin chin, though it was not sore down there. Eiji knew too but never said; his eyes, I remembered, had lingered there for a second as we walked. Knowing he knew, I didn't panic. He was not like other boys. He knew, simply from instinct. Outside my door there were rags and pins left for me, and I felt safe then, with the dark cloth blotting me up like diapers. Eiji kept my secrets for me, for ever.

The last time I bled was just after he died. It didn't surprise me that it stopped. It didn't worry me because I knew right then what my life was to be. It was startling, really, when I think back. For a girl of fourteen to know this, accept it. Wiping the steamed mirror now, I half expected to see that young face of an old soul.

At that moment, downstairs, there was a knock at the door; I recognized it as Sachi's, her tentative rhythm. I pulled myself together as best I could and slowly made my way down, rehearsing in my mind what I would say to her; how I would smooth over that night when I had heard her little voice on the telephone and not responded. It now seemed light-years ago. I put on a smile as I opened the door.

There she stood, agitated as ever, bobbing up and down in that way that set me off immediately. I lost my smile. Her hair still hadn't been washed, but she wore a little clip that pulled it to the side severely. Her braces were still clogged with food bits. How could Keiko let her out like this? Not that she could be stopped. I watched her through the screen, hesitant to open the door.

"Aren't you going to let me in?" She pulled the handle,

shaking the door, which remained locked as it usually was at night until I opened it to take my morning walk. Something I hadn't done since I'd heard about Chisako.

"Let go," I ordered, my tone perhaps a little too clipped. Sachi stepped back. She didn't lunge for the door as I expected once I released the lock; instead she stood there meekly, waiting for me to invite her in. I had barely opened it an inch when she slipped her scrawny body inside.

"So," I stammered. "What have you been doing with yourself?" Instantly I chided myself for such a question.

"Nothing," she answered, listless. "I wait for the newspaper every morning. The delivery boy thinks I'm crazy." Before I knew it, she'd propped herself up in my chair in front of the window, staring out at the Yanos' house. "You can see everything from here, can't you?" She turned to me. "Everything."

"I suppose," I replied. "I have nothing else to do."

"You should," she said, rather loudly; then, not without kindness, she added: "Don't you have friends, Miss Saito?"

It took me aback, this question. She knew me; she knew my life. Was she playing tit for tat, paying me back for the phone call?

"I did," I finally replied. "I did have a friend." I nodded towards the Yano house. With that she was silenced. When she turned back from the window, she seemed pierced by deep pain, hunched over by it. How petty of me to suspect her of vengefulness; I felt remorseful seeing her in the light of day. How selfishly I'd behaved that night on the phone. Thinking only of myself. When she was a mere child, really. In such pain.

"Sachi, about the other night—" I began, faltering.
She bopped to her feet. "Miss Saito," she interrupted,
eyes blank, expressionless. "I was wondering." The words
drifting down like snow. I understood then that there was to
be no mention of the call. She could be like this: lose her
memory of a thing when it suited her; expect the same of
me. I eyed her warily. She wanted something from me, I saw
that. She stepped close and a concerned look came over her
face. "Are you all right, Miss Saito?"

"What do you mean?"

"You look…"

"What?"

"You don't look like yourself."

I patted my hair self-consciously, smoothed my skirt.
"You caught me at a bad moment. I just came out of the
bath," I explained. "I suppose my hair is a mess."

"I guess that's it," she replied.

Just then there was a scratching at the door, but no one
was there. A blur of white and a black nose appeared, sniffing, barely visible through the screen. It was Yano's dog.
Before I could stop her, Sachi had opened the door to let it
in and, at the same time, picked up the morning newspaper
from the porch. "Nothing there," she said, handing it to me.
"She's been following me," she added, shrugging her shoulders innocently. Though the dog had always appeared docile
under Yano's strict hand, I was more than a little afraid,
unused to such creatures as I was. It seemed bigger and whiter
than when I'd seen it with Yano; it panted fretfully, quivered
and yawned; bared its teeth menacingly. I felt unusually faint
and weak, an after-effect of my bath, no doubt.

"Don't worry, Miss Saito," Sachi said. "She's gentle."
I nodded but stepped back to a safe distance. "Shouldn't
you have a leash for it?"
Sachi shrugged. "The lady next door didn't have one."
She ordered it to sit and it shrank under her outstretched
finger, then yawned and settled on its haunches. Sachi was
observing it closely. "Dogs yawn when they're scared," she
said. "It's not because they're tired. It's just a cover." She
scratched it gently at the neck. It was, I had to admit, a beautiful dog, almost feminine in its skittishness, and though it
belonged to Yano, it reminded me tragically, absurdly, of
Chisako. It wasn't only the animal's beauty: the stark whiteness of its fur and its dark eyes and nose. It was its nature,
both timid and surly. Mercurial, you might say; changing
from moment to moment. For I'd seen the creature many
times with Yano, cowering under his broad, threatening
hand; then growling, baring its fine, even teeth at me, its
plumish tail high in the air; then whimpering with an almost
coy piteousness. It peed under my rose-bushes with embarrassed modesty.

Sachi sank to her knees beside the dog and clung to its
neck, burying her face in its fur. I couldn't tell if she was
weeping. "She must've seen what happened," she said, her
voice muffled by the dog's fur. "She knows. Don't you, girl?"
The dog squirmed at first, then sat oddly still, its dark eyes
glistening with a feral knowingness. Already it seemed to
cower less than it had with Yano. "Don't you, girl?" Sachi
cooed gently; more gently, lovingly than I'd ever heard her,
even when she was with Tam, alone. "Don't you?" she
repeated, looking into its eyes.

"Now, Sachi," I started to say. I was about to tell her to pull herself together; a stern hand was needed. But before I could, she'd bounced to her feet again, dry-eyed, frenetic as ever.

"Miss Saito, the dog could pick up their trail. You know. Sniff them out." She looked ridiculously hopeful.

"Now, Sachi," I repeated. "It's not that kind of dog."

"All dogs follow a scent. Their sense of smell is the strongest of all."

"I hardly think—"

"Let's take her to Mackenzie Hill. Please, Miss Saito. Please. To that place. She can catch the scent there. We'll see where she leads us." She pleaded like a child, growing excited and demanding as a child does. She couldn't keep still, fidgeting, jumping on the spot.

I was shaking my head, trying to resist her. Slow and even. "No, no, no," I said.

"Why not?"

"Leave it to the police," I said, seizing on that idea. "Tell that nice detective—"

"I already did!" she shouted, rocking back and forth. "He won't listen." She hugged the dog once again. "He's like you," she wept into its fur. "He doesn't care."

"That's not true—"

"This dog should've been Tam's," she cried fiercely. "It should've! Yano is so selfish!" She was clinging tightly to the dog when it began to whimper hoarsely, then made a high and hysterical noise, struggling with itself to stay sitting as it had been told.

"Sachi!" I said, as gently as I could, taking firm hold

of her arm that held the animal too tightly. "Let go." The dog reared up and bared its teeth, barking and snapping at us both. I raised my hand over its head and it cowered and sank. I felt a small horror at myself; I'd done just what I'd seen Yano do hundreds of times as he passed by my window.

I felt sorry for the animal as it sat before us, obedient as ever, its ladylike paws neatly lined up; those dark wet eyes that glistened, almost human. Lost without its master, hard as he'd been. It went on whimpering quietly, as much as it would allow itself, as Sachi held me tight, her fingers digging in where they wrapped around my back, her face burrowed in my lap. "She's waiting, Miss Saito," Sachi said ominously, like one of those psychics. "Just like us." I stroked her hair, greasy as it was. I felt her rise with me the tiniest bit as I inhaled, and that made me give in, I suppose; it seemed the most wondrous sensation I'd felt in a long time.

It was a long walk to Mackenzie Hill; Stum had taken his car the night before, and even if he hadn't, I would never have let the dog inside it. We walked along the gravel shoulder, facing traffic, with Sachi holding the dog on a length of clothesline I'd given her. It amused me to think what an odd threesome we made, but I suppose I enjoyed the charade of appearing as a family, appearing as someone with a life different from my own. The hill loomed ahead, familiar and grey. I lapsed into my very old habit, a whimsical one I had as a girl, of walking with my eyes closed.

"You know who they named that for, don't you?" Yano would ask, testing me. "You know who that Mackenzie is, don't you?" Each time I refused to answer, refused his little history lesson, but he kept at me.

"It's not the same Mackenzie," I said.

"There's only one," he said. "It's him all right."

I shook my head, then scurried ahead, but he caught up with me. "He put us in the camps, Saito-san. He's the one."

It was so like Yano to be obsessed in that way. Living in sight of the hill made his wounds fester. It was an ugly hill anyway, a mound of garbage that had filled in a green field. They said the garbage would make a natural fertilizer, but the grasses and trees they'd planted on it years ago were still patchy, ashen, and frail.

"What's the matter, Miss Saito?"

My eyes flew open. "Nothing, dear. I'm fine," I told her, focusing again on the long road ahead, and the hill in the distance. When had I last done this, walked like this, blind? I suppose, as a girl, I was willing myself to trust: to trust I don't know what. I remember that dizzy fear, as my foot dangled in mid-air in front of me, of stepping off the edge of the world. Walking from school on a sunlit afternoon, dizzied all the more by the mysterious flashes of bright colour that filled my closed eyes.

On the way home, Eiji sometimes doubled back on his bicycle and followed close behind, haunting me like a ghost. He'd do anything—whoosh past, an inch from my shoulder. Out of the blue, shout, "Look out!" and dare my eyes not to open, then yelp in triumph.

"Miss Saito." Sachi was peering at me, like that capricious girl I once was. But her gaze penetrated me with awareness, the wise child momentarily come home to me. Then she raised her eyes to the hill, as if to some majestic mountain. "Miss Saito," she asked gently, "are you ever lonely?"

She never ceased to shock me; her honesty at the most unlikely times. In the midst of all this. How she disarmed me. I could seize this one chance to confide in her about my darkest moments; I needed only to hint and she, wise child, would grasp.

"What?" I stuttered, and in that instant my foot slipped on gravel sloping into a ditch; my hand clutched Sachi's arm to steady myself. The dog jumped back nervously. I had to blink twice at the road, which suddenly resembled the road from our house in Port Dover to the school. That bit of gravel I'd stumbled on could have been a pebble tossed by Eiji to startle me. "I'm sorry," I murmured half-heartedly, releasing Sachi's arm. "What did you say?" But she didn't repeat the question, and we walked on in silence, the dog keeping pace obediently. Before long, we came to the gravel road and turned.

"I have my family to look after, you know," I finally said. "Papa takes up so much of my time. Stum can hardly do a thing for himself. I have no time to be lonely," I nattered on. "I'll miss Chisako—Mrs. Yano—of course, but life goes on for the rest of us." Such gibberish from my mouth. I could barely look at her. We followed the road for some time, until the base of the hill was just ahead. We left the road to short-cut across the field alongside the hill to where the trees sprang up. I watched her small feet in stained canvas running shoes. It irked me that Keiko didn't buy her proper footwear.

"I don't know why," Sachi said after a moment. "But I was

thinking about when I was little and Keiko had these family dinners." She glanced over, checking, I suppose, to see if it bothered me, her mentioning this. If it stirred up my envy.

I'd watched those cars pull up to the Nakamura house one after another: doors opening to the frosty night, children pouring out; dishes wrapped and knotted in bright cloth, carried to the door. In the early days, when Keiko and Tom were more conscientious about providing company for Sachi. I'd look across the field at the lit-up house that seemed to bustle with movement, before returning to our small, quiet table—just Stum and me and Papa, before his last stroke, sitting down to our own New Year's gochiso, our feast; and I wondered what it would be like to have people around you at every turn. To talk freely about this and that, to So-and-so and So-and-so, without much time to contemplate what you would say. I tried it once or twice, chattered about the weather, about what I was reading, some challenging crossword, only to find Stum staring at me, stunned and perplexed.

"When everybody left, Keiko turned off the lights and the house was so quiet I couldn't stand it," Sachi said. "So lonely." Her voice, sad and thin, broke my heart. Then: "Like your house," she added. A parting jab. I let it go; I understood what it was in her, that spark or impulse to wound me when she felt something herself.

Was that when it started, I longed to ask but didn't dare. I longed to take her scarred hands in mine. Was that when she discovered she could cut and she could bleed?

"I miss Tam so much it hurts," she whispered, and her hand brushed her side, as if the pain resided there. "I know he's coming back, but I miss him." This time she was calm saying it. A little apart from herself. I couldn't promise her when he would return, but he would, I knew. He would.

When we reached the edge of the parking lot, where the woods thickened, I realized I could not go in, not again. "I'll wait here," I said firmly. I turned my back to her and stared up at that familiar fringe of sparse trees that skirted the top of the hill. I thought I could hear the creek not far off, where it took a bend and flowed east of Mackenzie Hill. I felt the dog swish its tail against my leg. She didn't try to change my mind.

"All right," I heard her say behind me. "Come on, girl," and I heard the snap of twigs under her canvas shoes and the dog's low whine. "Come on, Yuki," Sachi coaxed, and it was only then that it struck me, the name of the dog. Yano's homely face appeared to me, reminding me, on one of the morning walks that he joined me on, what it was and what it meant. "Snow," he declared. "I named the dog for the snow on the mountains in the camp. Remember? Remember how deep it was? How cold? Remember, Saito-san?" He was watching me, hugging himself, muttering: *samui, samui, cold, cold*, trying to make me feel the chill in my bones once more.

I paced towards the hill, then back again, almost curious enough to go in after her. But the thought of that place —the soiled, tattered yellow police ribbon on the tree, what traces remained of Chisako's dried blood—made me nauseated. I looked around me, affected no doubt by Sachi's imaginings. She clung desperately, morbidly to this place, convinced that clues to Tam's whereabouts lay here.

Everything was very still; the trees stood motionless, but I recalled how, in winter, their icy branches swayed with a cracking sound, like frozen bones fractured from within. The nausea in my stomach rose higher as a particular odour returned to plague me, or the memory of it, perhaps. That scent of burnt flesh that I'd detected here several days ago, that I could not forget. It made no sense at all, really, since there had apparently been no fire, only gunshots. I squatted down to quell the sickness. I stared at my shoes, Mama's, now more than a little muddy from traipsing across the field. The sight of their blunt rounded toes, the creased leather, made me all the more ill, reminding me of the day I removed them from among Mama's things.

Abruptly the dog came whipping out of the lot, away from the trees and into the open field. Sachi stumbled after it, breathless, the loose clothesline in her hand. The dog tore in circles until it became a white racing ball, with the fierce motion of its paws gouging the ground under it. All either of us could do was watch.

As I did, I thought of my ride with Eiji, the whirr of it up and down, so quick and so light, we could lift off into the air. As the dog slowed, its shining eyes searched and found us, the animal drawn back to whatever it knew. It returned to us, white fur splattered with mud, white paws brown, tongue slopping out of its panting mouth.

Sachi threw down the useless clothesline; the poor creature had no one else to go to.

"Well, that dog's not going to lead us anywhere," I said.

"I know, I know," Sachi broke in. Slowly she began trudging up the side of the hill. I was about to ask her where she thought she was going when I had to get back home, to check on Papa, but saw she was in no mood to explain. All I could do was follow. I felt a cold wet slither across my fingers, familiar from the other night, yet I recoiled; the dog had bounded up behind me, panting messily, anxious for the salt on my skin, I suppose. I pushed it gently away. I lost my breath momentarily, absurdly imagining, in a glimmer of deceptive sunlight, a dot of red dust on the creature's nose, but when I looked again there was nothing. I wiped my hand on an old tissue found stuffed up my sleeve as the dog clambered along beside me. Above us, a peculiar band of rose extended across the sky.

When I reached the top, Sachi was squatting, gazing down at the spot where we'd begun our climb. The trees looked out of place from up here, the way they sprang up from the flat field. They should have been levelled a long time ago, or the whole area left wooded as it was when they put in the hill. An odd spot for a lovers' lane, hidden in plain sight. Scarcely anyone went there, and yet lovers' lane was what the newspapers called it.

Sachi beckoned to me and, as I reached her among the tufts of crab grass, she was smoothing out a piece of paper she must have found in her pocket for me to sit on. By a strange coincidence it was one of Yano's flyers for another meeting at the school, two days earlier. *Redress the wrong*, it said, the letters fat and clumsy. "Oh" was all Sachi said when she realized.

I pushed her hand holding the paper away; she let it sail down the hill. Who came to Yano's meetings anyway? I knelt beside her.

"I know you used to watch us here, Miss Saito," she burst out. "Tam and me."

I froze, did not dare look at her, did not dare move. As if, by staying absolutely still, I might be forgotten; I might disappear. My wise child might return, my wise, silent child who kept my secrets, even from me.

"I really should go now," I stuttered. "Papa—"

"This is our spot, Miss Saito," she said quietly. Then she glanced from me to a nearby cluster of bushes.

I could only stare down at the bottom of the hill, at the trees that surrounded the parking lot.

"It's all right, Miss Saito. I'm the only one who knows. I never told Tam."

All I could do was nod. Let her go on.

"You see, Miss Saito," she continued. Repeating my name in that disturbing way. As if to show there was no mistake it was me. "That's why I brought you here. You're the only one besides Tam and me who understands. Keiko would never. Nobody would, except you. Because you saw with your own two eyes how it was for us."

She fixed her eyes on me; they were fired with desperation. "Don't worry, Miss Saito. I'm not mad." She paused in that way I had learned not to trust. Calculating how she might hurt me. "I know you get lonely."

I stood up warily and touched her shoulder. I wanted only to slip away.

But she grabbed my hand and would not let go. Her hand held mine so tightly that I had to squat down once more. "All right," I murmured.

She paused again, calculating further. "Miss Saito,"

she said slowly. "Tell me the story about your brother again."

"You've heard it enough times," I said. I had no wish to bring Eiji into this. It shamed me, for him to know this of me. "No, no," I said. "Not today." I was shaking my head. But I felt dizzy, and the whirring ride Eiji and I rode at the fair at Hastings Park came back to me again, myself light in the air; it lasted but a second.

"Tell me another one. One you haven't told before." I thought I glimpsed a threat in her eyes, a glimmer, and her hand tightened around mine.

I sighed, giving in, and she let go. I looked to the sky, trying to decide what to tell her. The pink band had melted away, and the clouds went up in ridges to the north, like distant mountains. At the moment there were no airplanes passing overhead. I tried to concentrate on Eiji, to give myself over to him and forget my shame.

As usual, I didn't quite know where to begin. "Did I tell you how he took me with him to deliver newspapers every morning?" I asked. She gave a half-nod that could have been a yes or a no, but meant for me to go on.

"Every morning at six o'clock, Eiji lifted me out of bed and put me on the front of his bicycle. In winter it was so cold," I laughed, "that my fingers stuck to the handlebars." I hung there on the bars by my hands and knees, the same way I'd swung on his arms as he held me over the outhouse benjo when I was afraid I'd fall in. He had his bundle of papers on his back and I'd feel his body and the bicycle pumping up up up as we rode to the hakujin part of town, up away from the mill. I learned not to look down at the rush of ground under the turning wheel as we rode; squinched my eyes shut when we flew downhill.

When we reached those blocks of big frame houses with porches that wrapped three sides, Eiji slowed down, pulled one paper at a time out of his bundle, and tossed it onto a porch. In three steps: pull, aim, toss. I felt the bicycle sway each time he turned and thrusted, as if I were one more muscle or tendon on his body.

"Ara?" I exclaimed. Sachi was nudging me. "Miss Saito, you're leaving parts out again," she said, holding back her irritation.

"All right, I'm sorry," I said, clearing my throat. "On collection days, he brought me right up to the houses with him," I told her. What I remembered about the hakujin women who came to the door was their eyebrows, perched fine and lonely on their big faces as they dropped extra nickels in Eiji's hand at Christmas and Easter.

"Sometimes they didn't pay," I said. "Can you imagine? Hiding away in their big, rich houses when we came knocking. What Eiji did," I told her, winking, "was sneak up onto the porch and wait until they came out for their paper, thinking we were long gone." We squatted there on those porches, still as another piece of their wicker furniture. Eiji clamped me between his legs, his hand ready if I let out the tiniest sound. When the door finally opened, he sprang up with his tickets, me tumbling from his lap.

"Once we were waiting at a big, big house. They hadn't paid in weeks. Eiji had to get the money. They'd take it out of his pay otherwise." Thinking back, it made me angry that Eiji should be treated that way, a young boy like him.

Sachi was nudging me again. "Go on, go on," she prodded, less gently this time.

"Maybe it's not such an interesting story to you," I said, perhaps more gruffly than I meant to. The spell seemed broken, or not yet cast. Perhaps I was too disturbed by being here, sitting in sight of the place where Chisako had died. Disturbed by Sachi's outburst.

"I'm sorry, Miss Saito. Go on, please," Sachi said. "I want you to." There was a yearning in the way she said this, so I went on.

"We were sitting there, just like this. The door was about to open, I was sitting quiet as could be, holding my breath, and—" I started to giggle. This wasn't the story I'd meant to tell.

"What happened, Miss Saito?"

I must have looked a little sheepish. "Onara," I whispered, embarrassed to tell it.

Sachi looked a little confused, then gave a loud guffaw. "Miss Saito!" she said, embarrassed herself.

"Eiji was furious with me. 'They were coming,' he yelled. 'Now there's not enough money!' Like that." I tried to imitate him. "He left on his bicycle without me," I told her. "Who could blame him? I was disgusting," I said, giggling again.

"Just for that? He left you for that?"

"I was bad," I exclaimed. "Baka." I remembered that sensation of being clamped between Eiji's bony legs, eyes closed, safe and still in that suspended moment, and the small lumpy bundle inside his left leg, warming my thigh, pulsing through me with a tiny rhythm. Like the *eee ahh yoo de ya booeee booeee* from

Eiji's jazz records throbbing through the wall in the Port Dover house late at night. Me swaying between his strong legs with muscles that could carry me anywhere. Then, inside the house, hakujin voices; the whoosh of the door starting to open. Eiji's breath rising, his body poised to spring, and a burning low in my belly. I tried to hold back but I couldn't. Onara. The sound I made! The smell of me, kusai! Eiji threw me down so the porch shook, and the door quietly shut. Eiji rode off. I was laughing now, harder than I'd laughed in a long while. I tried to cover my mouth but it seemed to stretch so wide, like a horse's. My eyes were streaming. I felt a little out of control. Sachi was watching me uneasily, but not laughing; she didn't find it quite so funny.

"Then what?"

"I screamed but he didn't come back. Screamed and screamed." I laughed again, dabbing my eyes with the crusty tissue. "Baka," I said again, through my laughter. I needed a moment to calm down and collect myself. I laughed for another spurt, hiccupped a little, then forced myself to take several deep breaths. As if drunk on my own memory. Sachi had turned away now, staring across to the ravine. I could only guess what she was thinking of me. She stood up suddenly and whistled for the dog. It seemed almost rude in the middle of my story, but perhaps she found it a little too crude. Perhaps she had never imagined me as a girl; the story made me ludicrous in her eyes.

"I followed his tire marks in the snow," I went on, "and walked back to the house. All morning I walked to get there." Finally Sachi settled back down beside me.

"When I got there, Eiji was in trouble for leaving me

behind. He was bent over the kitchen table, with his pants down, tears coming. Papa had his belt out. I'll never forget the look in Eiji's eyes with his red face," I said. "But he was not one bit sorry. Not one bit," I told her.

"That's it?" Sachi asked. "That's the story?"

I nodded. It was true that I'd left out parts. Things I might tell her later, when she'd understand better. I might tell her that afterward, that night, I crept into Eiji's room. I crouched beside him. "What?" he muttered. His voice was weak; Papa's beating must have hurt him more than he let on. I inched my hand under his pyjama bottom to the welts. At first he pushed me away, but then he gave in. He shivered as I traced one welt after another with my finger. They were raised so high, wriggling on his skin with a life all their own. Worms. He grinned, lopsided, lazy-eyed, no longer disgusted with me. No longer annoyed. I stroked with my cool fingertips, soothing him until he slept, drooling into his pillow.

Sachi was standing again, waving at the dog, her back to me. She seemed to want to hide her face from me; her shoulders heaved. Laughing at me, not at my story, perhaps. It had meant nothing to her. Tam was on her mind. Tamio. Distorting everything. The clouds that had climbed up the sky in ridges had smoothed out into an even wall blocking the sun.

"I must get back now," I called out hastily, already marching down the side of the hill. Sachi shouted to me, something about the dog going off towards the ravine, about wanting to follow it, but her voice had grown faint; I couldn't quite hear. Papa would be wailing for me by now, I knew, and I had no more patience with her. I waved and descended

briskly. I was irritable now; frustrated at having been brought
here, at wasting my morning. The same thing all over again,
what I'd resolved not to let happen. I thought once more of
my chores piling up, the dust on my window-ledge, the vac-
uuming, and so on. I felt small under the large sky; to distract myself, I studied it for patterns as I walked, marking my
progress by little hooks and swirls among the clouds so I
wouldn't feel lost under it.

I thought of Chisako up there, floating serenely, I hoped,
in her bright, rich colours. In the kimono I'd never actually
seen her wear, yet imagined her in more than a hundred times.
Watching me from above, going here, going there, pulled
along by Sachi in search of Tam and his sister, and Yano.

Miraculously, Papa was still sleeping when I got back, and he
was dry. I'd eaten nothing for breakfast but the nausea I'd felt
earlier had worked its way to my bowels. I sat down on the
toilet and emptied myself with the relief I'd withheld all
morning, and scanned the newspaper thoroughly. Though
Sachi had assured me that nothing was in today's news, I
wanted to see for myself. When I reached the obituaries,
there was nothing under Yano, predictably enough. But every
few days, the years going on as they did, there were smatter-
ings of names I remembered from Port Dover or camp days.
Today a name caught my eye: Yamashiro. It wasn't a common
name, but its familiarity came rushing at me despite the tiny
type and the sameness of all the entries. *Beloved wife of the late
Shigeru Yamashiro. Survived by daughter Sandra, son Robert, and brother
Takemitsu Iwata.* Yamashiro, Yamashiro-san. I whispered it over
and over to myself. *Passed away peacefully in her sleep.* Then, as if

he'd heard, Papa groaned and called for me: *Asako, Asako*. Jolting me just as Yamashiro-san's face or voice seemed about to materialize in my head. I got up and went to Papa, and those thoughts left me; I had no time or room left in my jumbled head.

After I fed and changed him, I read the local news to Papa, sitting on the edge of his bed. I had not done so in a long while, it seemed. My reading, no matter what it was, calmed him, especially when he was fidgety, annoyed to be trapped in his decrepit body. I could be reading an article about the most violent and hideous crime, and it would soothe him—the sound of my voice, the monotonous rhythm of my speech. His mind was long gone. He never had comprehended English well, and his Japanese had dwindled years ago, belonging, as it did, to the bygone era before he'd left Japan. Yet he could be quite content, I knew, muttering away to himself.

As I read out the latest traffic accidents from drunk driving, the unemployment rate, and other such things, I glanced at Papa now and then, to find him resting quietly enough. Then my dream from the night before came back to me. I was on the beach again and I was carrying Papa, his legs curling around my torso, his knees hitched under my breasts as if grown into my flesh. He was shrivelled and small, smaller than in real life, shrunken to the size of a baby monkey, except that his arms were monstrously long. So long they dangled near my knees, stretched from simply hanging, from their own weight. He had no clothes on. I felt his chimpo, tiny as it was, against the small of my back. He barely weighed anything, and yet, as I went on, each foot

sank deeper into the sand, and finally I had to sit, dropping
him to the ground, his stringy arms flopping back.

It was hard to believe that this dream could come from my
own mind yet feel so eerily real. Even now, I could not resist
peeking under Papa's covers at his arms. I laughed at myself
when I did, seeing the familiar mottled flesh of his arms,
which were in reality short in proportion to the rest of him.
The dream had ended abruptly, as many dreams do; I remembered nothing more. I stopped reading then; the air began to
feel close in the room, and Papa's odour, despite my having
changed him a short while earlier, felt suffocating to me.

I went on through the day with more chores, summon-
ing some energy, grateful to be left alone. I did not even let
myself pause at the window to watch for Sachi's return. She
did enter my thoughts now and again, her desperation about
Tam, but there was nothing more to be done at the moment.
I thought of her wandering aimlessly, absurdly following
that dog. It was not helpful to either of us to go sleuthing
about, dog in tow. For the first time I felt some sympathy for
Keiko, having to contend with Sachi, demanding child that
she was. I did not envy her as a mother, not at all.

Stum arrived home at his usual hour for once, without his
Angel. Not that I expected him to bring her; he knew better
than that. I thought of enquiring after her, to show my concern, my willingness to try to accept her, but I could not
bring myself to do so. We would have to wait until it came
from my heart, freely and sincerely. In the meantime, as Stum
himself said, who knew how things would progress between
the two of them, if at all?

We sat in the living-room after dinner, both of us reading quietly, almost as it had been in the past. We were being careful with one another, trying to regain, in silence, the rhythm of things. I began to make out my shopping list, looking forward to some concrete task to take me away from the neighbourhood. For the electrical towers, the hill, the Yano house itself—all were constant reminders of Chisako's absence; reminders that, as I'd told Sachi, I had lost my only friend.

There was an interruption to our calm as Stum paused over something in the newspaper. He rose all at once, crackling the paper, and came to where I sat to show me the Yamashiro obituary. He was jabbing at the item with his finger, open-mouthed, as if that motion alone could prod his memory, as I had tried to do myself earlier that day.

"Yamashiro, Yamashiro," he repeated, just as I had, only aloud. "Yamashiro." He looked out the window but by now it was dark. Beyond our reflection I thought I spied movement out in the field.

"Look." I pointed. "Somebody's out there." I pressed close to the glass. It could be Sachi; it could be Tam or Kimi. Or Yano.

"Look," I said again. "Maybe you better go out there." I sounded a little hysterical, but I couldn't help myself. I tried to snatch the newspaper from Stum's hand and draw him to the door. He pulled away.

"What are you doing? There's nothing out there." He looked me up and down, as if I were crazy. "You're trying to distract me, aren't you? Something about this Yamashiro woman. I know you, ne-san. I know you." He smiled smugly.

Perhaps he was right. I took one last look out the window, blinked at myself: nothing there. Briskly I drew the drapes and went into the kitchen to clean up the last of the day's dishes. "What a day," I said, clattering some plates. But Stum ignored me, simply sat there mouthing the name. Yamashiro. Yamashiro. Such a cumbersome, ungraceful name.

Later it came to me, unbidden. Yamashiro. I kept muttering it quietly to myself as I padded down the hall past Papa's room, past Stum's closed door. I paused by the door for a second, and was gratified to hear his low, thick breathing behind it, not quite rising to a snore. It was good to have him home where he belonged, I had to admit. I went downstairs to the cabinet where I kept our few photographs —not many, since we didn't have our own camera, hadn't had one since before the camps. I'd stored away the odd token too; nothing of any significance really. I found it there: an old leaflet from one of Eiji's memorial services at the church downtown. I suppose Papa had kept it for the prayer written in it. Papa wanted the service held there since he had switched to that church many years earlier because of Reverend Ono.

It was an annual event then, every November 16: an extra donation for the church, a gift for the reverend, two bouquets of chrysanthemums for the altar. We were waiting for the rows to clear so Stum could bring out Papa's wheelchair. I was tired. Weary from the drone of Japanese and English lagging in your ears, neither this nor that. It was several months later that Papa had his second stroke and could no longer go to church, and I was relieved of this duty. I had

little feeling for the church or the reverend, though he was
kind and well-meaning enough. He could be irksome, carrying things on for years after the war in his wishy-washy manner. He had been no different in camp, always urging us to
sing, sing, sing our troubles away. In the midst of that din,
what chased my bad thoughts away was how the hymn-books
fell open in my hands. The tiny precise letters *unto the hills*
printed on old paper so fine it was the skin that slakes off
after days in the sun. If only I could sing, I thought; that
would make me happy. The voice in my head was sweet, but
out of my mouth came a bitter squawk I let only myself
hear. During the service, my fingers would curl tight into a
ball at the sound of those silly voices starting and stopping
in ten different places, on five different notes. As if I could
hold a precious thing there where my fingers balled up, a
pure, sweet note. I ran my fingertip all around the sharp pink
rim of the page, faint as blood in water. I tucked the notes
from my memorial speech that day into the book, a small
slip of paper lost long ago. I was adjusting the lopsided
spine of the book as a woman came near.

"My dear," she said. "Such kind words you had for your
brother. Kind, graceful words." She was stooped a bit, well
into middle age. A little older than I was now. There was
something timid about her, crouched as she was, as if something might fall on her at any minute. She took my hand and
cupped it between her own white-gloved ones, murmuring,
so, so, so.

"It was nothing," I said, and stepped back. The tweak of
nerves I'd felt standing before the congregation returned for
a second or two.

"He was special, ne? Otoko-mae ne? Handsome, ne?" What everyone said about Eiji.

"Yes," I replied.

"You wouldn't remember me," she said, smiling. "Yama-shiro desu." I nodded. "Of course," she added, "that's my married name."

The woman stood staring up at me for the longest time with her small, clouded eyes. Fortunately Stum came rattling up the aisle on the opposite side of the pew with Papa's wheelchair then, and motioned me over.

"It's difficult, isn't it, Asako-san? Even after all these years." I found myself only able to nod my head.

"I know." She went on, just when I thought she would move away with her too-kind smile. "I know because I had feelings for him. But he never had time. Not for me, ne?

"I remember the two of you swimming, crossing that river outside the camp, back and forth, all afternoon. You know how the current was. You held on so tight to his neck, I remember..." and she waved her hand in the air, clenched and shook it a little before us. "I thought..." She didn't continue, but instead looked up, startled that she'd gone on so. She studied me closely again, standing up a little straighter.

"I used to think you two didn't look alike at all. Your brother was so tall and slim. And you..." Her eyes moved over me. "But now I think I see something—chiisai, something small. But it's there." She traced a finger over a patch of skin beneath one eye, then dropped it. "You didn't know, did you?" Again I shook my head. I held out my hand.

"Thank you for coming, Yamashiro-san. I'm sure my brother would have been very pleased."

We bowed to one another. She paused before turning away. "You do know who I am, don't you, Asako? You remember me, don't you?"

Again I bowed, as graciously as I could. "Thank you for coming, Yamashiro-san," I repeated, and watched her amble down the aisle and disappear behind the large door into the bleached white sunlight of the afternoon.

The cavernous church felt cooler and darker than ever as I helped Stum ease Papa into the wheelchair. Papa watched as I moved his body about, a helpless child who must assert his will any way he can. He wanted to know who the woman was I'd been talking to.

"Yamashiro-san," I answered. Papa's memory had long been ailing by then, and any name or incident could start it bleeding, like an unhealed wound.

"No, no. Iwata-san," he said. "Ne?" He was insistent, prodding, never content with my silence.

"No, Papa, that's somebody else," I finally replied.

When we came out into the sunlight, Mrs. Yamashiro was standing off to one side, alone, clutching a small shabby handbag, clearly waiting to be picked up.

"There she is again," Stum announced, a little too loudly. I almost pushed him away. He could be so backward.

Dare, who, who, Papa wanted to know. His eyes darted this way and that, his wheelchair rattling from his strong arms batting about.

"What's the matter, ne-san?" Stum tugged at my arm. "Ne-san, what is it?" The two of them staring up at me. With alarm I noticed that the paper I'd written my remarks on had slipped from my hymn-book. I watched it float to the ground through watery eyes. I snatched it up, and before I could stop myself I'd crumpled it in my fist.

"Ne-san," Stum repeated once more, softly. I felt him patting my back, the fleeting warmth of his awkward touch. "It's all right. You did a good job today. Good job."

At that time I could not place Yamashiro-san at all. Yet it all upset me; in light of the memorial service, I suppose, and the few words I'd said about Eiji. I was overcome. Tired, as I recall, because I hadn't been able to sleep the night before. My memory was blank, at least at that moment. The woman talking about camp days had done nothing to jog it. There were so many families there, all living in tumbledown shacks, one no shabbier than the next. It was just another adventure to me at my tender age. I was little more than a child when we first got there. Of course, after four years I was still young, barely older than Sachi was now. I could hardly be responsible for remembering a girl much older than myself, for at that age four or five years' difference could seem a lifetime. And yet she'd been there, watching Eiji and me swim in the river; watching so closely that she'd seen how I'd held him.

After dinner that evening, determined to show his tattered memory intact, Papa wheeled from the cabinet drawer to where I sat on the chesterfield. I flinched as he did so, watching him bump against the furniture, watching the wheels grind their thin tracks into my carpet. For years after he became confined to his bed, I could still follow his winding path through my living-room.

He pointed to a photograph, shaking his finger at it. This woman he remembered as a youthful girl. It was a skill,

I had to admit, reading a face across the decades. "Dare?"
Again he was asking who she was, but now he knew the
answer. He was testing me and showing off at the same time.
But I didn't have to look closely at the picture to recognize
Yamashiro-san. It wasn't just her face; it was the particular
way her legs were bowed below her skirt; the way she stood
on the patchy terrain, squinting, legs apart, holding a bucket
just as she'd held her shabby handbag earlier in the day. Papa
poked me with his bent finger. "Iwata." Her maiden name.
Iwata-san. And there beside her was Eiji.

She was the sister of a friend of Eiji. The brother I barely
remembered—an average boy, below average, really; a little
runty. When Stum joined us in the living-room, I quickly
put away the photograph. Stum had been just a baby then,
toddling about in the gloom of the camp, and there was no
need to open a can of worms to explain what was well past.
Yet Stum did have his suspicions and his questions, as if the
past were some puzzle, some game to him. One I did not
indulge him in.

Perhaps he'd spied me tucking away the photograph when
he came in from the backyard, for he immediately grew
cranky and glum. "Who was that woman at church, ne-san?"
he kept asking. "You know but you won't tell me. Why not?"
I let his childish questions hang in the air, unanswered. Papa's
head was dropping to his shoulder and I motioned to Stum
to take him upstairs. "Go on," I finally ordered, when he
slouched back in the chesterfield.

I hated watching that long, slow struggle up: the way
Papa clutched Stum, when they never touched otherwise. It
was unbearable to me. I went outside. At that time Stum had

not yet put up the fence that would separate our yard from the tangle of wild growth around it. Alongside the house I spotted four of my good jars that I normally used for pickling radish. All empty except for one with holes punched in its lid; a firefly blinked inside it. Stum must have caught it, stupidly thinking it would survive in there. By the time I unscrewed the lid, its little light had gone out. The tiny creatures flying through the darkness with their bodies momentarily aflame fascinated me too, but I'd never think to keep them in a bottle.

Stum called them kamikaze, those fireflies. As he called Yano and Eiji. In his jealousy, Stum had always made it sound as if Eiji were to blame for his own fate, as if he'd in some way brought it on with his recklessness. What did he know, being little more than two years old then?

When Stum came out he saw the empty jar in my hands. "Did you put the extra blanket on Papa?" I hadn't been thinking of Papa, but my mind, efficient as it was, had moved on to the tasks at hand. I found it necessary to tell Stum every single thing. Otherwise it would never get done. Back in those days, he could be hopeless.

"Where is it?" He nodded at the jar, ignoring my question. I held out my hands to show him that it was gone. He looked perturbed; the surfaces of his eyes shone, trapping what light came from the kitchen. "It took me all night to catch it." There he was, the little boy again, his little eyes drooping in disappointment.

"It's cold tonight, he'll need that wool blanket," I said. Stum could be distracted by the smallest things, and I felt bound to keep him on track. Instead of answering me, he wandered deeper into the yard and slowly moved beyond the perimeter of my then modest garden. With his dark clothing he was soon invisible, but I heard his rustlings through the weeds and bushes; the crush of twigs under his broad feet. As I think back, it was as if he were walking out to sea.

"Stum!" I called. "Stum!" But he didn't answer. I thought of following him, but stopped myself. I knew when to leave well enough alone. I hastily set down the jar and went inside. There was the rattle of glass that echoed on the stone patio behind me.

Upstairs, Papa was shivering under a single sheet and the thin bedspread. What was Stum thinking? The window was pushed up as far as it would go, up to the sky, flat and dark as slate. It was an ugly night sky. When I was a child it never entered my head that a sky could be anything but pretty, but there it was: desolate and empty of stars. The sight of it robbed me of my irritation with Stum, as I thought of him alone out there. How would he ever get along without me? Poor, sweet, foolish Stum.

By the time he returned that night it was past one o'clock, and I was sitting up waiting for him. Papa had long been asleep and I'd been mending a pair of socks to keep myself occupied. Somehow Stum's expression appeared tangled and weedy with too many thoughts, like those woods beyond our yard.

"Why do you keep things from me, ne-san?"

"What things? I don't keep anything from you."

"About our brother. About what happened. You never talk about it."

"There's nothing to say, ototo-san."

"That woman at church had something to do with it, didn't she?"

"It's not important." I sighed, exhausted. "Erai. It's late. Time to go nen nen."

"Stop that baby talk! I'm not a child any more!" I tried to shush him, fearful that he'd wake up Papa, but he stomped over to the cabinet drawer and began rifling through it. "Where is that photograph?" he demanded.

"It's just an old picture," I told him, as calmly as I could. I rose and went to his side and tried gently to pull him away from the drawer.

"If it's just an old picture, why can't I see?"

It was clear there would be no reasoning with him, so when I realized that he was searching the wrong drawer I coolly stepped back. "You hid it," he said, glaring at me. He closed the drawer.

Instead of indulging him, I concentrated on mending his sock. Suddenly he put his hand over mine to still my busy needle. He came close, his breath coming at me in gusts. "Is it me, ne-san? You think I won't understand, I'm baka?" His face had collapsed a little, and I had to look away. Stum had moments like this. When he took things too seriously; as if everything in the world were only about himself. I gave a mirthless laugh, muttered something, then yanked the sock away from his hand in order to carry on stitching. He grimaced, his cheeks bunched with pain. He raised his hand and sucked at his palm, then shook it. He gave me another look, of anger, bitter anger; sadness, I suppose. He seemed on the verge of saying something, but thought better of it and scrambled up the stairs. As I resumed my mending, I noticed a drop of blood on Stum's sock. The tip of the needle was tinged with red as well. He must have stabbed himself with his own impulsive gesture. I found myself irritable now that it was hours past my bedtime. He could never leave well enough alone. As always, he had to prod and poke at things.

I could smile now, remembering all this as I tucked away that leaflet. The thought of my poor baby brother fretting about nothing, about a past that had little to do with him.

Before shutting the drawer, I glanced briefly at the words on the leaflet once again. It did still pain me to see Eiji's name, and those meaningless dates that told nothing, nothing about him. Just as my words that day had meant nothing. I had half a mind to throw the flimsy leaflet in the trash. Yet I kept it; for whose sake I didn't know. I rummaged a little for the old photograph of Eiji and that woman, Yamashiro-san, or Iwata-san, as she had been called back then; I didn't recall her given name. But I dreaded the sight of it.

For she was just another one of those girls in the camp I tried to ignore, those girls who wanted Eiji. Who watched him greedily every minute of the day. It disgusted me the way they fawned, harmless as they were, their shrill voices teeming around him. He was beautiful, after all, with his smooth, glowing skin. I searched—half-heartedly, I admit—but the photo was not to be found. I must have misplaced it somehow, somewhere, over the years. I suppose I was grateful to be rid of it, if the truth be told.

Back in bed, I slept fitfully for a time, and in the middle of the night I found myself wide awake, staring into the darkness. My body felt heavy and swollen; something was happening to me, something frightening and gradual that no one, no doctor, could help me with, that much I knew. I held my arms out above the covers. They were heavy, so heavy; my hands were bloated, the skin a queer parched white. As enlarged as they'd appeared to me that day when I was a girl, coming back from the Port Dover beach, but more unsightly now that the skin was aged, no longer fresh. Then I saw her in my mind, Iwata-san—Sumi, that was the name I'd known her by—standing that day in the camp as she was in the photograph, holding her bucket as she called after Eiji and her brother, Tak, waving with one hand. They both called back to her. She'd seen me, but she was gone now, dead. Who else had seen? She'd seen my hands on Eiji's neck, holding too tight, those afternoons at the river outside the camp. I'd held too tight even after the time in Port Dover when Eiji sputtered at me to let go, then forgiven me because I'd held on as a drowning person does, drowning another.

SIX

THE SKY, WHEN I looked out, was thick and swollen with ashen clouds as if from a fire. It was Sunday; the field remained deserted. I could not detect even the shadow of a shadow at the window of the Nakamura house. I was worried but assured myself that, if Sachi hadn't turned up at home yesterday, Keiko would have been at my door, day or night. I busied myself, yet kept coming upon things I'd left behind: half-chopped vegetables on the cutting board, dishes standing in water, my dustrag abandoned on the ledge. I was about to retrieve the rag when there was a knock at my door. A crisp and clear *rat-ta-tat-tat,* unfamiliar to my ears.

"Is it here? With the girl?" It was the woman I'd seen last week, the Yanos' next-door neighbour. No sooner had I opened the door than she poked her head in, peeking around my hallway and behind me into my living-room. She would have stepped right inside, uninvited, if I hadn't wedged myself in the doorway. She coughed the scraping cough of a smoker, and now, in the light of day, I noticed the cluster of vertical lines on her upper lip, raying out from her lipsticked mouth. As her hands batted about beneath the longish cuffs of a man-sized windbreaker, I saw that, all over, her skin had the parched look some hakujin skin could have. I smelled the smoke.

"It's just that I'm responsible, see," she said. "I told the police I'd look after it, or else they'd lock it up in the pound."

"I see."

"I let the girl take it yesterday and she never came back."

"Why don't you try her house?" I suggested coldly. It was, after all, up to Keiko to contend with this; I had no patience for a useless conversation with this strange woman. I felt the draft coming in at my legs, and noticed that I'd forgotten to put on my stockings. I started to shut the door.

"There was nobody home there," she said, ignoring my hints. "I saw you and her go off with the dog yesterday. That's why I'm here." She looked at me blankly, waiting for a response.

"Well, yes, that's true," I stammered. "But that was yesterday. I left them at Mackenzie Hill and came back here myself early in the day."

The woman murmured something unintelligible, I suppose meant only for herself, and I went to close the door again.

"Mrs. Saito?"

I turned back, a little jolted. The woman knew me.

"That's your name, isn't it?" She smiled, stretching those lines across her upper lip.

"Why, yes, it is."

"Just thought I'd let you know. One neighbour to another." She almost reminded me of Yano for a second, with her conspiratorial tone.

"Yes?" I said, noting the flash of a thin gold band on a finger. "Mrs.—?"

"Frean. You see, I saw you that day when the kids disappeared. You were talking with Mr. Yano. Having a bit of a disagreement, it looked like. Out there." She pointed to the electrical field behind her.

I could only nod, trying to take in the meaning of all she was telling me. "I see," I said.

"When the detective asked me, I had to tell him. Maybe it slipped your mind. He said he already questioned you and your husband."

"I see," I repeated. I thanked the woman and firmly shut the door. Laughed to myself about her mistaking Stum for my husband. I didn't even go to the window to watch her cross the field. Instead I put the whole conversation out of my head. Such a nosy busybody, I thought, swatting the air still tinged with smoke.

I took up my rag again, determined to finish my dusting, but when I touched it the ledge was farther away than it appeared. In my living-room, I felt small, and my senses dull.

Yet when I lay down to rest, an alarm blared in my head and wouldn't stop. Like someone else's emergency that I was helpless to attend to. It went on for some time before I realized that the sound was actually a cry, a scream at high pitch. It was human, reminding me startlingly of Sachi, as she had been when I'd left her on the hill the day before.

"Get away!" she was screeching. Shrill enough to pierce

my eardrums. She'd frightened me, confused me so that I was not fully aware of what was happening. I had decided to leave, worried about the time away from Papa, that much was clear. I suppose I was hurt by how little she seemed to think of the story I'd shared about Eiji. How she'd seemed even insulted by it.

"Go!" she'd screamed. "I don't want you here anyway!" She'd cursed me violently, using words I could not repeat. It was no wonder that I'd not fully taken in all that had happened up on the hill; that I'd put it out of my mind right then and there. I recalled stumbling down, her screams chasing me away. I'd stopped for one second, thinking to reason with her, and she'd screamed again.

"You're crazy!" she shouted. "Just like Yano!" She wound up her finger to her head, as Yano had when talking about his brother. "Your stupid stories. You tell the same thing over and over."

She was upset, I told myself, didn't know what she was saying. I nearly fell over myself in my hurry to get away. But then I stopped myself again. Halfway down, it struck me: that poor girl, afraid and alone; her cries, they were cries for help. I thought of her left behind after Keiko's New Year's dinners. And the cuts on her hands; what would become of her if Tam wasn't found? I turned around and climbed back up; I held out my arms to her. I felt them trembling. I even said her name.

She came down slowly, tentatively. I tried to let my eyes speak to her, gently, as a mother would, to beckon and comfort. But just then a cloud burned away, the sun blotted out her face. To a faceless dazzle that screamed once again, the blare, the alarm sounding once more, pushing me away. Down the hill I retreated, as quickly as I could. Because then it was clear, painfully clear, that I had gone too far. How could I blame her? It wasn't me she wanted. It had never been me.

I now took my place at the window. I dozed there fitfully until Sachi's cry at last began to subside in my head. Soon I became aware of familiar voices muffled by the window glass. I looked out to see Stum and Sachi at the edge of my yard. The dog circled, shot past them to the field several times, and each time came back to them. It sniffed at my bushes, then, sure enough, squatted ladylike to pee, and once it finished its business it glanced up, seeming to meet my eyes dead on through the window. In a second it was racing about again. Such deceptive creatures, dogs, with their shining human eyes. In the end leaving you as alone as ever, racing after this or that. They'd give you up for a bit of bone. Yano must have found that out.

Stum was leaning close to Sachi, listening. She stood there forlornly, more unkempt than she'd been yesterday, if that was possible: shoulders slumped, feet planted too wide apart, as if they weren't a pair. Stum was standing too close, too greedy. Wasn't the company of his Angel enough? I paced back and forth noisily, wanting their attention, but of course how could they hear me? At last Stum straightened up. Sachi headed across the field, in the direction of the school, the dog trailing after her. But there was no school. She might have been coming to see me, before Stum scared her off. I thought of running after her. What if there'd been news, what if Sachi had been coming to tell me? What if she needed me?

Stum didn't see me when he came in, distracted as he was. Women still made him awkward, even a little thing like Sachi. Despite his recent manly experience. He set down the brown paper bag he'd taken to carrying whenever he stayed with her, his Angel friend; a crude, bald thing, I thought. Containing his underwear, perhaps, and who knew what else? When he looked up, there I was, startling him.

"Ne-san. I didn't see you." Clearly he hadn't worried himself over me. So soon forgotten, I mused, nodding to myself. He was about to go upstairs when he glanced at me again, this time with concern. Perhaps I'd mumbled the thought aloud.

"Ne-san, what is it?"

"Nothing," I said, cheerfully. "Nothing at all."

Abruptly he grew alert, surveying the living-room; even sniffing the air, as if something disagreeable was wafting about. I looked around too, seeing what he saw: the rumpled cushions, my coat and sweater and shoes strewn about, the dirty teacups here and there. The dusting rag still on the ledge.

He smiled tiredly. "There's no news. They haven't found out anything. Sachi talked to Detective Rossi last night."

"Would they tell her if they had?" I shot back. I paced to the window, irritated by his naivety. I glimpsed the tumble of his feet as he quickly climbed the stairs. Eager to escape me. I'd let myself go a bit, I had to admit, but everyone was entitled to a day off. A day of carelessness.

I was gathering up the teacups when Stum came stumbling down the stairs, out of breath.

"Ne-san, Papa, why didn't you...?" His confusion made me feel my own state of calm. He pointed helplessly upstairs. Instantly I heard Papa's wails, louder than ever, piercing, angry one second and pathetic the next. As if a radio's volume had just that moment been turned up.

"Why didn't you go to him, ne-san?" There was an accusation there but I wasn't sure what.

Stum was staring in horror. He opened his mouth to say something, then thought better of it. Instead he grabbed me roughly by the wrist and led me upstairs. "Come, help me," he urged nervously. "I can't do it. Not by myself. You know that." He glanced back, the accusation there again.

As we approached Papa's room, his wails grew more pitiful in my ears, like an old child's. The covers were kicked aside and that shocked me; I thought the strength had long ago left his legs. His eyes locked on me, and his cries grew smaller but more wretched, the urgency wrung out.

"If you had to leave, ne-san, why didn't you tell me? How could you? I don't understand."

I looked down at my father lying there so pitifully, and somehow I was stunned yet unmoved by what I saw: the spreading stains across the sheet, where he had overflowed his diapers; the vomit crusted around his mouth; his eyes, lolling and then locking on me, with the same accusation Stum had held in his voice. He was trembling, too—ice-cold, soaked in his day-old shikko.

Stum's hand pushed the small of my back towards the bed, his thumb pressing near the top of my buttocks. "Do something, ne-san," he whispered. "Clean him up. Hayaku! Please!" He wanted me to hurry, to take this from his sight. I moved slowly, as if every thought in my head resisted. I struggled for some bit of memory of how this had come to be, how I could have made myself so absent.

"Get the bucket and fill it with hot water," I ordered, forcing myself into the moment. "Bring some towels and a plastic bag." Stum obeyed without hesitation, grateful for an excuse to leave the room, relieved I'd taken charge, efficient as ever.

Left alone with Papa, I avoided his eyes. The accusation, harsher, more than I could bear. *Why did you do this to me?* And on the table by his bed, shoved back almost out of sight, to make room for the food tray, a photograph of Mama, taken during the years in the city. In that gabardine dress I'd sewn, the round collar that made her face rounder. Smiling the meagre smile that was never for me, reminding me how little she cared.

By the time Stum returned, I'd stripped half the bed and rolled Papa over to that side so I could replace the soiled sheet. Even the mattress pad was stained. "Ara!" he'd cried faintly when I eased his body over. Only his sounds left, the look in his eyes; no words. I removed his pyjama bottoms from him, tearing them at the seams, then threw them in the plastic bag Stum had brought, along with the sodden diaper. Stum drew back at the smell, sharper and more sour than usual. I took the towel from his hand and began cleaning Papa, plunging my hands in and out of the darkening water to rinse out the towel. I sent Stum back to the washroom to change the water and he did so dutifully, flinching now and again at the roughness of my gestures, but without a word. I was about to put a fresh diaper on Papa when Stum tried to still my busy hands. "Shouldn't we give him a bath first, ne-san?"

I shook my head. "He's too weak. Tomorrow." I made

Stum bring a fresh mattress pad and sheets, and threw the stained ones away. Moments later Papa was tucked into a clean bed. His eyes were closed and he seemed to have given in to sleep. Yet as I turned off the light I saw his eyes flick open, glassy and wide, as if in fright, before shutting once again.

I sat in the living-room, at last alone to piece together what I could not remember. Had I fed him today? Who else could have? The image of a fork raised to his quivering mouth floated into my head, the feel of its cold handle between my fingers, yet that could have belonged to a thousand afternoons. I recalled an off-taste in my mouth, acrid. I remembered a cry growing loud in my ears, someone calling me, needing me: Sachi haunting me from the day before, I had thought, but it had stopped, the volume clicked off without warning. Just as it clicked back on this afternoon when Stum came in. In between, the day seemed to pass peacefully enough.

When I looked up, Stum was staring at me intently. I'd forgotten him. I looked at my watch and saw that it was well past dinner time. "Dinner hoshii?" I offered, trying to appear cheerful.

Stum frowned moodily. "I have no appetite. Not after all this. What's wrong with you? How could you do that to Papa?"

He tailed me doggedly into the kitchen. "Ne-san, answer me! How could you?" I tried to ignore him, tried to concentrate on the task at hand, clattering pots and pans, but he kept after me.

"I didn't do it on purpose!" I said.

"But how else...why...?" Then his face released its

frown as a new realization came into his head. "I see." He nodded to himself, then turned away.

"What? What do you see?"

He stood there stupidly, with a stupid superiority. "You're afraid, aren't you?"

"Of what?" I gave a small, strained laugh.

"Afraid I'm going to leave you. You're trying to make me worry that you're not capable of taking care of Papa any more. Just so I'll stay."

I laughed out loud, long and hard. Until there were tears in my eyes, streaming down. My little brother's imaginings were at once too elaborate and too childish.

"Did your Angel tell you that ridiculous story?"

"How could she? I haven't seen her since this morning."

I turned away, embarrassed to have shown my pettiness once again. Then I wheeled around. "No, little brother. It's you who's afraid. Afraid to leave us!"

We sat in the living-room for hours, it seemed, silent as the evening light turned stale, then black, and the streetlamps blinked on. Both of us slumped in our chairs.

"I am afraid, Asa-chan," he finally said. My name, uttered like that. I couldn't find his eyes in the dark, didn't want to, really. But to leave him there alone, unanswered, would have been cruel. I reached for the light and turned it on. He squinted at first, shielded his eyes with his sleeve. His cheeks were wet with tears; his shoulders heaved. It took all my strength, all my resolve, not to run from the room, to see him like this.

"There, there," I muttered mechanically, in a doll's voice, reaching my hand out uselessly to the space between us.

Stum's voice burst into the air, as if from under water. "Is that all you can say, ne-san?" I struggled for something in my head, something an older, wiser sister would say. Nothing to fear but fear itself. Some such thing. But nothing came. I saw Stum's hand take mine, but I barely felt it. His skin was still youthful, thick and smooth across his knuckles.

He was half kneeling, absurdly, one hand resting on his knees, his head down, resigned. "Can't you say it, ne-san?" he was pleading. His breath came in audible gasps. "Tell me you're afraid too," he implored in a slow, muffled voice. "You want me to be the only fool?"

I wanted to say it. With all my heart, I wanted to let go. To say, yes, Tsutomu, I am afraid. For once to release us both, so I could begin my days alone, without him, with only Papa. To face that truth. Too tight, that was what Sumi had meant—Eiji's friend, Iwata-san, that day in church. I saw her saying it to me, holding up her two hands to show me mine at Eiji's neck. Too tight, let go.

But when I gazed up at Stum, I imagined I saw Angel with him, too dark and smiling with her high round breasts. I saw Stum touching them, patting them gently; kneading them. I felt his hand on mine, sickly warm flesh; I yanked mine from his and stood up.

"This is a game to you, is it? I'll show you mine if you show me yours?" Shock came over Stum's face, at my crudeness; then the eagerness there a second ago hardened to a mask. "I won't fall for such childishness," I kept on, ignoring the change on his face. "I won't."

With that, he got up off his knees, where he'd been bent down like my suitor. He did not squabble, didn't try once more, as he usually did, and it froze my heart; into my mouth trickled something acrid and burning, that taste I remembered. In my head, this silent shrieking, it was me: *Don't go! Don't leave me! Tsutomu!* His name just there, as only I could pronounce it. He was leaving me. Not this minute, not tomorrow, but soon. This was the disgrace I imagined for myself, not before some stranger but before my brothers: that I'd be pleading, crying shamelessly not to be left behind. To be held by familiar arms, with the smell of familiar breath on me. To be held by one who had known me, every ugly bit, since long ago, since the very beginning, so that it was all only me, Asa-chan, my old flesh, my sour breath. My love.

Before he opened his mouth, I said it; I asked what had been going round and round in my head for years, in a timid voice that almost disgusted me. What I had never dared ask anyone, even Chisako.

"What is it like, ototo-chan?" For a moment he was the little brother I could be tender with, could entrust myself to. My ototo-chan. What is it like to let yourself love someone? To be loved back? I needed to know.

He returned to me then. He raised his eyebrows, so very tired. "It's different, ne-san," he sighed, "and not so different."

I bustled about to disguise my embarrassment, my disappointment. "Don't talk nonsense," I muttered gruffly. Different from what, I almost asked. Almost betrayed myself. For it was obvious: different from the hundred small things that made up my life. I wanted more, he had to tell me more; he must have known that. Because it had to be the most difficult thing, to give yourself. And yet here he was, the same person, ototo-chan.

"You never came to me about it—about her," I started to say. But he had come, he had, that one evening, not long ago. Something wonderful has happened, he'd said. "You should have come to me earlier," I said, scolding him, scolding myself. "I might have tried ..." I didn't finish. Tried harder, I meant, if I had only known, had understood.

He was nodding slowly. "It was Yano who helped me," he said finally, measuring his words.

"Yano?"

"Yes." He looked to see if he should go on. "I know it sounds strange, ne-san. I know you didn't—you don't —like him. But he asked me all about myself, he wanted to know. He was a crazy kamikaze. It was easy to tell him about Angel. We talked one, maybe two times. I thought, what could it hurt?"

I was shocked. I'd watched and seen nothing. When had these talks between the two of them taken place? How could I not have known? "He wasn't your friend, really."

"I think now he was."

"What did he tell you?" I demanded. "What advice did this kamikaze give you?" I tried to keep the bitter chill from my voice, but it crept in, I heard it, and so must have Stum; he knew me well enough. I waited, seething, for his reply.

Moments went by. Then he answered: "Yano told me that if his beautiful wife could be with an ugly man like himself, then I should have some hope too."

Across the electrical field, Yano's house sat still and empty. Yano was ugly, repulsive. Chisako was beautiful. Countless times, sitting by my window, lying in bed sleepless, I'd asked myself how she could bear his touch. I even once, in one of

our last visits, asked her as much. She tilted that beautiful face
to me.

"But he isn't ugly, Saito-san." Her expression was serene
but perplexed. I was about to remind her of what she'd called
him—hidoi hito, a monster—but her smile silenced me. I
felt ashamed. For this was her husband, after all. The man
she'd married. Yet it plagued me, this question, petty as it
seemed. How an ugly person could be loved. Could I have
been wrong?

Stum gave a gentle laugh. His lips twisted. "But you see,
ne-san, in the end she couldn't. Chisako-san couldn't stand
him after all. You must have known that."

I was unwilling to give anything away. "But how could
you trust a man like that? A crazy man?"

"We only talked a few times, ne-san," Stum said.

"You said only one or two."

"Three, maybe. That's all."

"If he was so full of wise advice, he should have at least
told you to bring home a nice Japanese girl instead of a—"

"It wouldn't have made a bit of difference," he cut in,
"whether she was nihonjin or not." He stared at me hard.
"You never would have welcomed her."

I'd spoiled things between us. But all I could think was
how I'd watched and watched, all that time, and seen nothing.

"Ne-san, calm down," he said, suddenly concerned. He
shrugged his shoulders. "After all, it's not that serious yet
between Angel and me. It's too early to tell. She may get fed
up with me." He yawned and indicated that he was going
to bed.

"Why should you be tired?" I snapped. I wanted the last

word. "It was me who did the dirty work. Me who cleaned up Papa tonight. As usual." Instantly I regretted it. But it was said, and with that I switched the light off, leaving him in the dark as I quickly climbed the stairs.

I sat in my room, nothing but the dark shapes of my dresser and night-table lurking around me. Chisako came to me then, as she had been the last time I'd seen her. The spilled green tea, my clumsiness; a stain on their ivory carpet in the one room, a small den hardly more than a walk-in closet that Chisako had kept for herself. Had kept from Yano and the dog, from her homely Kimi, even from Tamio.

I remembered the overgrown path to the house that afternoon, the weeds seeming to choke my ankles as I waded through them. The heaviness of my feet as I climbed the porch steps to her front door, lifting one after the other with all my strength. I grasped the handrail slick with rain and my breath came in gasps. Breathing took all my energy, as if I'd caught Yano's asthma, as if it were contagious.

I knocked on the inside door; the buzzer dangled from the frame by a red wire. I clucked my tongue at Yano's sloppiness; the whole house was a shambles. I knocked once again. Chisako had to be there; she'd telephoned me moments ago, in a panic, asking me to come as soon as I could. How odd, the call, hearing her voice high and twittery through the telephone line. The sound of the ring itself had jolted me; we so rarely received calls that I could often guess who the caller was. My heart was thumping that morning, it seemed to take on the rhythm of every little thing that made noise around me.

At last I heard footsteps, a giant's reverberating heavily in my heart, and the whoosh of the door as it was opened.

"Ah," Chisako sighed, clearly relieved to see me. Graceful as ever, even in her distress. As I removed my shoes, she set down a pair of her dainty brocade slippers, which I tried in vain to fit my broad feet into, my face growing heated as I bent over. She adeptly pushed before me a pair of brown tweed slippers that easily fit. She then led me through the living-room, every surface cluttered with Yano's things, his useless propaganda: the flyers piled high; the envelopes strewn around the old typewriter; a half-typed letter clamped in its roller; newspaper clippings here and there—every last object coated in dust and dog hair. The musty, dank odour, like Yano himself. I shuddered at the thought of the mind behind it, the person, his dirty fingernails, the greasy scalp he scratched at continually. Chisako led me through smoothly, ignoring the mess.

She drew me into her room. Clean and dustless, with nothing but one chair and a loveseat arranged at the window, and a portable television set on a bureau. Closed the door, shutting out that other dirty, hectic world, then collapsed onto the chair at the window, which overlooked the neighbour's yard. As I sat down, I saw from the corner of my eye a woman flitting back and forth in front of what seemed to be her kitchen sink. It was the next-door neighbour, the same wheat-haired woman who later came to my door.

Chisako let out a long sigh. I saw traces of tears streaking her face. Instantly her eyes filled, as they had that day she'd sat beside me on my living-room couch. The sight of those eyes, those drowning eyes—I felt such pity in my heart for her. I felt at that moment that I had weathered nothing, risked nothing; I had no heartache to compare with hers.

"Chisako-chan!" I cried, daring to call her that, to show the fondness I suddenly felt for her: my sincere desire to be of some comfort, no longer a bystander to others' pain. "Is he, did he...hurt you again?" I ventured to say it aloud, to pronounce between us words to make real what I had not been able to see on that pale flesh beneath her blouse.

She quickly drew the curtains then turned her lovely eyes to me, seeming to regain hold of herself. She patted my hand. "What are you saying, Saito-san?" She gave a quavery laugh. "Yano would never harm me." She laughed again, the tinkle of shattered glass. "Baka-rashii sa," she murmured and patted my hand once again, a little harder, just shy of a slap. "I hope you're not repeating such things to your friends."

My hands loomed grotesquely large in my lap. "You are my only friend, Chisako," I said quietly. Yet a friend, I told myself, would not call the other stupid. She was telling me that I'd overstepped, said too much. But she'd hurt me, using that word; even dressed up, it was Papa's word, baka; she should have known better. I could not, would not, forgive that. Quickly I gathered my coat around my shoulders but when I stood up to leave, I felt Chisako's fingers grasping at mine.

"Please," she said, looking away. "Chotto." She bowed her head slightly. "Asako-chan," she whispered, as if pained. "Please don't go." With that she swished out of the room. Sounds drifted in from the kitchen, dishes clattering, cutlery, the refrigerator opening and closing. I contemplated my feet on the new ivory carpet, in slippers which I suddenly, with horror, realized must belong to Yano.

Chisako reappeared, carrying a tray with teapot, cups,

and a plate of cookies which she set down on a folding table. She must have noticed me examining the slippers, for she said: "He hardly wears them. Never takes his shoes off, chanto." Not like a proper gentleman, she meant.

"Stum is like that too," I told her, eager to skip past the awkwardness hovering like a third party in this tiny room. "Urusai, ne?" I exclaimed too loudly. What a bother these men could be, I meant to imply, with a casualness I could never muster, but the unnaturalness of my situation was instantly brought home to me: comparing her husband to my brother. I blushed, but there was no reason to, not with Chisako, who considered me smart, kashi-koi, and fearless. Fearless in the face of any gossip that might be spread about me. But what gossip? Whose? Those nisei women who stood in line in front of me at the Japanese grocery store downtown? Who barely remembered me from old camp days? Who had chased after my Eiji? Whose mothers had tsk-tsked about Mama being too old to be pregnant there? Now all they could do was politely ignore me. Perhaps they called me ki-chigai baa-chan behind my back, crazy old woman. But I wasn't an old woman yet, even though I wore the clothes of one. One who was already dead.

We drank green tea, nibbled at cookies that had a chewy texture and mouldy taste. Finally Chisako set down her tea-cup carefully. She held her hand to her throat, its poreless flesh a shade darker than the makeup on her face, a difference I could have detected only in this particular light. The fingers curving around her neck. "I think he knows," Chisako said tentatively. She stared down into her empty teacup for the longest time, waiting for I didn't know what.

"About my friend," she added.

"I see," I said. "Are you sure?"

"No," she said impatiently. Meaning, how can one be? She stood up abruptly, shook her hands at her side with dainty violence. Just then we heard the front door opening, with the hum from the outside world, and shutting. Chisako went to the door of the room and opened it a crack, wide enough for me to glimpse Kimi passing: a sullen fragment of her mouth, downturned like Yano's, and an eye that darted at me through the slit. Come home alone, Tam long gone from her, taken by Sachi. Chisako blurted words in Japanese, too quick for me to catch, in a surprisingly harsh tone, an octave lower than when she spoke English. The girl shrugged.

"Kimi-chan. You promised." Chisako swung the door a little wider and leaned into the opening, closer to her child, softening. Something passed between them in the next quiet moment, before Chisako closed the door.

Down the hall another door closed, and the rattle of music from a radio started up. As she returned to me, Chisako caught her reflection in a small mirror mounted on the wall, watched herself pivot, then parted from her image as she lowered herself into her chair. "I want her to join the clubs after school," she said, flicking her hand to say it didn't matter what. She scarcely looked at me saying this. "Kimi has a pretty voice," she added, "like mine, not like Yano."

Despite her carelessness, I was reminded that she was a mother, one who kept track of these things. "She could join the choir," I started to say. "It's important for a young girl—"

Chisako flicked her hand again, this time to say she wanted no more of the topic. She stared into her teacup. I thought of how she'd lingered before her reflection; I was convinced that if I now returned to that abandoned room, I'd find it there in the mirror, just as she'd appeared to me that day.

"Do you read tea-leaves, Saito-san?" she asked, holding out her cup to me. I looked at the meaningless scatter, the disorder trapped there.

"No, no." I slid back in my chair, away from the cup. The sight of those fragments set off a churning inside me, a wariness of what was to come. I feared more was expected of me than I was capable of giving. "I don't know these things," I muttered.

"Come now, Asako." She coaxed me forward. "Just tell me what you see. There's nothing more to it." She laughed gently and grasped my wrist, pulling me hard towards her and the cup. "Please," she let out in a desperate singing whisper. "Please," she repeated in a squeal that was no longer her voice but simply a sound, one I'd heard once before. It threatened to disturb me now as it had then. I pulled away from her with equal force as she tugged me towards her, unrelenting. My hand was white from her grasping; she was a strong, vital woman, after all. This was how it happened; it wasn't entirely my fault, my clumsiness. For as I resisted her, my other elbow jerked back, knocking my cup, from the tray to the floor, the tea casting its shadow of green over the ivory carpet. Instantly she let go.

I gasped. "Gomen nasai," I uttered frantically, scanning the room for a cloth to blot up the stain. I dropped to my knees and began scrubbing with my sleeve. I could not bring myself to look at Chisako. I felt her hand, gentler, place itself on my arm, urging me up. "Now then, Asako. You must do as I ask. As a kindness. Don't worry about the carpet. Green tea doesn't stain, you know that."

Once again she held out the cup. I looked and still saw nothing; I felt like one of those little leaves, doused and flung about. But slowly, undone as I was, an image began to collect, or rather it was there waiting, like an eye, watching and waiting to be met by my own.

"What is it? Tell me!" Why it was so vital to her to know what I'd glimpsed in that cup, what it meant to her fate, I could not understand. In the end it could not have meant much. But I reported what I saw: what seemed plain as day to me there.

"It's Yano's dog," I responded dutifully, pointing to the cup's curving wall.

"No." When she shook her head, she reminded me of a doll whose stuffing has thinned at its neck.

"There's the snout," I said, pointing. "And the tail." The plume was what had caught my attention; it was unmistakeable.

Chisako stared intently into the cup for a second, shook her head again, then set the whole tray aside. "No, no, no," she repeated, emphatically. "There must be something else. It's only because you see that dog all the time. Now you're imagining it here in my cup. How silly." She began to pace the small room, which barely took a few steps back and forth.

Her response was perplexing. Why it should bother her so, this image that had shown itself, was a mystery to me.

"Baka no inu," Chisako muttered, still pacing, her hands twisting. "Stupid, stupid dog," she exclaimed, louder now, with such vehemence. Then it struck me. If I had only thought of it before I spoke, I would have said something else, anything that popped into my head: a cat, a pig, a tree.

"We—Mr. Spears and I—we were visiting together at our spot. The little lot by the hill." She paused briefly. "Perhaps you know it, Asako." A vexed look danced across her face, as if this referred to something she wished to take up with me but would drop for the time being. Then a smile spread on her lips, the memory come out to play.

"Of course, we considered...a hotel, but that seemed too...well, you know. But Mr. Spears, he enjoys being out of doors. Especially now that summer's almost here. Out in the wilds, he says." Perhaps I imagined the flush of red beneath her powder as she told me this.

"It's like a picnic, ne? I make those little sandwiches cut in triangles. A bit of tuna with parsley. I trim off the crusts just as you told me to, Asako. So they are smooth and white all around. He likes them like that."

I lowered my voice. "Is that how Yano found out? The dog?" I began. I tried to recall seeing Yano without his dog, some late afternoon when I heard him calling out for it, when it might have strayed.

Chisako grew vexed again. "Baka no inu," she repeated, cutting me off. "Dogs are such filthy creatures, aren't they, Asako? They sniff around everywhere. They clean themselves with their own tongue."

"Was Yano there, with the dog?" I dared to ask.

Chisako shook her head vigorously, if only to stop me from saying more. "Yano is a smart man after all. He may not know, yet he suspects." She closed her eyes. "A man knows his wife." She must have learned this from one of her soap operas. Without opening her eyes, she sat back in her chair and stretched herself out, like a yawning animal. "He knows her body," she said. Was this the voice she'd used to seduce her Mr. Spears? Or, I wondered bitterly, did she play the Japanese coquette? Covering her mouth when she giggled girlishly? Suddenly Chisako seemed quite ludicrous, even hateful, to me: a middle-aged woman, a mother, pretending to be a girl, playing the exotic temptress. I could see she was savouring some private moment, reliving it even as I sat there, and I was even more ludicrous, if that was possible. Waiting patiently, obediently, as she did so. I felt nauseated watching her with her eyes closed too long. I felt like some peeping Tom. She'd reduced me to that. I cleared my throat, rather too loudly, but I wanted to shake her. I wanted to punish this greedy woman, she who thought she could have everything she ever desired. For the first time I felt sympathy for Yano. This poor, ugly man being deceived by this heartless woman, beautiful as she was.

But suddenly she seemed to fall apart. Her face dropped into her hands, cupped as if to catch it. I'd witnessed her tears before, been moved by them, then later become suspicious. She sobbed silently at first but then her cries began to rack the air, and she waved at the television, and I, not understanding, looked in vain at the nick-nacks surrounding it. In that instant I glimpsed among them the glass dome with the rose, Mr. Spears' gift. Chisako shook her head angrily, then flung out a hand to the knob. Instantly the screen flashed, blaring with crass voices and faces as she sobbed.

"He won't leave her!" she cried. I tried to conceal my

impatience with her; what had become, for the first time, not
envy but disdain.

"Who? His wife?" I had to say the word that she could
not. "Of course he won't leave his wife. Did you think he
would?" She nodded meekly, acknowledging for once how
naive she'd been. I felt the callousness in my tone, the superiority, and her cringing from it.

"He said he would."

"And you believed him?" I was shouting above the noise
of the television. I glanced at the screen, into the large faces
of women, a jumble of colours and shapes. A soap opera,
which told me it was already past noon. I reached over and
turned it off.

Instantly she clicked it back on, angrily. "Kimi-chan,
she'll hear!" and she pointed to the wall. In the midst of it all,
Chisako did not forget her daughter, her homely, sullen child
in the next room. She slumped down, cradling her face in her
hands. The rhythm of her sobs, of her body's tremors, did
not stop. It was a punishment inflicted on me, to have to
watch. To see such passion, such pain, which I would never
have in my life. Revenge for I didn't know what.

At last her sobs turned to weeping. In spite of the puffi-
ness and redness of her eyes, the blotches, there was a frightening clarity there, an understanding directed at me.

"You are so cold, Saito-san," she said. "I would never
want to be so cold."

I was not stunned by what she said. I was not insulted,
not wounded. For it was not the first time she'd said such
a thing. I'd come to know it to be true. All my life, what I'd
felt had been the promise of nothing. The risk of nothing,

which had frozen me to ice. Even as a child, as a girl ador-
ing her older, handsome brother, I had been capable of great
restraint.

I went to the window and clipped the curtain aside.
Across the yard, the woman had disappeared from her
kitchen. The window-ledge she had been cleaning was now
neatly lined with small potted plants.

"You will not understand this, Asako." Chisako's controlled whisper reached me through the television's blare.
"But I have been special to him." I turned not to her but to
those plants at the neighbour's window, the first in line with
its budding blossoms.

"I suppose you're going to tell me he made you feel special too," I spat. I was steeping her love in bitter brine. Even
I knew these clichés. Hadn't I myself said such things on
more than one occasion, blindly, blithely dispensing advice
to a young schoolgirl experiencing her first love? And hadn't
I known that in every word Sachi had detected my ignorance,
my despised naivety?

"If you mean to ask me about our sexual relationship,
Asako, then I will tell you that yes, it is wonderful." Chisako
was ruthless, bringing me face to face with a certain experience of life I'd been denied, rubbing my nose in it.

"And I suppose you're wondering if it's true what they
say about hakujin men, compared with nihonjin. Aren't you,
Asako? Ne?" She seemed to jab at me, in her delicate way,
with these loathsome words. It was not the first time she'd
brought up this topic, this crude preoccupation, though I
was never certain if it was merely to taunt me.

I continued to stare at the flowerpots set in the window

across the way. African violets, alternating purple and white. I clung to them, unblinking, concentrating as hard as I could —in so doing, forbidding her to utter another word. She could go too far. "I'm sure I don't know what you're talking about, but I don't doubt your superior knowledge in this matter," I snapped back.

This seemed only to encourage her. "Well, Asako," she replied, bristling, "I cannot say for all, but I can say that with my friend I feel very—" For some reason she froze then, watching me.

Several seconds elapsed. "Yes? Go on." I was completely composed by then. Had drawn myself up. I urged her on with my cold, cold authority. It was true what Stum had said of me: I could be formidable.

But she remained frozen there, staring at me, unable to go on. After a time she closed her eyes again, shutting out the sight of me. Suddenly she relented. "I tell you these things, Asako, only because I wish for you to experience them too, some day. But not for you to suffer as I do. I want you to find pleasure in what is good." She said this gravely, solemnly; as trite as it sounded, I almost believed her. Her eyelashes pressed into the puffy flesh beneath her eyes, which were locked shut. I almost laughed, with the rattle of my nerves, but controlled myself. I reminded myself of the reason I'd been summoned here; me, Chisako's lowly lady-in-waiting.

"You see, it's true: I am special to him." She leaned back in her chair, eyes still shut, entirely at ease like this. "But perhaps not special enough.

"Mr. Spears is a handsome man. To see yourself in such a man's eyes, as he holds you—" She grew breathless, absurdly so. Yet I was touched, I could not deny it. "I find I can't stop myself." I believed her; I believed her powerlessness. Her wanting to be powerless.

"His eyes," she murmured. "So deep and large. Not like nihonjin." Her voice turned petty, against herself. "So small, like slits."

I found myself poised at the edge of my chair. Wanting to touch her, console her. Be of some use. "But Chisako, you are...utsukushii." Tearfully I said this, believing it with all my heart. It was the word Eiji had used to describe cherry blossoms to me. When they first bloom. Their fleshy pink in spring. This is what I recalled as Chisako sat with me, her eyes pressed shut, each a furled bloom.

Blindly she shook her head. "No, Asako. You are being kind, I know. Yano says that to me too. Not often, but he whispers it in my ear now and then. He can be a fool too, you see. After all the ugliness he saw in Japan, I am beautiful to him." I thought of Yano as he had once stood before Chisako's haphazard arrangement of withered daisies. Utsukushii, he'd murmured, amid her derisive laughter.

Sitting in her small room, opposite me, Chisako was smiling a private smile into the darkness before her. That same darkness threatened to engulf me as well, even as I sat wide open to the light. "It was terrible," Chisako went on. "Maybe Yano told you. Such sickness, ne? People shut themselves away. It was better they kill themselves, to spare their loved ones the sight of them, day after day." She shuddered. "But you must know all this, Asako. Ne?"

I nodded, though she could not see me. She seemed to sense my movements, to move in sympathy with me. She paused to let me take all this in, even as her eyes remained tightly shut. Now it appeared, from the twisting of her lips, that she was attempting to quell a nausea arising from these thoughts.

It was not entirely true that I knew what Chisako spoke of. I understood the facts of it. I could recall sitting by the Nakagawas' contraband radio in the camp, hearing the news unfold, distant and elusive as the speck Eiji had pointed to on Port Dover's horizon. In my girlish mind I saw a tiny upward rush of dust; I thought of those patches of matsu-take deep in the forest, away from the camp, when they said "mushroom cloud".

"Yano told me it was like paradise for you, coming here," I said quietly. I scrutinized her face for the slightest twitch or tremor. She didn't move. I wondered if she had fallen asleep.

Her eyes finally opened with a startled yet languorous expression, as if she were waking from deep, satisfying slumber. "I would not say paradise," she said, "but I am grateful Yano brought me here, away from that place." A tear rolled down her cheek, melting away what was left of her makeup, exposing the marred skin under it.

"I'm so sorry, Chisako," I stammered. "Your family, your parents, they were in Hiroshima..."

Chisako's eyes suddenly seemed to hold a smile, though her mouth did not, and the trace of that tear remained. "Asako, you are confused," she said. "My parents died before the war. I never saw those things, but of course I heard." Her eyes shut.

I was about to repeat what Yano had said on one of our

walks. How he'd told me she was from Hiroshima, what he'd implied about her family. I could not have mistaken his meaning. For I had, I believe, in some way held it in my heart all this time, through the endless confiding, her stories about Mr. Spears. I'd held it there as she sat before me, eyes closed. I was on the verge of blurting how betrayed I felt, having my sympathies played upon, when her eyes flicked open again.

"Do you know what my secret wish is, Asako? You will be quite shocked." The crystal of her voice coarsened to glass: a new sound, a different Chisako.

I shook my head. Her eyes were wide now, rounder and larger than ever, unwavering; for a moment she looked foreign, no longer nihonjin. "My wish is for the bomb to drop on the ones who did it." She seemed shocked at herself, at her own cruelty. "Just because we're nihonjin, they think they can do anything to us." Her hands clenched and shook. She reminded me of Yano, the hands in fists, the anger.

"That is the reason for Yano's meetings and letters, the petitions to government people. He isn't crazy. He wants to change things. It's important to try, ne?"

I nodded, if only to appease her. It was true that her anger, her venom shocked me. Yet I wanted to tell her how useless it was to dwell on the past, to waste her words. Words that were not even hers. It dawned on me then that Chisako was a woman who could never be without a man; who must believe in that man. The world was too frightening to be alone and on your own.

Her thoughts seemed to take another turn. "I am a plain woman, Asako. Not special at all. Only with hopes and dreams for herself." Her lips rested sullenly behind the carefully shaped red of her lipstick. She sat forward, brought herself close to me. "You and I are both lucky," she said sombrely. "You may feel that life offers you little, but really, un no yoi, ne? You are one of the lucky ones."

I pondered her remarks now, trying to decipher the meaning beneath the surface. How I could be lucky. Was Chisako telling me I'd made myself needlessly pitiable? Felt sorry for myself when I had no right? When others had greater cause? I chided myself for probing too deeply, stirring things up for myself. When in the end, Chisako thought only of herself, always, never of me.

"Perhaps, Asako," she sighed resignedly, "perhaps Mr. Spears is not truly special to me either. Ne?"

Chisako paced a little back and forth, then sat down beside me. I felt the warmth of her legs alongside mine, both of us sinking into the soft cushions.

"Asako." She said my name with some tenderness, and pressed my hand between the two of hers. "You haven't, have you?"

I stiffened. "Haven't what? What nonsense are you talking, Chisako?" I turned once more to the window.

"You have never been with a man, have you?"

Now I was stunned; I was—there were no words for the distress, the shame I felt at being asked such a thing. But she would not let me go, and her face hovered so close; I could not conceal myself. I strained for words, some small offhand comment, some adept change of subject, but could find nothing. My voice had drained away. I rasped, as if we sat before a crowded audience of strangers eager for my secrets:

"Please, Chisako. Please," I pleaded, barely audible to myself. "Do not embarrass me."

As I recalled the moment, my cheeks burned, but my body was cold as if without clothes. Stum's padding steps now came up from behind and in a second he was patting my shoulder. I was oddly warmed by it, the intimacy of his touch here in my room. My brother's face, in spite of our conflicts, was a solace to me during this moment in which I regained myself. The things we'd shared all these years. Our discomfort in the world. The consolation of one another's company, which had sustained us within the walls of our home. I'd forgotten about him, lost in my reverie. Assumed he'd left to see his Angel once again.

"Tell me, ne-san," he prodded. "What was going through your mind just now?" I shook my head. "I was daydreaming," I answered. On any other occasion he'd assume I meant about Eiji.

"You were mumbling strange things," he said. "What did you tell Chisako? What were your last words to her, ne-san?"

I shook my head, absolving myself. "I don't remember just now," I said, watching his searching, doubting eyes. "But soon it will come back to me."

"Tell me. Tell me," he repeated, unwilling to let it go. In my confused mind his voice became twinned with another's, Yano's; the two huddled conspiratorially all along, unbeknownst to me. The eyes of my brother, then of Yano, whitening with rage, hungry for me to tell him what he already knew. As I watched Stum's back turn to me, that familiar back with its particular bent angle at the left shoulder, as I

watched him leave, I was compelled to call out to him, to
stop him from leaving me alone, to tell him what I had in
fact remembered of that night. But then it was Yano I saw
too, Yano turning away from me in the electrical field,
stooped to catch his snagging breath in the midst of his rage
and jealousy.

My voice grew loud suddenly, boisterous in my ears. "I
told her to tell him!" I was shouting, the blood coursing
through me was thick and pulsing, vibrating with this news.
"I did!" I declared baldly into Stum's disbelieving eyes. "I
demanded she tell Yano about her Mr. Spears. How she
preferred him. I told her to. I insisted! I demanded she be
honest!" I cried, on fire with shame and uncontainable excitement. A torrent of thoughts rushed into my head. All she
had confided, every private detail that I had tried to cast
aside was still stored inside of me. The painful intimacies
that I had yearned to hear, that I was helpless to shun despite
the envy they raised in me. The envy that now burst from me,
victorious and vindicated. Stum knelt in front of me again.
He clutched at my knees, hoping against hope that it was not
true, that I had not made Chisako tell Yano such things, yet
he did not dare ask. It was his pure good nature, I knew, his
naive faith in me. "And now," I sobbed, crying for my childish innocence that was spoiled long ago, the burden of it.
How much a victim I'd made of myself and everyone in all
of this! "Now she's gotten what she deserved, hasn't she?"
I cried.

"Yes!" Stum shouted back, emphatic, equally vindicated.
His anger, his envy now shockingly revealed to me. "Yes, ne-
san! She has!"

It was the kind of dream that does not deceive you at all, but simply lulls you into reliving a treasured time or sensation, and you know it is a dream of pure memory. I was a girl once more, and I was walking with Eiji through the orchard of the camp. It was spring, and the apple trees were in full bloom. Eiji clambered up the side of one tree and snapped off a small branch. "Utsukushii," he said, handing it down to me. I remember it was a new word we'd just learned at the Japanese school in the camp. Up close, the blossoms were more like insects that wriggled with the breeze than flowers. The petals were skimpy and the stamens fine as nostril hairs. They made me go cold. I dropped the branch; Eiji picked it up and put it back in my hand. "Utsukushii," he repeated, then pointed to where the blossoms were thick and pretty on the trees. He was showing me the kind of pretty glimpsed at a certain time, in a certain light—a special light. A pretty that can't last; a pretty that can even turn ugly. As we walked, the blossoms on the trees curled up and blackened before my eyes, just as I remembered them doing in real life a week or two after blooming.

Papa groaned as I fed him his porridge, but he didn't seem resentful towards me for forgetting him the day before. Everything that had happened last night, my conversation with Stum, wrenching as it was, seemed far away. I felt fortified by the sense that, whatever the circumstances, I could rise above them. I had my daily tasks, I thought, wiping the porridge from Papa's chin; responsibilities that could only carry me forward: a tide. Life itself, I laughed. I was formidable. Besides, there was the chance, as Stum himself had said, that this situation with Angel would pass, and life would resume as usual. But no, I vowed; not as usual. Things would change for the better. I would change. I would welcome life into this home, I thought, remembering the flowers I'd put in the living-room. I'd throw open the doors, encourage my brother to make more friends. I would make new friends myself. Perhaps invite that hakujin woman over for tea, the Yanos' neighbour, to reminisce about Chisako, after more time had passed.

Come what might, whatever the outcome of these terrible happenings, I told myself, what I wanted was the happiness of my family. Of Sachi too. Once Yano and the children returned, that was what I would pour all my energy into.

For the first time in the years since he'd lost his wits lying in this bed, I searched Papa's face for signs. I wiped his chin and waited, watched for some link between my touch and his sense of it, any at all. I sat on his bed beside him, listening to the sputter of his body's eroded parts; outside the twitter and ping of birds and leaves on trees echoed in a comforting way. He perceived this too, I thought, for the marsh in his eyes seemed to clear with the light and sounds coming from the window.

Not knowing what possessed me, I lay down beside him on his bed. "Ara?" he exclaimed, wondering what was happening, what this quaking was I'd caused. I felt the coldness emanating from him even as I tucked the extra blanket under his chin; Dr. Honda had told me that it was common for the body temperature of old people confined to their beds to drop below normal. I ignored the sourness his body exuded, the old smell that could never be scrubbed away without peeling the very skin from him. Instead I lay there and watched him close: the plastic-wrap skin around his head, the birdlike bones beneath; I felt the slow drip drip of blood through his veins. It was a marvel, really, to exist for nearly ninety years, the body still breathing, still alive. I wrapped my arm across the mound of him, pressed myself close to warm his body with my own, and felt the crushable bones beneath the layers of bedding. "Papa," I whispered. "Papa, all right? Genki?" I wanted him to hear, to feel me close.

I often forgot it had been Papa who was tender with me after Eiji was gone. Mama blamed me, I know, for his death; but that did not embitter me, for I understood that she was grasping desperately for some peace of mind. Some consolation. When I stopped eating and sleeping, it was Papa who watched over me. There was nothing my body could take in. It was hateful to me, the thought of my body succumbing to sensation with any relief or pleasure when all I wanted was to be numb. To be closed over. Yet, however deadened, alive to my own misery. Though I wished for it as for nothing else before or since, I did not deserve to die with Eiji. Or to survive without him. Stum once told me that, in his infant memory, I was a skeleton that stalked his dreams. I remembered little of that time; only that Papa stuffed me with steamed napa grown in the mountain soil, and beans: beans pushed between my teeth with his brutish fingers as I lay there. Papa feared the same thing happening to me, the pneumonia, though it could not; would not. It was Eiji who had been weak, and not I.

Papa had been kind even when Eiji first turned from me. Eiji was fearful, I came to understand, of his little sister, his little ojosan with the soft lumps swelling on her chest and the furry spots sprouting here and there. He was just a boy, after all. It was endearing, one might say, and, I came to understand, not the least bit unnatural; for perhaps a year ago I had noticed how Tam, in the smallest yet most telling ways, flinched from his sister's touch. How she scurried to keep close when they crossed the field, and each time he strode ahead. Instead of clinging all the tighter, she drew back. Of course, that was only after Kimi had stumbled onto them down by the creek, just as I had. I had watched Sachi shoo her away with a glance, a mean, darting glance. To keep Tam to herself, as I had tried to keep Eiji. Kimi let go, seeing how her place had been taken. It was difficult for me to hold back, not go to that girl to explain, but wisely I did not. She would learn, I told myself, just as I had learned.

I could even laugh at myself over it now: the doubts I had harboured those many, many years ago; how panicked I was. As if Eiji could ever stop loving me, even with Sumi and the others flocking around him. But many things were changing then, and I was so young, and he not much older; it was understandable, this confusion. One day I was different for him, and he for me. It was Papa who kept me company then. He tolerated my meanness, because I'd earned it by enduring the burden of his drunkenness those Saturday nights in Port Dover. He had little to do in the camp, and began to mutter sayings, sayings meant in his rough way to soothe me; I could only guess at their meanings with my bits of schoolgirl Japanese. "Nan-to, ojiisan?" I lashed out, jeering at him as Mama did. Old fool, I called him, what are you saying? Baka, I even dared to call him. Him with his foolish sayings, telling me I'd live past this; as if my love for Eiji were a phase I'd outgrow.

I sat with Papa on many sullen, lonely days, waiting, waiting. Staring out across the muddy road at an ugly old boot stuck in front of our shack since the snow had melted.

I dozed off lying at Papa's side, just as I eventually did in the old days when I was spent from my crabbiness. When I awoke, Papa was sound asleep. I choked a little at the sour odour, in that first deep and languid intake of breath on awakening.

Stum hadn't yet emerged from his room so I tiptoed past it. Perhaps he was exhausted from our exchange last night, and taking advantage of his day off. For the next hour or two I busied myself with chores, tallying those completed with my old efficiency. Gently I pushed open his door with my dustmop to find it empty. I could see that his bed had not been slept in. At the instant of my discovery, there was a knock at the front door. I hurried downstairs. I knew immediately that it wasn't Sachi, yet I did not inch to the door in nervous anticipation. I revelled for an instant in the uncertainty. This was how life could feel—not knowing, from moment to moment, what awaited you.

I threw the door open wide, to blinding sunlight and a hush of moist air held inside the screen door. Out of the dusty light a voice emerged—a man's, ever so slightly familiar, tapping, as it did, on the door of my recent memory. He shifted so his head blocked the light and his face materialized.

"Hello, Miss Saito."

The care he took in pronouncing my name this time. "Hello, detective," I answered briskly, efficiently.

"I have a few more questions to ask. Is this a convenient time?"

"Of course," I promptly replied, "but my brother isn't home just now. If you'd like to come back later..." I started to close the door, my natural cautiousness returned.

"It's you I need to speak with," he interjected, in a friendly tone that did not intimidate me in the least, even with his hand pushing firmly against the door. "I see," I said. "Of course," I added graciously. I let go of the door and ushered him in. After all, I had nothing to hide from the man, nothing at all. On the contrary, I welcomed the opportunity to add to what little I'd been able to tell him before. To be helpful in whatever way possible. Since his last visit, various recollections had popped into my mind, events and conversations that might be useful in his investigation. Though it occurred to me he might find them trivial. One never knew. But this business of cobbling facts together was, I told myself, the detective's, not mine.

As he stepped into my living-room, I was struck by how tall he was. I didn't recall noticing that before, perhaps because on the previous visit he had sat most of the time. Today I felt quite small beside him, like a little girl or an old woman, I didn't know which. But I felt surprisingly comfortable; I felt safe. I was certain that he, if anyone, would get to the bottom of things. That, after all, was his job. I indicated the armchair he'd sat in before but he shook his head. "I'm fine right here," he said, rocking back on his heels. I must have frowned at his shoes digging into my carpet, for he immediately straightened up, planting his feet carefully, evenly in place. He took out his little notebook, which I noticed was new, though identical to the one he'd had the other day. He gave a brief, vanishing smile. His dark, greyless hair was as immaculately arranged as ever, and I observed once again, in the light flooding my living-room, how impressively its broomlike thickness held its coiffure.

I almost started telling him about Sachi's absurd attempt at tracking Tam's scent with Yano's dog; in fact, I'd just opened my mouth and a chuckle had come out, a little high and jarring, if only to my ears. I had wanted to confide that from the start I'd known how futile her undertaking was, but that I'd indulged her because the poor child was so distraught over the missing boy, Tamio. Tam, who was, after all, her special friend. It occurred to me to wonder if the detective knew this or not; if it would be considered at all relevant. I was contemplating this with open mouth, I discovered to my embarrassment, when I caught the detective staring at me, taking note of my appearance. A self-conscious hand flew up to my hair, patted down strands here and there. It dawned on me that I'd done nothing to care for myself in the last two days. With horror I caught a musty odour rising from my armpits, and saw that my dress was rumpled from my having slept in it. I looked down at myself to see the body of someone else. Someone sloppy, forgetful, unrecognizable. Perhaps a little crazy. Even criminal.

"Miss Saito, are you feeling all right?" he asked, with such sympathy. "Maybe all this—" and he gestured gracefully with his large, broad hands towards the field and the Yanos' house on the other side of it framed by my window. "Maybe it's throwing you off a little?" His eye seemed to catch on the vase of flowers I'd put out.

I nodded gratefully. Instantly whatever fears had crept into my mind retreated. "Yes, yes, I suppose it is. A little.

You're probably right," I said. It seemed perfectly reasonable. The tone of his voice reasonable. A violent murder in a quiet neighbourhood, our neighbourhood. A woman, my friend, murdered. Two young people missing, along with their father. I felt warmed, protected, in the tall shadow of this man in my living-room. He wasn't some hakujin stranger in my home; he was a detective; Detective Rossi, who had grown up in the neighbourhood across from ours.

"I wondered if there was anything else you wanted to tell me, Miss Saito."

I realized then that my head was a hive swarming with voices, none of them mine. Making no sense, no sense at all. Growing louder, above my own thoughts, which I could hardly sort out as mine. I didn't know where to begin, what to say. Even Eiji's voice was teeming in me in that moment, *Asa, stop, stop.* Then mine, shouting the same: *Stop, stop.* Stop what? Who? I didn't know, didn't know at all. I swayed, my knees buckled; the room blackened.

I was walking. Briskly, as was my routine. There were the electrical towers marching into the distance. The Yano and Nakamura houses just across the way. I was my neatly groomed self, in my quiet navies, my jacket just back from the dry cleaners. I recall glancing down at myself, thinking they'd done a good job. Nothing else was in my head really. I'd visited with Chisako the day earlier, that was true, but it was not up to me to sort out the mess she'd gotten herself into, despite what she'd confided in me. How she'd wanted me to help her, to talk to Yano, to try to explain; to reason with him. She hadn't said it in so many words, but her desperation had been unmistakeable, her cry for help. Yet I'd

resisted. It was not my business at all, I told myself. I purposely timed my walk an hour earlier to avoid an encounter
with Yano. It was just after five in the morning, when that
dull underlight of darkness still hung in the air.

The detective's voice intruded. His hand on my face, a
small biting slap; I pushed it away. The same hand, then two
of them, gentle but I felt their strength holding my wrists.
"Miss Saito. Calm down. You're all right now."

There he was, the detective, bent down in front of me
as I sat in my chair. His large face very close. "Hooked you
a little too hard there, did I?" He rubbed his large hands
together, a faintly reassuring gesture. "I was trying to bring
you to. You had a little spell. Have you eaten anything today?"
He placed in my hands a glass of water he must have gotten
from the kitchen.

I shook my head as I drank. "I really couldn't," I said
after swallowing. "Not a thing. This helps." He clucked
his tongue, apparently to scold me for not eating. My stomach felt queasy. The detective's face was still very close; so
close I could see the pores of his skin pooled with fluid. The
sharp scent of his cologne stung my nostrils. There was his
little notebook in his jacket pocket, gaping a little, so that
I saw the loops of his handwriting folded within the first
few pages.

He stood up. "Maybe I should come back when you're
feeling better," he said, but there was reluctance there. He
was clearly anxious to get on with his business, and I saw no
reason, weak though I felt, not to oblige him.

"I'm fine now, detective." I gave a smile to convince him,
and was relieved when he finally sat down on the chesterfield.

"So, detective, you were asking if—" I started to say, but then noticed that he was sitting up very straight, both hands on his knees, feet planted in front, looking at me. He took a very deep, audible breath, and I realized that this was for my benefit; he was urging me to breathe along with him, even though I'd assured him I was all right. "Detective, really, I'm just fine—" He wagged his finger and motioned for me to take a deep breath with him, stretching upward, then to exhale slowly.

"There," he said at last. "Better?"

"Yes, thank you, detective," I replied, and it was true. I did, for a moment, experience an invigorating surge into my body.

"You like to take walks, don't you, Miss Saito?" he asked, slowly retrieving the notebook from his pocket.

"I haven't had the energy lately, but yes," I said. "Every morning."

"With Mr. Yano."

"I beg your pardon?"

"You took walks with Mr. Yano."

"Not with Mr. Yano," I said. Such a ridiculous idea, I thought. The detective continued to look at me expectantly.

"But you did walk together."

"Well, I suppose, yes. Sometimes he'd catch up with me."

"How often did the two of you meet?"

"Not very often, really." I looked up at him scrutinizing me so intently. "It wasn't ever planned," I added. "Not on my part." Suddenly, absurdly, I burst into laughter. The thought that had occurred to me was so humorous, I could hardly contain myself. "Detective, you weren't thinking—" I broke off, unable to continue, so racked with laughter was I. "You weren't thinking...that Yano and I...," I stammered.

The detective sat there, notebook and pen in hand, plainly perplexed. He shrugged. "I'm afraid you'll have to explain, Miss Saito."

At last I caught my breath, calmed down a little. "You weren't implying...?" Again I trailed off. The look of confusion was still there on his face. Perhaps I was not seeing things too clearly. I still felt queasy; inside me was a giddy rhythm of panic and embarrassment. "Please excuse me, detective. I'm not quite myself."

He nodded graciously, then turned a page in his notebook. He cleared his throat, as if anxious to get on with his business. "Your neighbour, Mrs. Frean, said she saw you in the field the day before Mr. Yano took his son and daughter out of school. It looked to her like you were having an argument."

"Hardly." I gave a mild snort at that. To think I'd actually considered inviting that nosy busybody into my home.

"You mean she was mistaken? You didn't talk to Mr. Yano that day in the field?"

"No, I did. I only meant that we—"

"Do you recall the conversation?"

"It's coming back to me," I said, holding a hand up to beg his patience. I struggled to collect my thoughts from the buzzing hive. The detective waited.

The words were taking their time returning to my head, but the look on Yano's face that morning—I closed my eyes and there it was. It was a bitter cold morning that, in mid-May, hadn't quite left winter behind. Though the day was early, I knew it would remain grey and lifeless; a day when you feel not so much the cold as the absence of warmth. When you can imagine how it will be when the sun at last burns itself out. He was waiting by the north tower, my first destination each morning once I crossed over to the field. He had his golf jacket on with the collar turned up, and his hands burrowed in his pockets, as if, his reptile skin worn thin, he was feeling the cold for the very first time.

"Da-me, Saito-san. It's no good" were the first words from his mouth. In resigned disgust. His homely face seemed to have broken out in stress and grief. He never had that smooth, poreless skin that so many nihonjin have, but his face was worse than usual that day. Swollen, oddly chapped, his features more lumpy than ever. A large ugly blemish, perhaps a boil, was forming on his left cheek.

"She has no shame," he said, still in that low, ominous tone. "But I said that before, didn't I, Asako? Told you that myself, right?"

I suppose I nodded at that point, aware that his exhaustion had progressed to a state of nervous alertness. His eyes were feverishly bright, even attractively enlarged from lack of sleep. He'd called me "Asako", perhaps for the first time.

"What did I say back then, Asako? Tell me. You remember everything. You see it all. Tell me."

"I don't remember," I said.

"I know you do. Say it. It helps me."

"You said," I began hesitantly, not certain if I should continue, "you said Chisako didn't know how it felt to be ashamed to be nihonjin. Not like you and me."

"That's it." His eyes flamed even brighter. It was what he

wanted to hear, I suppose, and I'd felt compelled to oblige him. For once, he was keeping up with my pace, though I realized I'd unconsciously slowed down a little. "See, Asako, that's why she feels no shame to be with a hakujin man. She's proud. That's the difference between her and us, right?"

I was quiet at first, until he nudged my elbow, some of his usual emphatic energy returning. I could not help thinking of the secret wish Chisako had divulged to me, the bomb she'd wanted dropped, the anger she'd expressed. "Just because we're nihonjin," she'd said. Yano never grasped it, how well she'd learned from him. I thought of telling him, but didn't. Instead I told him what he wanted to hear.

"Yes," I said after a moment, decidedly firm. "Yes," I clearly said, "she's proud," thinking of her arrogant words, her telling me that I was without feeling, that I was cold. Parading her love before me, lording it over me. When she'd hardly taken the time to know me, to know my heart. "That's the difference," I said.

But Yano wasn't hearing me, not now. He was hardly concerned about me, either. He'd rushed on with his frantic, searching thoughts, trying to make sense of the betrayal. "Maybe it's not her. It's him. He came after her. He's the boss, right? A big shot, right?" He was fighting with his fists now, punching the air with every word. "You know those kind of hakujin. I saw enough of them over there after the war. They get a taste for nihonjin women." He said all this so crudely. To try to spare himself.

Now it was I who could barely keep up with Yano. His pace matched the fury of his thoughts. "I wouldn't know those kind of men," I started to say, but Yano had even

moved ahead of me, so that I had to scurry to catch up. He
was briskly rounding the south tower.

"There was a change," he said. "I didn't know it then. But
now...it was a month ago, that's when it started. Right,
Asako?" He turned to me. How I longed to shake him free
of his ignorance, his self-delusion, to tell him Chisako had
been carrying on with her friend for many months now.
From back in December, with that first insignificant gift of
the rose inside the glass dome. Through the winter, when the
trees in that tiny wood had drooped with ice and I'd seen the
car windows steam up in no time from the heater. But I
could not. It was up to Chisako to fill in those details, not
me, I thought irritably. Why I should have to answer such
questions was beyond me. It seemed I was trapped for ever
in this situation, bound up in the concerns of others.
Though I felt sorry for Yano—and, I suppose, Chisako—
they really had nothing to do with my life.

Yano had moved on yet again. He was shaking his head
in agitation. "We're so full of shame, aren't we, Asako? We
hide away, afraid that they'll lock us up again. That's it,
isn't it?"

I could think of no way to respond. I nodded my head
sadly, knowing whatever I said would have no effect on him.
"That was such a long time ago, Yano," I said. "Things have
changed in thirty years."

"Chisako saw it in me," he said, not hearing me, not a
word. "It isn't attractive, Asako. Especially in a man. I don't
blame her." He tugged his fingers through his coarse hair. For
the first time that morning he gazed directly into my eyes,
and it unnerved me, seeing myself there in his. I could not

help thinking of Chisako thrilling to her own reflection in
Mr. Spears' eyes. "I can see it in you too," Yano was saying.
"You hide in your house taking care of Papa and little
brother. You should get on with life. Have your own family.
How old are you now, Asako?"

I struggled to contain the indignation I felt. "My age is
beside the point," I said. I tried to stay calm, reasonable; not
to say anything I might later regret. "You can make all the
excuses you want for her, but Mr. Spears did not make
Chisako do anything she didn't want to." I barely paused to
ponder what I was inflicting on Yano. "She thinks she's better than us," I found myself further declaring. I heard a
vibration in the air, as if we were gliding over an earthquake.
"But she isn't," I said. "Not one bit." I saw Chisako then, her
eyes closed, in that private, forbidden world with him, her
Mr. Spears. A world that I, no matter how close I came to it,
no matter what I witnessed with my own two eyes, could not
touch, or tell of with any true feeling.

"When you spoke with Mr. Yano, did he know about the
affair, Miss Saito?" the detective was asking me. I might have
imagined a change in his tone, ever so slight. It made my
living-room seem small, just the two of us in it.

"Of course," I replied.

"You know that for a fact?"

"Of course he'd suspected for a long time. A man knows
his own wife, detective," I declared brazenly, slightly impatient
with him. He must know these things, I thought; I'd spied
the wedding band on his finger at our first meeting. "He
must have gone to her with his suspicions, don't you think?"

"I see," the detective said, but he wasn't writing anything into his notebook. "What did you argue about with Mr. Yano, Miss Saito?"

"That woman is mistaken," I said, keeping the disdain from my voice. I thought for a moment. "I slipped on a patch of mud at one point, I think, and Mr. Yano helped me catch my balance," I said. "That must have been what she saw. People jump to all sorts of conclusions," I added irritably.

"True enough."

"She got it completely mixed up," I said.

"Is that right?" the detective remarked. A laziness seeped into his tone. "How so?" He glanced at me almost absent-mindedly, doodling, it seemed, in his notebook. His heavy lids appeared to droop. I was about to explain that, though we'd spoken that morning, it had in fact been the night before that Yano and I had words.

I was about to say that it had been late, creeping past my bedtime, following the afternoon I'd met with Chisako. I'd rarely been out at such an hour; the darkness had a different quality, a density that pressed in on me. Yano was late coming out with the dog for its nightly walk. I recall seeing every house lit up in the row across the way, and growing cold waiting in the biting wind that swept across the field that night. The wind wound and howled around me, tossing up the flaps of my coat, and when the dog came it bellowed strangely with each gust, and I strained to be heard above it all: I shouted each loathsome word louder and louder, as loud as I could, to make Yano understand. The secret torn from my throat, cast to the wind. How grateful I was for the cover of night. After it was done, and I saw, even in the dark, that Yano had grasped my meaning, I felt purged, having done my duty. I had no doubts; no doubts at all. For I knew what Chisako expected of me, hoped of me, though it had remained unspoken. Limp, will-less doll, limp before her desires, she needed me to act for her. To clearly speak them.

I resolved to leave him there with his thoughts; not to exert any influence on him as to how he might now act. But as I stepped away his hand gripped my shoulder, close to the neck, where the bones meet; I felt it through my sweater and raincoat as he pulled me back. "Chotto." Wait.

"I don't believe you," he said into my ear, as biting as the wind. His hand still holding my shoulder. I thought his breath would be foul, curdled, but it wasn't. He pinched me tighter when I didn't answer. Of course he'd already known, I told myself. Long before. A man knows his wife. He knows. He shook me, and finally I struggled free.

"Mixed up?" the detective was saying to the confusion on my face. "You said Mrs. Frean got things mixed up. What did you mean, Miss Saito?"

Now I truly was confused. For it occurred to me that Mrs. Frean probably could not have seen that night when I wrested myself from Yano's grip, because it was too dark. Her lights had been on, which only turns the night to slate beyond your window, once you look past your own reflection. Perhaps it had been the next day, that morning, when she saw us and assumed we were arguing.

We'd been circling, circling, once, twice, three times around the field, looping the towers. I'd grown tired. We'd halted at the north tower. Suddenly Yano grabbed hold of the steel rails and shook, shook with all his might, so that a rattling echoed into the thickly clouded sky. I looked away and fixed my eyes on Mackenzie Hill in the distance, as one steady, immovable thing, expecting Yano to stop after a few seconds. But he kept on, as if trying to uproot the whole tower.

I stood there stupidly, not watching, but hearing the rattle go on, and his hectic, laboured breath. As I backed away, he finally stopped, gasping: "Why did you tell me? Why?" Quietly, but there was violence lurking in those words, on their underside. He came close, sickly sweat rolling off his face, his neck, splotching his jacket at the armpits. He held out his hands to me and there were faint lines of blood pressed into them. "Stop, stop!" I cried out.

"Why? Why did you tell me?" He stood there, gasping still. I feared another of his seizures coming on.

"I thought you knew," I stammered.

He shook his head in a resigned yet frightening way. "You should have left it to Chisako."

I shrugged innocently. "I didn't mean to...I thought she'd already told you...." I was a child fretful with excuses.

"What do I tell my girl and my boy now?" he asked weakly, plaintively. "What do I say?" Like Chisako, almost begging me, in her helplessness, to do something.

"Tell them nothing," I said simply, seizing my chance to be strong. "Leave them out of it."

"How can I?" Yano held onto the beams of the tower again, but this time only to stop himself from wobbling. "We're a family." The sky was suffocating; its thick clouds would neither move nor dissipate.

"Yesterday," he said, slowly regaining himself, "it was you waiting for me," and he jabbed his thumb towards me, then at his chest, to make his point. I felt the old irritation return. He shook his head again, in that manly way that shows regret for an action that must be taken, whatever the consequences. He lurched towards me and I stumbled back in alarm; he grabbed me roughly by the shoulders, but at the same time his body leaned into me, drained and weakened. I must have cried out, tried to push him away, and perhaps that was the instant witnessed by Mrs. Frean. He steadied himself, then released me.

"I don't blame you for telling me, Saito-san," he said, with a ruthless eye, as an untrusting stranger would, protecting his own. "I wish you hadn't. I didn't need to know. But it's done." He shook his head again, in that same way. Muttered, half to himself. I knew the words but I did not then understand what he intended by them. "Mottai-nai," he'd said. What a waste. What Mama would say when Papa threw out scraps of left-overs, when we had so little to begin with.

"Miss Saito." The detective's voice intruded once again. This time he was wide awake, and suddenly insistent. "You'll have to speak up," he said. He sat forward, his notebook on his knee. He'd been scribbling away. He paused. "So you told him?"

"Yes, but he already knew," I said. My heart was beating fast now, and I felt warm, feverish. "He knew," I insisted. I clung tight to those words, Chisako's words. "A man knows—"

"His wife. Yes, you said that."

For a moment everything slowed, and I saw it all with clarity. I saw Yano's expressionless face in the darkness of that night. I stared at the detective as if he were Yano himself. "He might have thought he didn't know," I said carefully, determined to sort this out; understanding things for the first time myself. "But he did," I said with conviction. "He did." I calmed myself with this insight. Yet my heart was still pounding in my chest, pounding in its cage.

The detective was truly agitated now; he blinked several times, trying to comprehend something in his head; he inched so close to the edge of the chair that I thought he'd fall off. "Miss Saito, tell me if you can, please. Did Mr. Yano become angry when you talked to him about this?"

"The first time, yes, you could say—"

"You spoke to him more than once?"

I nodded and continued, determined to keep my train of thought. "The second time he was more resigned. But angry then too, I think." It was difficult to sum up, even as I saw how impatient the detective was. Angry, not angry—it wasn't that simple.

"Miss Saito, did you know that he'd bought a gun?" The detective was staring so hard at me that it was difficult to concentrate. My heart went on, no less violently.

"Not then I didn't," I said. "If I'd known... Of course, I read about it in the newspaper."

"Was Mr. Yano angry enough to use that gun?"

"I really couldn't say. I couldn't imagine...." I trailed off. A gun, a gun. I tried to comprehend. The detective was about to ask another question, but I forged on. "I wasn't afraid of him," I offered, and I could feel my heart skipping, pounding randomly, and myself seeping away in those missed beats. "He wasn't dangerous," I said, frantic to convince him. "I'm sure he wasn't. Not at all."

The detective seemed not to hear me. "Did he know about the lot in the woods, Miss Saito?"

"I wasn't afraid," I repeated, sternly, I thought, but my voice veered high and away. "Do you understand?"

The detective shifted back in his chair; smiled in a kindly yet forced way, to calm me down. But the falseness of his smile only made me more desperate.

I tried to recall the feel of things, the sounds that night, my voice and his, but the wind, the dog's howl, everything buzzed deafeningly in my head, like a threat. The detective's face blurred. His questions churned relentlessly in my mind; without logic, without meaning, they buzzed into the hive. For if Yano had not known about the parking lot, I tried to think—if he'd not known where to find Chisako and Mr. Spears, if he was enraged enough, desperate enough...Did I tell him? Did I know he'd bought a gun from Canadian Tire? Had I seen him take it from his trunk, or put it in? Had I seen him lead Tam and Kimi to his navy Pontiac that afternoon? Had I imagined it, dreamed it? For couldn't I see them now: two little soldiers dutifully climbing into the back seat of that car? Could he do such a thing? Was he capable? What had I seen? What did I know? What had I done?

"I'm sorry, detective," I stammered stupidly. "I'm quite tired now," I heard myself say, with surprising calm. "Exhausted, in fact." Behind my words, the hive was a fierce whirr. Behind that, a distant sound, a familiar rattle and creak. The clunk of a car door shutting; footsteps. "If we

could continue another time, when my brother, Stum—"
Stum was all I could think. *Stum. Tsutomu. Tell me what I know.
What to say.*

"Miss Saito?"

"Yes?"

"Did you tell Mr. Yano about the parking lot?"

"I don't know. I don't know," I sputtered. I wanted to cry,
to scream; I groped for some release but I was dry, dry.

But then Stum, my Stum, my Tsutomu was there with
me. Traipsing into the living-room, paper bag rolled under
his arm, the twang of the screen door behind him. Gazing
at me, not with suspicion. Neither timid nor irked, but tender. Loving. Towering above me, the two men shook hands.
Stum had never stood so tall, so straight. My ototo-san.
I was exhausted. I felt the tears coming. Soon. I longed for
sleep.

Stum sat down opposite the detective, faced him. "Yano
knew about the parking lot," he said. "He knew everything.
For a long time. Months maybe. Yes sir. He told me so."

Stum shut the door and at last the man was gone. I could
only stare numbly at a patch of carpet, lost in its minute
canyons. I watched my brother's feet shuffle over that patch,
halting before me. Such a familiar sight, those broad, stubby
feet in their worn, stretched brogues. Shoes I'd bought for
him. Beloved sight. I could not raise my eyes to him. "Ne-
san," he gently prodded. Then, finally, I was violently seized:
I sobbed and sobbed. What had I done? A monster, that was
what I was, what I'd always been. I could not stop. *No, ne-san,
no. He knew, he knew, it wasn't your fault. Asako.* The words drifted

down as I sank, a dead weight. I was drowning, drowning; a sensation I knew so well; slipping away, but I would not reach out, not this time.

"Ne-san, stop," Stum was urging. "Please." So calm. "It wasn't you."

His hand on my sleeve. "It was me," he said. "I told him."

I tried to push him away but he stayed put. Stum could not save me. No one could. I would not allow it. I simply nodded at that patch of carpet, pretending to accept his kindness. His lie. I stared at his shoes, and finally they stepped back.

"Are you all right, ne-san?" the voice from above said.

"Yes, I'm fine."

"We still don't know, ne-san."

"We don't, no."

"I have to leave now." He gave a sigh; his feet made a half-turn, then paused. "Those flowers, they're no good now. I'll bring you some fresh from the supermarket tomorrow. Let me throw them out."

"No, no. I just cut them." I waved him away.

"I'll be back tomorrow. You all right?"

"Yes, yes."

I watched his feet lift, one then the other, then shuffle towards the door. Heard the crunch of that paper bag rolled under his arm. Out the door, down the porch steps they went, into the car and away.

I sat for I don't know how long. Performed my duties for the rest of the day, feeding Papa, settling him in for the night. Each time returning to my armchair, unable to bear the day's final routine climbing of the stairs, the steps down the hall, the desolation of my room at the end of it. In front of the window I sat through the night. Not bothering to close the drapes. No wind, no birds, no children. The darkness thick, like snow, settling on me, piling up silently. My limbs drained of blood and feeling. From the corner of my eye, I glimpsed my drooping flowers, gone black. Outside, the clouds stayed black, invisible in the night. The end of the world. I slept a short, blank sleep.

The door must have been left open for I heard nothing, no familiar knock, until Sachi was standing in the hallway. The sky, the clouds, all blindingly bright, starting to move with the sun. Sachi teetering on her limbs, skinny and spindly as a wishbone, outlined by the light. The dog beside her, panting. The morning paper, still rolled up, dangled from one hand; her other hand lingered over the dog's finely shaped head. It raised its nose to sniff at her, no longer cowering. Slowly the newspaper slipped from her hand and dropped to the floor. She let it sprawl there, and watched, like a cat that has dragged in a carcass.

There it was: bottom corner, front page, that same family picture they'd run before, this time with only Tam and Kimi and Yano. Where Chisako had been, a sliver of her dress showed, a line at the very edge remained. Beneath it: *Man shoots son, daughter, and self.*

Everything was quivering, everywhere I looked. Tiny quivers, side to side, quick. Sachi looked blank, numb. The floor under my feet began to sink, pitched to one side, the house was falling, the things in it trembling. I held a hand out to the wall to steady myself; we stopped sinking.

Sachi took a step closer. "Keiko won't let me keep it," she declared, her voice too loud, too clear in my ears. She knelt down beside the animal, leaned her head against its fur. Obediently it sat, its dainty paws lined up, the wildness I'd glimpsed in it banished.

"I wish it was Tam's," she cried.

"Maybe it is," I might have said, "in its heart." I could not bear to look into the creature's gleaming, helpless eyes. Eyes that did not blink, like Tam's. But I could not conjure him up, not his eyes or any part of his face.

I left her sitting in my chair at the window, with the dog at her feet. Went into the kitchen and began pouring a glass of milk, arranging cookies on a plate, too many. I stalled there for a time. She was staring across at the Yanos' house when I returned, its empty window, and fingering a darkened petal in one hand. I set down the plate and glass, not daring to touch, to pat her back or smooth her hair. I did not deserve that.

I bent down beside her. "I might have been the cause of all this," I whispered by her ear, choking, just as Yano had whispered his refusal to believe into mine. I could no longer endure myself. In that dark night with Yano, Chisako's secret burning in my throat, aching to be let out. His face, how it looked in the dark; the next morning.

"No, no, no, no," Sachi muttered, over and over, wincing with hurt eyes, flailing her arms against me. She didn't want to listen. She got up, shoved the dog aside. "No, Miss Saito. You don't know," she said, making no sense, flustered, cringing, her cries tearless and dry, coming from her throat like raised dust. She pushed at the air that crowded her, bruised her. "There are things you don't know." She banged her leg against my table and the untouched glass of milk tumbled to the floor. She tore out of the house, the door shuddering behind her. From my window I saw the wind come alive to whip her dress and her hair as she darted out to the field first, then doubled back towards the creek. She was gone. By my feet, the dog was licking the spilled milk from the carpet. I pushed the creature aside to scrub the spot with my kitchen sponge, scrubbing and scrubbing in spite of my exhaustion, greater than any I'd ever felt. The dog sat silently beside me as I went on, wearing down the pile. I could not stop. As I scrubbed, the flesh of my hand grew pink.

On the carpet the newspaper lay where Sachi had dropped it. The words, the miniature faces blurring as I went on with my scrubbing, back and forth.

It felt natural that Yano's dog should be here with me now, I thought, settling into my bed at midday, strapping myself in between the sheets. Strangely so. I considered retrieving Eiji's picture from the drawer downstairs but my body would not move. The thought of that photo sitting inside its darkened drawer, silent, serene, was more comfort than I deserved: Eiji at rest, intact, as I now wished to be. The mattress gently buckled as the animal eased itself up beside me to rest its small head on my hip, tickling me in the slight dip beneath the bone there, not used to touch even through the thickness of my covers. So I dozed, my hand buried in the soft fur at the dog's neck. A fever crept into me instead of sleep, a hotness went into my bones, my head. I wanted to sleep. I wanted peace.

At last I did sleep. A dreamless sleep that floats you on its surface. The kind of sleep you have only in daytime. Yet somewhere, somehow, in the midst of it, I realized that I understood Yano utterly and completely. *What will I tell my girl and my boy?* he'd asked me in desperation. *We're a family,* he'd said, answering himself. *A family.*

Of course I understood. *No good,* he'd said. *No good. Dame.* All along I'd understood. How one thing turns everything bad, taints all of it, and there is no going back. There is no return. For hadn't I longed for that too, a hundred, a thousand times? Hadn't I fooled myself into believing it possible? The slate wiped clean. The electrical field in winter, glimpsed from my window after a night of snowfall. Almost pristine that December afternoon I'd sat with Chisako at the bus stop, before my walk home, before I sank my footprints into it. And when I did, how I'd wanted to take them back, to somehow erase them.

Asa, Asa-chan. Someone was calling. I did not want to wake up. But the voice was sweet and reassuring; a woman's. Like no voice I knew. It was pleasing in my ear, drawing me in. I could have resisted but I did not. I was too weak. I cared too much for myself. A hand, a hand that did not go with the voice, was shaking my arm, shaking it like a rattle.

Asako, please wake up. Wake up.

I opened my eyes to find Angel sitting on my bed, leaning over me in concern. Beside her, gripping my arm, was Sachi. She was pale, the rims of her eyes raw and pink, my wise child, wizened and old. Waiting. The pleading in her eyes at once brought back all I'd left behind. Her hand was cold on my arm, a touch that chilled, another reminder, and without thinking I recoiled. Immediately I cupped her icy hand in the two of mine, but it was too late. Her eyes clouded over, became distant, unreachable.

"Asako, you slept for two straight days. We were worried about you!" Angel exclaimed. "We even called Dr. Honda to make a housecall."

"Two days?" My voice was a croak from nothing passing through for such a time. It seemed incredible. So much time. And yet nothing had changed. Nothing was forgiven.

"You were grieving," Angel said, momentarily solemn. "For your friends."

"Sachi, are you all right?" I asked. Stupid, stupid question. I tightened my grip on her hand. Nothing could warm either one of us, at least not now.

"She's been brave," Angel answered, patting Sachi's head.

I stopped myself from saying his name, the one first on my lips. Sachi pulled her hand free. She got up and went to the window, listless but calm. She began to hum faintly, something she never did, fingering a small black box left on the sill. That song of hers I recognized from before, about how easy it was to love someone who is beautiful. With that long and piercing high note that gradually fell at the end of its chorus.

"They're all...? Yano?"

"The newspaper says yes," Angel replied.

Stum hovered by the door, too shy, it seemed, to enter my room in Angel's presence. But Angel waved him in. "Come, come. Say good afternoon to your sleepy-head sister." He stumbled in, nearly tripping on my small throw rug.

He bent down beside me. "Genki, ne-san? Are you all right?" He said this as if I were fragile, a feather he might blow away with a big breath. I looked around me. My room, usually so dark, so dry and folded in shadows, had never felt so bright, so open.

"She's very genki," Angel said.

"Genki," I said. "Much better now. Thank you." And as I said this, I did thank him with all my heart. Silently I poured out my love. I thought I might cry, not knowing why or for whom. Perhaps it was only pity for myself.

"The dog...," I muttered, the instant its absence struck me. I strained up from my pillow to search the floor around the bed. A little rush of panic.

"Shush, shush, Asako," Angel said, gently pushing me down. She went to the open window overlooking our yard, stood beside Sachi to show me, as if I were a slow child. I didn't mind. She leaned her head out and cooed. "Yuki. Yuki," she called, and a familiar whimper and bark rose up, sifted through other yard sounds. "She's just fine, Asako. Don't worry." She gave a kindly pat to Sachi's head, which the girl flinched from.

But now there was an insistent press into the palm of my hand. A dig of nails into my flesh that was almost painful. Angel and Stum exchanged a knowing glance, then moved towards the door together. "They didn't suffer, Asako," Angel said gently. Then, "We'll be downstairs." Such ease, no longer the stranger, the guest in my home. It did not pain me. I did not mind when I saw her slip her hand into my brother's on the way out.

I twisted my head to see Sachi better as she let herself be

pulled nearer to me on the bed. I caressed her hands, careful where there were fresh cuts deeper and longer than usual. Her hands were grey and cold: bloodless, like mine. I no longer had words for her; I had nothing to explain. The terrible urgency I'd felt to tell her what I'd done, how I was to blame; the burning wish to unburden myself, selfish, selfish wish: I let go of it all. She dropped her head onto my breast, ear to my heart. The scent of her crushed close, young and unspoiled. She'd never let me hold her like this before. She squinched her eyes shut, tight, because everything hurt.

"Miss Saito," she whispered. A harsh, sandpaper whisper.

"Yes, Sachi."

"Miss Saito, you have to take me." Her hands were clawing my hands, my forearms under the covers.

"Take you where?"

"To that place. The ravine."

"It's no use, Sachi. He's gone," I said, as gently as I could. The words lifting off my tongue, light as air. She dug her nails into my arm then, making me feel my own callousness, my heartlessness.

"They could've made a mistake," she said, sucking her breath sharply. "A mistake."

She clung to me like a monkey, hugging me, stabbing me, all the while humming snatches of that song. I didn't know whether to hold her tighter or push her away. I couldn't help remembering her clinging to Tam this ferociously, her legs climbing. Their bodies rolling and twisting once the game was almost over and they'd stopped taking turns, so her back was to me, and he held still, letting her do it all, and I saw his face above her shoulder, what she couldn't see.

So fierce and aching, it pained me to see. Looking so much like Chisako.

"Please," he'd groaned. I'd seen him with Yano countless times, a small, stiff soldier, doing what he was told.

"Tell me," Sachi had coaxed. "Come on." She was smiling, I knew, though I could not see her face. Because he wanted it, he'd pointed to it in the game. I could tell the tone in her voice. The teasing. Holding out what she knew you wanted most, making you reach for it. She nudged him with her shoulder, giggling. He seemed to stare right at me crouching among the bushes, yet did not see me.

"Chin chin," he whispered at last, and his face broke open, the fear giving in to her. That baby word. I saw her take his hand and push it down the front of the light blue jeans she wore that day, planting it in the dainty jungle there, her mystery. She was never gentle, with him or herself; she pushed and pushed when his hands were like spiders. I'd stuffed my fist in my mouth to stop from gasping, snorting, from crying out, I don't know what. But I saw their faces, both of them, I saw how they looked. Her mystery.

Sachi's tears were spilling onto my chest like sweat; they ran between my breasts.

"Please. Miss Saito, Miss Saito. I have to go. I have to."

I heard the dog just then, its plaintive bark echoing up through the window. "What about the dog?" I said, reaching for something, anything, to distract her. "Tam's dog. Go see her, she needs you to stay with her."

"He should've shot the stupid dog!"

She sobbed onto my breast; sobbed and sobbed. I felt the front of her teeth press against my skin; her lips pulled back, trembling. Her cries a keening in my ears. "Please take me, Miss Saito! Please!"

"It won't do any good."

"It will! It will do good! Don't you know, Miss Saito?" She groaned as if physically pained. One hand went to her temple, the fingers stiffened and flayed. She held it there as if against an intense flash of light. Then she drew herself up and brought her lips to my ear, pressed them right inside it. "I have to see him." A bird's whisper.

"Sachi, I—"

"Don't you trust me?" Her lips tickled my ear. She relaxed her body into mine, willing herself to be patient.

"I trust you," I said.

"Then take me!" she cried.

"No, Sachi, no," I murmured.

"Keiko will never. Only you, Miss Saito. Please!"

"I can't." We both heard it: for the first time I was saying no to her.

She tore herself from me then, grabbing that small black box from the windowsill. She ran down the hall. I heard the rumble of her feet on the stairs, and the slam of the door that vibrated upward; a distant cry I couldn't make out. Outside the dog began yelping and did not stop. The coldness stole over my breast, the wetness of her tears abruptly chilled; the child gone from me.

EIGHT

I SAW THE SPOT in my mind, in Yano's mind, the place
he would have chosen. A place seemingly untouched.
A temple in the forest. A place Sachi would know how to
find. She would have done anything to get there—hitchhike,
cycle, if it took all day and all night. The sight of Sachi's
hands, the snaking cuts along them, filled my head; her voice,
ominous: *There are things you don't know....* And at the same
moment, a lurid slash of yellow at the side of the road
caught my eye. I backed up to find a police ribbon tagging a
tree. I parked the car. The trees and bushes were too green
and lush and sparkling from the rain. I sprang from the car.
I could be too late: the air felt spent. Already the sun was
dropping.

The dog tumbled out after me. It paused in front of a
dirt path, glared at me with its quick, dark eyes, and darted
down among the trees. I went after it, lurching clumsily, for

I hadn't exercised in days, weeks, bedridden for what seemed like an eternity. Twigs and leaves scratched my cheeks, poked my eyes, I didn't care; and orange sunlight needled in between the trees. Just ahead, only the white blur of the dog. With every step my feet in those stupid shoes sank into the muck from the rain, but the white ball kept rolling down. Abruptly it vanished, and I reached an empty clearing, gasping for breath. There it was, sitting obedient as could be on the grass, as if Yano had ordered it to sit. Only its tongue flopped wildly, not fitting back in its mouth.

I clapped my hands, cracking the air. It had to move, had to tell me where to go, where to find Sachi. "Yuki!" I shouted. "What is it, girl? What is it?" I tried to talk to it as she did, as if it were human, as if it were wise, but still it sat panting, staring; wanting to move, it seemed, but compelled to sit. I scanned for more police markers, for signs of disarray. But nothing.

I was deep down in the ravine, far from any source of light, far from the sky. There was the creek, the same creek that ran behind our house, now rushing wide and fast, brown and swollen from the rain. The place where Sachi had skipped across the creek on stones was miniature, remote in my memory, miles away. Everything was too big here, dwarfing me as in a dream, and I felt lost, shrunken. Where was Sachi? Was I too late? For what, I didn't know, I couldn't think. I shooed the visions of her welted hands from my head. I began walking, following the creek as fast as I could, urged on by the current, full of force and omens. I called to the dog but still it wouldn't come. I looked back to where I had landed, now a distance off, but no one else came.

No one. Hours earlier I'd pulled myself from my bed, crossed the electrical field, climbed the steps of that house I'd never been welcomed into, knocked on their door, to say what? To do what? It was only for Sachi that I found myself there, obeying my conscience. To tell Keiko, to warn her of I didn't know what. I had to say it, the danger of what she might do. To act unselfishly for once, urging a mother to her child. Not to come between them.

They'd stood there dumbly, Keiko and Tom, tired from work, I could see that. Nothing to say. They would wait, stupidly silent, never ask why I was there; why their daughter came to me and not to her mother to confide every single thing, everything that mattered. Too proud, too timid to ask me, to have asked her in the first place. I thought of Yano then, amid the salty smells of shoyu and fish, familiar smells that did not lessen my discomfort. I thought of what he'd said about our shame.

I told them about the ravine, the park named in the newspaper, frantic because every moment counted. I don't know if I made any sense, if I conveyed what I meant to. What was at stake. I spied the ghost of a smile on Keiko's lips, slow in showing itself—that amusement at my expense, at Sachi's. Wasting precious time.

"You must believe me," I said, breathless.

"Sachi has a mind of her own," Keiko finally declared. Of course she would speak first, hard woman that she was. Indignant that I should be telling her about her own daughter, her own blood. "Don't make a fuss, Miss Saito," she snapped. It was a command, an order.

"It's Asako," I barked back. I don't know why, in the

middle of all my worry over Sachi, I had to say it. Refused to be that old schoolmarm to them. Keiko's mouth hung open. "My name is Asako," I repeated, ready to walk out.

"She would never keep still, even when she was little," Keiko said suddenly. Looking at me to say, *You must understand.* "She wouldn't keep quiet." As if that was the worst thing to be in the world, not quiet. For once I saw how desperate they were, how angry. "She'd scream and scream." Keiko looked to Tom anxiously, pointed at him to share it. "Once he even had to throw water over her to calm her down."

But she was only a child, a child! The thought pounded in my head. Why couldn't Keiko see that? A child.

"What?" She was staring at me, the hoods lifting from her eyes, now bright, exposed. "What did you say? Asako?"

Slowly I repeated what must have slipped out. "She's only a child," I told her, careful to keep the accusation from my voice.

We stood in silence, we three, I unable to leave, unable to entrust her to them.

"It's the boy," Tom finally said, in his brusque, clumsy way, watching himself tap his smallish foot, in brown Hush Puppies. He reminded me of Stum then, unbearably awkward, unbearably timid. For all the bluster, it was difficult for him to speak up to a woman, to Keiko. But in an instant he could, like a man, surprise you with a glimmer of what was going on inside, what you'd never fathomed there before. Tom knew about Sachi and Tam, more than he might have known from carting her away from the electrical tower that day. More than I thought he'd ever try to find out. "She and the boy used to go to the hill together, and the creek." He lifted his smooth muscular arm in the air and let it drop. It was beyond him to say more.

"Ara?" My first time hearing Japanese from Keiko's lips. The helplessness in that exclamation, what even she fell back on. She looked from Tom to me and back again, stunned, in panic: what she didn't know, had never been told. Could not have guessed, when the rest of us had. "Why didn't she tell me?" Keiko half shouted, and in those moments of fury, of humiliation, I knew Sachi would be forgotten.

"She'll be back," Keiko declared, calm and hard once more. "She always comes back to me," she said. This to hurt me, I suppose.

I withdrew then. Leaving her to them. I resisted every impulse in me to stay.

"Miss Saito." I heard Tom call after me, half-hearted, divided between us. Calling me "Miss" again. But nothing more.

I let myself out and faced my trek across the field. It was alive with echoes, a minefield. It was the kind of day—misty and changeable with rain and bursts of intense sunlight— that could have brought on one of Yano's attacks. Such a day as when I, striding along, was called back by that stooped, wheezing man, his breath stopped. For a moment vulnerable, choking. What if I'd hurried home to my window, left him there? What if?

At my window once more, I waited, watching for them to get into their car, to go to her. But they did not. I blamed Keiko, blamed her with all my heart. Cold, cold woman, I must have muttered, over and over. As Chisako had called me.

I waited, trembling with anger. Stum and Angel tried to get me back to my bed, not understanding, but I refused. Stum knelt beside me. No longer the suitor, he shook my arm: overgrown, inarticulate boy, late in learning his own strength. I could not begin to explain to him. It upset him to see me like this, his strong, capable ne-san, but I could no longer look after him; he had his Angel. Then Angel laid her hand on his shoulder, to calm him. "She blames herself, Tsutomu," she cooed, saying his name with as much care as I ever did. "Poor thing," she sang. I could not be consoled by her, ignorant as she was of my part in all that had happened. What I was coming to understand.

"Please, ne-san," Stum pleaded. "Stop this. Please." He bent close, rasped: "The man was a kamikaze." Believing it would heal me, vindicate me to hear this. He clung to the word without knowing what it truly meant. It could only be a picture in his head, as it was in mine: a newspaper cartoon of hideous flying insect-men plummeting in flames. Photographs of Japanese soldiers in magazines, squashed faces, hundreds and hundreds of them, all the same. Not one recognizable. Not one Yano. In spite of all I now knew him to be.

At last I left. Tiptoed past Angel and Stum huddled together on the chesterfield, finally surrendering to their own exhaustion. They stirred against one another as I carefully retrieved Stum's car keys from his jacket and slipped out the back door. The dog followed me from the backyard to the car, the silent, knowing ally Sachi had always believed it to be.

The woods now crowded thick around me, dense, impenetrable. The creek roared low in my ears, out of sight. The dog was long lost behind me. Above, in the narrow sky, birds swooped down and up, recklessly, it seemed, their wide wings buckled by the wind. The air was close, insects brushed my face.

Kamikaze. Stum's fireflies—nightmarish creatures, really, seen up close, their bellies in flames. Yano came to me once again, unbidden. "Kamikaze were very clean, Saito-san," he was saying. Smiling a strange, shy smile. We were sitting in my garden on a sunny afternoon three weeks earlier, under a wide-open, blazing blue sky. He was not so ugly to me that day. He wore fresh, clean clothes; even his fingernails, habitually long and dirty, had been clipped. He was a different person. Almost handsome. Yet clownish and sad, because he was being deceived at that very moment, and I, as a favour to Chisako, was helping.

She'd telephoned me that morning. Mr. Spears had dared to call her at home, she told me breathlessly. His wife had gone away for the day and he wanted to see Chisako. Demanded to, spilling with passion for her, which she was helpless to resist; herself burning in his eyes. I could barely stand to hear it, the excited twitter in my ear that would not stop. "I have to see him, Asako. Only you understand. You're the only one." She was relentless; she would not let me go. She'd scurry to a side-street deep in the neighbourhood, unrecognized; the eely shimmer of that beige Eldorado catching the light as it pulled up beside her. Her tiny feet in high heels lifting from the pavement, one, then the other.

"The kamikaze cleansed themselves and prayed before they flew off to die for the emperor," Yano was explaining. How had we gotten on to that? The war? His years in Japan?

He was different that day; even the way he spoke, without the usual roughness. On his best behaviour because I'd let him into my house. He sat up straight in the lawn chair I'd set out for him, sipping his tea. "Ocha is good," he said, holding up his cup a little too eagerly. "You keep your house clean, Saito-san." He twisted in his chair to look back through the kitchen window. "Better than Chisako," he laughed. "It's like a temple, ne?" he said gravely. Mocking me, perhaps, but I couldn't be sure. "Today I cleaned myself up to enter your temple." He laughed and patted his pressed white shirt.

It was not long before Yano slipped into his familiar rant, much as he'd tried to hold himself back, keep up his good behaviour. "They were hoping we'd all commit hara-kiri in the camps, don't you think, Saito-san?" He laughed a dull, sour roar, but it pierced me just the same. "People say it wasn't so bad. Easy to say now. But it was bad, wasn't it, Saito-san?"

Abruptly he fell into a sheepish silence, realizing how he'd already misbehaved. It was bad, I suppose: the waiting, not knowing how long, Papa not knowing how he would start up again once we got out. Stupidly, I kept thinking of that boot stuck in the mud in front of our shack, stuck all through one winter until the snow melted. How I waited for someone to claim it. Wondered how a person could lose one boot and not come back.

He cleared his throat. "You know, Saito-san, there were a few who did kill themselves. Out of shame."

"Don't exaggerate," I scolded, but he ignored me, staring out beyond our neatly fenced yard—drifted, almost dreamily.

"I thought about it myself," he murmured. "Once or twice."
In an instant he came back, alert, watchful. "How about you,
Saito-san?"

I must have stuttered then, utterly confused, for Yano,
seeing me, was suddenly remorseful, and waved a hand in the
air, shooing his words away like bad air. "Remember how I
brought you and Chisako together? The ikebana? Chisako
didn't have any idea. And here I am. We stick together now,
don't we, Saito-san?" Already his face had begun to assume
its old ugliness, the freshness worn away in spite of the gleam
of his white shirt.

"At last Chisako's making new friends," he went on
brightly. "I don't have to worry about her any more, ne?"

I shook my head.

"She's been working overtime for her hakujin boss. Some
important executive, she says." He guffawed. "No extra pay."
He tilted his chair back to survey the sky. "I tell her, make
him pay. Who does he think he is?" He shook his fist, about
to pound the table I'd set out beside him, but stopped
himself, looking sheepish. Instead he downed his tea in one
scalding gulp. "These hakujin think they can do anything
they please, ne, Saito-san? We're just mushi they can squash."
He swiped at the air as if to catch a fly. "Same old story,
right?"

I rose with my teapot to refill his cup, stumbling on the
uneven grass, and before I knew it the hot liquid flew out the
spout onto his shirt. He stifled a cry.

"Gomen, gomen," I muttered. I dabbed at his shirt and
the spreading stain I saw there.

"Iie, iie. It's okay." He stood up and stepped back, away

from me. For the first time in Yano's presence, I felt my own clumsiness.

"It's all right, Saito-san," he repeated, examining himself. Abruptly he unbuttoned and removed the shirt, rolled it into a ball, and dropped it to the ground. Stood there crudely without an undershirt, but I saw a reddened patch of skin on his chest. "It's an old shirt anyway," he said, though it appeared hardly worn. I bent down to retrieve it. "Let me wash it for you," I started to say but he snatched the shirt from my hands so roughly that it burned my palms.

"Please," I said, reaching for it again. "Allow me."

"No, no, Saito-san. You shouldn't wash for me," Yano said more firmly, and no sooner had I opened my mouth to insist once again than the tearing of cloth startled the air; he'd ripped the shirt in two. I could only stare at the tatters held in each of his hands. The man was crazy.

"You see, Saito-san, it's no good. Nothing but a cheap old shirt of no value, really. Anyway, green tea doesn't stain, you know that." Without another word, we both settled back in our chairs.

Then I could only stare at the ground, the thickening, deepening grass under us, and a small mushroom that had sprouted under Yano's chair. "It's getting chilly," I said. "I'll lend you one of Stum's shirts." I half rose. I needed to be relieved of his company, if only for a few moments; to have him clothed and covered.

"No, no, Saito-san, don't bother. You know me. Cold-blooded. A snake." He smiled his jumble-toothed smile.

This time I did not insist. I could not help noticing that, for a nihonjin, Yano had a fair bit of hair on his chest; not as much as hakujin men in magazines or on TV, but more than Stum or Papa, or Eiji. Thinking back, it was ridiculous, even obscene, to be sitting in my backyard with Yano like that, and yet I remained there, continuing to sip my tea politely. Relieved, I suppose, to have Yano's comments about Chisako and her Mr. Spears diverted, to not have him ask me anything.

I felt sullied by the memory of Yano and that whole afternoon; I despised myself for letting him occupy my mind, for granting him the slightest bit of understanding. After all, wasn't this running through of events in my head a way of making sense of all that had happened, of the unspeakable act Yano had committed? How could there be any sense, any understanding? I wanted him out of my thoughts. Away from me.

Yet he stayed, as he had that day, as I'd let him. In these woods his voice kept intruding, his face. Too close, too alive. "Hear that?" he'd said, and I'd heard nothing. Before I could stop him, he'd sailed into my living-room, scampered up the stairs. I had found him with Papa, tipping a glass of water to his lips. "Ojiisan, genki? How are you, old man?" Such tenderness from such a crazy, half-clothed man.

"He's holding on tight, isn't he, Saito-san?" Yano whispered as he set the glass down. Yes, I thought to myself, observing the purse of Papa's thin, thin lips.

"I would not," Yano stated, watching Papa in his bed, the trickles of water from the corners of his mouth. Watching without a trace of distaste or hint of recoil. "You would not either, Saito-san, would you? Not with your pride. We're not so different, you and I."

I said nothing. But to myself I thought: no, I would not.
I knew better. Papa on my back, the jut of his bones into my
sides. The burden of him, my chances meagre as they were,
dwindled down to so little. My life. Yano was watching me
closely, slyly. He wanted to make me see how little difference
there was between us. Between me and a murderer; brutal,
brutal man. Yano had meant to leave no burden behind, but
he had.

It was late and the light in the ravine was changing; bright-
ening in that muted way that showed up every beating thing
in the air before dying away. I could fool myself into believing it was an afternoon like any other by the creek behind
my house, when I'd find Sachi with Tam in that spot by the
willow, spy their tipped-over cans of soda, their jackets flung
onto the grass, arms wrung inside out. I'd never meant to
stay. No more, I told myself. I ran home, snagging my stockings, sweating like a pig, praying I'd get there without anyone
seeing, before Stum arrived from work.

I started to run now, now that I wanted to be caught. I
called out, expecting her to appear at any time but the bushes
here were different, thicker; they smothered my cries. I
stopped, unsure if I should turn back, if I'd been wrong and
she was someplace else. How I longed to be at my window
behind glass, safe and blameless, home free. I longed to take
back time, take back the words to that silly game between
Sachi and Tam. *Chi chi, chikubi, chin chin, chimpo.* I'd convinced
myself it was harmless babble. But word by word I'd sent
them into a forbidden place, so tiny and dark that they would
never climb out. *Tell me, Miss Saito, just this one more word, I won't*

tell anybody. I made her beg for it and cling tighter to me than to her own mother. I whispered in her ear and she raced away, down to the creek or up to the hill to meet him. This web of secret words knit them together, and they fell in love with the feel, the smell, the sound of themselves, held in their bony arms. In love. How she ran home to me, calling my name from far out in the field; how she flew up my steps, eager to report back.

"Tam told me everything," she trilled high up, delirious. "I can't tell so don't ask."

I knew full well that she yearned to tell; my seeming indifference could only tempt her more. For why would this boy's secret not be safe with me? She sat unusually pensive, watching the electrical tower. "He's never told anybody. Not a soul."

I did not press her, not that time. I gave a long sigh, a surrender. She would not betray him for me. It was no longer a game.

And now he was gone. Didn't I know how it felt to be left alone, deserted by the only one who knew you and loved you just the same? Pulled you close, took your secrets and gave some back, and then was gone? I would have done anything to make things the way they were before and to never be alone again.

The dog suddenly zigzagged in front and I let out a shriek. I chased after it as it flew among the bushes and came out alongside the creek. I heard voices, familiar, echoing, but I couldn't tell if they were from memory or if they were real. The dog must have heard the voices too, for it halted and sat again, ears up, obedient once more. One had to be Sachi's;

she had to be all right, but the sound was tinny and monotonous, as if from a radio. Before I could make out a word,
the voices faded. The dog reeled, snapping at air, barking
wildly. "What is it, girl? Where?" I flung myself around
coaxing the dog to some trail, some scent. A small light
pierced my eye then vanished. I nearly collapsed at the sight
of it, the relief; it was her, it had to be her. If I'd blinked I
might have missed it. But the light flashed again, closer this
time, as sharp as ever. As it was on nights when I'd seen that
same beam from my window: Sachi's, tunnelling out of the
darkness to meet a second one, Tam's, flickering across the
electrical field. Then *click* and they disappeared. I thought I
heard the rustle of grasses as they ran to meet one another,
voices overlapping, delirious, but they were far away and my
windows were shut. Long after they were gone I imagined
lines of light, traces of their flashlight beams converging;
incisions healing over in the sky.

I approached the copse where the light had seemed to
come from and called again. Softly, I warned myself, fearful
she might flee, but I heard my own cry, a scream barely held
back. I must have been blind until this moment, because only
now did I glimpse the yellow police ribbon all around,
looped from tree to tree, loosened and tattered, but still
lurid. I glanced down at where I stood, at my feet; could I be
trampling the ground where Tam had lain? Where Yano had
struck himself down? I lifted one foot, then the other, and
beneath was a patch of green flourishing from the rain, clean
from it. Cleansed the way Yano would have wanted.

"Sachi!" I cried. The sound was muffled as in a dream
where the air is a pillow and everything floats, half dead.

"Sachi!" The dog was barking with my cries. I dropped to my knees, my body throbbing, aching. I felt my palms sink into the lush grass, too exhausted to recoil from it. I was sobbing dry, hollow sobs. "Sachi," I called once more. "Come out! Please, come out!" I half lay down, spent. I felt the paper-thinness of my skin; I was melting into the dust of this special light.

She was holding her fists out to me, clenched, sitting cross-legged at my side. Grimier than I'd ever seen her, and beneath the grime she was pale, deadly pale, with a ghostly calm. Her eyes and nose were gummy, her hair matted into a nest. I detected the tiniest tremor she could not control. She'd been out here all through the day's rain. She nudged my shoulder, and I saw that the cuts were festering, the scabs scratched away, the blood dark. I could only stare and she nudged me again, hard with her knuckles. "Which one, Miss Saito? Left or right? Pick one," she demanded. Another of her games. Through everything, she kept it up.

"Left," I finally said.

Slowly she opened her fist and held it out to me. A miniature flashlight, a metallic cylinder, small enough just to fit in her palm, to be squeezed. "You picked Tam's," she said. She clicked the switch back and forth. "It's dead," she mumbled, and threw it down on the grass. She rose to her knees, clicked on the flashlight held in her other hand, focusing it yards away, on the foot of a tree tied with a tattered ribbon.

"That's where I found it," she said. "He left it for me."

I took my coat off and tried to drape it on her shoulders, but she pushed me away. Suddenly I remembered the dog.

"Yuki!" I shouted. "Yuki!" Instantly it came bounding out from nowhere, circling us, half playful, half fearful, pausing to stare with its human eyes. Sachi called to it softly— "Come girl, come"—but it wouldn't. "Yuki!" she finally bellowed, harshly. It came, responding to the brutality in her voice that was familiar, lost as it was without Yano to smack it down. Then the dog was licking her streaming eyes and the runny business from her nose, the slime of its tongue sliding across her face. She hugged the dog so tight it squealed, so tight, and I remembered how close she and Tam had held one other, as if their prickly, sore bodies were in the way. Finally the creature broke away from her and sat again, sentry-like, at the edge of the wood.

Carefully I inched closer to her, and at the same time pulled her down onto my lap. She was limp in my arms; she let me drape my coat over her. She gave in to me, as I knew she would, as she always did sooner or later. She held on, her arms not quite reaching around my thick waist, bunching my skirt in her fists. I touched her hair and it was rope in my hands, coarse and strong enough to tie things with, hang them up, bind them.

"He was going to die anyway," she said, matter-of-fact, poking her head up from my lap. "That was the secret he made me never tell."

I was about to say that we all do, eventually, or some such absurd thing. Be silent, I chided myself. Be nothing but silent, wordless, blameless comfort.

"Tam had this lump on his neck." She lifted her nest of hair, pointing to the back of her head. "Cancer," she said bluntly. "It was growing and changing colour." She eyed me warily, my doubt. I was beginning not to know her, this adult-like acceptance. "It was this big." She suddenly opened her mouth wide, distorting her face to show me her tongue; there was the disturbed, rebellious child once more. She looked pitifully hideous; too sad to laugh at.

"I know you don't believe me, Miss Saito. He never went to the doctor, but it wouldn't have done any good."

I nodded.

"You never believe," she said with a resigned sigh, heaving in my lap. How I disappointed her, how I fell short.

I lifted her chin; I wanted to be gentle with her, this child, to think only of her and leave my despised self behind. "I believe that you believed it," I said.

"It doesn't matter," she said callously.

Tam and Sachi. Nothing, no one else counted.

He was lanky, stretched too thin, more than ever that one day up on Mackenzie Hill; perhaps it was true, perhaps he was already dying. His hair was a sickly blue-black bruise covering his head under the sparkling sun. She was whispering a word—one of the words I'd given her, I couldn't guess which—into his ear. This time she'd surprised him; he didn't know, couldn't know where she'd gotten it. He let her lie on his back with her arms stretched out into wings, like the planes that sailed over them. What was she, she whispered, just loud enough for me to hear between the planes. DC-10, he burbled, his belly pressed into the grass. Their games, their secret codes. Other times, he'd named the planes, watching their silver bodies soaring overhead: DC-7, 707, 727, Boeing 757. She buried her mouth into his neck, biting, sucking at something, while he howled and giggled. She licked and licked, hard and with care, as if she could heal it.

He'd rolled onto his back then, playfully, tumbling her off, both of them face-up to the planes. The mood between them changing minute to minute, gathering up, then floating away, like clouds. Tam lay there; the boy could never show he wanted anything too much. Not like Sachi, who always wanted, wanted so much; she clawed you for it, for what Keiko never gave. Tam could wait. Not like his father, not like his mother. Wait there, sweaty and bundled up. Lie there, still as could be, eyes closed, the sun beating down just enough to collide with the cool edge of the breeze.

Sachi had moved from my lap and was clawing at the grass now, but it was thick; thicker than the flimsy sod of our lawns. She took the key that hung from her neck and stabbed into the ground; sawed out a ragged patch, gripping it, solid like flesh. She tugged it fiercely as she did so; I winced at the sound, the ruthless tear of its roots, like hair from a scalp. The reddish clay soon lay exposed, parched despite the rain. She smoothed the earth, sifting out pebbles, and dragged her finger through it to scratch: T A M, then below that: S A C H, and a fat heart around them, then a line with two slashes through it. "That means for ever," she said. Methodically she replaced the patch of grass and tamped it down with her foot, a surgeon stitching up the wound.

The light, what there was, was leaving. Sachi sat down, planting her bottom right on the patch, guarding a treasure. Another game. The clouds had bloated up grey, smothering most of the sky at the top of the ravine. The creek rushed on with a low roar. I wanted to ask how long she would stay, but was afraid of the answer. I wanted to take her by the hand, back to my home, tuck her in my bed, but knew she would not come.

Around us, the air was crackling. I thought I saw the exact moment of day turning to night. It wasn't, as I'd always believed, a light put out, the sun gone; it was a seeping in of the dark. It filled in the pale of Sachi's face right there before me. She laid that dark face in my lap again. She was hugging something to her stomach, tucked in the waistband of her pants. She wriggled in my arms and I heard a click then the tinny voices that had echoed through the ravine. Singing, wobbly and messy, but I knew the song; the melody wore through: it was the tune Sachi had hummed at my bedside. Abruptly the *lala lala la* stopped, and voices started up, thin and childish—a boy's and a girl's, giggly and self-conscious.

Today is May the fifth, 1975. It is a sunny day.

Now say your name. Say when your birthday is.

No, say yours. Say when you were born. Say . . .

My name is Sachi Nakamura. I was born on January 14, 1962—

The tape clicked off. The ravine was stiller than before. Sachi huddled into my lap, pressing the tape player into my stomach; I caressed her, and she let me.

I recalled the day when I'd heard them practising those lines, so shy, fumbling for things to say, when really they never needed to string together much. That wasn't the way they communicated. But I could not help feeling the envy leak into me, wishing I had Eiji's voice in a box to keep me company, to bring my picture to life now and then. To help me remember my blessings. I wanted to tell her this. The darkness had reduced us both to shadows, and I felt a kind of safety in that, a freeness. To feel the damp creeping cold of night, the brush of grasses, to hear the creek flowing onward and the prickle of sounds, and to see nothing. I was not afraid.

"You have your memories," I whispered in her ear. "Hold on tight to them, and Tam will be with you always. His love. His secrets. I know. Believe me." I did believe it myself, for hadn't Eiji lived with me always, all these years? And yet my words sounded hollow and false. A silly old woman's romance.

She stayed a lumpy shadow in my lap. I didn't know if I'd reached her. If I'd convinced her, after all those times feeding her my romantic ideas, that this time I was being as true as my heart knew how. My arm was growing numb under her weight but I had no wish for her to move away. I leaned down to touch my chin to her forehead.

"Tell me a story about Eiji," she said softly, just when I thought, from the rhythm of her breathing, that she'd fallen asleep. She surprised me, touched me, thinking of Eiji at such a moment. But it wasn't the first time.

"Another time." I tried to ease her up gently. "It's time to go home now." I scanned the ground for the flashlight to take us back.

"No," she said. "Tell me a story. A happy one about Eiji. Please, Miss Saito."

I paused.

"Please?"

This time, I would not fail her. I knew the story to tell.

"Eiji, you know, loved the ocean," I began. "In the summer, he went in the water every day in Port Dover. Every day, rain or shine. He taught me how to swim there." She already knew this but it didn't hurt to tell her again, to remind her.

"When they moved us to the camp, Eiji missed the ocean so much." How many times in summer had I looked out my window at the electrical field, squinting at the reedy grasses swept in waves by the wind. How many times had I seen Eiji there in the grasses, treading them like a current.

"One summer day, we discovered a river not far from the camp. He was so bata bata he couldn't keep still; he was like you," I said, nudging her. I recalled how his body had twitched and burned with unspent energy in bed next to me those first nights in the camp; it was the energy he had always used up in the ocean. "The river made him happy." I remembered those days—carefree, running through the orchard, away from the rows of ugly shacks, down to the river. There was nobody to stop us, nowhere to escape to; we were already nowhere, deep inside the mountains. I felt Sachi stir against me.

"I ran back and forth, back and forth," I told her, laughing at myself, recalling the bridge that went over the river, and the sensation of my hand in the air, waving each time Eiji's head came up. Of course, there was that shadow spidering up my back—Sumi Iwata, Yamashiro-san, four or five years older than me, running behind; Sumi with the bucket she'd have on her arm for some chore or other, chasing after me, asking about Eiji's favourite songs and colours and dishes. How erai she made me, so tired when she'd catch me saying "I'll Be Seeing You" and "green" one day, then "Skylark" and "blue" the next, and badger me to tell her which it was.

One day—it may have been the last day of summer—Eiji

made me come down from the bridge. Our first September there, and I felt fall lurking in the edge of the breeze.

"Last chance." He winked. He liked that I was tough, that my skin wasn't pearly and delicate. It didn't matter that I was afraid. I wasn't that fragile; he could toss me into the current. "I won't make it, I won't." I could hear myself pining for Eiji's attention, for his protection. As foolish as all those other girls who watched him.

"I'm scared, nii-san. Nii-san!" I tried to tell him, tugging at his arm. Saying it out loud, as I could not now. Now when there was no one, no older, stronger brother, so that I could be the weak one. He smiled back, fearless for me.

"You, urusai, ne?" he threw back over his shoulder. But I wasn't a nuisance, I wasn't, I knew that.

"It's only water, Asa. Look, just water making bubbles." The river was rushing forward, on and on. Where it came from I didn't know; it had no start or stop and I had to cross it. How could my small body resist that force for even a minute? But Eiji would not let go of me.

"All right," I said finally. My soft giving in to him. The things he could make me do. The things I thought terrified me.

I remember him making me climb on his back. I was heavier than at Port Dover, and even he groaned under my new weight, small as I was. We inched towards the water, tottering, I watching his feet, his toes, clenching the rocky ground that led to the shore of the river. This shore was different from the ocean, where the water rose to greet you in a frightening embrace. This water surged past you, shunned you without a care. I felt the goosebumps rise on his skin against me, and it was contagious; they rose on my chest and arms, wherever his skin touched mine. In my middle I felt that familiar pulsing, gaping: my mystery.

"Nii-san," I whispered, desolate. He ignored me. "Nii-san," I said again, for comfort. The water foamed, inched icily over our bodies, and then suddenly the ride tumbled us, speeding faster than anything, thrashing us. I heard tiny screeching cries: gulls circling, or Sumi on the bridge, I didn't know which. I saw Eiji's head disappear into the bubbles, then come up, and I felt my body alone, bobbing, pushed and pulled. I didn't try to cry out, because Eiji was there in front of me, but we were no longer linked.

"Asa!"

"I'm all right, I'm all right," I cried, giddy to be feeling strong, my head high above the surface. I spied the bank of the river and it was not far.

"Asa!" Eiji's eyes, frightened eyes, disappeared under the water. He was afraid, my nii-san was afraid. For the first time I was seeing that.

"Nii-san! Nii-san!" I screamed.

His head bobbed up as if separated from his body, then down again. Then there was nothing but those fists of current churning over him.

"Pull him up, pull him up!" Sumi's voice from above, urgent, commanding.

I remember filling with strength, despite the numbing cold, the fear. Repeating her words to myself as I went down seconds after him, wriggling every muscle in my body, lashing out my arms in the murky water. *Pull him up, pull him up,* the voice went again, half my own. I remember curving my hands as Eiji had taught me, cupping the current like balls in my palms, throwing them aside until I reached him. He grabbed my hands, held them tight, his fingers gouging mine, and I loved that, how our arms resisted the water that beat at them. He smiled at me, coming up to the bank, and the water bubbled around his teeth as he coughed.

"You see, Sachi," I said now. "I saved him. I saved my brother."

I remember pulling ourselves out of the water and collapsing onto boulders on the shore. The air so dry and crisp there in the mountains that it cracked your throat and skin. The children I had thought were gulls flocked like hungry orphans; Sumi had come down from the bridge, her bucket somehow lost. I recall only then glimpsing the blood leaking from his toe onto the rocks. He'd scraped his toe on the bottom, hard. I winced at it, we all did except Eiji, seeing how the nail was half off. But I smiled a secret smile at that bit of blood, the brightest colour there, knowing it was why he had gone down, the only reason.

That was the best day of my life. I knew it then, even with Sumi there. I never took Eiji for granted, not for one second. That was a gift to me: knowing that so young, in the moment. It didn't take me years to come to. "He could have drowned," I told Sachi.

"It's a happy story, isn't it?" I felt a surge of strength in my limbs folded under me on the damp grass, remembering how I'd taken his arms and fought the current. Behind Sachi and me, the creek seemed to roar louder. Sachi was very still in my lap, so I gently nudged her. "Isn't it?" I asked again.

"Yes. You saved him," she said limply, without emotion.

"What is it?" I whispered, after a moment went by in silence. "What did I say?" I'd fallen short once again. Hadn't I told the right story?

"Then how did he die?" she asked. "If you saved him, how did he die?"

"That was another time," I stuttered, grateful once more for the darkness. "Another time." Sumi's voice commanded me again: *Pull him up, pull him up.* But she hadn't been there that last time, in the night; no one was there except Eiji and me. I didn't need to pull him up; he was strong that night, though I fought him and my nightgown was heavy in the current. He pulled me up, as always. For the last time.

"You didn't save him. He's dead," she said. "All you have is that old picture."

"That's not true, I—" I could not find the words to tell her that I had his love. His love.

"You keep telling that story when you know it isn't true. Can't you say what really happened?" She slipped from my arms, and in the darkness I made out the scramble of her figure as she struggled to stand over me. "I would never lie about Tam. No matter what."

The confusion of her words—I did not understand, yet I knew she was accusing me of something, and at the same time herself too. Of something awful, something that could never be taken back. *There are things you don't know,* she'd told me, long ago it seemed. I was drowning in the darkness and I wanted to let go, to push off for ever.

"I didn't save Tam and you didn't save your brother." Her voice came out of the darkness, which made her words seem truer.

Didn't save your brother. Didn't.

I stumbled to my feet, my cold, damp skirt flapped against my thighs.

"I told Tam," she said. "I showed him and he told Yano." Her voice was firm, solid in the marshy blackness. She was walking away from me, deeper in, towards the sound of the creek. Somewhere, somehow, the dog was scampering behind. I tried to follow the tinkle of its collar, tripping after the sound. Once again she paused and turned back, the barest tinge of light drawn to her face.

"I saw them in the parking lot. Tam wouldn't believe me so I took him there. I made him look. I dared him." I could imagine the purring of the car's engine; they left it running even in summer. That would have drawn Tam and Sachi in. The radio would be on with some old song Chisako sang along to, the words not quite right with her accent. The memory of it all. How you felt your breath so tight inside your stomach and chest, rising up, and you felt the tininess of a world inside a world, inside your skin, your breath. Not wanting to stay but not able to move, and the car chugging gently on the spot with the music. Until she sat up in the back seat, her hands climbing up to repin strands of hair. There was no mistaking who it was, even if you didn't see her from the front. Nobody else had hair like that, so long and so black, and nobody else twisted it up like so, into a fat, spiralling roll. Her mouth caught in the rearview mirror, opening and closing over the words of the song.

Then he came out of the car, sliding along the seat, never showing much of himself, wily and so tall. You'd see only the back of him, but you'd catch the gleamy nape of his neck before he tied his tie back on, that creamy whiteness, the strangeness of a stranger, a hakujin, a kind of man you'd never in your life known or even been close to. The dark colour of his hair that was not quite black, not quite straight but wavy. He never turned to you, but slid into the front seat of the eely car and closed the door without slamming it, knowing how hard was enough because it was his car. I never saw his eyes, the eyes that Chisako glimpsed herself in.

"It was a dare. That's why I did it." She still had that adult calm.

In a second she would be gone. What could I say, what could I do to make her stay with me? "It was because of me," I at last whispered into the dark. "I told Yano about the woods. About Chisako. I told him."

She wouldn't listen. Now, when I was speaking the truth, what I'd hidden from myself. "I showed Tam his mom in the woods, with that man," she said, steadfast. And Chisako's face came to me then, as she turned in the car once, for a brief second: her makeup smudged, her hair fallen, her face drawn down, anxious, and drained. She was the old Chisako after all, plain in the end. I thought of the sandwiches, the triangles left behind, half-eaten. The other things they did not clean up.

"I know what I did. I know what's true and what's a lie," she said, "even if you don't." She had moved away, out of my arms.

"Sachi!" I cried, unable to restrain myself. Was it for me or for her I was crying out? Left alone, I would never find my way out of this place. How would I find her in the dark? How could I stop her from doing what was my worst fear?

What I would do? The awful resignation in her voice, the terrible calm. "Sachi, please don't!" I cried again. "Don't leave me!"

But she did. I was alone, left behind as I'd always feared. I had no sense of time, of how long I'd been there, what time it was. Everything pressed in too close, all at once, blaming, suffocating me. The sky closed its lid over me; the half-moon was pocketed in the clouds, behind the trees. The water roared in my ears, became a lion. I'd had my chance to save her from herself: my one chance, now gone. It was me I should have saved her from, I saw that now; all along it had been me. How would she do it? It hardly mattered. She would do it, smart girl that she was, with that will of iron, with her shattered heart; she would do it, whatever way.

I heaved myself forward, towards the creek, drawn into the roar. I held my arms in front, blindly pushing aside branches that twanged back to scratch my face. Stumbling down, calling out. In one step the air was different: cooler, moister; there was mist on my skin, and the creek hardened to a machine's roar instead of an animal's. Yards ahead, a small figure, darker in the night, teetered at what had to be the edge of the creek. I did not dare cry out; I scrambled forward, and the figure seemed to see me coming; its eyes, catching some moonlight, glittered like the dog's.

She fell. With a strange, crashing sound she broke the surface. Her glittering eyes vanished. Before I could think, I was falling, my clothes heavy and sinking, pulling me down. I opened my mouth to call out but it filled with water. I saw nothing, felt only cold, burning. Light poured over me, and I saw myself, bloated in the water, and I was crying, trying to point upstream to where I knew Sachi had fallen in, but my arms were weighed down. Then Sumi appeared above me with her bucket, frantically waving, running from side to side of the bridge, calling me, calling Eiji. *Let go*, she was crying, or something. *Stop, ojosan, stop*; but only Eiji could call me that. Sumi's face came close, grimacing, pained, was there and gone. *Sachi*, I called feebly, but the sound died in my mouth. I know what's true, I know what's a lie, I meant to tell her. I know what I did and I will say it. For you I will. Sachi. I didn't save him. I longed to say this; to have these be the last words in her ears. Instead, I closed my eyes and sank.

NINE

"WHAT KIND OF MAN would do this?" Detective Rossi looked at me in that way of his that had grown so familiar. As if nothing I said or did could change it. The same way he had looked pulling me from the creek, not more than an hour ago. When he had shouted, "Take my hand, take it!" and I had obeyed. When he had pulled me up, wrapped me in a blanket, and I had glimpsed his face above me before collapsing against his tall frame. It was the same as in my living-room, with his questions, his pad and pen. "Sachi!" I must have cried out; I must have pointed to where I'd heard her fall, where I couldn't see.

Because he shone the light and there she was on the bank of the creek, bundled in a blanket as I was, with Keiko and Tom holding her. Holding her as a mother and father should. Their faces opened by the light, the lingering terror, like walnuts cracked from their shells. She waved and mouthed something to me, and it was all a game once more, one of her silly games. I was too exhausted to decipher the curl of her lips.

"The case is closed now," Detective Rossi was saying as we drove on, one eye on the road that tunnelled into the darkness. In the flash of oncoming headlights I glimpsed the sweat across his brow. He had turned the car heater on high so I wouldn't catch a chill, but I felt nothing, neither heat nor cold. He went on. "I keep thinking he had to be some kind of…" He didn't finish.

The road bumped under us, and as my body lifted and sank into the car seat in that barely airborne second, I was taken back to being small and light, bounced on the handle-bars of Eiji's bicycle at dawn. Without a care.

"Monster," I said softly.

"Was he crazy?"

"No, no. Yes. Maybe." The blackness crouched around us until Detective Rossi flicked on the high beams. "You might not understand," I murmured.

"Why? Because I'm not Japanese?" He said this too quickly, with the first hint of bitterness. It brought the echo of Yano's words: *They thought we'd all commit hara-kiri.* I heard his sour laugh at the expectation of every last thing going against him. I thought of the nod I'd given him on our morning walks; the smile to loosen the clenched fist, to tell him that I knew there was an impressive man inside who'd had his chances taken away. How I held back, the time when it counted most.

"No, no," I said quietly. I pressed close to the window and the passing darkness. I did not wish to see the detective's face, the change there, however fleeting.

Yano had stood at my bedroom window that day, the first time any man who was not my father, not my brother, had set foot there. His shirt, ripped in two, left on my lawn. I'd followed him up from the garden. My room filling with his scent, once so repugnant to me. He raised the blinds I always kept down, loosing a flurry of dust.

He was looking out at Mackenzie Hill. Thinking, *wrong, wrong, wrong. That bugger Mackenzie*, he was thinking. As if it could have been just one man, the same man, this hill. When all the time, in the woods at the foot of the hill, Chisako was lying with her Mr. Spears, and he didn't see. Blind man, fool. He began to wheeze then, from the dust I'd let collect on the blinds.

I drew him away from the window, sat him down on my bed. I went to rub his back, as I always did during his attacks out in the field, as he'd shown me—so long ago, it seemed—but this time my hands met his flesh instead of the thickness of his clothes. My hands sticky with secrets. He didn't notice; how could he, coughing and wheezing as he was? "Lie down," I told him, with the sternness of a nurse, or a wife who knows her husband's stubbornness only too well. "Chotto. Lie down and close your eyes," I ordered. I surprised myself.

He did not flinch from me when I began to rub his chest with my cold damp hands, the place where, inside, the fluid had thickened in his lungs and kept back the air. His face was red and contorted in my lap, ugly; he tried to struggle up, shamed, I suppose, but still I held him.

I turned to the detective now, pulling the blanket close. "Everything was ruined for him, you see," I said wearily.

"Everything went wrong. It was no good any more. No good." It was Yano, his words, what he'd left me, in my mouth.

Detective Rossi fell silent and focused once again on the road. If he was surprised by what I'd said, how I had tried to understand Yano, he didn't let on. We drove like this for I don't know how long. Long enough for the sky to brighten, abruptly it seemed, the light coming on like a siren out of nowhere, in a single, climbing streak.

"She knew, didn't she?" the detective asked, as if no time had lapsed, as if we hadn't left that dark world behind. "Mrs. Yano knew what her husband would do when he found out."

I saw her now as I had seen her then, as I had felt the press of her thigh beside mine on the loveseat in that small room she'd made hers alone. Her breath smelling of something, of manju, its sweet-bean filling. "I think I understand you, Asako," she had said, as if seeing me anew. "You want to think badly of him. You want to believe he is a monster so you can hate him, ne?" She nudged me with her dainty slippered foot. "You want to believe he would harm me." I could only stare into my lap.

"You have feelings for him, don't you?" Again she nudged me with her foot, harder this time, then stood over me. My cheeks burned. "It's all right, Asako," and she reached down to pat my hand, not so gently, for it made a sound, a soft slap. "Perhaps you didn't know this about yourself." She went to the window with its view into the neighbour's kitchen, half watching me still.

"The way you wait for him to come out and walk with you every morning. It's obvious, Asako, can't you see? Even my son sees." My face burned and burned, the tears hot and unspilled in my eyes. "You want them to see, ne, Asako? You have no shame," she chided, with a harsh, teasing laugh.

"It's not true," I cried after a moment. "It's him waiting for me! *He* waits!"

She sat down again, to calm me, I suppose. Refusing to take in what I said. "Your feelings frighten you. I understand." She looked me in the eye, hers so fixed, so startling inside the black lines drawn across her lids. "He's just a man, Asako. Nothing to be afraid of. Different from us, and not so different." I tried to protest, but she went on.

"It's true he likes you, Asako. He has respect for you." She rose. I felt something then—the ride, Eiji's ride—rise and tumble inside me. Sensing this, she added: "Of course, not in the way of a man having feelings for a woman." Again she paced two steps this way, two steps that.

"Asako, you must understand that Yano would never—"

"Of course not," I interrupted, if only to stop her words.

"He's not that kind of man, Asako. If he knew..." She touched her hand to her breast. It was not me she was speaking of. She did not finish.

I glanced at the detective, afraid that, in his wisdom, he'd divine my thoughts. The truth, whatever that was. Now I felt the sweat on me, a cold clamp on my buttocks, the fiery ring of the blanket at my neck, amid the blare of heat from the car vents. A sickly sensation. I rolled down the window and instantly the detective reached to adjust the heat setting.

"You all right, Miss Saito?"

"Yes, yes." I nodded as fresh air streamed over my face. *A man knows his wife. As she knows him.* "Yes, detective," I said finally, gulping the wind. "Chisako knew him. She knew her husband very well." I paused. "You see, she loved him." I glanced again at the detective's profile, unmoved, and his hand with its band of gold on the steering wheel; then said: "Surely you understand, detective."

After a moment, he took something out of his pocket and placed it on the dashboard. "They found it nearby, in the parking lot," he said. It was the glass dome Mr. Spears had given Chisako, with the pink rose inside. A terrible thought came to me, seeing that perfect blossom bounce in its watery vault as the car bumped along.

"Where is she? All this time...how did they—"

"Her body's been kept in facilities downtown," the detective said. "They'll be buried together. When there's no family—"

"No family," I repeated. There was no use mentioning Yano's crazy brother. I took a deep breath and exhaled, just as Detective Rossi had once shown me.

We rounded a corner and the electrical towers, Chisako's cages, my giants, swung into view, and I saw myself there, foolish and clinging, insignificant beneath those monstrous beams. Clinging to another, no less dwarfed—to Yano, on that morning as grey and early as this: two ants struggling in that empty field. I had not given him the comfort he deserved that day, the comfort I knew how to give; what I'd done was far worse.

The field came into view now, blank as snow in mid-summer, and a panic struck me. "The dog!" I exclaimed. I heard myself; the hysteria still lurked there, my heart was still racked; after everything, nothing, nothing was settled.

"It's with the Nakamuras," the detective answered, pointing to the road behind us. "The girl wanted it with her."

"Of course." I calmed myself.

We pulled into the driveway, and there were Stum and Angel huddled in the window. How odd to see them there. Detective Rossi opened the car door for me, cradling my elbow in his palm. He slipped the glass dome into my hand. Quietly said: "It was a brave thing you did, Miss Saito. You saved that girl."

No, not brave. Nothing but fear. I looked into Detective Rossi's eyes, the kindness there that would accept anything I said, anything that was the truth. "I didn't save anyone," I told him. I wanted him to understand. He was about to reply, but just then Angel came scurrying towards us, Stum lagging behind. Angel cried in her fussy way: "Asako! You're safe!" and I let her take me in her puffy arms, I let her chastise me as if I were a child who'd wandered off from home.

I slept and slept. Did not wake until late the next morning, when the air was already stale. My fever gone. I felt the busyness of my heart, of a lingering presence and the exhaustion of having dreamed, yet I remembered nothing of it. Angel came in as I started to push away the covers, Stum hovering behind her. She scolded me to lie back and rest. I surrendered to her fussing, avoiding Stum's little worried eyes, and told them to go off to work before they lost an hour's pay. "I'm fine, fine," I said, closing my eyes. I opened them and I was alone. This was how it was to be: fuss, fuss, then gone, forgotten.

I sat in my garden, my neglected garden. It seemed so long since I'd tended to it properly. On my fingers I counted seventeen days since the first news had come of Chisako's death.

That long since my routine had been disrupted. I wanted the number to hold some special meaning, but when I searched my mind, my memory, nothing came. How quickly the weeds had encroached to threaten my precious blooms. Only my roses were unwilted. I began clipping the withered flower heads vigorously, digging up thorns and stray grasses. As I surveyed the heap of weeds and petals, his voice entered my head—Yano's—as I knew it would, as I knew it would for years to come.

"Mottai-nai," he'd said, the day when I, Chisako's accomplice, invited him into my home. He was holding up my Eiji, clumsy fingers pasted half over that tiny face. Holding the picture above us as we lay back on my too narrow bed, his breath regained. I might have giggled, like the girl I had been with Eiji. But Yano was an old man, muttering his old refrain.

The side gate creaked and the dog came bounding in, startling me out of my thoughts. Its tail was flickering, that white flame that had guided me through the forest. My impulse was to touch, though I never had; it resisted even Sachi's embrace, time and time again. It was not a creature like others, to be cuddled, to know itself only in your eyes. "Yuki!" I called, and the dog paused to stare, and in the particular cock of its head I saw that it remembered me.

Keiko appeared then, neat and in order as always, not broken open, as on that night in the ravine. She looked to the ground, to my heap of weeds. "Thank you for telling us," she said after a moment. "Asako. Gomen."

Sorry for what, I wanted to ask. For one night? For the years of averted glances, cold shoulders? For Sachi? For herself? She took one more step. Carefully she embraced me as

I held out my soiled hands helplessly. She was a slight thing, feathery, not wiry as I'd thought all these years. Seconds later I was released.

She was weeping, dryly, quietly, to herself. I could only stand there. I wanted to console her, to leave her be, whatever would ease the moment. But abruptly she stopped.

"Gomen," she repeated, in her frugal way. As if English would be too plain, too bald. The perfume of my roses overpowered me then, I don't know why. On impulse, I went to the end of my garden, where they'd begun to bloom on the bush. I snipped a branch. "Nakamura-san...Keiko," I started to say, for we were, it seemed, friends now. But as I turned, with a smile and my modest gift in hand, I heard the gate creak and found her gone. Myself alone. The embarrassment of the moment, her shame at what had happened, not to be overcome.

A sudden wave of fatigue overtook me, though it was early afternoon. I sat down in my lawn chair, roses in my lap. I was reminded of the dream of Eiji I'd had days ago, the dream that had seemed so much like life. But in the dream, the blossoms Eiji gave me became grotesque in my hand. My roses here were velvet up close; no ugliness in them at all. A word sprang to my lips. "Utsukushii," I said aloud, forgetting that I was alone, that Sachi wasn't with me. I must tell her, I said.

Of course, she'd already know. From Tam. She more than anyone would grasp that word, just from the sound of it. The prettiness of a thing that will soon die. As a child she had known by instinct, when she broke the baby blooms off my roses.

I had no wish to bring the cutting inside, to wake to its drooping petals in the morning. Instead I tossed it into the heap of weeds. As I did, I could not help but hear Yano behind me, the wheezing from his lips. I glanced down at the last bright, lovely thing at my feet.

Alone in my living-room at night, Stum and Papa fast asleep upstairs, I made a faint circle on the cold glass with my breath in the moonlight, as I'd done when I was a little girl. Circles and circles, big and small, that wouldn't stay. Night after night I had seen the two beams of light meet and fade out there. I clearly recall my thoughts on one such night, my wistful thoughts. They are happy, I told myself. In love. They could die tomorrow, I even whispered; I did. Thought to myself that it would not be such a cruel thing. Believed it.

Inside the refrigerator, I found two foil-wrapped plates labelled "Papa" and "Asa" in Angel's flowery handwriting. Such a waste, I thought, smoothing out the creases and tucking the foil back in my drawer. On another night it might have irked me, but tonight I was tired enough to be grateful. Papa was unusually quiet, meeting each spoonful with a dutifully open mouth. "Yano-san wa," he muttered, pointing to the window, "don-buro." As he had some days ago. Down below, his word for basement. I pondered that; a senile old man's premonition, perhaps, but there was nothing in it. After he finished, instead of hurrying downstairs to sit by my window, I brought a hot washcloth to his face, wiping slowly and carefully, as in the old days. Back then, I could take an hour to clean him, top to bottom. Each day a fresh start. Each day some hope. Now I twisted my finger in the cloth and gently picked at the corners of his eyes until he pushed me away. Bi-bi, I said with my ridiculous clown-smile, holding that bit of crust up to him, rewarding him with such nonsense. As Eiji had once said to me, and I to baby Stum. Bi-bi. If someone were to hear me.

When I sat down to my own dinner, the sky was still bright. I did not once go to the window, my chair there; I had no interest in gazing over the empty field, at the empty house across it, and the light inside that must have burned out by now, or finally been turned off by the police. I wondered what would be done with the house, with no one to claim it. I thought of Yano's crazy brother out west, all alone in the world now, who could never stand the sight of his own.

By the time I finished, the room was half dark. Mazui, I clucked at Angel's overboiled vegetables and tasteless bits of chicken that I'd downed. Stum would not like this, I thought; it would not do. Cleaning up, it struck me: the two identical plates wrapped in tinfoil, my name and Papa's. The same sad mush for two old ojiisans. This, I sighed, this was how things were to be. Any other day, I told myself, I don't know what I would have done.

I didn't know what to do with myself—any more, I laughed bitterly, than Angel did. I went from this armchair to that, to the chesterfield. I was tired but listless, my body, my mind both a nuisance. I half rose to go to the butsudan, dusty and neglected in its corner for years now; I made out only a shape, the outline of Buddha with his hint of a smile. The prayers left unsaid, in spite of Buddha's boundless compassion. I had known all along that it was too late; I'd had no hope, no faith. I sat back down. No solace in that corner.

Only this persistent fatigue that was, it occurred to me, like jetlag, though I'd never travelled far enough, never flown in a jet to know. Still I was sure it would feel like this: part of me here; part of me there, never catching up.

The next morning, after breakfast, they bundled me into the car, though I protested. Stum driving, with Angel beside him in front. Going so fast that it seemed the trees were hardly trees; I wanted him to slow down so I could see them, hear them whisk by. I had no wish to nag him, though; things had changed between us, ever so little; the way he exchanged a look with Angel only to cast a watchful glance over me in the rearview mirror when he thought I didn't see. Their conspiracy, well meant as it was. Whenever I found my mouth open, about to say waga-mama, to complain, I shushed myself. Be grateful, I told myself. Over us, the clouds were still and heavy as ice floes, even as we raced on. A hint of my dream from the night before revisited me, but only the sounds, the swish, the giggling, the breath held and let go: it was Sachi, with Tam, by the ravine under the willow. Utsukushii. Not a cruel thing.

"It was Angel's idea," Stum was saying. "She thought you might want to come. You've never seen, all this time—"

"Asa, there are thousands of them. Busy, busy, cracking open, all day, all night in the hatch room." She was hunched over the seat and reaching for me; planting a cluster of fingers in my palm. "Their fur tickles at first, it's so soft," she told me. "After, they're like part of your hand." She pinched me then, a little scratch for barely a second. "Just a little squeeze open, just to see, that does it. Stum's been teaching me." She got on my nerves, telling it but all the while really keeping it to herself, this know-how meant only for them, her and Stum. The little squeeze open that does it, does what? What they did with their hands, what they saw that told them—it was not for me to know.

We pulled up to a white brick building, one storey high in the middle of an empty stretch of land, and Angel bounded out with such energy, reminding me how young she was, robust—how much younger than Stum, who lumbered behind, slow and steady. She doubled back to urge me out. I caught Stum's worried look, even from a distance. "Go on, you two," I said, "I'll follow." I shooed them away. They joined up happily enough, clasped hands, and disappeared into the building.

I thought of waiting in the car, but Stum had locked the doors. I couldn't disappoint them, not Stum, proud for once, anxious to show off. Around the building the ground was muddy, from the recent rain, I suppose, and before I knew it my shoes were chunked with dirt. It was strangely quiet here. I waited but the quiet persisted, except for the few cars that passed on the road. There were no planes crossing the sky, that was what it was. I'd lived with it for so long that it was the quiet I noticed, not the noise. I remember how it was at first, when the airport came. Suddenly one day the planes coming and going. Rattling the house. Soon, I suppose, my mind ceased to hear them, but my heart took longer to; I felt it shudder inside my chest, rising and rising every single time.

"Asako." I felt a hand shaking my shoulder. Too roughly. A touch that didn't quite know its own strength, that could only be a man's. The name rushed to my lips—Yano—but

I caught myself. I looked up and there was Mr. Fujioka, Stum's boss.

"Fujioka—Kaz," I exclaimed, trying to compose myself. "You shouldn't sneak up on me like that." No sooner had I scolded him than I realized I'd wandered quite far from the car, come around the length of the building to the back. He had hardly snuck up on me. All this added to my embarrassment at seeing Fujioka. Back in his bachelor days, he used to call at our home for tea. Papa wanted to impress him, since it was Fujioka who had taught Stum chick sexing when he arrived after the war, having been trained at some special school in Nagoya. Of course he'd been served tea in proper style countless times back there, but what did I know? Afterwards, Papa would scold me for the tea being too weak or too strong, not enough this or that.

"You were looking at my trees, ne?" he said with some pride.

"Yes, yes," I responded, looking just at that moment. They were beautiful, unexpected, hiding there behind the building. The soft pink of their blossoms that became something else, less pretty when you came close. For a second they took my breath. Once again I recalled the time with Eiji, the branch in my hand. "They remind me—" I stopped myself. A silly thought.

Kaz stood patiently, waiting for me to finish. Kind enough. "Well," I said, "they make me think of the orchard in the camp." Pointless as it was to bring up such things, nothing else was in my mind at the moment.

"Those were apple trees, Asako," he said, with a little snort. "These are sakura. I ordered them special from Japan.

Takai desu," he said this in a confiding way. Of course, having to mention their costliness, to show me how well he'd done for himself. It seemed to me that over the years he'd become more like his wife, a home-grown nisei without tact; that he'd lost the grace of his bachelor days, when he first came here from Japan. In the past, I had to remind myself to call him Kaz, as he insisted, trying to be like another of the boys. Once he brought me a box of pretty pink and green sugar candies sent by his mother from Kyoto. I was such a naive thing, quite unaware of what it could mean, that box, I hardly thanked him. For Mama had taught me nothing, nothing at all.

"No, no," I said, waving him away. "Besides," I added, suddenly brazen, "you weren't even there. How would you know, Kaz?" I tossed a little laugh at him.

"Asako," he said, clearing his throat. "Sakura in the middle of the mountains? Not with all that snow."

I shivered when he said this, surprising myself, for the afternoon was quite warm for a June day. It was Yano, his memory of cold, still in me.

"Apple blossoms, apple," Kaz repeated stubbornly, going on admiring his trees. "Saw them last summer when we visited the in-laws." He stood waiting for some reply, I suppose because he knew his wife and I had been in the same camp. Though she was some years older.

"I see" was all I said. I gave in, remembering how stubborn he could be, even back when he was still a gentleman. How he stopped me from pouring tea to turn and wipe the cup, making me feel oafish but all the same grateful. How odd to imagine Fujioka there in the mountains, sipping from some chipped teacup, no doubt, in the dark of an old shack the family had stayed on in; I always pictured him in a teahouse in Japan, kneeling in kimono by an open shoji, looking out onto a rock garden. The same way I'd sometimes imagined Chisako, though I'd never seen either of them dressed so. I'd never seen a teahouse, never seen Japan.

I couldn't care less what he claimed; I knew what I knew. I knew that orchard. Hadn't I walked through it with Eiji a hundred, a thousand times, day after day, back and forth, to school, to the bath, to the youth club? Up and down the wide mud street after the first thaw, the boot uncovered. Then into the orchard. "Was it dark?" I asked.

"Ara?" Kaz looked puzzled. Lost in his thoughts too, I suppose. "Dark?"

"The sky, the clouds. It was always dark." He had never lived there, how could he know? The mountains cluttering up the sky, the street wide and messy with mud, your feet sinking if you didn't step quickly. The cold at night, so stark in summer. It was the cold that woke me each morning, the heat that leaked out once Eiji left. That one night I'd kept myself awake even though the breathing mound of him stayed warm beside me. When Eiji finally woke, it was because I had gone, my heat. I'd left our bed, run down the street, past the shacks, past the crooked doors like rotting teeth and their peeling burnt tar-paper skin. Everyone asleep row after row, sleeping as they should, staying put. In my nightgown I was white as a ghost running in the awful mud in the middle of the night. Through the orchard, out onto the road. Down to the river. The strange light that lit my legs pink, the moon.

"No, Asako," Kaz insisted. "It was sunny. Like Natsuyo remembered."

Yes, that was true. I'd forgotten; if it wasn't dark it was bright, ice bright, so your eyes smarted, so it was hard to see sometimes. But the light seemed unnatural in a way; it could never warm the dry, dry air or shine for long. I didn't remember things the way Kaz's wife did; but who was she to say, she wasn't so special, I had no memory of her. She was old, she must have gone with the older crowd to the dances and such; older even than Sumi. And all I could see of Sumi was her bucket, held at one side, and her bowed legs showing below her skirt, coming out of the woods with Eiji. Where her face should be was empty. There was only that older woman, Yamashiro-san, in the church, holding her finger under her eye, showing me where Eiji and I resembled each other. I touched myself there, that bit of skin.

"I know what you're thinking, Asako," Kaz was saying, and I looked up but he was hardly paying attention, still staring off at his trees.

"You think, why would anybody want to stay there?"

"Yes," I said, all the while thinking of Sumi. The bucket in the crook of her arm when she came out of the woods that time, with Eiji behind, when all day long I'd been looking for him, missing him. Sumi held out her bucket and it was brimful of matsutake. She held out her hand with one of the mushrooms in it, the first time I'd seen one whole, just picked. "Look," she said, and she pressed her finger into it to show me how easily their tender flesh bruised. They hid in the woods at the bases of trees, or in patches of shade. For your mama, she said, take it, holding the monster ear at the stem, reaching for my hand—just like Angel taking my hand, planting something there. Sumi knows all the best places, Eiji said. Sumi giggled.

"Kirei, ne?" Kaz said. Pretty. "What do you call that place? A shangri-la?" He laughed. "Folks there don't seem to age much."

The mushroom ear sitting in my hand, black gills on the underside, breathing and listening in the woods. Paying attention when nobody else did. Sumi gave it to me with the finger-bruise she'd made on top of it. I didn't want it, didn't want it touching me, but I took it just the same.

"Natsu's auntie looks the same age as her, like her ne-san. Natsu didn't like that." Kaz shook his head. "Didn't like that." Now he was frowning at his trees.

"It's the air," I muttered. "It's so cold and dark. Here the sun can make you old, weatherbeaten."

"So, so, so." Kaz trudged off. I saw how his shoulders had already become rounded, like a woman's. Before he might have given a stiff little bow, a respectful smile at the ground, before leaving.

It was enough that I knew, I told myself. I knew they'd be there if I went back. If I went back today, I'd find those trees in the orchard with their blossoms, the very one Eiji snapped a branch from. The very one, all pretty from the road a ways off. Kaz was dreaming, of course; no doubt remembering only those blossoms he knew in Japan as a boy. I understood those kinds of dreams. The dreams that hid away secrets, kept them behind a closed door, closed even to yourself.

"Did Eiji love someone?" Sachi had asked, sitting on my

porch one day after school, when I wanted her company to last. Startling me.

After a moment I smiled. "Of course. He loved me," I told her, with the confidence of one who does not doubt her place in the world, the value of her person. *Eiji loved me.*

"I know, Miss Saito," she giggled, laughing at me. Tapping on that closed door. "But I meant, did he love somebody?" She said it differently that time. *Somebody.* "Did he," and she giggled once more, "did he have a girlfriend?"

She wouldn't take my hands, or let me take hers for long. I couldn't blame her, mine were old and ugly—for the longest time, the oldest thing about me was my hands. They were sticky, and they ate away at my picture. But Yano's hands were always dry and warm, not like the rest of him. When he put my picture back on the night-table with care. Setting down my poor, sickly Eiji with such care. So unlike Yano.

"Everything would have been different," Yano declared sadly, so sure of himself, so convinced of how things worked in the world. "Ne, Asako? We would be different people. We might not be here." He flung his arms up, as he had count-less times on our walks through the field. "I'd be educated." What I'd heard a hundred times from him, but he went on. "Wouldn't have got shipped to Japan." He was touching his hand to the tops of my things throughout the room, plant-ing his prints in the dust.

"They didn't make you go," I told him.

He rested his hand on my dresser, palm down. "Coerced, Asako! Coerced!" I waited for that hand to curl, to clench into its fist, but it stayed open on the dust.

"I know, I know," I murmured, regretting my few words.

He seemed to brighten. "But then I never would have met my Chisako, would I?" He smiled. My Chisako. *My.* "And she..." He paused, lifted his hand, and returned to my bedroom window, unusually quiet. Looking out at Mackenzie Hill. I waited but he would not say more.

"What? What about her?" I prodded, desperate for him to say it.

He seemed not to hear. He wouldn't answer. I didn't dare prod him more. He returned to my night-table and picked up my Eiji again, staring at him. In a second he started up, out of nowhere, shouting, filled with rage, spitting on my picture: "Your brother would be alive today, Saito-san! That's what! He'd be alive!"

I almost cried out, but nothing came. He fell silent then, understanding instantly that he'd gone too far. I did not cry at him that he was wrong, wrong; that I could blame no one but myself, that I had never meant for Eiji to come after me that night to the river, though I knew he would, as he always did. I went out to the river, not knowing why then, as I knew now: it was so Eiji would come for me, for me and no one else. I was a child, wanting his attention when it was slipping away, grasping for it any way I could. I could not tell Yano that I threw myself in at the first sound of Eiji coming, fooling myself that I hadn't been waiting, when the truth was that I would have run back dry as a bone, slipped into bed without waking a soul, if he hadn't come. The water was cold that night, colder than in the day, the current dark with pummelling fists. I didn't struggle against him when he came in after me; I let myself get beaten back by the fists, into his strong arms, angry arms. But he'd come for me, I told myself, for me. I could not tell Yano how after, in bed, Eiji couldn't get warm. I gave him all the blankets and he couldn't get warm. All night he was ice when I dared touch him, and by morning he was hot, burning. The cloth turned sickly warm on him in seconds each time I cooled it, wrung it out. I would not let Sumi near. Not her or any of the other girls who came knocking at all times of the day, when what Eiji needed was rest and quiet. When just to lie there took all his strength, and his breath came out of him like bits of broken string. Even when he was fading away, I didn't let her in.

At the end, after the Reverend Hashizume said his part, after the chanting and after everyone went home, when Eiji's men friends took the box to the edge of the camp and sent Mama and Papa and me away, I made sure Sumi left too. I crept back in the night, and watched and smelled him burning in the pine wood with the grass underneath. I waited until Papa came with the cocoa tin that we would take with us no matter where we went. We'd never leave Eiji there, never.

I did not tell Yano it was me, selfish, hungering child that I was. It was me wanting the world my way, never to change, ever. It was my fault, all my fault—not the war, not the government, not some hakujin stranger named Mackenzie.

Yano brought me no comfort, none at all, he and his reckless anger meant for someone else. I felt him behind me, felt him around my shoulders, lurking near, wanting to leave but not leaving; his sweat was rising, his nervousness. For him, for Chisako, for Sachi and Tam, I would keep it all to myself; I would not say a word. I would not fling my own anger back. I vowed to myself, I bit my lip until it bled. But in the final moment I couldn't help myself. When he was almost gone I stopped him, there at the foot of my stairs, in Stum's plaid shirt I'd lent him to cover himself. I called down with the words on my lips to tell him he'd been made a fool of.

It was Stum at my shoulder. Stum putting his jacket around me, not Yano. The sun was bright in my eyes. "Asa, what are you doing out here? Angel's waiting."

I nodded, but could not move.

"Angel's waiting," he repeated gently. There was something in Stum's voice. His taking care of another's feelings. I'd never heard it before.

Out in the electrical field that morning Yano had said, "You shouldn't have told me, Asako." He was thinking of Chisako, protecting her from himself, as he no longer could. He must have known everything then and there. He knew his wife, knew how things might turn out long before that December morning four years earlier when he first moved them in; when his boxes toppled out front, and he kicked at them until bright clothing lay strewn across the snow as Chisako watched from the window with Tam and Kimi.

Stum tucked the jacket close to my neck, though the air was mild. I let him lead me back to the building. His touch reminded me of the last kind thing Yano had said to me. The last time he would think of me and only me.

"Things would have been different for you too, Asako," he had whispered in my ear. "I know."

We drove back on a different road—the scenic route, Stum called it. He drove slowly this time, after I mentioned a new dizziness in my head, passing groves of trees on both sides, then empty fields fringed with birch trees pitched away from the road. I pressed close to the window to see them, the papery bark that flaked sadly from their trunks. Stum and Angel sat quietly in front, Angel unusually so. Stum, his two hands on the wheel, his jacket back on, the jacket he'd draped over my shoulders just an hour earlier. He'd never done such a thing before; Angel must have shown him. The look of it on him now, filled out where it had drooped on me, I don't know why it struck me; he was a man, my brother, different from before, and yet not so different.

I felt a tickle on my palm but there was nothing there; perhaps the ghost of Angel's fingers planting a baby chick in it. Perhaps a tiny feather I couldn't see. I'd watched them at work, the two of them. Stum standing very still at a table, feet apart, concentrating, hands busy and small over the boxes, under the hanging light. Angel bringing in the carts, taking out the boxes to be sorted, feeding them to each sexer, taking them away, this box here, that box there. Angel had to be wrong when she said the creatures became part of your hand. One day out of their shell, they were so soft you could crush them. How could you forget and mistake them for part of your own big, ungainly self? The noises they made— the pipping, Stum called it—the males deep and rich, the females thin and clear; they reminded me of my dream. In an instant I knew my dream had not been a dream; the swish and whisper I'd taken to be Tam and Sachi revisiting me, they'd come from the room next door, from Stum and Angel in his narrow twin bed in the early morning when my sleep had been shallow.

In the front seat Angel was doing what Stum had taught

her, in slow motion, her hands like puppets. Scooping up one imaginary chick in her right hand, another in her left, dipping its head down, turning up its bottom with her thumb.

"Ah," Stum interrupted.

Angel glanced back at me. "I forgot this part," and she gave a tiny squeeze and a scratch. "So you can see." Clearing away its business, I guessed. She seemed to tighten her grip and give a push and a squeeze at once; then she wriggled her thumb about with its fingernail, grown long like Stum's.

"Inside there's a little mark—"

"Invisible to the untrained eye," Stum added, smirking.

"So tiny," said Angel, squinting at her thumb where she held it pressed to her palm. "If it's raised and shiny like a ball, then it's—"

"A rooster."

"If it's flat and faint, then it's a hen."

"She'll be the first girl sexer in the area," Stum told me, beaming. Keeping one eye on the road, he reached over just as Angel was picking up a fresh chick. He stilled her working fingers and thumb.

"Look." He pointed at her cupped hand. "That one's no good. Two marks."

"That means it's male and female in one," Angel explained. Their eyes seemed to twinkle, a secret between them.

Stum looked back at me. "It happens sometimes, ne-san. You have to watch for them. Go on," he urged Angel.

Angel grimaced, holding onto that poor unseen chick until Stum nudged her shoulder. She closed her eyes and squeezed hard for several seconds. I saw the imaginary chick in her fist choke, saw a flutter of feathers.

"See, not so bad," said Stum, smiling, in some way proud, I suppose. Slowly, gingerly, Angel placed the lifeless chick to one side, into a third box, and pushed it away. She pushed them all away, and let her head fall, with a sigh that wasn't quite a sigh, onto Stum's shoulder. "You didn't know your Tsutomu could be so cruel, did you, Asako?"

Stum was watching me in the rearview mirror, worried that all this might have upset me, that I hadn't taken it in the right spirit. I shook my head. "No, I didn't know." I settled back in my seat. But without thinking, I blurted, "But think of all the ones he lets get away. Seven hundred and ninety-nine in one hour." They both laughed at that, at the little joke I'd made. On a whim, without pausing to ponder how funny my remark might be, to wonder if I'd make a fool of myself. They went on laughing a little too long, I realized; laughing at themselves, I suppose, at their delight in each other.

The thought of the two of them tucked away in that dark room where soon enough you understood everything that happened or could happen inside it, what you could expect, day by day. The cycle of things, the routine. And yet. It dawned on me that this was how they fell in love. Sharing a worker's specialized knowledge, a secret from the outside world, a secret of life under the dim light of hanging bulbs, the shadow cast by the rice-paper wrapped around them; an indescribable smell, the *pip pip* of newly hatched chicks. Girls here, boys there. It was simple, really.

ACKNOWLEDGMENTS

I AM DEEPLY GRATEFUL to my wonderful, brilliant friends who encouraged me in writing this book. For their incisive comments, I thank Richard Fung, Dalia Kandiyoti, Ruth Liberman, and, for her close readings and unerring judgment, Ellen Geist. I thank Helen Lee, Deborah Viets, and Lynne Yamamoto for their invaluable support.

My special appreciation to Teruko Sakamoto for the inspiration and insights; to Gordon Hideo Sakamoto—who bought me my first typewriter—for the lessons in perseverance; and to Laurie Michi Sakamoto for the bolstering cheer.

Many thanks to my intrepid super agent, Denise Bukowski, for her relentless enthusiasm and stalwart support. Thanks to Diane Martin for the deft touch and to Jill Bialosky for her helpful comments. My appreciation to Gena Gorrell, Charis Wahl, and Mr. Ryuji Nakahara.

For financial assistance, my gratitude to the Banff Centre for the Arts, the (now defunct) Explorations Program of the Canada Council for the Arts, the Japanese Canadian Redress Foundation, the Multiculturalism Program of the Department of Canadian Heritage, the Ontario Arts Council, and the Toronto Arts Council.

KERRI SAKAMOTO WAS BORN and raised in Toronto where she currently resides. She earned her master's degree from New York University. She has been a scriptwriter for independent films, and has written extensively on Asian North American art. Her short fiction was included in *Charlie Chan Is Dead: An Anthology of Contemporary Asian American Fiction*. *The Electrical Field* is her first novel.

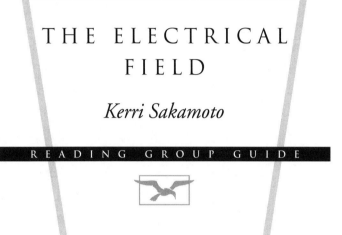

THE ELECTRICAL
FIELD

Kerri Sakamoto

A CONVERSATION WITH
KERRI SAKAMOTO

Q. *Your book draws much of its emotional intensity from the legacy of the Japanese Canadian internment experience. What was your family's experience during the war?*

A. My parents, my aunts and uncles, and my grandparents were all interned in camps during the war. After the bombing of Pearl Harbor, all Japanese Canadians living on Canada's West Coast were herded into the exhibition grounds in Vancouver where for several months they slept in horse stalls. They could bring only what they could carry, leaving most of their belongings behind. Families were split up with able-bodied men sent to set up camps and work on road crews. The others were transported to the camps—in hastily resurrected mining ghost towns—in the mountains of British Columbia. There they lived in tarpaper shacks. It was a very arduous existence. My mother was one of the oldest in a family of eleven siblings. One of her brothers died in the camp after being injured on a baggage crew. His death may have been partly due to inadequate medical facilities.

Once the war effectively ended with the bombing of Hiroshima and Nagasaki, Japanese Canadians were released from the camps and allowed to resettle only in designated areas of eastern Canada. My grandparents lost the homes and businesses they had worked so hard to acquire before the war, which were sold off by the government. My mother worked as a domestic and then as a seamstress. School was not a possibility for her. My father luckily had finished high school by this time. Like my mother, he came from a large family and had to work immediately to help buy a new home for them.

Q. *How does the history of internment in the United States differ from that in Canada?*

A. When I lived in New York, I was often surprised to learn that many people didn't know Japanese Canadians were interned in camps just as Japanese Americans were. Although the history and events are very parallel, in some ways the Canadian government's treatment of its 22,000 Japanese Canadian citizens was much harsher than in the United States where 120,000 individuals were interned.

In Canada, the government seized and sold land and personal property and the proceeds were used to build the camps. In other words, they made Japanese Canadians pay for their own incarceration. In the United States there were panic sales, looting, and depreciation, but no government sale of property because of constitutional protections. Families were not broken up in the United States as they were in Canada. American citizens were permitted to return to the Coast in 1945 while Canadians were not allowed back until 1949. And in Canada, a policy of exile to Japan and dispersal eastward continued for years after the war ended. These policies were intended to permanently destroy the Japanese Canadian coastal communities.

Q. *In what ways has the internment experience affected those who were interned and their descendants?*
A. My parents were teenagers at the time of internment and I believe the experience affected their lives profoundly. My parents' schooling was curtailed, and I believe their generation (called nisei) lost its sense of possibility for the future. The loss of opportunity is difficult to quantify.

No one talked about internment—not the history books at school and certainly not my parents at home. There was a collective silence among Japanese Canadians that had to do with a sense of shame, a sense that somehow they were to blame for their incarceration. As I recall, I first learned about internment from reading something in a magazine, then I began to ask my parents questions that made them very uneasy. It was not until the redress movement—the lobby to secure an apology and restitution from the government—gained momentum and public support that Japanese Canadians started to speak out. I worked in the movement for two years, and in the beginning my parents refused to attend the meetings I helped organize; so did many others. It was the idea of being visible once again that was uncomfortable for them, even threatening.

Things have changed over the ten years since redress was attained. More people speak about their experiences, memoirs have been written, films have been made. But certain scars still remain. It seems sad to me that there is no Little Tokyo or Japantown anywhere in Canada—only vestiges of the original one in Vancouver. This is the legacy of the Canadian government's policy of forced dispersal. There has been, as a result, a kind of cultural impoverishment for my generation. I believe this is because our grandparents and parents were forced to relinquish the artifacts and rituals of their cultural identity, leaving behind family heirlooms when they were evacuated, sometimes destroying items fearful it would signal disloyalty to Canada and an allegiance to Japan. Of course, for many, Japan was a country they had either left behind decades earlier or, as Canadian-born citizens, had never even seen.

Q. *How did this personal history affect your writing?*
A. I grew up in the shadow of internment. I felt that history cast itself over the present because it remained perpetually unspoken. I grew up in the suburbs of Toronto, which in the '60s and '70s were predominantly white. Racial taunts were a fact of daily life. My response was silence—not unlike my parents' response to the internment. As I got older, I felt compelled to articulate my response to that racism. My work in the redress movement helped me to do that and my early writing grappled with the difficulties of expressing the anger and sadness I felt. As a child of internees, I felt and witnessed its residual effects. I felt compelled to write about that.

My book focuses on the trauma and repression associated with the experience of internment and the particular ways individuals carry this history. I wanted to portray the characters in my book as individuals with their own personal experiences that were colored by internment in very different ways. For example, the protagonist, Miss Saito, is traumatized by memories of her brother's death; the trauma and tragedy are compounded by the fact that he died in an internment camp.

My mother often talked about her teenage brother who died in the camps. There was a photograph of him on our dining-room table. At family gatherings, I'd hear stories of his kindness, his winning charm, and how handsome he was. He became a mythical, tragic figure to me—all the more tragic because he died without a country, without a home. My uncle was the inspiration for the character of Eiji, although in the book, his death has been completely fictionalized.

Q. *Where did the image of the electrical field come from?*
A. I grew up in the suburbs where those vast open hydro fields cut a swath through the landscape and you see those huge, oppressive towers going on in the distance. I walked past those fields on my way to and from school every day. After living in New York City for several years, I revisited the place where I grew up and saw those fields with a fresh eye. And after viewing the old sites of the internment camps, I sensed an odd connection between the two landscapes. At one point in *The Electrical Field*, Miss Saito looks out onto the grassy field, the houses on the other side, and Mackenzie Hill in the distance and is reminded of the camp: the floor of the valley in the mountains where the rows of tarpaper shacks stood. It's a reflection of her psychological state: she hasn't yet left the camp behind. She hasn't yet let the memories surface.

Q. *Miss Saito is such a distinctive character. How did she come into being and why did you choose her to narrate the story?*

A. I suppose Miss Saito is what one would call an "unreliable narrator" because the reader cannot trust her to consistently tell the truth about events and her role in them. The murders that occur at the beginning of the book function as a kind of flashpoint for her memories—memories of what actually led up to the murders and, at the same time, of the death of her brother in an internment camp thirty years earlier. Because her memories are painful and repressed, they surface in fragments that, over the course of the book, gradually piece together to form a complete picture by the final pages. In that way, *The Electrical Field* is a kind of psychological mystery.

What results, more than an unreliable narrative, is a kind of narrative of self-delusion, of trauma. It was important to me that there be a unity between the story being told—about the pain of remembering or forgetting a traumatic event—and the way in which it is told. I know that Miss Saito is a challenging character to contend with; I wanted to imbue her with a psychological complexity so that it would be impossible to see her simply as a victim of racism. She is difficult to love—perhaps because she finds it difficult to love herself—but I'm hopeful that readers will ultimately feel a compassion for her. I believe the book culminates in redemption for Miss Saito.

Q. *The book has received a great deal of attention in Canada for a first novel. How do you feel about that? Does that put pressure on you in terms of your second novel?*

A. To be honest, it's been both thrilling and overwhelming. When you're typing away in your solitary hovel, it's difficult to imagine an audience for your strange little thoughts apart from your best friends and your loving mother. Now that it's out, it's a wonderful relief and pleasure. At the same time, the public aspect of publishing a first novel is such a contrast to the private experience of writing it. It's definitely a challenge to reconcile those two experiences. But I'm learning. With regard to a second novel, the way the first has been received in Canada has been a great encouragement to me. I feel more confident to call myself a writer. I'll be a novelist when the second one is written.

Q. *What will your next book be about?*

A. I'm in the midst of research for a novel that will be set partly in Japan where I've just returned from. It's about twin sisters of Japanese descent who only learn about each other's existence on their thirtieth birthday.

One has been raised in Tokyo, the other in Toronto. The Canadian sister goes to Japan in search of her twin. Like *The Electrical Field*, the book will address issues of history casting its shadow over the present, specifically the legacy of the bombing of Hiroshima.

It will also deal with the experience of a third-generation Japanese Canadian, not unlike me, going to Japan for the first time, not being able to speak the language—being, in effect, a cultural outsider. I'm very interested in the idea of "return" to a mythical homeland—a reverse of the more familiar narrative of east to west migration.

READING QUESTIONS

1. Kerri Sakamoto describes *The Electrical Field* as a "psychological mystery." In another sense, it is a traditional murder mystery: a woman and her lover are found killed, her husband and children are missing. How does it both use and subvert the conventions of the mystery novel? Think perhaps of the interview with the detective and of Miss Saito and Sachi's searches for "evidence" at the murder sites.

2. How do questions of guilt and blame play themselves out, not only in the murder but in the death of Miss Saito's brother Eiji and the legacy of the internment? How, especially, do Miss Saito and Yano deal with these issues?

3. Which of the characters did you sympathize with most? Why?

4. Why is the novel named *The Electrical Field*? What sort of emotions and memories do the electrical towers evoke in Miss Saito?

5. Compare that backdrop to the ocean of her childhood, even to the internment camp. How does Sakamoto use landscape to convey both mood and meaning?

6. What do you make of Miss Saito's obsessive cleanliness? Is it merely a ritual that helps her pass the days or is it linked to her attitude toward the past, trying to simultaneously circumscribe and preserve it?

7. What do you make of the scene when Chisako pulls up her shirt to show Miss Saito something—presumably a bruise or a cut—and Miss Saito sees nothing?

8. How different are Yano and Miss Saito's feelings about the internment and where exactly do they differ?

9. Miss Saito is cast as a witness, even a voyeur—she stands at her window looking out, she spies on Sachi and Tam, Chisako enlists her as an audience for her stories of Mr. Spears. However, much of the novel is concerned with that which cannot be seen: the whereabouts of Yano and the children in the days following the first murders, the goings-on in Tom and Keiko's house, what Stum does when he is away from home. How does the novel use this tension to explore the limits of Miss Saito's perception? Perhaps tie this to her role as what Sakamoto calls an "unreliable narrator."

10. The fact that the two sets of murders that frame the story are remote, relayed back only through the newspaper, helps emphasize the alienation and isolation of Miss Saito. In what other ways does Sakamoto heighten Miss Saito's distance from the world around her?

11. Miss Saito is unable to keep her thoughts to herself; her memories always bleed into the present so that she catches herself participating in decades-old conversations. What do you make of this habit? In light of this, do you believe her when she says that her past "mattered little now"?

12. What does Japan represent to Miss Saito? To Yano? To Chisako? How and why does Chisako play off of others' conceptions of Japan?

13. How does Sakamoto use issues of naming or translation to highlight relationships or power dynamics? Think of Sachi and Tam's "game" of naming and touching or Miss Saito's relationship with Sachi or Keiko or Yano's hatred of Mackenzie Hill.

14. Sakamoto claims that "the book culminates in redemption for Miss Saito." Do you agree? If so, what realization brings about that redemption?